MY YEAR AS A FRAUD

MY YEAR AS A FRAUD

JOHANNA SWANBERG

HUTCHINSON HEINEMANN

UK | USA | Canada | Ireland | Australia
India | New Zealand | South Africa

Hutchinson Heinemann is part of the Penguin Random House group of companies whose addresses can be found at global.penguinrandomhouse.com

Penguin Random House UK,
One Embassy Gardens, 8 Viaduct Gardens, London SW11 7BW

penguin.co.uk

First published in Sweden by Albert Bonniers Förlag 2024
First published in the UK by Hutchinson Heinemann 2025
001

Copyright © Johanna Swanberg, 2024
Translation copyright © Agnes Broomé, 2026

The moral right of the author has been asserted

Penguin Random House values and supports copyright. Copyright fuels creativity, encourages diverse voices, promotes freedom of expression and supports a vibrant culture. Thank you for purchasing an authorised edition of this book and for respecting intellectual property laws by not reproducing, scanning or distributing any part of it by any means without permission. You are supporting authors and enabling Penguin Random House to continue to publish books for everyone. No part of this book may be used or reproduced in any manner for the purpose of training artificial intelligence technologies or systems. In accordance with Article 4(3) of the DSM Directive 2019/790, Penguin Random House expressly reserves this work from the text and data mining exception.

Set in 13.5/16pt Garamond MT
Typeset by Falcon Oast Graphic Art Ltd

Printed and bound in Great Britain by Clays Ltd, Elcograf S.p.A.

The authorised representative in the EEA is Penguin Random House Ireland, Morrison Chambers, 32 Nassau Street, Dublin D02 YH68

A CIP catalogue record for this book is available from the British Library

ISBN: 978–1–529–15575–4

Penguin Random House is committed to a sustainable future for our business, our readers and our planet. This book is made from Forest Stewardship Council® certified paper.

MY YEAR AS A FRAUD

MAY

I

She wasn't always like this.

It's Saturday and her alarm goes off at half past four in the morning. Last night's wine still coursing through her, a near-empty glass sitting on the nightstand. Cassi starts the day, as she does every day, by knocking back what's left in it. It's as if she'd thoughtfully prepared a small breakfast in bed for herself before passing out a few hours earlier.

The brown, eighteen-kilo lump at the foot of the bed, aka Maine, doesn't even bother to look up, but he does stretch all four paws before going back to sleep, while she herself unsteadily throws her feet over the edge of the bed and onto the cold floor. She puts on the same trousers and hoodie she wore yesterday – not a stylistic choice, just one of convenience. That seems to be her thing these days.

In the bathroom, Cassi downs two toothpaste-smeared glasses of water but doesn't brush her teeth. The fact that her hair, with its split ends and greasy, mousy roots that are a good ten centimetres long, has grown halfway down her back isn't something that she can be bothered dealing with, so she ties it in a messy ponytail. Her clothes, clearly too big for her newly small frame, hang off her awkwardly. She never looks at herself in the mirror if she can avoid it, but for some reason she decides to do it now. She hardly recognises the face reflected back at her, with chapped lips, hollow brown eyes and washed-out skin.

Anyone who knew the old Cassi would barely recognise her now. The person she once was would have despised anyone who looked this grimy, let alone letting herself get this way. The person she once was had needed at least forty-five minutes to complete her morning routine, an internal checklist for the day she finalised every evening. The old Cassi had had no time for half measures.

If you're doing something, do it properly would have been her life motto if she'd been the kind of person who needed peppy catchphrases to motivate herself. Before everything happened, Cassi worked out with a personal trainer twice a week and three more times without him. She kept her bright, newly renovated, tastefully decorated flat neat and tidy, with fresh flowers delivered every Friday. She scheduled facials and Botox and hairstyling and eyebrow threading and mani-pedis at a salon as frequently as the beauty therapists recommended. Her clothes always looked brand new. She spent at least ten hours a day at work – doing a job she loved! – and had a relationship with a man she – also! – loved. She put time and effort into her friendships, made sure she kept up with current events as well as the weather forecast and celebrity gossip. She was the one who threw birthday parties, bought presents, issued dinner invitations. Cassi had trained herself to make do with four hours of sleep, her waking hours divided into fifteen-minute increments, her calendar chock-a-block and colour-coded months in advance. She made sure everything turned out the way she wanted. That everything turned out the way it *should*.

These days, the chances of Cassi running into someone from her old life are remote. She's no longer in contact with *anyone* she knew back then. And by 'back then', she means a little over a year ago. The undeniable fact of her continued existence is the only proof that former life was actually hers.

One thing, out of all the things, that has happened over the past year is that she has stopped caring so much. She's learned to shut down. It was a process that took several months, but she came out on the other side a purer self. Stripped down. Clear. As though everything that could be deemed unnecessary had been scraped off, leaving only her core. Her core doesn't need perfectly plucked eyebrows and lip filler. It barely even needs a bra anymore. She goes through her days thinking as few thoughts as possible.

The basement room she lives in now – or 'garden flat with en-suite bathroom', as the ad put it – is in a house owned by a divorced woman she doesn't know. Her tenancy is a practical solution for both of them. The woman gets to keep her home while making some extra cash and Cassi doesn't have to worry too much about taking care of it. She leaves her tiny room only when she has to use the kitchen – and every other week she does her best to avoid that too, not wanting to run into the woman's two sons when they visit. Six and eight years old, they have only one redeeming feature between them: they like Cassi's dog and don't mind taking him for walks.

Changing her ponytail into a messy bun, she climbs the stairs to the kitchen and turns on the tap. She grabs an empty plastic bottle from under the sink, which she sniffs half-heartedly before pouring in instant coffee granules. Once the water is hot, she fills the bottle halfway and adds a splash of milk from the fridge. She shakes it a few times then grabs her bag, puts her shoes on and leaves the house.

Getting to work takes only fifteen minutes on the bus if she's lucky, and on this particular Saturday morning she is. Cassi sits next to the buggy space, drinking from her plastic bottle of coffee while gazing out at misty football fields and desolate roundabouts. The driver listens to a foreign radio station, the incomprehensible words filling the silence.

She clocks in at work no more than five minutes late. She changes into her uniform – beige trousers, a beige chequered button-down shirt worn with a brown gilet – and steps into the hypermarket.

Eight hours later, she changes back into her own clothes and makes the same trip in reverse. At this hour, the buses, the roundabouts, and the football fields are populated by a sprinkling of weekenders. The evening driver is singing a jingle to himself. Children are screaming and phones are ringing all around her; the sounds feel like they're perforating her eardrums so Cassi gets off two stops early. She takes a shortcut through the woods. Well, maybe not exactly woods – more like a stand of trees, just big enough to play hide and seek or secretly stash issues of *Playboy*.

She knows this small town like the back of her hand. When she and her friends moved away to Stockholm after school, Cassi had sworn she'd never come back. And yet, here she is. And even though it is in many ways the opposite of where young her had imagined she'd be living at this stage of her life, her basement room is the only place where she feels truly comfortable. Most of her days now are spent waiting for them to end. It's not that Cassi wants to die, not really. It's more that she doesn't want to take part in that thing other people, the people out there, call life. Her own life is lived on the outskirts of society. Her life is what's contained between the four walls of her room, and when she has to leave to go to work, that life is put on hold. Once, not long after she'd moved in, temporarily buoyed by the relief of being in a place where no one knew who she was or how to find her, she'd organised a treasure hunt for her landlady's sons and Maine. A simple map with tricky riddles and hidden treasures in the form of tinfoil-wrapped treats for both children and dog. The joy in their little shoulders, the admiration in their eyes had warmed her heart. But that creative surge had been a blip; afterwards, she'd sunk even deeper into lethargy and isolation. The boys still talk about it and ask her when the next treasure hunt will be every time they see her. This saddens her if she thinks about it too much, but it's not her fault, it can't be. They need to accept that Cassi's not their fairy godmother. If anything, she's more like a troll, only she pays rent to a divorcee and her cave has a mattress.

This Saturday, the house is empty when she gets home. This isn't unusual, in fact, it's the very thing that makes it possible to live with a stranger and her joint-custody children. The residents of the house live their lives on different levels, both figuratively and literally. The others spend time together, barbecue, have visitors. They make lasagne. Laughing and shrieking, they chase each other around with water pistols. They watch TV together on Friday night, cuddled up on the couch. Cassi can hear them from the basement, but she wouldn't dream of joining them.

Maine meets her in the hallway, his tail wagging – at least someone is happy to see her! Even though she knows she's not supposed to, Cassi lets him out into the small fenced front garden so that he can walk over to his usual corner and do his usual business. Once done, he immediately comes back inside. He's a dog with the right level of expectations in life.

Cassi boils macaroni and pours herself a pint glass of boxed wine. According to Cassi, red wine is a daytime drink. It's more like food, nourishment, because it's opaque and compact. White wine is for the evenings, because it's abstract – it's barely even there, really. To the old Cassi, these new habits would have been unthinkable. Absolutely insane, drinking wine at all hours of the day, going to bed with a glass by her bed to drink first thing in the morning. But in the here and now, it feels like a perfectly logical routine. Nothing weird about it. Cassi doesn't view herself as someone with an alcohol problem. Wine is a tool that helps her get through things. Getting through her days with as little friction and pain as possible, aided by a constant and comfortable alcohol level, that's what Cassi's all about now.

When the macaroni's done, she carries everything down to her cave, where time has stood still since the morning. Maine used to be on a special diet for his stomach, but now he gets regular supermarket dog food. It's hard on the air quality in the room. The transom windows are hidden behind tartan curtains that match the bedspread that hasn't been discarded on the floor since she's lived here. The cushions on the sofa are invisible under piles of clothes but Cassi sits down anyway, pulling her legs in under her. Maine settles in with his head on her thigh. She devours the pasta in a few bites, it's the first thing she's eaten today. In many ways, Cassi feels like she lives the life of a seventeen-year-old (she's actually thirty-seven). It becomes quite obvious when she opens her laptop to watch a show in which British couples, desperate for a change, tour properties in warmer climates. She simultaneously scrolls through her social media. Someone's been to a family get-together while someone else has stayed at a spa just a few minutes away from her place. There's also a hen night in full swing made up mostly of girls from her old life. Cassi was invited, but obviously never acknowledged the message.

Now, she has a sudden urge to go away. Far away. Where's that spa place? No, she doesn't want to go to a spa. She can't imagine anything worse than being in a crowd of wet bodies sipping from glasses of lukewarm bubbly, stale strawberries floating on top. What does she want? Present-day Cassi usually tries not to think about things like that, but sometimes the thought pops into her head and every time it's more annoying than the last. She reaches for her plastic fan and directs the breeze at Maine, who lets out a smug-sounding sigh (the sign of an impending bout of flatulence).

She heads up to the kitchen to refill her pint of wine. When she gets back downstairs, the full box in hand now, the hen night has, according to the most recent pictures posted, moved on to a go-kart track. The party is nowhere near this town, but they still feel intrusively nearby. As though they could appear outside Cassi's window at any moment and laugh at the state of her.

Should she leave the country? Go join the Britons in Costa del Sol? She sips her wine and googles 'flat Nerja', because that's the town that was just recommended to the prospective buyers on the show. The excitement fades as soon as she sees the prices. She clicks absently on a few other properties, but her interest is already waning. Weariness takes over and as the go-kart winner is celebrated with a plastic trophy and a gazillion jubilant group photos from the most prolific poster of the hen night, Cassi lies down next to the dog and shuts her eyes.

She wakes up a few hours later when the divorcee comes home and yells 'Cathrin!' at the top of the stairs. Cassi realises she's left the used pasta pot to soak in the sink – rookie error. She checks the time on her phone, it's still early. Cassi chooses a film she's seen before, tops up her glass, and tries hard to stay away from her social media, to no avail.

2

In other words, Cassi was definitely drunk by the time the Facebook algorithm served her up a derelict cottage for sale, on which she clicked 'like'. She was probably still drunk when she woke up the next morning to find that some rural estate agent had, in a fairly desperate manner, sent her a message about viewing times. His profile picture made her vaguely depressed. His hair was neatly combed and thinning above the ears despite his seemingly young age. He had a forced smile and was wearing a paper-like grey suit that looked as stiff as a theatre backdrop.

That must have been the reason why she didn't immediately delete his message. She felt sorry for him! Her account was private, so he hadn't been able to see the utter lack of content on her page. But Cassi's profile picture – her in an intricate yoga pose on a beach at sunset – could definitely be one of the reasons things turned out the way they did.

Cassi's had the same job for a long time. Forever. At least that's what it feels like, when in reality it's been just over six months. Before that, weeks could go by without her leaving the basement. She can barely remember it, though she does recall dragging Maine out for walks in the rain and freezing cold on nights when she couldn't sleep.

She wasn't actually looking for a job. It was Cassi's landlady who had told her about an ad, urging her to apply. The woman was probably sick of always having her around. Cassi doesn't expect people to do things for her without an ulterior motive. There's always one. But even though Cassi wasn't particularly interested in working, it felt easier to say yes than no. A no would have required her to explain herself to her landlady. And she had to say yes because she'd decided at a very young age that she was never, ever, ever going to end up on benefits. Logically, that meant working, even if she currently had enough savings to get by. A job was the necessary penance to uphold her principles. Had she been a medieval monk, a whip would have been a much better choice.

When she's at work, Cassi does what she's supposed to, more or less. Or at least she tries to do things right, although she does clock off early every day. Looking at her now, no one would believe that she used to be a senior manager in charge of fifty employees and every aspect of one of the capital's most popular restaurants, with queues around the block from opening until closing.

Nowadays, Cassi is a supermarket shelf stacker. She works in silence, doing everything she can to avoid contact with both customers and other members of staff.

'Don't just restock where you see big gaps on the shelves,' her shift manager says in his muted way of speaking. It's been a few hours since the sad estate agent messaged her and Cassi has yet to reply. The manager points at a lonely marmalade jar. 'Keep your eyes peeled for smaller ones. They're easy to miss.'

'Absolutely.' She always replies the same way. Her shift manager, who in Cassi's head is called Tiny Face, studies her, stroking his chin, pondering whether he should clarify his instructions further. The fact that Cassi has replied 'absolutely' doesn't mean that what he's asking her to do will get done, and he's probably aware of that by now.

If it were up to her, Cassi would get through her entire shift without stopping once. Unfortunately, she's required by law to take a thirty-minute break in the middle of the day. Tiny Face doesn't want anyone else to burn out, so he's meticulous about the rules and regulations. Thankfully, he can't dictate what she does on her break – which is everything but sit down and eat. It would never occur to her to eat at work. Not only because she's so rarely hungry these days, but also because of the revulsion she feels when watching others wolf down food. The smells from her colleagues' lunch boxes annoy her as much as how badly put together their meals are. Brown goop. Instant noodles with corn. Spaghetti drowning in anaemic-looking sauce.

If Cassi is in the breakroom, it's only because she's wasting time. She sits at one of the plastic tables, surrounded by framed motivational quotes like 'There's no I in team' and 'First coffee, then we change the world'. The one Cassi despises the most says 'Inspiration. Joy. Community'. The three words feel alien to her.

Old newspapers stagnate on the communal tables for weeks at a time. Cassi cares as much about current events as the detailed list of workplace rules someone has taped up above the sink: very little. One time, when no one else was in the breakroom, she'd replaced it with a child's Christmas wish list, which she'd found on a seat at the back of the bus. People had laughed. Then the workplace rules had come back. A week or so later, she'd put up a list of that year's most common baby names, which she'd ripped out of a magazine. People had laughed. Wondered who was behind it. And the workplace rules had come back. The third time around, she was growing tired of her own shenanigans, but was still entertained by her colleagues speculating about who might be behind it. Early one morning, Cassi swapped the workplace rules for an infographic listing the people who earned the most in their small county, which had just been published by an evening paper, and on which the owner of the hypermarket held second place. After that, the workplace rules had come back laminated, secured to the cabinet door with long strips of sturdy duct tape.

It's raining outside now. Sitting in the corner of the sagging sofa, Cassi tries to focus on her breathing. She has, reluctantly, let go of her fantasies about being sucked into a black hole, but she still reckons it should be possible to, bit by bit, fold her body into itself, a clump of atoms and nothing else. A kind of advanced origami resulting in her complete disappearance. Her focus is disrupted by a discussion about relationships at one of the tables. Or actually, more of a monologue.

'It's time you left that loser. He doesn't deserve you,' says the woman who's in charge of fruit and vegetables to the woman who usually mans the customer service desk. 'Move out, try living alone for a while. Focus on taking care of yourself. *Self-care*, sweetie.'

Fruit and Veg reaches across the table, grabbing Customer Service's hand.

'Loving yourself is the start of a lifelong romance. I read that somewhere, isn't it beautiful?'

Fruit and Veg doesn't wait for a response, just ploughs on.

'You deserve the best. And only by looking after yourself can you truly shine.'

Customer Service nods, wiping her eyes.

Cassi sighs, far too loudly. She finds it pathetic that people think they can tell others how to live their lives, as though they know anything. Both Customer Service and Fruit and Veg glare at her.

'You don't have to listen, you know,' Fruit and Veg snaps. 'This is a private conversation.'

Customer Service and Fruit and Veg exchange a look of mutual understanding. There's a brief pause.

'Speaking of which,' Fruit and Veg adds, sounding suddenly more energetic. She turns to Cassi, her big forearms resting on the table. 'I'm going to have to give you notice.'

Cassi doesn't have time to filter her reaction. She looks up and meets Fruit and Veg's beady eyes.

'Eh, excuse me? You can't fire me, you're not my boss,' she says.

Fruit and Veg purses her lips, pulls her mouth to one side. 'The basement,' she clarifies. 'I'm going to be needing the room.'

The last part is delivered with a quick glance at Customer Service.

Fruit and Veg isn't even trying to sound personable. She and Cassi passed that stage many weeks ago, probably around the time Cassi yelled 'SHUT THE FUCK UP ALREADY' at Fruit and Veg's sons, who were playing at the top of the basement steps. Because yes, Fruit and Veg happens to be Cassi's landlady, who also happens to have found her the job she so hates. Cassi obviously knows

Fruit and Veg's name, but she can't bear to let it into her mind. Acknowledging Fruit and Veg's name would be like admitting her own inferiority. Her debt of gratitude. And Cassi has no intention of doing that.

'No problem,' Cassi says, studying her nails, chewed and splintered. She can still remember how smooth they would feel when she'd step out of the salon with a fresh manicure. 'I was going to move out anyway.'

Then she stands up and walks out into the warehouse. She nods at Burnout, who's recently returned from sick leave. Burnout's hunched over in her chair, writing slowly with a quill on thick paper. It's a mindfulness exercise her therapist recommended; she explained that to Cassi at some point when Cassi was feeling receptive to small talk. Cassi has noticed that she has an easier time putting up with people who are depressed. Burnout's also an older woman, quite possibly the last segment of the population Cassi still has some empathy towards.

She goes to fetch the flask she's stashed for emergencies behind the smoke alarm at the back of the store. It's precious to her in more ways than one, even though it's practically empty, and Cassi brings it out to the loading dock, tracing the engraved logo with her fingers before drinking the last few drops. When she goes back to the breakroom, her eyes meet Fruit and Veg's again. The latter looks like she's about to say something when Cassi's phone dings. It's that sad estate agent again. This time, he's texting her to 'gauge her interest in an afternoon viewing', even though she still hasn't replied to his last message. To avoid having to look at Fruit and Veg again, Cassi keeps her eyes fixed on the screen.

She hadn't planned to respond. Why would she? Owning a shack in the woods was never a dream of hers. Liking this ad yesterday had been nothing but a sloppy impulse, if that, possibly just a finger slipping on the screen. The basement room has worked out well for her, she'd intended to stay there until she came up with a better plan. But now, the situation has changed. And action needs to be taken. Her heart hasn't stopped racing. Cassi feels a powerful urge to get away. It wouldn't hurt to look, after all. That estate agent might have some other, more appealing properties they could discuss.

As she starts typing her reply, Tiny Face enters the room. He looks at his watch as if to ask why Cassi isn't back at work – her break ended two minutes ago – before going over to the sink to rinse out his thermos. She can't bear this place for another second. Not one second. She has cut everyone she knows out of her life and finds it unfathomable that she still has to exist around these people. Which is why she sends the estate agent a thumbs up, then grabs her bag from its hook and announces: 'I have a temperature, I'm going home.'

The door shuts behind her with a sigh-like sound. Cassi takes a deep breath and smiles to herself.

3

There are still, as a matter of fact, things that feel like crossing a line for Cassi, albeit fewer than before, when the list would have included drinking a Riesling out of a pinot noir glass, being three minutes late without letting someone know, keeping improperly folded towels in her bathroom cabinet, wearing the same top two days in a row, eating solid food before noon, damaged cuticles, and people who pronounce bruschetta 'brushetta'.

Even if Cassi doesn't give much of a shit about anything – not even Tiny Face's 'expresso' bothers her anymore! – she still draws the line at drunk driving. It's the reason she doesn't drive to work despite having a car, which has been sitting unused outside Fruit and Veg's house for months. She loves the bus, the convenience of being able to drink as much as she wants without putting anyone at risk. Besides herself, that is.

On this particular day, having kept the car feels like fate, even if all she's doing is driving to the countryside to look at a derelict shack. As she pulls away from the kerb, Cassi feels sorry for herself – what is she even doing?! But the self-pity slowly dissipates as she puts mile after mile behind her.

She should do things like this more often. She'd forgotten the freedom of an empty motorway. Cassi applies her personal speed limit with a 20 per cent gratuity. It comes naturally to her, a pointless nod to all her years in the restaurant industry. She flips between radio stations, which gradually grow fewer and further between. She finds half-eaten bags of sweets in the glovebox, the driver-side door and the centre console. She doesn't even remember buying them. She finishes them anyway, one after the other, all except a bag of salt liquorice that must be absolutely ancient because the pieces have fused into a greyish rat king that's stuck to the plastic.

She feels almost *cheerful*. When was the last time that happened? The fact that she doesn't have to see people while she's driving is likely a contributing factor. Just nature and the occasional motorist, but other than that, this is a world in which only she and Maine exist. The dog is in the passenger seat, sighing a cloud of steam at the window. From time to time, she rolls the window down, airing out the cab, letting him enjoy the wind. Around halfway through her journey, Cassi stops to refuel, buys a coffee and lets Maine out to pee. Other than that, she drives without stopping, without thinking about much of anything at all.

On the GPS, the village of Bäcken is located between Berg and Berget. Solid, literal names, no frills. Cassi nods approvingly when checking the directions, as if someone had asked her opinion. There are acres and acres of forest on either side of the road, the green a constant presence around her. She slows to a crawl as she reaches the high street, where faded signs reveal that there was once a petrol station, a café, a beauty salon and a hardware shop here. All that's left is a supermarket and a pizzeria that, according to a blackboard propped up on the pavement, also does burgers, Thai food and kebabs. The three-storey buildings look lonely. By the church, Cassi spots what looks like a florist's, but it's shut. On a Sunday afternoon? Cassi wonders, then continues past the cemetery, driving down a street lined with budding birch trees. When she turns right by a spindly for sale sign, the asphalt turns into a gravel track with sizeable potholes. Finally, she spots the red cottage.

A green Jeep is parked in the drive and the sad estate agent is there in the flesh, leaning against it. He looks like he's making a show of being busy, flipping through a stack of papers, pretending not to see her. His hair is less thin in person, and blonder. His suit, blue today, is slightly too small, clearly struggling to contain his shoulders. He's young, but probably not as young as he looks.

The relief and confidence Cassi felt during the drive begin to wobble. The estate agent is here in the clearly defined role of a professional, but she's just a person who's about to be homeless, who barely has a job, let alone a life to start somewhere. But she just has to get through it. See this as a break from things. A role play scenario, perhaps. She's going to try to come off as a completely normal person looking for a summer retreat, and then she's going to say thank you and get out of here and never speak to him again. That should be doable. He knows nothing about her. And she was a pro at dealing with people back in the day. My God, that's all she did every day. It shouldn't be too difficult to temporarily access that skill again.

She takes a deep breath and climbs out of the car in one fluid motion, hoping to radiate confidence. Shooting the estate agent a smile, she opens the door for Maine. The dog trots straight over to the man and gently licks the palm of his hand. The estate agent flinches in a way that reveals he's not an animal person, but he quickly slaps his rehearsed smile back on, wipes his hand on his jacket, and holds it out to Cassi.

'Hey there, hey. I'm Max,' he says. 'Welcome to Bäcken. No better place for country living, as I like to say, he-he.'

Close up, the estate agent's age remains difficult to pin down, but she guesses somewhere around thirty. His ruddy cheeks show almost no sign of facial hair, his blond hair looks baby soft and spontaneously parts on one side. Cassi can tell he's trying to get a read on her, just as she is on him. He's probably taking note of her dusty but relatively modern mid-range car, and her – deceptively – sporty outfit consisting of navy leggings and a grey hoodie. The silver necklace with a pink stone around her neck. On her feet: worn Nikes. Cassi's hair is pulled into a bun. Make-up? Hardly any. She puts as much time into her appearance as she wants people to spend thinking about it on noticing her. None.

'It's pretty out here,' she says, realising her voice sounds tentative. She clears her throat.

It's not that Cassi likes her current living situation, but finding an alternative feels overwhelming. She does need somewhere to live, though. And the best option would definitely be a place of her own, without a grumpy Fruit and Veg landlady dictating the terms. Cassi looks around. It probably won't be here, but this outing is a means to temporarily escaping her reality. Maybe draw some inspiration.

From the intense look in the estate agent's eyes, she can tell he has high hopes for this showing. She may be a twat in a lot of ways, but she's actually quite self-aware. She knows this man is not to blame for her life being what it is. True, you might be able to say the same of her colleagues at the supermarket, that they're not to blame either; Cassi's never claimed to be consistent in her thinking. Besides, the way she feels about her workplace is inextricably entangled with the way she feels about where she lives, which is in turn entangled with her feelings about previous events in her life. This complicates matters.

But this place, this man, are completely free of associations. They're untainted. A clean slate. The least she can do is behave as a prospective buyer. She can always hold off on asking about properties located elsewhere.

She raises her arms above her head and her shoulder blades crack, cool relief coursing through her back and neck like a balm.

'I haven't been out here before,' she says. 'Seems like a peaceful place. And this air!'

She inhales deeply – is she putting on too much of a show? – and looks around. The front yard is overgrown. Glimpses of gravel emerge between wilting blades of grass on the path that leads to the house. Behind the house, the forest extends like a velvet curtain. The front steps are covered in bright moss. There seem to be no other houses in the immediate vicinity, no neighbours at all. Maine sniffs loudly as if wanting to help with Cassi's eager-buyer act, eyeing a barn over by the treeline with obvious interest.

Max nods, looking pleased the way only an estate agent can – deviously yet cluelessly.

'Yes, a place where it's easy to feel at home,' he agrees, before being interrupted by the loud fanfare of a text notification. After a quick glance at his phone, he slips it into his jacket pocket, folds his papers, and shoves them behind him. Then he turns his gaze to the house, smiling, hands resting on his hips. He looks as though he would high-five the cottage if he could.

'It's a lovely place,' he continues. 'Wonderful. Needs a bit of TLC, of course, but who doesn't, he-he.'

Cassi studies him and forces out a smile. She tells herself to not worry, that Max will soon be a distant memory. She adopts the same pose, mirroring him.

Max breaks the silence and tells her she's the only prospective buyer attending the viewing.

'I like to keep it personal, you know. Give people some space. Some privacy. But I had a couple out here yesterday, and they're pretty keen. There's a lot of interest. But I obviously want to find the *right* buyer, too. And that can take time.'

If there is one thing Cassi has mastered during her many years as a restaurant manager, it's reading people. Granted, that confidence got knocked badly, but this baby face of an estate agent is an open book to her. She knows Max *really* needs to get this particular property sold. That it has taken longer than he'd thought it would.

'The house has been empty for a few years now,' he says, confirming her suspicions. 'The owner's elderly and the property's being sold by relatives who don't live locally.'

He digs a key out of his pocket and holds it up in front of him. They walk towards the front steps. The door is stiff and doesn't open right away. Max pulls on it and then leans against it while lifting the handle to get it open. Rattling windowpanes, squealing hinges and stale air welcome them inside.

'Yeah, so right now, that requires expert training, but a bit of oil on the hinges will take care of that,' he says with a grin.

Straight ahead from the hallway is the living room. The kitchen is on the left and a poky bathroom is on the opposite side. Cassi follows Maine, who's gone straight over to a pile of rag rugs next to the fireplace in the living room and begun to make himself comfortable. The room's painted in a pale blue colour, the medallion pattern of textured wallpaper clearly visible through the paint. Cassi walks a lap around the room, pausing to look out of the window, towards the barn.

Beyond the living room is a small bedroom with a single bed. The thin, sun-bleached red cotton bedspread looks as though it has been there forever. A dark-blue blind covers the window, secured to a hook on the windowsill. The blind snaps open with a bang when Cassi unhooks it. The forest murmurs outside.

A narrow staircase leads up to two rooms on the first floor. In one of the rooms, there's a double bed with wooden slats but no mattress under a half-moon window. The ceiling is slanted and Cassi notes a tall person wouldn't be able to stand straight in here. Just like downstairs, the floor consists of wide, grey wooden floorboards.

'So, you should also know that the house is sold as is,' Max, who stayed behind in the living room, tells her when she comes back downstairs. 'There's a septic tank and a well. Both probably need to be looked at. But the water was tested last year and there were no issues. I would recommend that the pipes, wiring, roof and foundation be inspected, but as you can tell, there are no obvious problems. I've been here quite a few times now and have seen no signs of mould or damp. Solid construction. These old houses were built to last.'

He knocks on the wall next to the door and clears his throat when there's a sudden rustling sound.

'The sellers are motivated and willing to accommodate a quick sale – to the right buyer, of course,' he says loudly.

He keeps talking about the size of the property, how close it is to Norway, about an 'as-is clause' and 'chattels' and 'property taxes' and 'title registration fee' and 'domestic well'.

Cassi only listens to the sounds of the house. A fly bouncing against the window. A draught from the door, carrying the smell of the forest. When Max clears his throat again, she realises she'd closed her eyes. When she opens them again, he is regarding her with a curious expression, but then he quickly looks away and shows her the breaker panel, demonstrating that it's functional by turning on the main breaker. The refrigerator rattles to life and begins to hum. The kitchen is outdated and has a mottled vinyl floor. Cassi runs her fingers over the well-worn hardware on the cabinets. It has a lived-in feel, seems familiar somehow. Maybe her family had the same kind when she was little? She turns on the tap and brownish water bubbles out, hesitantly at first, then in a steady stream.

'A bit of discoloration's no big deal,' says Max, who has appeared in the doorway. 'That's just because no one's lived in the house for a while.'

Cassi nods. Through the window, she spots a currant bush, or maybe gooseberry, next to the red building over by the treeline.

'Could we have a look at that too?' she says, pointing at the barn.

Max breaks off his monologue about the local amenities and says 'Of course!' Then he picks up where he left off as they walk out of the kitchen, down the steps, across the gravelly grass and a mossy lawn towards the barn, which has tractor-sized double doors in the middle of its front wall. A smaller door within the bigger one swings open without a sound, as though it were part of a completely different property.

Inside, it feels like time has stood still. There are dark haybales scattered randomly on the dirty concrete floor. The ceiling is covered in cobwebs and Cassi can hear birds rasping against the metal roof. Max touches a switch and a greenish-white fluorescent light flickers to life above them.

'There's no limit to what a person could do with this space!' he says with renewed zeal. 'Some people might just think "barn", but I say "annex"! The right person – a person with vision – could make anything they wanted happen in here. It's easy to imagine a stable, chickens, an artist's studio! Yes, and yoga, meditation – anything along those lines would be a natural fit for the place!'

He presses his hands together in front of his chest, then smiles and winks at her, as though they're both in on some secret. Cassi doesn't want to ruin the mood or dampen his obvious enthusiasm so she nods encouragingly, as though she's completely on board with what he's saying. Then she inhales and exhales slowly.

'Yes, it's a great space,' she says with conviction. 'Incredible energy. Almost spiritual. The past meets the present with an indoor-outdoor feel. There's a harmony that I can just *feel* in the air. It's definitely quite magical.'

She takes a few steps, pulls herself up straighter, and spreads her arms like a pompous actor attuning to her stage.

'There's a lot of space here . . . you could fit twenty, thirty people.'

What is she talking about? She probably doesn't even know herself, but Max seems thrilled. He's nodding almost frantically, his head bobbing up and down. The validation encourages her to take it even further. She points at one of the walls.

'Imagine a picture window here, facing the woods, and proper flooring. It could be a place for . . . inspiration. A blank space to start over with new energy. What's the situation with planning permission? Could I build on the property? If I were to start a business here, I mean.'

The fantasy becomes suddenly so clear to her, so palpable, even though she just pulled it out of thin air, that she's given herself goosebumps. That the phrase 'planning permission' popped out of her subconscious and arranged itself neatly in a fully functional sentence is nothing short of astonishing. Are these things she's learned through osmosis by bingeing all those property shows? All the barns turned into villas. Max looks as though she's asked him to elope with her.

'I honestly don't know off the top of my head, but I could look it up. Between us, I don't think there will be any problems. There are no close neighbours and it's a sizeable property. I can see big-city people wanting to come out here to experience the tranquillity of the area. Meditate, unwind. It's an up-and-coming region, this one, a lot of things in the pipeline, but there's also plenty of nature here. Forest retreats, isn't that the latest craze?'

He surely seems knowledgeable about everything woo-woo.

'Forest retreats, yes, they're a gateway to heavier stuff,' she says, half-jokingly, mostly just to say something, anything at all to cut through the awkwardness. He seems to be into things like that, and she's not above going with the flow. She listens to herself and is surprised by the words coming out of her own mouth.

'I suppose hugging a tree can have the same positive effect on a person's well-being as hugging another human. Once you've experienced the transcendence of being in and with nature, you never want to be without it. Some people find happiness in their big-city neighbourhood, others need to travel further.'

It's a hodgepodge of quotes from various things she's watched recently. The last part is definitely from that British property show.

Max nods, smiling broadly.

'Personal development and wellness, those are fast-growing industries,' he says. 'I listened to a podcast about that only the other day. A lot of interesting things going on in the world. People need guidance. Good for you!'

Cassi doesn't quite know what to say so she just smiles back. What on earth would be good for her?

They step back out onto the gravel. Max flips through his papers, checks his phone, and announces solemnly that the bidding's expected to start any moment.

'So if you're interested, I'd advise you to be in touch

soon,' he says. 'No pressure, obviously. But you never know. Things can happen quickly. They usually do. Like I said, the sellers are motivated, and the buyer could take possession immediately, if they wanted.'

He'd said roughly the same thing when she first got there, but for some reason, the words land differently for Cassi this time. Max is studying her with the same look in his eyes that Maine has when you hold a piece of banana in front of him.

It's a strange day. Too many things are happening. All she was supposed to have to do today was get through it. Work, then pour herself some wine and watch something to shut her brain down. This wasn't how it was supposed to go. There was no inner storm on today's forecast.

Cassi looks at the house, wondering what it would feel like if someone else moved into it. She steps onto the porch. Rings the small bell next to the front door, pretending to be a visitor. She takes another deep breath. The country air feels like it can travel all the way down to her toes. Her heart's racing. Cassi presses a hand against her chest to steady her thoughts.

'I'll have a think and let you know,' she says, bowing slightly. 'For now, I thank you for your time.'

'Of course, of course, no rush,' Max says. 'Any other information I can give you right now?'

Cassi walks to her car and opens the passenger door for Maine, who reluctantly jumps in. He probably would have preferred a walk in the woods.

'Nah, I'm . . .' she replies with a vaguely pointing gesture, before climbing in and shutting the door awkwardly and starting the engine.

'Oh! Of course! Namaste to you too,' Max replies, putting his palms together and bowing a little. 'Give me a shout if you have any questions!'

Namaste?! Cassi doesn't linger or reply. She turns the car around and drives back along the gravel road before heading towards the village, speeding as soon as the traffic signs allow her.

Cassi knows nothing about houses. Aside from the fact that she's currently residing in the basement of one, she's never lived in anything but flats. But as she stood there, in the timeworn kitchen with its spongy floor, staring out through the grimy window towards the forest, she felt almost the same way she did when she saw Maine's adoption details online. This house needs her. She's the one who should paint the walls and clean out the gutters and make sure the barn doesn't collapse. She should look after it. And maybe, just maybe, it will look after her.

4

On her way to work the next morning, just after getting off the bus, she texts Max to place a bid slightly below the asking price. When she got home late the night before and squeezed the last of the boxed wine into a pint glass, she read up on house buying on various online forums. Despite the nausea churning in her stomach, she actually feels as though she knows what she's getting herself into. As though she has the kind of confidence and determination that can be sensed by strangers as she passes them on the street, the kind that's unstoppable. She feels euphoric until she enters the supermarket and is once again forced to interact with her colleagues. Tiny Face is standing in the breakroom, eating tuna out of a can with a teaspoon and washing it down with diet soda.

'Where did you go yesterday?' he asks, and Cassi reiterates her lie about having had a temperature.

'But I'm OK now. I reckon it was just an awful bout of PMS,' she adds, mostly to make him feel uncomfortable about asking any follow-up questions. Menstruation's a woman's last refuge. It can still save you from all kinds of situations, the same way parents of young children can always play the 'stomach bug' card when they want to back out of any commitment they regret making.

Cassi runs a hand through her unwashed hair and pulls it into a ponytail as she heads out to the warehouse, where

Burnout tells her she's chosen relaxing music for the shop floor today – as if Cassi cared. Cassi would roll her eyes at that if it weren't for the fact that her eyes have already rolled so many times this morning – her bus ride to work was one long cavalcade of irritation – putting her at risk of severe chafing in her orbital sockets.

To distract herself, Cassi thinks about the cottage and its forest backdrop. The serenity of it fills her mind. She imagines starting over, recharging, being completely alone. No people around. Just her and her dog, free, in the bosom of nature.

Burnout has dragged out the day's first pallet of goods to be brought onto the shop floor and is now leaning back in the chair by the computer, eyes closed. At that moment, Cassi's phone buzzes in her pocket. Since everyone knows Burnout can react strongly to unwelcome noise and that it would be pure idiocy to trigger her migraines this early in the day, Cassi rushes into a corner of the room, answering in her softest voice.

It's Max. Who else would be calling her? Nobody cares about her the way he does – after all, he wants that commission.

'Wow, is this a bad time?' he asks, probably on account of the music, but he doesn't let that stop him. He informs her that the sellers have accepted her bid.

'When can you come sign the papers?'

Cassi suddenly feels very tired. Almost sick. Moments ago, this was what she dreamed about, now all she feels is a raging wave of anxiety. Do people have to keep bothering her? Why do they even know she exists? Can't they just leave her be and agree never to talk again, thanks. A sudden silence on the phone makes room for the plucking of strings, now complemented by a pensive pan flute, a bellowing humpback whale. Cassi hears herself tell Max the Estate Agent, still in that soft, almost whispering voice, that it's great news, but that she'll have to call him back.

'Of course, I'm sorry if I . . .' he starts to say, but then he cuts off because she stabs the red end-call button several times really hard, as though it were a real button, and as though it could pause the world around her.

Burnout lifts her eyelids, shooting her a look as she passes, but she says nothing. Cassi stares back at her as she pushes the pallet out of the warehouse.

The money's been sitting in her bank account for almost a year. When Cassi checks her email later that morning, hidden behind an eighty-foot wall of cereal, Max has sent over a flood of documents. She forwards them all to the Bank Woman who occasionally contacts her to ask if Cassi would like to invest her money rather than have it sit idle in her current account. Cassi figures the two of them can work this out.

During her lunch break, she walks over to the pizzeria on the corner and orders, without so much as a glance at the menu above the counter, a pint and some *pizzasallad*.

'We don't do *pizzasallad* here. You need to order a pizza and a separate side salad. Which is five kronor.'

Cassi nods at his answer. If either of them was doing better mentally, this could have been their inside joke, since Cassi has tried to order *pizzasallad* on its own – unsuccessfully – every week since starting her job. But the man behind the counter is as sick of her as she's tired of him, so she pays for her beer without tipping and walks over to her usual corner. The tabletop's made of faux wood and the small promotional tablecloth in the middle of it is faux cloth. Her glass leaves circles of condensation, real ones, and the man behind the counter, a towel slung over his shoulder as though he fancies himself a proper chef even though it's simply a practical solution for messy hands, jots down an order for a capricciosa and a kebab pizza.

Where Cassi sits, she's invisible from the outside. Not that she's ashamed that she's having a liquid lunch. Why would she be? She just doesn't want to have to talk to anyone. She feels talked out. She pictures herself on the front porch of the cottage again. Nothing but the trees murmuring around her. Maine lying next to her. The thought makes the area behind her eyes feel soft.

She pulls out her phone and plays a game where you have to line up different types of candy.

That afternoon, the property sale seems to have gone through, and Cassi has been forced to commit to going out there the following week to sign papers and pick up the keys to the house. She feels weak, dizzy. But this is what's happening now. And how bad can it be? Anxiety burns in her stomach – or maybe it's the beer. Doubt and self-loathing and a feeling akin to fear rush through her bloodstream. What is she going to do in the countryside? Why not stay in town, work in the hypermarket, let life just pass by her? But it's too late to back out now.

Digital contracts have been signed. From their emails, both Max and the Bank Woman seem to feel they've done a good day's work. For her part, Cassi feels truly ready for some silence.

5

The road to the house is bumpier than she remembers. Poor Maine, who's sitting in the passenger seat like a rally co-driver, almost falls off the seat every time she hits a pothole. On smoother roads, Cassi would have absolutely floored it, but not here, not now.

She parks by the front steps. It seems that someone has mowed the lawn. When she turns off the radio and opens the car door, the absence of sound feels like a scream in her ears. It also makes her feel like she needs to pee. Not even the trees are moving, and when Maine suddenly barks at a hare brazen enough to show itself over by the treeline, even he seems jarred by the echo.

'You'll get used to it,' she tells him, and, probably in equal measure, herself.

The lock and door give her little trouble, unlike at the viewing – maybe Max oiled them? The rooms, however, feel somehow unwelcoming when she enters. She turns on the kitchen and living room lights and starts bringing in her belongings.

Her material world doesn't take up much space. It's made up of two sets of blankets, sheets and pillows, a camping mat that Maine likes to sleep on, a carrier bag full of kitchen stuff, a smaller carrier bag containing her toiletries, a bag of clothes, her grandmother's old lamp, which she places in the poorly lit bedroom, and a box of further miscellaneous light sources. She hangs a string of fairy lights in the hallway and another in the living room.

These are the remains of Cassi's old life. She'd gotten rid of almost everything when she sold her flat, the one from her previous life, pre-Fruit and Veg. The wishbone chairs, the designer table, the white sofa, the art prints, the heavy candlesticks, the trendy cutlery, the monster blender, all gone. Never again will she force herself to make, let alone drink, a green protein smoothie.

But she's been unable to part with a large potted plant, which was the first thing she'd bought herself when she moved into the gorgeous flat. Looking at it now, Cassi notices that the small tree has shed almost all its large leaves. Something about its obvious suffering makes it impossible for her to consider throwing it out. How can she kick it when it's so down? She places the scraggy plant on the floor between the two tall windows in the living room. She decides the planter will serve as the new hiding place for her silver flask in case of emergency. Why an alcoholic who lives alone in the middle of nowhere would need to hide a flask in some dirt, Cassi can't say. But its presence makes her feel more at ease.

Cassi always thought it practical to be a person who barely eats, but even more so on moving day. Her kitchen stuff fits in a single plastic carrier bag, which she empties on the counter: a bag of oats, instant coffee, two tins of tomatoes, and a box of instant mac and cheese, olive oil, salt and pepper.

In the bedroom, she flips the stained mattress and makes the bed. In the old days, she would never have touched a mattress this old and grubby, but dirt no longer concerns her. If it's not crawling, there's no need to worry about it.

Afterwards, she feels pretty much moved in. Through her bedroom window, she spots Maine chewing a stick and rolling around in the grass. Wasn't there a stack of logs in the barn? It might be nice to give the fireplace a try. Cassi finds an empty wooden log basket next to it and heads out. Maine follows her.

The barn smells of damp. It needs a good clean, but Cassi can't be bothered to think about that now. She shoves as many logs into the basket as it can hold and lugs it back to the house.

Surprise, surprise – the logs don't burn properly. The cottage quickly fills with smoke, so she opens the door wide and leaves the basket on the front steps.

The pile of rag rugs that was in the living room the last time she was here is in the hallway now, and she drags the whole lot outside to hang them on the tilting clothesline behind the house. For lack of a more appropriate tool, she finds a rusty rake and beats the dust out of them.

It's not long before it starts drizzling, which frustrates her even more. How many setbacks can there be on her first day? She fetches her raincoat from the bag she left in the kitchen and the lead from the passenger seat of the car. She leaves the front door open – that's how people do it in the countryside, isn't it? – and calls for Maine, who ignores her. It really is quiet around here. She calls him again and this time he obliges, possibly having perceived a hint of desperation in his owner's voice.

The two head down the gravel driveway. Cassi looks around for a sign of human life. There's what looks like a farmhouse a few hundred metres away, but it's hard to tell from this distance. A screeching sound suddenly erupts in the air. She glances to her left, where an old lady on a bike seems to have narrowly missed running her over.

6

Or maybe old lady isn't the right word. Let's say a perky woman in her sixties, who has come to a hard, wide-legged stop in front of Cassi and Maine, in the middle of the road. She squints her steel-grey eyes, lined with black kajal, a hint of a smile forming on her lips.

'So, here you are.'

Cassi nods, confused. The woman extends her right hand.

'Welcome to Bäcken. Max told me you were incoming. He's my nephew so I know most of what there is to know about the people selling and buying houses around here. Or, well, I know most of what there is to know, period. I'm Marlene.'

Marlene's voice is deep and slightly husky and her handshake is robust. Cassi tries her best to suppress the *ouch!* that threatens to escape her lips.

'Cathrin,' she says, because her legal name comes automatically to her when introducing herself to someone older than her. 'But everyone calls me Cassi.'

Marlene has greying, curly hair that falls just below her jaw. Large gold hoops dangle from her ears. Her outfit is quite an eyesore – a pink quilted jacket paired with bright red trousers. She clearly doesn't believe in helmets.

Marlene turns her attention to Maine. She purses her lips, bends down to scratch his head, neck and back with red-manicured hands.

'He's a cutie, isn't he? So gentle! I don't have one anymore, but we kept one for hunting back when I was married. A mean bastard, he was.'

Cassi still feels overwhelmed by the sudden company. She was unprepared to make conversation. All she manages to get out is a: 'Is that right?'

'The dog, I mean!' Marlene adds with a raspy sound in her throat that might have been a laugh but sounds more like a growl. 'But I don't have much good to say about the husband either!'

She straightens up and adjusts the cloth tote in her basket before sticking her hand into her jacket and performing the motion usually associated with a bra strap having slipped down and needing to be pulled back into place. Then her hand digs a ball of *snus* out from under her top lip, flings it into the ditch flanking the road, and shoves a fresh one in.

'It's been a long time since anyone has lived in that house,' she says. 'Karl-Adam moved out several years ago, and we haven't seen hide nor hair of his kids since.'

Marlene looks beyond the gravel road, where a trace of red emerges from the foliage.

'And did I hear you're going to be living here permanently? Did you leave the city for the country?'

Cassi swallows, her mouth suddenly dry. Her fingers move reflexively to her necklace with the pink stone, clutching it.

'That's the plan. I felt it was time for a change.'

'I have to say I find this *green wave* business odd. Isn't that what you call it?' Marlene says, looking around. 'What are you young people coming out here for? No offence, but surely you can find adventure elsewhere.'

She shakes her head.

'I guess it's all thanks to Max – who you obviously already know – and the Desgoffes. They've taken over the campground. They're entrepreneurs.'

Marlene pronounces the last word as though it were in italics.

'They're not as posh as they sound,' she adds, her mouth crooked into a smile. 'Just normal-posh. They're the ones who keep alpacas. You haven't met them, I know that, because I was just over there, and we talked about you. Lollo's helping me with some interior design.'

Marlene pats the tote in her basket, from which the ends of two candlesticks are sticking out.

'But Max said you're starting a business. Something New Age-y, or whatever? Converting the barn?'

Marlene raises her eyebrows inquisitively but leaves no room for a reply. Cassi's head feels like it's been beaten down with a baseball bat.

'I'm not criticising, obviously. It's not for me to dictate how other people live their lives. I've gone through that enough myself.'

She shakes a fist at the sky to illustrate her frustration, looking at Cassi to make sure she's getting how sick Marlene is of the lifestyle police.

'As far as I'm concerned, it's great that you're bringing something fresh to the town,' she continues. 'I'm the kind of person who likes change. But I don't understand you people.'

Then she falls silent again, her eyes locked on Cassi's. Cassi realises she has to be strategic. What she says to Marlene will clearly spread far and wide. She doesn't want to look like a hippie (or worse: a yuppie), but she doesn't want to come off as too closed-off either, risk rubbing someone the wrong way. Mostly she just wants to be left alone, but she can't tell Marlene that.

'Sounds like there's a lot going on around here,' Cassi says. She speaks slowly, especially compared to Marlene's torrent of words, giving herself time to weigh hers before letting them out.

'What I do is quite different . . . but I'm happy to be here. I feel inspired. I can really feel the tranquillity.'

There, that wasn't so bad, upbeat but not too enthusiastic. In time, the people in this town will see what she's like. They'll notice that she keeps to herself and will respect that. Cassi bends down to stroke Maine's head.

'The sale and the move happened so quickly,' Cassi continues. 'It was all done and dusted in what felt like a second.'

Marlene studies her, one eyebrow cocked.

'Said the actress to the bishop,' she quips, pausing briefly before continuing. 'I'm open to things, you should know that. As I said, I like when there's stuff going on. Be it parties, New Age nonsense, whatever. I want to hear more about what you're up to.' She adjusts the gears of her bike. 'But I'm meeting someone, so I have to go. Let's meet up soon, though. Come by for a cup of coffee.'

Cassi replies, without any intention of following through, that she'd love to. Marlene throws Maine a kiss and pedals off. Cassi stays where she is, watching Marlene's pink silhouette grow small and disappear.

What she said about 'a business', that she wants to hear more about what Cassi's up to, makes Cassi wonder what

Max the Estate Agent has told the people of the town. Running away from your life hardly qualifies as being an entrepreneur. Besides, Max knows nothing about her. Cassi has done her best to shut down any attempt at small talk when they've spoken on the phone and when she stopped by the agency to pick up the keys. She didn't say anything out of the ordinary, did she? The whole thing was over so quickly, it's as if she witnessed it from afar, rather than made a huge decision and uprooted her life. There were a lot of papers to sign. She did it sitting cross-legged on a chair, scarfing down complimentary chocolates from the bowl on the table, which prompted Max to start talking about an 'indigenous cocoa ceremony'. Cassi had just kept eating in silence. Yes, maybe she'd given the wrong impression, acted too much like a bohemian city girl looking to settle down in nature. But it was never her intention to mislead anyone. Could it be that Max – and in turn Marlene, and who knows who else – thought that she came to Bäcken to shake things up? And why on earth does the thought of actually doing it excite her?

7

Most of Cassi's first night in the cottage was spent listening to the house creaking and some mysterious sounds coming from the forest. Or maybe she's just not used to being surrounded by nature.

Cassi feels better now that the sun's up. She rubs her temples before getting out of bed – embarrassingly, she slept in yesterday's clothes – and slowly makes her way through each room of her new home, as if to check whether anything's changed overnight. The floor is cold against the soles of her feet.

Everything's the same. Coffee, she needs coffee. When she turns on the kitchen tap, the water comes out a pale brown colour. Not as pure looking as she'd imagined country water to be, but Max said it was drinkable, so she tries not to overthink it. She lets the water boil for quite a while in a small pot before mixing in instant coffee and a splash of milk.

Cheerful morning light dances through the kitchen window. Cassi takes her cup, unlocks the door and spreads one of the tattered rag rugs out on the top step. She wonders if she should scrape the moss off the steps, but wondering's as far as it goes. Maine sniffs the air, then heads out into the garden with his nose firmly planted on the ground.

Is this first cup of coffee on the front steps of your

new home a rite of passage? A moment to instil in your memory? Cassi tries to sense if this is a truly pivotal life event. If this is where she's going to be sitting from now on, if this is the step she will remember as the place she always had her morning coffee, come the winter of her life. Before she can fantasise too much about it, a large spider scuttles by her bare feet, as if to encourage her to explore other coffee-drinking locations.

Cassi stands up and looks around. The adrenaline rush from the spider encounter, combined with the caffeine, has her engine revving. She thinks to herself that she should make a list of things that need fixing. A to-do list of all the practical chores she didn't have to deal with when she rented a room, and that she never had to worry about in her newly renovated flat – all those things that are a hundred times more impractical when you live in an old cottage in the middle of the woods. Every little part of the house would benefit from being looked at, she knows it. Over the past year, she's watched so many derelict homes turned into luxury condos, she ought to be an expert on the subject. Her coffee break on the front steps could have served as the opening sequence of the first episode on her renovation, followed by a snappily edited montage. Quick cuts of Cassi, happy and sweaty in dungarees, tearing down wallpaper, replacing old insulation, tiling, laying pipe, painting, installing new wiring, damp proofing, decorating.

But no. This is the kind of thing she was trying to get away from. The ridiculous demands and must-haves of modern society. Here in nature, she's going to view scarce resources as a blessing. Her savings, the money she made from the sale of her flat, which buying the cottage only took a bite out of, will last her a long time. If she's prudent, that is. Instead of turning her nose up at her tap water, she should see the extra iron as a welcome dietary supplement. Use rainwater to wash. Pee in the forest and use her poo as fertiliser. Stop being so prissy in general. Live like in the good ole days, maybe. Learn to grow things. Use the things growing around her. Rise with the sun and hit the hay when night falls. Or acquire some kerosene lamps. She makes a note to google whether human faeces can indeed be used as fertiliser and if kerosene still exists, and if so, where to buy it.

Cassi sets off towards the Big Road. It's hardly big, but bigger than the one her house is on, and paved too, so that's what she'll call it. She looks in the distance, her gaze fixed on her closest neighbour's farm. It's a yellow house, half-hidden behind trees. There's smoke rising from it.

Her phone buzzes in her back pocket. From time to time, they still come: messages, like tentative digital nudges from her old life, from people who might think that this time she'll reply. But she doesn't. She deletes everything immediately, doesn't even look at the words, doesn't want to let them invade her, eat their way into her consciousness. She turns around and walks back. Manages to avoid the deepest holes in the road, where the puddles have now dried and turned into mud. She studies the walls of the cottage, a rusty gutter that has come detached over in one corner, and the roof, where the tiled symmetry is broken around the chimney.

Wellies, she thinks. Wellies.

8

Truth be told, the cottage is not the first life-altering impulse buy Cassi's ever made. Maine, for example, came into her life three years ago, just like that, after an intense spin class at the gym. She was drenched in sweat, high on endorphins, invincible, checking her work email before she'd even made it out of the studio. She'd pedalled her way to solutions to both human resource issues and buying problems that had been grating on her for a while, and just before the class she'd had a highly sensitive, passive-aggressive non-row with her boyfriend Jarmo about the protracted work trip he was on. And she still hadn't stopped bleeding after a pregnancy that hadn't ended the way she'd wanted.

It was a feeling of strength, euphoria, defiance, of everything being possible, mixed with a stifled bass note of despair. And suddenly, there it was! An advertising link to a dog shelter among the endless spam in her inbox. When she clicked it, the first thing she saw was Maine's slightly cockeyed gaze. Underneath, a brief description:

Breed: Mixed
Age: Approx. 7–8
Sex: Male
Can live with children/cats/other dogs: Unknown

Maine is a very gentle and affectionate dog who loves to snuggle. He enjoys walks but prefers to take it easy. Loves bananas. Surrendered after death of owner.

Cassi looked at herself in the mirror of the changing room, wiped the sweat from her forehead, grabbed her bag, and left the gym. Called the shelter on her way home and in less than half an hour, she talked them into letting her bypass every one of their usual routine checks. She picked up Maine that same night.

Her impulsivity sometimes scares her. It reminds her of her childhood, her mother. Cassi didn't, doesn't want to be like that. She's not like that. She's in charge of her life. She's in control.

And yet, sometimes, these things just happen.

Not that she lets it show. Cassi's quick-witted and solutions-oriented and any impulsive decision she can't return, paint over, or gaslight her way out of afterwards, she simply pretends was thought-through. Meticulously planned.

Maine was not returnable. All the arguments she could have made, she'd used up when she talked them into letting her take him. So instead, the story she told people was that she'd always wanted a dog. That he'd been a carefully considered decision, that she'd wanted to adopt, and that this dog was right for her because he was used to being home by himself. Granted, she only used that last argument once, since the look on the face of the person she said it to made it clear she was on the wrong track. After that, she instead leaned hard into what a beautiful thing adoption was. To anyone who wanted to know, and everyone else for that matter, she explained that it's the only proper way to get a dog, in fact the only way a sane person could and should consider doing it. She threw herself into the role of rescuer. Got involved with dog charities, helped connect lonely pooches with new owners. She was even asked to participate in a panel discussion on the evening news when there was a public debate about imported street dogs, but she declined because she had to work.

In all honesty, it was a process for her, learning to share her life with Maine. But now, she genuinely believes they were meant for each other.

9

Cassi had thought she'd feel complete and utter bliss the second she picked up the keys to her new house. But today, on her second day as its owner, she still feels restless. It must be the abrupt change from the city to life in the country. She tells herself it's natural her head's all over the place, it will take a while for her to get used to it and find serenity in the silence, the solitude. Those are the very things she was yearning for. Those are the things she used her savings for.

She needs to remember that here her previous life doesn't matter. She's finally managed to get far away from it. This is her fresh start, complete independence, and everything will happen on her terms from now on. This is where she's going to be able to be who she really is. Gradually emerging, as if out of a thick mist, new and crisp. Any moment now, serenity is going to crash over her. Any moment now, she tells herself.

She lets Maine out, makes coffee, sets up her recycling bin.

It's raining when Cassi sets off into the forest. This is the moment her life as an outdoorsy person begins. Lingonberry shrubs graze her legs, dry themselves on her jeans. Ah – the magic of water! Yes, nature *is* magical, she says out loud.

Then she trips over an exposed tree root. The moss is wet like a sponge against her bottom.

Any moment now.

10

She's finally managed to sleep. She wakes up late on the third day, in the same position she fell asleep in. She lets Maine out, puts the empty wine bottles in the recycling bin, boils water for coffee. Her shoes are still wet from the day before.

Wellies, she thinks. Wellies.

She goes outside, her socks already damp. The weather has cleared and a few faint rays of sunlight are finding their way into her clearing. Maybe she should turn it into a garden. She walks her usual lap around the house and shakes the tilting clothesline on which the rag rugs are still hanging, now soaked. She walks over to the barn, opens the small door, and ventures in, ready to get to work.

Behind the haybales, Cassi makes serious progress. She finds a round, green plastic garden table, a foldable beach chair, a shovel, a wooden stool, two buckets, a tied-up plastic sack of what appears to be Easter decorations, and a stack of old magazines. She hauls all of it into the light and wipes the worst of the dust and grime off the furniture with a kitchen towel. Then, she arranges an improvised outdoor seating area at the bottom of the front steps, using her finds as props. She carries out a large ceramic planter, which had been sitting just inside the front door, and puts it on the porch.

'This place is starting to look lived in,' she says out loud. Cassi checks her phone. Then, she goes into the kitchen and picks up the corkscrew.

11

On the fourth day, Cassi wakes up late. She lets a rather desperate Maine out, puts more empty wine bottles into the recycling bin, boils water for coffee, slips her feet into her shoes. At least they're dry today. She boils some oats in milk and eats them from the pot, her stomach rumbling loudly with every bite. When was the last time she ate a full meal? Cassi can't remember.

The forest looks the same as yesterday and everything is still. A movement over on the gravel road sparks a glimmer of excitement inside her, but it's only a deer walking by.

Cassi would never admit to herself that the silence and solitude are getting to her. Once she has finished her coffee, she grabs her car keys and opens the passenger door for Maine, who jumps in eagerly. She drives aimlessly past fields and tall trees, passing the village which is deserted even in the middle of the day. Only the pizzeria shows sign of life, with three cars parked out front. She considers going in but quickly realises she doesn't have her wallet on her.

By the church, she gets stuck behind a tractor with a trailer for a while, until a wider lane allows her to overtake. A few metres away, a woman wearing gym shorts and a purple bra is fetching post from a row of post boxes. Marlene. Cassi waves with her hand out the car window.

She keeps driving. And here's the forest. And the Big Road. Again. A feeling of emptiness that has nothing to do with food settles painfully in her stomach, like an undigested seed. Can she think of a reason to turn around and drive back to Marlene? Does she have some kind of errand she could use as an excuse?

Just as she's about to turn left onto her own gravel, another car approaches from the opposite direction. It's so surprising that she stops to let the other car pass. Maine wakes up when she brakes, climbing up onto the seat and sitting down. The other car slows down too, coming to a halt. The driver, a gaunt, baseball-capped, big-nosed man of indeterminate age, possibly sixty-five, but likely closer to eighty, rolls down his window. Cassi does the same. The man looks as though he regrets it the moment he meets her eyes. At first, he stares at her as though he's seen a ghost, then he looks past her, his eyes finding Maine. He doesn't look like he wants to talk, but he does anyway.

'I noticed you'd moved in. I just wanted to stop by to see if you needed anything. I know that house well. I used to help Karl-Adam too, back in the day. I'm Pavel.'

Pavel turns his head, eyes fixing on the road ahead, as though he were still driving.

'Thank you, that's so nice,' Cassi says, smiling. Raising half a hand from the wheel in a small wave. 'I'm Cathrin. But everyone calls me Cassi. I admit, there's quite a lot that needs doing and I'm sure I haven't discovered half of it. But at least I can now open the front door without almost breaking my wrists!'

Pavel's eyes stare into the distance, a painful reminder that she's not good at small talk anymore.

'My dog is called Maine,' she says. 'He seems to like it in the woods. We lived in town before.'

'Oh right, another thing.' The man seems not to have heard her, or maybe he doesn't care for animals. He leans over to the seat next to him, which is piled high with unidentifiable stuff, and digs around for a while until he finds a single key attached to a colourful key ring.

'Here, I'm sure you'd like this back. I came to fix the door when I heard the house was sold. But it would be wrong to keep the spare key now that you've moved in.'

Cassi's about to take the key when the man retracts his hand.

'I wouldn't mind keeping this, eh, key ring, actually.'

He carefully removes the key and then holds it out to her.

'A key ring's always good to have,' Cassi says, hoping to cut through the awkwardness, but she's not rewarded with a smile. The man just looks at it and then slips it into the breast pocket of his less-than-clean, blue-chequered flannel shirt.

'All right then, I need to be off. But you can have my number. So you can call me if you need me.'

Cassi holds out her phone and Pavel types in his number, then checks it over, mouthing each digit to himself.

'This is really nice of you,' Cassi says. 'Thanks again. I'll try not to call all the time.'

She raises the phone to her ear, pretending to already be calling him. Another attempted and failed joke. It's not like her. She can't help but wonder what these forced jokes are in aid of. Cassi clears her throat, but before she can say anything else, Pavel puts his car into first gear and rolls away. Despite the stiff juxtaposition of Pavel's terseness and her own babbling, Cassi feels borderline cheerful as she drives up towards the cottage. She turns to Maine.

'Nice old man, don't you think?'

It felt good to have a semi-normal human interaction. Maine looks at her like he agrees.

12

Cassi has always known she's a perfectionist and a control freak. An only child born into a life of no boundaries, she grew up to be a persuasive individual, able to get things done her way – and get people to do them too. As a child, she talked her friends into quitting after-school activities that she herself couldn't afford, or that took up too much of their free time (meaning she was bored). She made sure she was crowned prom queen every year, until the school board changed the rules so that the same person couldn't win two years in a row. She controlled her circle's friendships and romantic interests like a puppet master. She was the head of the student council, raised money for charity, edited the yearbook, organised prom. Always with freshly washed, neatly brushed hair – from a young age Cassi had understood that a low-budget wardrobe could be concealed behind a seemingly expensive haircut. As an adult, she'd had to work hard to dial back at least some of those traits. She realised that they weren't always appreciated by others – quite the opposite, in fact. She always pointed out if someone had food stuck in their teeth, she brushed dandruff off the shoulders of jackets, used the best cutlery when a friend would come over for dinner. Yes, maybe she came off as stern, controlling. But she was always easier on others than herself.

After days of isolation, Cassi decides it's time to finally

venture into the supermarket in Bäcken. She needs pasta. Remarkably, the store is not one of the usual flashy chains and seems to be independently run. The exterior of The Market, as it's called, is completely devoid of advertisements. There are signs at the entrance informing Cassi that The Market also serves as the local post office as well as a liquor store. Good to know, she thinks.

The aisles are deserted. A man who reeks of manure seems to be the only customer, walking around aimlessly with an empty trolley. Cassi picks up her usual groceries – consistent, even after her recent change of scenery: pasta, tinned tomatoes, onions, instant coffee, oats, milk, washing-up liquid, hand soap, loo roll. Feeling energised and slightly overstimulated, she also grabs a packet of biscuits which, nearing their sell-by date, are on sale by the tills.

A middle-aged man in a knitted sweater vest tallies up Cassi's shopping without meeting her eye.

'You wouldn't happen to know where I can buy wellies around here?' she asks him.

The cashier shoots her a quick glance, his gaze surprisingly stiff, and replies briefly: 'You'll have to go to the Village Shop.'

Cassi has no idea what or where the Village Shop is and is taken aback by his obvious iciness. Surely her question wasn't that odd?

Without looking at her again, he adds: 'Drive towards Berg.'

'Thank you,' Cassi replies.

She starts to pack up her shopping and accidentally knocks a tin of tomato paste, which falls and rolls under the till.

'I know who you are,' the man says as Cassi awkwardly bends to pick up the tin. 'We're neighbours. My wife and I live in the yellow house near yours. This is our shop. I'm Hans.'

At first, Cassi thinks this is his way of apologising for his unfriendliness. Maybe he's about to invite her around for coffee? She waits for an invitation, but it doesn't come.

'Max told me about you,' Hans says instead, as the manure-smelling man pulls up to the till behind Cassi and begins to put his shopping on the belt. 'And I reckon I know what you're up to. Let me be clear, I don't stick my nose in other people's business, but I want no part in that kind of hippie nonsense.'

Cassi looks up at him, eyes wide.

'OK, good to know,' is all she says, because he's already turned his back on her and is now talking to the manure-smelling man about his newborn calves. What has Max been saying about her? First Marlene's enthusiastic curiosity, now Hans's hostility. She feels resentful and embarrassed. She came here to be alone, didn't she? That's all she wanted – to be left alone.

On the way back, Cassi listens to a radio programme in which a weepy listener has called in to get advice on how to handle difficult childhood memories. She thinks about a psychology show she saw a few years earlier on TV, where the recommendation given to a similar patient was something along the lines of: 'Imagine putting all your problems in a casserole dish on a hot burner. Then you put a heavy lid on it and keep it clamped on there as things start to boil inside.' The idea seems strangely comforting and familiar to Cassi now.

13

The full name of the Village Shop turns out to be the Garden, Forestry, Farm, Field & Home Village Shop, est. 1969 Morten Gunnarsson. It stocks, as the name implies, almost everything. Tractor parts, sheep-shearing equipment, dish racks, gas barbecues, sweets sold in bulk. The garden section has an impressive array of patio canopies, outdoor furniture and climbing frames on display, as well as everything you could ever need to grow plants, be it in small flowerpots on the windowsill or in a field.

Cassi finds herself drawn to the seeds and lingers there for a long time. Contemplates growing her own food, owning a farm. It would make sense financially – plus, it'd be nice to avoid crowded supermarkets forever. What goes into taking care of a cow? Are they like hamsters, do you need at least two? Maybe that's a step too far. She can think about it some other time. Maybe she should buy frozen vegetables and call it a day. Does she even have a freezer? She's forgotten to check.

Cassi walks around until she eventually finds a pair of wellies. She also grabs a rake and asks an employee hurrying past for something to cut bushes with and is shown to the hedge shears. A display in the home decor section persuades her to buy three geraniums and a bag of potting soil, too. Just because you're planning a life as a self-sufficient hermit doesn't mean you want your home to be ugly.

The girl at the till has platinum blond hair secured in a high, shiny ponytail and looks up at Cassi through fake lashes, jet-black and dense. Her nametag says 'Sofia', but the 'So' has been crossed out with a sharpie. Ever since Cassi turned thirty, people's age is always the first thing she thinks about, and she places this Fia at the lower end of her twenties. Fia smiles at her. Cassi smiles back. It's a relief after the awkwardness with Hans.

'The geraniums are four for a hundred,' Fia speaks at a leisurely pace. 'So go ahead and grab another at no extra cost if you want. Greed is good!'

Fia smiles again.

'All right, one moment, then,' Cassi hurries back to the geranium aisle, grabs a plant, and jogs back to the till.

'Hey, no rush, we're not exactly crowded,' Fia comments, glancing out at the virtually empty store. 'You're the one who bought Karl-Adam's house? Marlene said she met you. Nice!'

She starts scanning the barcodes of Cassi's purchases. As long as it's done with kindness, Cassi realises she doesn't mind people talking about her. Yes, maybe she has loose plans of becoming a self-sufficient, world-rejecting recluse in a cottage full of geraniums, but she can still talk to people. The two aren't mutually exclusive.

Cassi nods and tells Fia about the forest and what living in the house feels like, finishing off with a long harangue about how the purpose of living is experiencing things, that people have to break out of old routines and try something new. It's as though she's trying to persuade herself she's made the right choice. As though both her encounter with Hans and the anxiety that still sinks its claws into her at night need to be aired out, and Fia, with her kind smile, simply happens to be the one who bears the brunt of it. She might have been the best person for it, as she doesn't take her eyes off Cassi's once, attentively listening to every word she says.

Before she's done talking, a woman joins the queue behind Cassi. She has big, frizzy hair and seems slightly frazzled. Her trolley's piled high with bags of animal feed and a pitchfork. She reaches out and grabs a fistful of chocolate bars from the display next to the till, tossing them onto the belt. Then she sighs, demonstratively raising her left wrist, as though there were a watch there to mark the time.

Fia calmly turns to her. 'Hi, Alida.'

Cassi turns to the woman too and nods. They must be about the same age.

Alida says 'Hey' to Fia, not in the broad local dialect Cassi had expected, but in sharp Stockholmian, and shoots Cassi a sceptical look. Then she raises her chin in an almost imperceptible nod. One of life's little mysteries, how that particular motion has become a universal greeting.

Fia looks at Cassi again and smiles. She's in no hurry.

'Marlene told me you're going to convert the barn and do workshops there,' she says. 'Let me know when you're up and running.'

Cassi almost bursts out laughing but manages to stop herself. She realises the misconception about who she is and what she does has truly spread, with more and more details added to the mix. She knows she should set the record straight. She really should. But the real dilemma is how to rectify the situation without making anyone feel stupid. She doesn't want to create drama. Most of the interactions she's had with people have been pleasant. She has enjoyed the positive attention and wants to keep it that way.

There's also an element of flattery. All this attention, all these questions . . . it's as though she is *someone* again. Has something to offer. It's a feeling she didn't know she'd been missing.

'Well, I don't know about workshops,' Cassi says with a smile, which she hopes comes off as warm and not as stiff as she feels while chatting to these strangers. 'I'm not sure exactly what I'll be doing yet, I have to settle in first, I think. Do up the house, things like that. There's quite a lot to be getting on with.'

Is that enough of an explanation? She hopes so. Talking without knowing what you're talking about is a tricky balancing act.

'Sure, but, yeah, let me know,' Fia replies. 'I tried a bunch of things when I lived in Oslo, but around here, stuff like what you do isn't very common. People can be sceptical. So I'm really glad you're here!'

Cassi asks no follow-up questions, even though she wonders what 'a bunch' is a measure of. What 'stuff like that' could mean. Maybe it's best not to know. She simply nods, says: 'See you!', and carries her purchases to the car.

She's finished packing everything into the boot and is about to close it when Alida steps out into the car park with one hand raised to shield her eyes from the sun. She looks around and, spotting Cassi, points at her, calling out: 'Hey!'

Alida starts pushing her heavy trolley towards her, but

the wheels get stuck in the gravel. She gives up and pulls it behind her instead, leaving two deep tracks in her wake. Alida looks like she could be in her thirties, short and stocky. She's wearing a thick wool jumper with leather elbow patches, rolled-up jeans and sturdy boots. Cassi can sense she's a practical person who doesn't like too many frills.

It's not that she looks like Cassi's mother. Because she really doesn't. Other than the blond hair, there are no similarities. It's that insecure look in her eyes. That messy aura Cassi had sensed at the till.

Later on, when Cassi tries to figure out how things unfolded, she wonders whether she might have acted differently if she'd spent more time with her mother. If she'd had more experience of dealing with this particular personality type. Maybe she would have been able to fend off Alida, but in the moment, she'd been entirely powerless.

On her way home from the supermarket, Alida's words echo in a loop in her head.

'Can I come by? I want to talk to a professional.'

And her response – God, her response.

'Absolutely.'

14

Cassi's mother Bea had a lot of great qualities. When she was young, though, only one had seemed to matter to others: her beauty. She was drop-dead gorgeous, out-of-this-world stunning: legs that went on forever, hair cascading down her back like a silky, yellow waterfall. If life were a cartoon, chins would have hit the ground and tongues would have unfurled whenever she walked by.

Bea had started modelling in Sweden at fifteen, moved abroad a year later, and had never had to have a so-called *normal life*. She'd lived loudly and unapologetically from a very young age: parties, celebrity friends, trips abroad, fancy restaurants, designer clothes. Bea refused routines. Demanded spontaneity from everyone. Trusted crystals and astrology and tarot cards to solve all her issues. She'd gone viral long before the concept of 'going viral' even existed when she'd fallen into the lap of a famous actor at a Paris Fashion Week show, the photo making the front page of most gossip magazines. The brief and stormy romance that followed with said film star, he forty-seven, she nineteen, had actually helped her career. The world had talked and written about Bea. It was exactly how she'd wanted it to be.

But then Bea had become a mother at twenty-four. Earlier than her managers would have wanted. Life as she'd known it ended the moment her belly began to grow.

People as good-looking as she was were usually given extra latitude in society. The requirement to obey certain unwritten rules didn't apply to them. After giving birth to Cassi, Bea had spent a few difficult months trying to return to her old life, in equal measures convinced that things didn't have to change just because she'd had a baby and determined that no outsider would ever infringe on the bond between her and her daughter.

But not even a committed free spirit can lug an infant from bar to bar every night of the week, waiting for her recently pregnant body to slim down and tone up enough for the pages of *Vogue*. Besides, if you're always turning up in the company of a colicky baby, it doesn't matter how gorgeous and famous you are. Even a barman who has a crush on you will ask you to leave.

Spending time with her friends became impossible. Working was already out of the question. Bea couldn't keep up with her previous lifestyle anymore. Not even after selling all her designer luggage. She'd surrendered the whole lot, including a complete, if well-worn, resort collection, to Paris's most esteemed vintage shop, around the corner from Place Vendôme.

She had to go back to her hometown, where Cassi's grandmother could help out with childcare and cheap flats were easy to come by. The downside was, there was nothing for Bea to do but struggle with postnatal depression, mindlessly eating homemade cinnamon buns and sneaking shots of cream liqueur into her morning coffee in place of milk. As Bea quickly grew bigger, the chances of her resuming her modelling career shrank even further. It's unclear whether her modelling contract was actually terminated, but after she moved home she never had another job.

A normal life was out of the question. Bea was not about to compromise on her freedom. She believed life was meant to be lived without structure and with a completely open mind. True, her baby had forced her to give up her popularity and success, but her bohemian nature was never going to disappear.

And so Cassi – her name a misspelled homage to Catherine Deneuve – grew up without boundaries, with the wrong clothes for every season, breakfast for dinner and dinner for breakfast. More often than not, Cassi had to sleep on the couch – her bed was frequently occupied by someone else, or by an art project, or by last week's health-kick purchases, which had then promptly been forgotten and were now still in their bag, slowly morphing from root vegetables into mouldy, alien globs.

Bea smoked a lot and drank a lot but had a fairly even temper. Short bursts of emotion would quickly turn into self-pity, the column of ash at the end of her cigarette a sad pennant above glasses of red and the kitchen table, her fingers playing with the silver chain nestled among the folds on her neck.

There had never been a dad. But that was fine. It wasn't as though Cassi felt a need for another parent. She had her grandma. She had her mum. Her mum was enough. Enough of a burden. And besides, Cassi felt that there was nothing unusual about her living situation. In her class at school, most people were being raised by single parents.

But what Cassi quickly realised was that she preferred

the structured rhythms of school to her unpredictable homelife. On the weekends, she found herself longing for the neatly sorted markers, the clean drinking glasses, and the toilets that always had loo roll.

Her need for order was fully cemented on her eighth birthday. Cassi had had a great time at her party. She and her closest friends – Maggie, Andrea and Liza – had danced all day, thrown things from the balcony, repotted – or completely ruined, depending on your interpretation – their landlord's flowerbeds. Having been interested in smoke signals since Maggie had read some old *Lucky Luke* comics, that day they'd managed to start two fires in the courtyard before a neighbour had intervened with water and curses. None of them had ever laughed so hard. And to top it all off, Liza had fallen asleep with her head in the meringue cake! But the mood had turned sour when the parents had come to pick their children up.

'Did you give them alcohol!?!' Andrea's father had asked, and Cassi's mum would mimic that question for years to come in a squeaky voice, as though it were the most ridiculous thing she'd ever heard. Andrea, usually so capable, had been leaning heavily against the doorjamb as she attempted to stick her arm into her jacket sleeve, her lips pressed into a thin line of deep concentration.

'Oh, I didn't mean to,' Bea had replied in a husky voice, leaning against the bathroom door. 'And it was only cider. I didn't realise there was alcohol in it. And come on, the kids had a blast!'

Cassi could feel the mood in the room changing into something sour and scary. After her friends and their parents had left, Cassi had gone back to her room and instinctively started folding her clothes and putting things away. She found the act of cleaning calmed her down.

In time, Cassi and her mother became two polar opposites sharing a flat. One scattered things around, the other picked them up. It wasn't entirely unlike a normal parent–child relationship, just in reverse. Cassi was given new nicknames by her mother: 'Miss Pedantic', 'Buzzkill', 'World's youngest pensioner'. Bea took on random jobs that never lasted and developed drinking habits that intensified ever earlier in the day, her signature silver flask always in hand.

Cassi moved to Stockholm as soon as she was done with secondary school with Liza, Maggie, Andrea. For over a year, the four lived together in a stuffy flat they called the Smoke Signal, until Cassi's need for order forced her to get a place of her own.

As an adult, Cassi's relationship with her mother became complicated in a strange way. They rarely saw each other and yet on most mornings Cassi would wake up to long, sad, personal rambles in her voicemail.

'I don't belong here, Cassi. I want to sip rosé and do coke in the French Riviera. That was my life, Cassi. Handsome men. Luxury. Glamour. I'm not saying it's your fault my life took a turn, turned into this. But I did have to adapt, I did. And I did OK, didn't I? Hello?'

A brief pause for the rustling meeting of lighter and cigarette.

'I just want everything around me to be beautiful. I want to go to the ocean. The oooooooocean, Cassi. La mer. La mère. See, they're the same. The sea, the mother, we belong together. It's not pretty here, Cassi. This town isn't beautiful. It's *boring*. I didn't choose this. You chose, Cassi. Not me. I want to go to the Mediterranean.'

But she never did. Booking two plane seats, as her current weight would have required, was too expensive, taking the train was out of the question, and Bea had never had a driving licence, unless you count the fake one she used as her ID when she was fourteen.

But really, it was the heart attack that did it.

Then a burial by a lake, a final resting place next to Cassi's grandma, who had passed away four years earlier.

Had Cassi felt slightly relieved? No, you can't think things like that, let alone say them. Cassi loved her mother. But Cassi's mental checklist had always felt too long, her mother a checkbox perpetually flashing red behind her eyes. Now, it was gone. Only years later did Cassi realise guilt had taken its place.

15

Even more days have gone by. The restlessness hasn't subsided.

Cassi has watched so much TV that her eyes feel like they might melt any second. She's explored every inch of the house. Googled descriptions of every plant in her front garden, trying to identify them. Moved her growing collection of empty bottles into the barn. Read all the lifestyle magazines from the nineties she found in there the other day. Or was it the other week? The days are blending into one.

Something she read in one of those magazines has stuck with her. It wasn't the instructions on how to use empty beer cans as curlers, nor the article about swapping lives with your male friend for the day. Somewhere, she had come across an article on the benefits of 'saying yes' to everything. It had intrigued her, despite some of the examples being slightly dated, like 'say yes to whatever film your Blockbuster cashier recommends, it might just end up becoming your favourite!'.

If only there was something for her to say yes to in Bäcken.

When the woman from the Village Shop, the one with the frizzy hair and tangled aura, comes cycling down the gravel road on Cassi's sixth day of solitude, it feels serendipitous. And when she asks if Cassi has time to talk, Cassi says 'yes'. It takes no effort at all and isn't even a lie. Cassi has all the time in the world. The woman points to herself and says: 'Alida. No one can ever remember my name.' Which is lucky, because Cassi had in fact forgotten it. But she feels enlivened. The only thing she's worried about is what Alida meant by 'professional' the last time they spoke. Maybe she just needs advice. And that shouldn't be too difficult; Cassi should be able to provide some all-purpose regurgitated pearls of wisdom – especially after reading all those magazines. Plus, she has lived what feels like four different lives already. All she has to do, if Alida really needs solid advice, is add a dose of that New Age vibe they all seem to get from her.

Alida drops her bicycle on the lawn. She seems less frazzled today. Now that Cassi's actively looking for it, the resemblance with her mother is much more noticeable.

Alida studies Cassi closely. 'You look familiar somehow.'

Cassi smiles at her. Says it like it is, even though she's making it up. 'You too, actually. I was just thinking that you remind me of my mum – something about the way you come across. Similar auras.'

Cassi moves her hands in a circle around Alida's head, but Alida slowly shakes it.

'No, I mean, not anything like that. I was wondering if we've met before.'

Cassi's smile is wide and indulgent. She knows she's never met Alida before. She would have remembered her. But, to be on the safe side, she takes another good look at her. Like herself, Alida wears no make-up. She has small, squinty eyes, a full mouth and a freckled nose. She's wearing the same clothes as the other day, but her hair is down today.

'Perhaps that means we have a unique bond,' Cassi replies, inspiration flowing through her. 'Right now, our souls are existing in their physical form at the same time, but it's perfectly possible they've met before. We all belong together one way or another.'

Alida looks at Cassi, her eyebrows raising ever so slightly. Cassi keeps her smile firmly in place.

Her visitor bends down to pet Maine, who has come over to say hi, tail wagging. He pants welcomingly against her thigh.

'Hi there, are you the manager around here?' Alida says. 'You don't exactly smell like roses, do you?'

'He keeps eating something out in the woods, I think,' Cassi says.

'I live with alpacas, I'm used to most things,' Alida says, and shrugs. 'Shall we get to it?'

Cassi shows her into the house. Alida looks around the unfurnished living room. The only things worthy of note are the tall, leafless potted plant, a pile of fist-sized rocks sitting near the fireplace and Maine's camping mat, which she gestures Alida to lie down on. She wants it to seem like a deliberate choice, like the room has been turned bare and all her gorgeous, expensive furniture is sitting somewhere else in the cottage. In reality, there is no furniture. But practical problem solving has always been one of Cassi's strengths. At the end of the day, who's to say she's not just a minimalist? She smiles at Alida again.

'I believe it's easier for body and soul to come together when the body's relaxed,' Cassi says, running her hands over the camping mat.

Almost everything she's said so far has been taken from

an interview with a meditation-obsessed celebrity she watched the other day on daytime TV. Alida steps closer to the mat, takes off her shoes, putting them to one side, and lies down. Cassi fetches a blanket and spreads it over her, lights a candle in the window. Alida closes her eyes, but then opens them again to watch Cassi as she moves around. Cassi feels a sudden pang of anxiety, an urge to call this off and admit she knows nothing about this stuff, that this isn't her. But she doesn't. Instead, she closes her eyes and gives herself a mental pep talk. If this is what's expected of her, it's what she'll give them. She didn't ask for it. She didn't go looking for clients, Alida came to her. And how is offering to help someone feel better a bad thing? They're just going to talk for a bit, it's no big deal.

Cassi hums to herself as she walks a slow lap around the room, wasting time, trying to come up with her next move. Finally she takes a seat on a cushion next to Alida's head, since it feels like the symmetrically appropriate spot, and places her cold fingertips against the woman's forehead, since that feels like something she might have seen people do before (on TV, of course). She presses down gently for a few seconds, then lifts her hand. She pulls her mother's necklace out from underneath her T-shirt so that the pink gem sits directly below her chin, then places her hands in her lap. In all honesty, she's not sure what to say.

Relief washes over her when Alida finally closes her eyes and starts talking.

'I've been feeling for a while that I need to talk to someone, vent, you know.'

She sticks a finger in her ear, rubs her nose.

'But, well, I have a hard time trusting people. And the

people around here, my God! World's biggest gossips. I've tried online forums, but there was just so much drama. So when I heard about you, I thought this might be the solution. That it might be easier, since what I say to you is confidential, you know . . .'

Alida keeps talking, but Cassi's brain is stuck on one word.

Confidential. Is she obligated to keep things confidential? What does that even mean? And most importantly: does that mean there could be some legal liability here? She ponders how to get out of the situation. Should she make Alida sign some kind of waiver, just to be safe? But if so, what kind of waiver?

She defaults to her usual approach: handling the situation by not handling it. Cassi tells herself she wouldn't even know who to tell whatever it is Alida wants to talk about, so confidentiality isn't an issue anyway.

'People lie and make stuff up,' Alida says. 'Before I moved here, I worked in finance in a big city. It was even worse there. Long days, late nights. You know, shit happens. People talk behind your back. Rumours and lies. That's why I prefer to work with animals. They don't play games. When you're dealing with money . . .'

Cassi doesn't mean to interrupt, but she can't help herself.

'Are lies so bad, though, Alida?' she says. 'Isn't all of life a lie, to some extent? I mean, when are we ever completely honest with ourselves?'

A line appears between Alida's eyebrows.

'What are you talking about?' she asks, visibly annoyed, and makes as if to get up.

Cassi puts her hands on Alida's shoulders.

'All questions have to be welcome here, Alida. This is a place of trust and openness.'

Alida presses her lips together but seems to relax back into the camping mat.

Cassi continues.

'You said you used to be in a different line of work?'

Alida exhales through her nose and resumes her story.

'I'm not from here. I'm sure you figured that out already. You can obviously tell from looking at me I'm from the city. The posh part. If you met my dad, he'd make your ears bleed, talking about his endless titles. My family's of aristocratic stock.'

Cassi wouldn't have guessed. But she's not about to question Alida again. She waits silently, letting her talk.

'I got my MBA and it's no exaggeration to say I was the top of my class. Do you get the kind of pressure that puts you under? I went straight from graduation to a job at a top brokerage firm. I had a career. But it wasn't enough. I wanted more, know what I mean? I wanted to *feel* things.'

Alida talks as though she's reciting lines, Cassi thinks. Has she rehearsed this script in her head? Or is Cassi just not used to listening to people anymore? She focuses on giving her face a soft and empathetic look, even though Alida's eyes are closed. Cassi softly presses her hands together, bends her lips into a spiritual smile. When she thinks about how this scene would appear seen from outside, it almost moves her to tears. It must look so peaceful, with the single candle in the window and two people sharing a moment.

Meanwhile, Alida's picking up speed.

It's been a long time since Cassi has experienced such a torrent of words. She really has to focus on not getting distracted by the etymology of the word 'confidence' or by Alida's hair – is it bleached or natural? It's like in an American film, when someone opens one of those red fire hydrants in the summer and the water comes shooting out, raining down on the street, flooding it, children jumping around, playing in the shallow lake, barking dogs joining them, while the adults organise a spontaneous barbecue and a five-person band gathers on someone's front steps and plays and everyone dances. Flashing coloured lights illuminating the entire block. *Focus, Cassi, focus.* She gives out occasional 'hmms' and 'I sees' to appear engaged. Whenever Alida trails off, she asks, 'And how does that make you feel?' That's more like it.

It doesn't feel quite right, what she's doing, but at the same time, it's hard to put a finger on what's so wrong about it. Alida came to her, saying she needed to talk, and Cassi is allowing her to do so. Granted, Alida might have the wrong idea about her, but again, that's hardly Cassi's fault. She hasn't done anything to make people believe she's some kind of therapist. This therapy session notwithstanding. Her neglecting to set the record straight notwithstanding.

At one point, Alida looks like she's on the verge of tears. One hand comes up and wipes the tip of her nose. Cassi suddenly remembers watching Dr Phil console a crying guest by handing her a box of tissues that must have originally been sitting outside his field of vision. She thinks about the way he'd grabbed that box without taking his eyes off the sobbing wretch in front of him. At the time, she'd thought that Dr Phil's main strength wasn't that he solved his guests' clichéd problems with uniquely qualified advice, but rather that he was so skilled at adopting the role of listener. It was all theatre. Cassi has no tissues to offer but she did just wipe fly eggs from the windows. She reaches for the kitchen roll she'd left on the windowsill without taking her eyes off Alida.

'You OK?'

Alida blows her nose loudly and scrunches the kitchen paper into a small ball that Cassi has no option but to accept from her.

Silence falls again. Cassi figures it's probably her turn to say something, but she's been so focused on looking like she was listening that she hasn't actually heard a single word Alida has said. Why did she want to come here? Cassi clears her throat, fumbling for any wisdom that might sit well with her client.

'It's time for you to forgive yourself, to look forward rather than backwards,' she says. 'Life is complicated. You don't have to get everything right. Sometimes, it's good to take a chance on yourself. You can't live your life in fear of making mistakes. If you want to do something, just do it.'

It's Alida's turn to be silent. Cassi takes that as a sign she should continue.

'We have to stop striving for perfection,' she says, and this is something she's thought a lot about the past year, so it's not really a lie. 'What even is perfection? Unachievable, that's what. And what does it give us? Nothing, that much I can tell you. Not even perfection can protect us from misery. It's better to let go of your expectations. Be happy with what is. You don't have to "love" yourself. Bearing it is plenty.'

Cassi pauses. Surely that's enough. Her initial confidence is waning.

'I mean, that all sounds good, I guess, but I'm not sure what you mean,' Alida says.

Cassi neither intends nor tries to clarify further.

'Not everything has to make sense right away, some things are simply meant to be felt,' she says instead. 'Our souls need air and room to thrive. Room for all aspects of our personalities to breathe. Look inward.'

Alida seems to give up. The room's so quiet Cassi has to wonder if Alida can hear her heart racing. She places her now warm fingertips against Alida's forehead. Alida closes her eyes again. Cassi sits motionless for a long moment, then slowly starts tapping on the woman's forehead as if it was a tiny piano. She finishes by pressing the tips of her index and middle fingers against Alida's temples, then strokes her hair gently. A quick head massage would have probably been a nice way to end the session, like a good hairdresser's appointment. Too bad that Cassi finds other people's scalps revolting, so she lifts her hands, leans back and exhales slowly through her mouth.

Apparently interpreting this as a signal that the session's over, Alida sits up, stretching her arms wide.

'I needed that,' she says. 'It's as though my brain's been emptied. I feel clean. Talking to someone who doesn't judge actually feels good.'

Alida pushes back up onto her feet and puts her shoes on. Then she makes some puffing sounds with her hands on her hips, like she's just been through a gruelling workout.

'What are his worst traits?' she asks, pointing at Maine, who's asleep on the porch outside the open front door.

Before Cassi can respond, Alida continues:

'Does a dog even have bad traits? A dog is what it is, right? It has no hidden agenda. Doesn't play games. It acts on instinct and who's to say instincts are wrong, or even something to be judged? Who are we to say if any of them are right or wrong? Why do we feel such a need to compare ourselves to others? People who have a lot to say about other people's lives aren't usually doing too well themselves, that's what I've noticed.'

She almost glares at Cassi at this point, as though Cassi's silence has offended her. Cassi realises she's never given Maine's personality much thought. But she would agree that he is what he is. He's always been easy to live with. Apart from the flatulence, she has no complaints. He's calm, companionable, uninterested in playing. Cassi looks at him. He's lying on his side on the porch, belly facing the sun.

'Thank you for making time for me,' Alida says, holding her hand out. 'Imagine the good it would do a lot of people if they would just go talk to someone. How much do I owe you?'

Cassi's palms are suddenly sweaty. Alida wants to *pay* her? Could charging her be considered fraud?

'Don't worry about it,' she says. She bends down to roll up the camping mat.

'Oh no, I always pay what's owed,' Alida says, sounding and looking stern. 'Just tell me how much.'

If Cassi had kept bees, she would have been allowed to sell honey no matter how inexperienced in beekeeping she was. This is pretty much the same thing, isn't it? And it's the easiest money she's ever made. Granted, the plan was always to live off her savings, but having an active income wouldn't hurt. She snaps the mat out flat on the floor again.

'I usually charge five hundred a session or five sessions for two thousand,' she says.

It's cheaper than a haircut, but more expensive than dyeing your eyelashes. It feels reasonable.

'All right, then let's just book five sessions right now,' Alida says, handing her the exact amount in cash. Cassi takes it and prays Alida doesn't notice how badly her hands are shaking. She presses them together in front of her face, the money sticking out at the top, and bows slightly. Then she walks towards the door, stepping over Maine and jumping down onto the grass. Alida has no choice but to follow.

'I always hang this up outside. There's nothing more cleansing than moonlight, you know,' she tells Alida, holding up the camping mat.

She attaches the mat to the plastic clothesline with wooden clothespins that crumble between her fingers. Then she walks her guest, or maybe she should call her a client, to her bicycle.

'Go home, have a hot beverage, and take it easy,' Cassi tells her, since that feels like the kind of thing a person should say in this situation. 'All the answers are already inside you, you just have to let them up to the surface.'

Alida stares at her. Then she picks up her bike, flings one leg over and pedals off.

When Alida's gone, Cassi picks Maine up and sits down

in the beach chair with him on her lap. She stays there for a long time, until her body temperature has seemingly lowered and her heart has stopped thumping. She's not sure what she just did or what they talked about; she still has no idea what Alida's problem is. But they, she, Cassi, got through it and it wasn't a disaster. If it happens again, she'll be better prepared. She even feels moderately pleased with herself.

She fetches her jacket and the car keys and opens the passenger door for Maine, who jumps in.

16

Cassi has now made a habit of slowly driving up and down the streets of Bäcken. She needs time to see what's going on in her village, what her neighbours are up to. Many of the fences are surrounded by chicken wire, presumably to keep dogs from escaping, and almost every house has prepared for summer by installing white or grey canopies over their patios. A robot mower's doing hesitant laps around a lawn that's barely had time to start growing.

It's dinner time. Several cars are parked outside the pizzeria. She now has money in her pocket, thanks to Alida, and high hopes of seeing the words 'fully licensed' on a sign. Those hopes are unfortunately dashed, but she still leaves Maine in the car and walks towards the door.

There's a ding when she pushes the handle down. Six pairs of eyes turn to her. One person is behind the till, one pops his head out of the kitchen, two are in line to order, and two are sitting at a table with half-eaten calzones in front of them.

'Hey,' she says vaguely to everyone and no one in particular before turning her eyes to the boards above the counter. The menu is divided into four sections, each represented by a flag faintly visible behind a list of dishes.

'Would it be possible to order just a *pizzasallad*?' she asks, since it's the first thought to pop into her head.

'Yeah, I guess that's fine,' the woman behind the counter

replies and starts scouring the till for the corresponding button. 'Nothing else?'

Cassi, stunned and elated, shakes her head, but then changes it to a nod. Realising the gesture's confusing, she then adds words.

'No, sorry, I was just asking if you had it. I haven't decided yet.'

Cassi looks up at the menus again, focusing on the Thai section, suddenly in the mood for something spicy. She swallows loudly. She orders a vegetable red curry. She feels like she's being watched.

The serving section of the restaurant isn't very large. Cassi sidles past one of the calzone-eaters to find a window seat. There are two middle-aged women, one with short red hair, the other with long, black hair, both tousled-looking and red-cheeked. They've hung up their thick hi-vis jackets, which tell Cassi they work outdoors, and are deep in conversation about a film they've both seen. A cloth tote hanging on the back of a chair reads 'Park Workers Against Patriarchy'.

The other twosome is younger. Only when she gets closer does she realise the woman is Fia, the cashier from the Village Shop. Today, she's wearing her bleached hair down and styled into loose curls. Not a hair is out of place, each curl as precisely arranged as her make-up. Her red work fleece has been replaced by a black tank top under a cropped denim jacket. The man sitting across from her is no less well-groomed. His black hair is slicked back, his T-shirt hugging every muscle of his toned torso, arms sticking out, covered in tattoos.

Cassi has a hard time tearing her eyes away from the

couple. To a person who barely showers and rarely changes her clothes, their meticulous looks are fascinating. Maybe they'd be unremarkable in a night club in the city, but in this run-down pile of bricks, they stand out as if they were sitting under individual spotlights.

Which, in fact, they are. When Cassi glances up at the ceiling, she realises the spotlights above that particular table are brighter than any other in the room.

The couple notice her watching them. Fia raises her hand in a wave. Cassi smiles in response and tries to turn her attention to the world outside the window instead. But before she knows it, she's watching them again. They both get hamburgers and Fia squeezes out a dollop of ketchup next to her fries. Then she dips and eats them one by one, grasping them as though her fingers, with their long, pink nails, were tweezers. The man has removed the bun from his burger and is cutting the patty into tiny bite-size pieces with his knife and fork. His black beard is thick and neatly trimmed, and he's careful not to get any sauce on it.

Cassi can tell they're talking about her, even though they're careful to keep their voices down. From time to time, her eyes meet Fia's, and from time to time the man turns around to look at her with unabashed, intense eyes.

She checks her jacket pockets for her phone, anything that might offer a distraction, but she must have left it at home. It's a relief when her own food is brought out, giving her something to do.

Her vegetable stew is piping hot, topped by a layer of grease. The first spicy bite transports her to a balmy evening at a restaurant in Thailand, the sound of the ocean in the background, Jarmo in a white linen shirt, hand-holding across the table, two rings in a box between fizzy champagne flutes.

No, she won't go there! She can't, not today.

With beads of sweat on her forehead and tears in her eyes, Cassi shovels sticky rice into her mouth.

'How did the geraniums work out?'

Cassi looks up to find Fia standing in front of her. Her eyeliner has smeared a little in the corner of one eye, and there are, despite her careful table manners, a few granules of salt stuck on her upper lip.

'Great, thanks. Or at least they've been planted.'

Cassi smiles. Fia smiles.

Fia seems so calm. Cassi envies her, since she's experiencing a minor but impactful mental breakdown.

'So, we were just talking about you. Sorry if it was too obvious,' Fia continues in that leisurely voice. She points to her dinner companion. He smiles from his seat, raising a hand before going back to typing on his phone.

'We know you're, like, a guru or whatever, that you do therapy and whatnot. Yoga, right? But no one I've talked to seems to know exactly what you do. So I figured I'd ask you directly.'

Cassi feels exhausted. The Thailand memory that resurfaced unexpectedly still requires active suppressing. In lieu of three quick vodka shots, Fia has opened a door to something else for her brain to focus on. Seizing the opportunity, Cassi slips through it.

'I don't believe in labels,' she says, even though Fia wasn't exactly asking for a label. 'If I showed you all kinds of diplomas and certificates, what would they tell you?

They're just words. We are all who we are. It's what we do, how we act, that matters.'

She thinks that sounded pretty good, but she can tell Fia doesn't consider it an answer. Cassi has another go at it.

'I'm not sure about being a "guru", but yes, I don't mind offering people who need it some guidance and support. Mental coaching, I suppose you might call it.'

Reasonable enough. But she keeps going.

'Meditation. Breathing. Healing. Visualisation. Massages. Energies and flows.'

The words won't stop coming. They keep pouring out of their own accord. It's possible she's making it sound more like she's confirming Fia's 'guru' statement than denying it. Is it because she detected a note of distrust in Fia's voice? A hint of condescension perhaps? Maybe Fia does see her for who she really is: a shabby, jobless outsider.

Fia's companion joins them at the table, putting his hands on the back of the chair across from Cassi's. He's incredibly good-looking. Cassi lowers her eyes, admiring his round, neatly filed nails and immaculate cuticles. She folds her own fingertips into the palms of her hands.

'Energies, what do you mean by that? Hi, by the way, I'm Berzan.'

Cassi smiles, trying to hide the panicked frenzy she feels inside. Energies, what does she mean by that? Good question. She starts talking, assuming she'll work it out as she goes. As a strategy, it's been working so far.

'Simply put, it can be described as a version of physical therapy in which I create energy flows between my hands to alleviate stress and worry, ease pain. Anything from anxiety to digestive problems . . . But it's a bit difficult to describe in words, maybe it would be easier if I showed you.'

Where did that come from? She's not making this easier for herself. But now she has to deliver. Cassi gets up and steps behind Berzan. The T-shirt straining across his muscular back is blindingly white and seems freshly ironed. She rubs her hands together to make them warm, blows on them with breath that reeks of garlic.

'Now, this isn't how I normally do things. It's better if the surroundings are a bit more tranquil and harmonious.'

She looks around the room, meeting each person's eyes, as though urging them to keep it down.

'But we'll give it a go.'

Cassi puts her hands on Berzan's shoulders, letting them rest there for a while, until the heat of their physical contact begins to make her feel uncomfortable. At that point, she pushes both thumbs into a certain point between his shoulder blades.

'You're blocked right here,' she says quietly. Wow, he *is* jacked. Cassi hopes she didn't pick out some hidden muscle he's been working on deliberately growing and hardening.

Berzan lets out a puff of air. Cassi's own shoulders relax.

'Ow, right there. How did you know? Shit, seriously, that really hurts. But in a good way.'

Cassi keeps pressing her thumbs into the same spot for a long while before easing off. In her old life, she regularly massaged that exact spot on someone, someone who also did a lot of back work at the gym and didn't bother to stretch properly either. But she won't tell anyone, of course not.

Berzan and Fia stare at her in awe. The women at the table next to them have been watching with interest and are now squeezing their own upper bodies to feel where they hurt. Cassi resists the urge to shrug nonchalantly, and instead performs her signature bow to the group. It's becoming increasingly natural to her.

The mood in the room is upbeat now, but all Cassi feels is a sudden and overwhelming urge to leave. She only recently met Fia for the first time, but it feels like she's turned herself into a completely different person since then.

Cassi pulls on her jacket to leave.

'Good to meet you, I hope your back feels better. And the food was great!' she adds, turning to the chef, who has also come out to see what his customers are up to.

Then she does her best to make a composed exit before quickly driving away, the gravel sizzling under her tyres.

17

The cottage is a welcome sight. Her body's throbbing with anxiety, shame and self-loathing. What is she doing? Who does she think she is? It's all so incredibly mortifying.

Within moments of killing the engine, she's reached the pantry, whose shelves are still dusted with either flour or the leavings of some kind of beetle, and which she has turned into wine storage. Then she sits on the porch with Maine and a bottle until the light fades and the treeline begins to morph into eerie shapes. Should she go back to her old life? The basement, the hypermarket, the isolation. She considers getting behind the wheel and leaving this all behind. Only the empty wine bottle in her hand and the immeasurable weight of her body are stopping her.

How is she going to get out of this? Maybe if she stops saying yes to people it'll all simply peter out. She could lie low, find a regular job, and eventually people will forget she ever therapised them or rubbed their backs.

No, that's still too weird. She has to leave. Is there a grace period on cottages?

Cassi finds more wine. And as though she physically has to stop herself from acting on any more stupid whims, she hides the car key inside one of her wellies. It's a clever idea, so clever that it'll take her several days to find it again. She pulls out empty Ikea bags from one of the kitchen cupboards and starts half-heartedly packing up her things. A lamp in one. In another, her duvet and pillow, which she'll have to unpack again to use very soon. Through the window, she sees the geraniums in their new pot on the front steps and bursts into tears of self-pity.

She paces aimlessly, back and forth, back and forth. Dwelling in an endless figure-eight on how life turned out and who she has let herself become, how she's allowed herself to be treated. Remembering all the things from her previous life she desperately wants to forget, all the things she normally suppresses, every detail vivid as though it were yesterday. Her friends, her life, her job, her boyfriend, her travel. The unforgivable betrayal.

It is not until around two o'clock in the morning that she comes to a decision. She is drunk and weepy, and as she's standing on her moss-covered front steps with her fist raised above her head at the starry night sky, she wishes someone could have immortalised the triumphant moment with a photograph. Because she feels it so strongly. That it's enough already. It's her turn. It's time for her to take charge of her life. She's going to stay right here. She's going to start afresh. She's going to become the person she's decided she is. She's going to keep saying yes. She's going to step out of the shadows, she's going to give herself room and this world what it wants from her. Or at least what she thinks it wants and what she herself is willing to agree to. Cheered on by two empty wine bottles, she steps into the early morning to unsteadily hammer a sign into the ground out by the road, in the exact same spot the for sale sign stood not too long ago.

If she'd known then what it would lead to, if she'd

had any inkling of all the things that would happen over the months that followed . . . it probably wouldn't have mattered.

She would have done it anyway.

JUNE

18

The pipes are gurgling. When Cassi flushes the toilet, which she's still using despite the plan to start producing her own manure, the bowl has barely had time to drain from her last visit. In the kitchen, she does the washing up in a bucket she then empties outside, just to avoid having a sink full of water.

Wasn't his name P something? Paolo? Might he be able to help her with this? She searches for 'pa' in her phone and a contact for Pavel pops up. She's always preferred texting to calling and she hopes he's not too old to be a texter. She doesn't want to give him the wrong impression – she needs him to be happy and willing to fix her plumbing issue. Preferably for free. It's going to have to be a call.

She walks outside and dials. Pavel picks up after ten rings, so he's evidently turned off the voicemail function. That's technically proficient for eighty, Cassi thinks. Either way, Pavel says he can come by and have a look at the pipes. That it might be a blockage caused by the house having been unoccupied for so long. Cassi's happy to go with that, it's not as though she has any other, better ideas.

'I'll be home all day,' she says. 'Come by whenever's good for you.'

Pavel says he's going to the shops anyway, so he can be there in fifteen minutes. Then he hangs up on her, which might look normal when it happens in films, but anyone who has experienced it in real life knows it feels abrupt. A bit aggressive, almost. But Cassi appreciates Pavel and his directness. He's like her, no ambiguity. Except every single thing she has said and done since she first entered the cottage has been ambiguous.

Almost exactly fifteen minutes later, Pavel's old orange car turns down her road. In an attempt to get on his good side, Cassi has boiled water for coffee and taken out the reduced-price biscuits, ready to act like an exemplary neighbour being helped with her pipes. For free.

She goes out to greet him on the front steps.

'This is so nice of you, Pavel. I really appreciate it!'

Pavel climbs out of his car. From the boot, he takes out a rusty toolbox. He's wearing the same baseball cap and blue-chequered shirt as the last time she saw him. Neither's been washed in the interim. Another thing they have in common, Cassi notes.

Pavel stares off at the trees as though he can't see her but walks straight over to the house on his scrawny legs. She moves aside so he can get past her. He makes a beeline for the small bathroom and starts clattering about.

'Let me know if there's anything I can do, but when it comes to this house stuff, I'm . . . completely helpless,' she says. 'Can I offer you a cup of coffee?'

An echo of 'not right now' from the pipes.

Cassi goes back to the kitchen and pretends she has things to get on with. She faffs about in the cabinets, plates the biscuits. Puts them back in the packet. Boils the water again.

Pavel eventually joins her in the kitchen, does something

with the pipes under the sink, and drains something revolting into a bucket that he then empties over by the treeline. Then he tests the sink again, and it drains perfectly. He doesn't say a word, but he hums while he works, so he doesn't seem like he's in a bad mood.

'I'll take that coffee now,' Pavel says when he's done, which is surprising, because Cassi has almost assumed his unsociable style would have made him head off as soon as he finished the job.

Pavel washes his hands. Cassi makes two cups of instant coffee and hands him one. The kitchen feels cramped and overly intimate. She has no chairs, or a table for that matter, so they go outside. Pavel sits on the stool and Cassi in the beach chair.

'Would you mind telling me more about Karl-Adam? It would be nice to know something about the people who lived here before me,' Cassi says, mostly to break the silence once they've exhausted the subjects of the weather and the local area. Pavel still hasn't made eye contact; he keeps his eyes fixed in the distance, somewhere else, when he speaks. He turns his gaze to some point along the gravel road.

'Karl-Adam,' Pavel says, pausing to take a sip of coffee. 'He always lived here. First his parents and then him. And his family. Except his wife died, she got sick, so it was mostly just him. And their son. And then he moved.'

Cassi says nothing, because it feels as though Pavel might continue his staccato narrative, which sounds strangely melodic and has a hint of an accent, if she keeps quiet. But he doesn't.

'When did he move out? Since the house has been empty

for a while, I mean.' Pavel seems to know the answer right away.

'It'll be five years this autumn. The son came and got him, had arranged for him to go live in a home. After the diagnosis. I suppose he figured Karl-Adam couldn't live out here anymore, on his own. I haven't seen him since.'

There's a certain feeling in the air between them, ready to be grasped.

'Were you good mates?' she asks, wincing inwardly at having used the word 'mates' talking to someone so old. She changes her approach.

'Did you know him well?'

At first, he says nothing. Then, for the first time since arriving, he turns his head and looks straight at her. Light-brown, grave eyes that look straight into hers. Holding her gaze.

'He was my best friend for over fifty years.'

Then he looks away again. Up at the roof tiles, the chimney, the clouds. Blinking.

Cassi takes a sip of her coffee, pondering how to phrase her next question to avoid offending him. Then, it just comes out.

'But he's alive? Why don't you go see him?'

Pavel shifts on the stool, running a hand over his bony jaw and its grey stubble.

'I noticed you put up a sign. Out by the road. *Cassiopeia*?'

Now it's Cassi's turn to shift uncomfortably, though she tries to disguise it as a matter of seating comfort and nothing else. Pavel's presence has provided a bit of a break from her new life. She hasn't had to put on a performance with him, unless you count general behaviours associated with being around people, the kinds of things a socially functional human wouldn't even call behaviours, but rather just 'being'.

Pavel doesn't see her as someone she's not, he has no prejudgement. He expects neither a therapist nor a crystal waver, or even a mental coach.

When Pavel says 'Cassiopeia', which is the name she came up with for her business the other night, after the first bottle of wine and a documentary about astronomy, it almost makes her feel sick. 'In Sweden, Cassiopeia is a circumpolar constellation, which means it never dips below the horizon,' the narrator had said, and in that moment, the name of her new title, and identity, had come to her.

Now, it suddenly feels silly. Pretentious. In her sober state, she almost feels ashamed, as though Pavel can see through her and her new fake life. But she has decided not to back away from her decision, so she doesn't. It is what it is.

'Yes, I figured it was time to get things going. Since people are already coming to me – I figured I'd make it easier for them.'

If her voice sounds faint, Pavel doesn't seem to notice, nor does he seem to find her reasoning odd.

'And where did you live before? I remember Marlene telling me. But I can't recall what she said.'

Cassi once again weighs her words. She doesn't want to lie to him, but she also doesn't want to create gaps in her story that someone else might notice.

'I've been around. Most recently, I was just renting a room. It's a long story. And not a particularly fun one. At all. It's been a rough year.'

Shockingly open, for her. She's fundamentally out of practice when it comes to sharing her feelings. She's surprised at herself, but something about Pavel's social awkwardness makes her trust him. He doesn't force anything out of her she doesn't want to tell him. He's neither going to judge her nor spread rumours. He seems like someone who's used to keeping secrets.

He's staring straight ahead again, into the forest. Cassi's relieved the subject's been closed, that she didn't burst into tears, and she seizes the opportunity to take charge of the conversation again. Having sensed a chink in Pavel's armour, she wants to know more.

'What about you, have you always lived here?'

'No, I'm from Lithuania. Originally. I left when I was eighteen. Then I lived in Stockholm. Then I came here.'

So that explains the accent.

'And that's when you met Karl-Adam?'

Pavel looks at her again. Seemingly taking her measure.

'I met Karl-Adam in Stockholm. We studied together. He was the one who talked me into moving here.'

Then he's silent again. Pointing at the roof.

'You have some crooked tiles up there. I can bring my ladder some other day and check out the situation underneath. See if there's damage. Straighten the tiles.'

He stands up and rocks back and forth on his heels for a moment, as though to let his legs warm up before it's time to move. Cassi stands up, too. Is struck by a sudden thought.

'I have Karl-Adam's address. It's somewhere in my property papers. If you wanted to visit, I mean. Or write. Unless you already have it, obviously.'

Pavel is still staring off into the forest. He stands silent, motionless, for several seconds. Then he turns his eyes to her, and it feels as though something big is about to happen. A lightning strike, a heart attack, a massive tax refund.

'I'll think about it,' he says.

19

Some days, you wake up with a firm feeling something's changed. You just know it. The only question is when you'll notice, when someone will tell you, what exactly is different. But then, usually, nothing else happens. The hours keep marching on as before. The feeling subsides.

Or you're right and what happens is that the very same morning, as you're putting on your make-up before leaving for work, you realise the person you've been with for the past six years is a complete stranger. And after that, nothing's ever the same again.

This morning is, thankfully, of the former kind. Nothing has changed today. At least not since yesterday. Cassi's almost sure of it. But the memory of that feeling, the feeling of that memory, lingers, making her heart thump, a restlessness that can't sit at home. So on this specific late spring morning, she doesn't drink her coffee on the front steps, she takes it with her in a plastic bottle, like in the old days. She climbs into her car, determined to get things done. She's not the person she was back then. She's moved on with her life. What existed before doesn't anymore. If you tell yourself something enough, it'll become true.

But before she's even reached the main road, coffee bottle in hand, she's struck by a realisation. It comes to her courtesy of the potholes littering her gravel drive, and at first, it's painful, because the coffee sloshing into her lap was made with boiling water. But then it feels like a *ha-ha!* moment. She has to fill in the potholes. Literally and metaphorically. She has to commit to whatever she's doing to make sure the road ahead is smooth.

Her philosophical thinking gives her goosebumps. Barely able to fathom her own brilliance, she pulls over and types 'fill in your potholes' in her phone's notes app. It feels like playing guru has made her wiser, happier, transcendental almost.

Cassi takes out napkins from the glovebox to wipe up the spill. While she wipes, she reads over the small flyer again. She drew it last night. She's going to post it on the noticeboard at The Market, and it will inform customers that they can get in touch with Cassiopeia if they want to 'expand their mental universe'. 'With open minds, we can move forward. Coaching / Therapy / Healing / Fourdery', the second line reads. She made up that last word herself. She'd started to write 'fortune telling' but ultimately changed her mind, it sounded too made-up. If anyone asks what fourdery is, she's just going to wing it.

She knows people want to confide in her. And rightfully so. She can guide them. Her life experience and insights are invaluable. She's sure of it.

She's beginning to put the horrible start to the morning behind her. The future feels clearer, not poisoned by old memories. This new Cassi doesn't listen to some top 40 hot music rubbish in the car. No peppy radio voices. She tunes into an ad-free channel, which happens to be playing jazz. Cassi tries to find the rhythm and drum her fingers on the wheel. Thinks to herself that she should cut back on the wine and increase her intake of green vegetables. She should start growing her own veg.

When she turns into the car park at The Market, she does it with the confidence of a lorry driver. Cassi ties her jacket around her waist to hide the coffee stains and remembers to grab a tote from the back seat. She takes a deep breath, exhales through her mouth, and smiles, inside and out.

She takes the steps in a long, slightly bowlegged step, almost colliding with grouchy Hans right inside the automatic doors. He's bent over the bin in the space between the till and the entrance/exit. They usually do their best to avoid each other, he because he dislikes her and she because she dislikes that he dislikes her, but today, Cassi's in a different mood. Today, she's the Cassi who has relocated to this town to make it a better place. Cassi the Benevolent. She was going to say Cassi the Saviour, but that might be taking things too far.

While pinning her piece of paper, fringed by pre-cut strips with her number on it, to the noticeboard, she looks Hans straight in the eye and says: 'Hello, Hans, how are you today?'

Which is really nice of her. To make an effort like that, even though he's so unpleasant.

Hans looks at Cassi and straightens up, wiping his forehead. His hairline is receding, Cassi notices.

'Can't complain, thanks,' he says. He ties up the binbag, which is brimming with receipts and ice-cream wrappers.

Cassi lets her palms meet in front of her chest. She feels certain he'd be able to drop his aversion if he just got to know her.

'I'm so happy this is where I ended up,' she says, as though he asked. 'Bäcken's such a beautiful place and all the people I've met here are so genuine. So warm. There's room for the soul here, for it to both develop and rest.'

She adopts a facial expression she imagines underscores her sublime feeling.

'Mhmm,' is all Hans says back. She can see his face hardening, watches as he ties the bag up even more tightly.

'The air, the tranquillity, the nature. It gives me such energy!'

Cassi describes a sunrise with her hands to illustrate.

'I find so much inspiration in the sense of community here, which still leaves space for spirituality. I would love to invite you and your wife to one of my ceremonies this summer.'

Is she deliberately provoking him? It certainly feels that way, but she can't help it. It's like she's rising to his challenge at this point.

Hans clears his throat. Briefly looks up at the ceiling, but then fixes her firmly.

'Look,' he says, sounding fairly riled. 'I've already told you I'm planning to stay as far away from the kind of things you do as I possibly can. You should know my favourite programme on TV is that one with the bloke who goes around exposing fraudsters. Snake-oil salesmen. People who exploit the weaknesses of others. So don't even think about trying anything with me. I'll be keeping an eye on you. You make one wrong move and . . .'

Hans looks as though he's about to drag a finger across his throat, but probably realises at the last second that wouldn't be appropriate.

'Nonsense is what it is. I'm not having it!' He glares at her, holding the binbag in a tight grip between them.

She calmly raises both hands.

'All right, all right, no problem. We're all entitled to our own opinions.'

She lowers her hands again and picks up a shopping basket, preparing to enter the shop. Annoyed that Hans's refusing to be charmed, worried what his threat might entail.

'We can still be respectful, though, despite our differences, don't you think?'

Hans mutters something and leaves with his bag. She enters the shop, basket in hand and head held high.

Cassi collects what she needs. She's no longer feeling uplifted, more flattened, if anything. A little bit alarmed. What might that kind of aggression lead to? Hans feels like a liability. Cassi doesn't want any doubters around her. She walks over to the till.

A grim-looking woman is sitting behind it, working on her cuticles while she waits for the next customer. The woman has an asymmetric, grey hairdo and wears glasses with loud, squarish red frames. Cassi's seen her several times before, both in the shop and out and about, and she's noticed that her frames always match her nail polish. She knows she's Hans's wife, though they've never been properly introduced.

'I'm picking up an order as well,' Cassi says while paying for her shopping. She holds out her ID.

The woman gets up and heads over to the storeroom. Everything she does happens at a leisurely pace. Cassi waits. Soon, she can hear frantic clinking in the distance.

The sound slowly approaches. Other customers turn to see what's causing the racket.

'I had to get a trolley, I can't carry this many bottles,' the woman announces rather loudly as she pushes her load towards the till.

'My goodness, I think there's been some kind of mistake,' Cassi says, raising her voice so everyone in the vicinity can hear her. She hadn't given it a moment's thought before, but now she realises people might get the wrong idea about her alcohol consumption. Or, well, not wrong, exactly. But ideas nonetheless.

'All I did was fetch what was on here,' the woman replies, as though to make clear she's done nothing wrong. She holds out the order, recently stamped and signed by her.

'No, I'm sure, but they seem to have sent much more than I ordered,' Cassi says. Gosh, what a rookie mistake! She needs to rectify it as soon as possible. 'My goodness, what am I supposed to do with all this wine? And you can't return it either, I imagine.'

Cassi considers adding a 'Now I have enough wine to last me until next year' in a breezy tone, but realises that might come off as odd if she then were to return next week to pick up even more. Or could she claim the bottles all broke on the way home? It's a good thing she hasn't filled in those potholes yet; at least she'll have something to blame. How far is the next nearest place a person can buy alcohol? Driving for an hour might be worth it to avoid a repeat of this humiliation.

The woman just stares at her blankly. She looks as though it would be absolutely impossible for her to care less about anything than Cassi in general and Cassi's wine order in particular. Cassi takes the trolley from her and pushes it out of the shop. When she gets to the ramp, the weight of the wine makes the trolley start to roll down it by itself. While she does her best to control its speed, and the blabbermouth bottles do their best to make as much of a racket as they can, Cassi has time to notice out of the corner of her eye that her flyer has already been removed from the noticeboard.

Back in the parking lot, she loads the bottles into the boot and back seat. The positive energy she had channelled on her way here has evaporated. Cassi checks the order she's still holding in her hand. Her eyes linger on the woman's signature.

Every fairy tale needs a villain, or two. Cassi's, apparently, go by the names Hans and Gretel.

20

Cassi sits in the car, taking in deep breaths. She feels sick all of a sudden. The salt liquorice rat king is still in the door pocket and this time she doesn't hesitate. Cassi picks up the bag, pulls the lump off the plastic, and shoves the whole thing in her mouth. She chews and chews and when she has to sneeze, it's as though every part of her has turned into black goop. This wasn't the feeling she was looking for. It doesn't even taste good. She spits it back out, liquorice sticking in her teeth, smearing her hands and the bag.

She's not going to admit defeat. This isn't who she is anymore.

Cassi turns to the back seat and picks up one of her newly purchased bottles from the floor. It's like an automated reaction. This isn't who she is either. Anymore. She was going to cut back. Maybe even quit. But she still unscrews the top. She'll have to think of this as a break, a plateau in the cutting-back process. A few gulps, so small they barely even happened.

Cassi stays put a while longer. Gives herself a few minutes.

She stares out at the village. Red barns, the whitewashed church, the green fields. Then, her eyes circle back to The Market and over by the skips behind the shop, they suddenly meet Hans's again. Has he been standing there long? Has he been watching her all this time?

Hans is neither short nor tall, neither fat nor thin. His not-particularly-thick, but also not completely absent hair is somewhere between blond and grey. His eye colour is dark. Possibly brown but could just as easily be blue. And he's always leaning forward slightly, making it look from a distance as though he's remonstrating with whomever he's talking to.

Cassi shudders. What's his deal? She looks down, breaking eye contact. Just then, there's a tap on her window. Fia has parked her old banger a few spaces down without Cassi noticing. Cassi opens the door and climbs out, praying the draught from the door will air out any potential wine smell.

'We meet again,' Fia says. She seems to be heading into or coming off work, because her hair is tied up meticulously and she's wearing the shop's signature red fleece. 'I noticed the sign by your house. Good to see you're up and running!'

Cassi tries to smile. This day is draining. She wants to go home, shut herself in with her bottles and her dog. She tries to formulate an appropriate response.

'Yeah,' she manages.

Fia points to the large advertisement boards by the road, where some kind of forestry monster vehicle has just rumbled past.

'You should do something like that too, make sure people know you're here. Seriously, I know I keep saying it, but so many people in this town could use a bit of therapy. Do you have a website?'

Cassi obviously doesn't. But just the day before, she did google herself to see what would come up and realised sharing a name with a world-famous Danish entrepreneur in the field of online payment solutions can be a very good thing. At least if you're trying to launch yourself as something new, something you might not be. If a search returns a long list of results for a Danish entrepreneur, it will, by the same token, throw up proportionally fewer for a Swedish restaurant worker starting a new career as a New Age fraud.

'I'm not big on the internet,' Cassi slurs. She clears her throat. When she resumes speaking, she does it in a tone that can't be questioned.

'I prefer to make my contacts in the real world. So much of our modern life is conducted online, on screens, but it's important to be present in the moment, mindful. That might even be what's lacking. For me and for my process, being one hundred per cent in the here and now is crucial.'

Cassi places a hand on her heart, to underline her words. It's still beating at twice its normal rate after seeing Hans over by the bins.

Fia nods.

'I suppose that's what it's all about. Carpe diem. I think that sounds super exciting. I'm definitely going to book a session sometime soon. How did it go with Alida?'

Fia begins to pull a face, then looks briefly amused before adding:

'She's one of a kind, that woman. As I'm sure you've noticed.'

Cassi feels it's important to stay neutral, now that she's shouldered the role of local do-gooder.

'I saw a woman who needs someone to talk to.

Sometimes, that's all it takes. I'm so happy I'm able to be here for her.'

Fia shrugs and nods towards Gretel, who has appeared at the entrance to the shop with a carrier bag in her hand.

'I'm picking up my order. See you.'

As she walks backwards towards Gretel, Fia raises her fist with her fore and little fingers extended, a hard rock gesture Cassi interprets as an ironic statement about the mundane task at hand. Cassi gets into her car intending to respond in kind, but the wine has reached her limbs by now, impeding her fine motor skills, so as she drives away, the only finger that pops up is her middle one. Cassi has time to register the surprised looks on Fia's and Gretel's faces and quickly rolls down her window to shout an explanation as she heads towards the exit.

'It means something different in Sanskrit!'

21

Days pass. Cassi has polished the hinges on the kitchen cabinets. Pried off and cleaned the overhead light switches. Run a toothbrush along the gaps between the floorboards. Pulled weeds out of the lawn. Scrubbed the limescale between the washbasin and the tap. Trimmed back the plants growing along the foundation. Broken dry branches off the apple tree. Cut the verge along the driveway with shears.

It's as though she has become her old perfectionist self again, but only with regards to things that don't matter and details no one else will ever notice.

Maybe it's a peace-of-mind thing. She's noticed she can turn her brain off if her hands are busy. Has that always been the case? Did she make sure to keep busy so she wouldn't have time to think about what happened back in the day? To avoid falling down that particular rabbit hole, she decides to tackle the treeline that runs around her garden, which looks awfully unkempt. She would prefer a more clean-cut boundary between lawn and forest, between her territory and nature. And it would be great to not have to put up with all those long, sweeping blades of grass attacking her calves every time she goes for a walk in the woods.

Pavel's going to help her. He looked amused when she asked him, but he's shown up with his clearing saw and scythe all the same.

'Next time, I'll bring the ladder,' he says, his gaze shifting upwards. 'The roof tiles, Cassi. And the gutters. Important things in an old house.'

'Absolutely, Pavel,' Cassi says, 'can't argue with that. Still, it's made it to this point, so I reckon it'll hang in there a while longer.'

They've quickly fallen into place in each other's lives. Filled holes neither one of them had known were there. Even though their meetings usually revolve around Pavel helping Cassi with something to do with the house – yesterday, an electrical socket that kept giving her shocks, today, the offensively long grass – she has an underlying feeling he truly understands her. It feels simple.

Cassi sticks her feet into her wellies, grabs her hedge shears, and strides off toward the treeline. She shows Pavel what she means. Explains that the idea is to create a clear line between the forest and the lawn.

'When you step out of the trees, you should feel like you've survived an ordeal and you've finally made it to the other side,' she says. 'Nirvana!'

'You don't like the woods?' Pavel asks.

'I like them fine, that's not what this is about. But life is a struggle. Sometimes, you have to pause and feel good about what you've dealt with. Grateful you're still in one piece. And sometimes that requires a clearer contrast.'

She trails off, because she realises she sounds as though she's talking about something other than the existence of undisturbed nature. She picks up the scythe, swinging it at a patch of undergrowth, but having never used a scythe before, she handles it like an axe. Which she has never used either. A cloud of pollen bursts into the air around her.

Pavel has walked over to a scraggy bush at the far end of the garden. The leaves are densest at the top of the grey branches, above his head. He reaches out to touch them. He stands there in silence for a moment.

'This used to be an arbour,' he says at last. 'Before. We could try to restore it. If you don't mind it looking a bit sad this season.'

'Sounds good,' Cassi replies.

She'd like to come off as a normal person, a person who cares about gardening without underlying psychological motives. She leaves the scythe against a tree and picks the shears back up. Pavel's already going at the dry branches.

'Sometimes, the only thing to do is to cut everything down and start over,' Pavel says.

Cassi nods. She couldn't agree more. But is he aware of just how much this resonates with her? There are still so many things they haven't said aloud to each other. So many things she feels are nevertheless understood.

Lichen flies through the air. Soon, she can make out the shape of the arbour.

'We used to sit here a lot, back in the day,' Pavel says. 'It was like a secret place. We were invisible to the rest of the world.'

They carefully sweep the lilac shoots off the dirt floor.

Cassi asks questions about Karl-Adam and his family because she's noticed Pavel likes to come back to that subject. He's unusually talkative today. He tells her about the son's musical talent. Käthe's upside-down apple cake. About long moose hunts and nights spent in tents. The cray fishing and the parties that followed.

'Karl-Adam was always good at sorting things out. He

knew how he wanted them and made sure they turned out that way. Being with him was never boring. You're a bit like him in that respect.'

'Me?' Cassi says. 'I can't fix a single thing myself! And not much happens around here, it's hardly entertaining.'

She looks around, taking in her unkempt property.

'In my experience, it's easy to lose sight of yourself when you're around people like that,' she says. She would never count herself as one. 'People who simply plough on. It's easy to put your own needs second, because theirs feel more important. Things just happen and then suddenly, everything might have changed.'

Pavel shakes his head.

'It wasn't like that with Karl-Adam,' he says firmly. 'He really was always right.'

22

'I'm coming straight from work, but I figured I'd take a chance,' Fia calls out through her rolled-down window. She's pulled up outside Cassi's house in her old pickup truck, the engine still running. 'Do you have time for me?'

Cassi squints from her spot on the front steps. She's not up to anything in particular and has grown used to people just coming by.

'Sure,' she says. 'Any special requests?'

Fia kills the engine and hops down from the truck. She looks around. She hasn't been to Cassi's house before. The look she gives the motley collection of furniture Cassi has dubbed her 'patio' seems sceptical. This brings to mind the large pile of empty wine bottles just inside her front door, waiting to be carried out to the small mountain awaiting recycling in the barn. There's no need for Fia to see those.

'What do you feel you're in need of?' she asks.

Fia ponders that.

'Well, I suppose that's up to you. But I'd like some guidance, maybe? What do you recommend?'

Cassi's catching on to the fact that the thicker she spreads it on, the grander her gestures, the less likely people are to question what she's doing. She just has to sound confident and spout some woolly concepts, keep the definitions open to interpretation. She stands up, placing her index fingers on Fia's temples.

'My crystal healing's popular with people who feel lost. I don't know what types of treatments you've tried before, but I work holistically, with strong faith in the ability of our bodies and souls to heal themselves. Sometimes all that's needed is some encouragement along the way.'

Fia nods, saying that sounds good. Cassi puts a finger to her own lips, looking as though she's had a sudden thought.

'Hmm. It actually works best when you do it in a familiar environment.'

She raises the same finger in the air, as though she's just had a great idea, then points to the pickup.

'Do the seats fold back in that thing? Because we could do this in your truck. That would be perfect, I think.'

Fia turns around and starts turning knobs at the base of the driver's seat. While she's busy, Cassi bends down and quickly picks up a handful of small stones from the ground.

'Is this OK?' Fia asks from inside.

'It's perfect,' Cassi replies.

She opens the passenger door, climbs up, and takes a seat. The car smells of dust and petrol. Ancient cigarette smoke and air freshener, sun-warmed plastic. Fia has laid back in her seat and is carefully adjusting the angle of her head to make room for her shiny ponytail.

'I want you to focus on lying still,' Cassi says, placing the stones on and around Fia's forehead. 'But at the same time, you'll feel total relaxation.'

Then she stops talking. Swallows a wet burp. A diet that consists primarily, or exclusively, of wine and pasta with tomato sauce will do that to you.

The silence lasts until Fia breaks it.

'OK, are we ready? Should I start?'

Fia's eyelashes quiver nervously, but the stones on her eyelids keep her from opening her eyes.

'Mmm, so, it's about life, I guess, or, well, how do I put it, my choices. What I should do.'

Fia's quiet again. Then she gets going.

'It all started when I was supposed to get married, but the day of the wedding, I realised I didn't want to, so I ran away to, er, Oslo. I stayed with my best friend from school, she was nice enough to let me move in. She had a lovely flat.'

Cassi nods but says nothing.

'I found a job at a café. It wasn't a dream situation, exactly, but it was a start. My friend's brother was in love with me our entire childhood, or whatever, and his friends lived across from us now, so the five of us, and a sixth friend, a girl, would hang out almost all the time.'

It feels like a bunch of disjointed sentences, the overarching point of which is lost on Cassi. She waits to understand where Fia's story's going. Cassi's now used to saying 'And how did that make you feel?' to interrupt an incomprehensible monologue, but she's not sure it would work now.

'A lot of stuff happened, this and that,' Fia continues. 'The guy who was in love with me was getting divorced. He was having a baby with his ex-wife, who was a lesbian. One of the guys became an actor. My friend started dating this older guy. She opened a restaurant. Something new was always happening, nothing big, I guess, but just a constant stream of stuff.'

Fia falls silent again. She touches the stones on her eyelids as though she's considering removing them. Cassi pokes her elbow.

'Fia. Relax.'

Fia puts her hands back down, making fists on her stomach. Her eyelids stop moving. Cassi studies her eyelashes, which reach halfway down her cheekbones.

Several seconds of uncomfortable silence pass before Fia resumes her story. Cassi focuses on minimising the gassy movements at the back of her throat by swallowing hard.

'Isn't it weird that therapists just listen, while people you know, who might be idiots, love to throw advice around?'

Cassi doesn't know what to say to that. Is afraid to say anything at all.

'But I guess I'm mostly worried about work,' Fia says. 'How to achieve what I want.'

Cassi realises she has to say something now.

'I suppose that depends on where you want to go,' she says. 'You've worked in a café, and now you're at the Village Shop.'

'I have ambitions, I do,' Fia replies. 'I worked as a secretary for a successful woman for a while. That was in Oslo, too. After leaving the café. I helped her with everything, hoping to make it to the next stage in my career. I had lots of ideas, but I just didn't get anywhere. Then I found out my boss had stolen my ideas and passed them off as hers. So I decided to get back at her. When she was away, I pretended I was her. And I was really good at it. I even stole her boyfriend, or, well, I mean, he fell in love with me. But then she came back and, yeah, now I'm here. But I'm ready for more.'

'All right,' Cassi says, trying to wrap her head around the constant plot twists in Fia's story. 'So you're saying you have no problem playing dirty when you feel it's required? Or what?'

She still hasn't identified a clear issue to home in on. When the subject's this vague, everything she usually says sounds too . . . unremarkable.

Fia brings one hand to her face, scratching under her nose.

'Eh, I guess I mostly mean I'd like to do something bigger than what I'm doing now. More responsibility. I want a job with more heft. But what would that be?'

She smiles wryly.

'It's not as though I'm going to off Rumaan so I can take over as the manager of the Village Shop, exactly. At least not yet.'

This talk feels more like a catch-up over coffee than therapy to Cassi. She wonders if a more experienced person might have known how to steer the conversation to the right level. Not that she has an exaggerated respect for experience. If there are two things you can be sure of, it's that everyone could always try a bit harder and that no one's perfect. That's generally true. It's also undeniable that now that she's learning more about her industry, her new industry, the self-help industry or whatever you might call it, she's finding it a bit wishy-washy. Everything seems to be resolved by believing 'you're great just the way you are'. Cassi's not convinced everyone's great just the way they are. They're OK, maybe. They exist, mostly. Cassi would, for instance, give Fia's story a two out of five. It's not remotely inspiring.

'We can't control the wind, but we can adjust our sails.' Cassi shifts the tone of the conversation. She can see the words before her, misspelled, on the wall of the warehouse she spent so many days in, borderline drunk and definitely depressed. 'No one's built like you. All your dreams are within reach.'

Fia nods carefully.

'Life happens no matter what you do, but when you add intention, you're more likely to get the result you want,' Cassi preaches. She's finally finding her groove. She's left Fia's story behind, finding the inspiration within herself instead.

'To know which way to turn, you have to know where you want to go. Something as small as a butterfly flapping its wings can start a hurricane on the other side of the planet.'

She's aware that all she's doing is filling the silence with words. But if there's one thing she's learned over the past few weeks, it's that it's not so much about what you say, more about who's listening.

'The life you tell me you had before might have been more eventful, but were you happier?'

Fia hesitates before answering.

'I mean, it was great, but it's not really about that. It's more about where I go from here.'

Cassi enunciates clearly when she speaks, giving her pearls of wisdom time to sink in.

'The best way to tell the future is to create it yourself. Compare yourself to who you were yesterday, not to what someone else is today. Or, as Gandhi put it: our future depends on what we do in the present.'

Did he say that? Cassi has no idea. All the inspiring quotes she's taken to googling for research purposes are buzzing at the back of her mind, waiting to be let out. To demand that they always come out exactly right is too much to ask.

Cassi forces herself to smile as she keeps talking, trying to give Fia a sense of hopefulness.

'It's OK to not always feel OK. You're going to find your way, you just have to trust yourself and send your true signals into the atmosphere.'

Her hands rise into the air again, gesticulating to demonstrate all the magic contained within the gravitational field of planet Earth. Not that anyone can see what she's doing, but it feels right.

'I'm going to give you something to guide you in your contemplations going forward.'

Cassi takes the biggest of the stones she picked up off the ground a moment ago. It's white and smooth, the size of a biscuit. She's been holding it in her hand, so it's warm, and now she opens Fia's right hand to place it on her palm. She closes Fia's fingers around the stone. At the same time, she begins to mumble since she can't think of anything else to say.

She stops after a few minutes, another burp threatening to come to the surface. Fia seems to be asleep. At least she's done something, right? Cassi clears her throat gently.

Fia startles. The stones roll off her face, rattling against the car door and gear stick. She wipes the corners of her mouth with the sleeve of her fleece.

'My God, I think I dozed off. I'm sorry.'

'That's fine, nothing to be ashamed of. That means you experienced complete relaxation, that you're now able to rest even when awake. How do you feel?'

Fia stretches a little.

'Um, yeah, pretty good, I think. Kind of shaken, maybe.'

'Crystal healing can stir up a lot of emotions. It's common to feel confused, both happy and sad, afterwards. And I'd like you to keep the stone you're holding now with you at all times.'

Cassi puts her hand on Fia's.

'The stone's gone through an ancient, homeopathic karmic process. It's been cleansed by forest rain and shooting stars. It will help you on your spiritual journey, help you focus on what you want, and it's going to shield you from harmful energy.'

It hasn't and it almost certainly won't – it's highly possible Maine even peed on it at some point – but the words sound amazing leaving Cassi's mouth.

Fia looks amused, so Cassi arranges her features into a stoic smile.

'Take good care of the stone and treat it with respect. Touch it and talk to it as often as you'd like, as often as you need. And then come back in a few weeks and we'll see how you're doing. I think you'll feel a lot more certain about things then, Fia. There's a lot of strength in you. Your aura's super powerful, I mean, wow.'

Cassi mimics an explosion with her fingers. Fia sits up, looking at the stone in her hand. It looks like a fairly ordinary stone, but she smiles and whispers: 'My precious' to it before slipping it into the pocket of her tight jeans.

Cassi opens the car door and climbs out. She closes it with a bang, slapping the bonnet. She contemplates whether she should go straight to the pizzeria once Fia has paid her. She always feels better when the money's been eaten into a little, when it's no longer the same sum she charged. Once the money's been spent, it's as though her feelings of guilt subside ever so slightly. No one can come and point to the exact amount that was handed over, it's already been transformed into something else.

'I'm so sick of feelings,' Fia comments while she digs around the glovebox for her purse. 'Why can't people just be?'

23

'Yes,' Cassi replies.

The question comes from Marlene one afternoon. She's been given Cassi's number by Pavel and what she wants to know is if Cassi reads tarot cards.

'Then get yourself over here right now,' Marlene says in her husky voice. 'I'll have the coffee ready.'

Cassi's not busy. She also doesn't own a deck of cards. So, on her way to Marlene's, she creeps through the aisles of The Market. Unfortunately, she's still unable to avoid Hans, since he's manning the till again today.

When he notices her joining the queue, he starts to talk loudly about a programme he watched the other day, in which people confronted 'quacks and fraudsters'.

'Zodiac signs and astronomy. Nothing but flimflam and quackery if you ask me. People who push things like that should be on some kind of watchlist. Most of them likely belong behind bars.'

That last part is said with a pointed, lingering look at Cassi. It sticks to her like gum, only to then come off again, slowly and stickily. When it's Cassi's turn, she pays for her deck of playing cards without saying a word. She knows she has to tread carefully around him. Not push his buttons. But even so, she can't stop herself from correcting him on her way out.

'I think you meant ASTROLOGY, Hans,' she says as she pushes the door open with her bum.

But as far as vengeance goes, correcting him is so minor it's virtually no consolation. And the animosity in his eyes when he looks at her is frightening. It's as though he knows how easily he could destroy the façade she's worked so hard to create. It's as though he's waiting for the right time to do it. It feels both unsafe and unfair. Hans doesn't know anything about her. He's never even given her a chance. He just dislikes her, and that's that. Cassi's not used to being met with such prejudice.

One of her own prejudices, the one about how all rural ladies enjoy baking, becomes reality when she gets to Marlene's and Marlene sets out a packet of biscuits and a shop-bought frozen cake on the garden table when it's time for coffee. But before that, the cartomancy session is nearly derailed before it can even start.

Marlene's yellow sand-lime brick house is located on the outskirts of Bäcken, with a view of the village, fields and the main road. Scattered around the property are projects at various stages of completion. Some look like recent additions, like the pile of blindingly white wooden sticks by the gate, which Marlene proudly describes as her 'rose trellis'. Others look like they've been going on for a while. A bird feeder, intended to be hung from a branch, has become part of the lawn beneath the cherry tree. The 'outdoor shower', which Marlene points out to her, has not been installed, and consists only of a small square of snap-together decking by the garage wall and a damp-warped cardboard box with a picture of a rain shower on it.

Marlene, who's dressed in a short, purple cardigan over a floral yellow top and a wide red skirt, leads her to the back garden, where a wooden deck houses a swing seat, a table and chairs. The sky is overcast but there's no wind. A combine harvester is rumbling across a meadow beyond the nearest field. Half the deck is encircled by a fence with hanging planters. Along the other half, the planters are sitting on the wood, serving as both decoration and frame. A kettle grill is lying on its side in the grass below. Cassi sits down near the wall, Maine ambles about with his nose in the grass, and Marlene walks this way and that, eager to find a spot that's just right for their session. She pops around the corner to see what it's like in the shade, then declares that it may be too cold if they were to open the umbrella. She shifts the chairs around the table.

'I'm going to put up more fence here, but I haven't got to it yet,' Marlene explains. She squats down, poking at the fresh soil, her back to Cassi. Her shirt comes up a little, revealing the top of a black thong. Above it, across her lower back, a line of tattooed words, seemingly underlined by the waistband of her knickers. Cassi squints, hoping the words might give her some inspiration, but the letters look too small and blurred from where she's sitting.

'I always get started on one thing and then immediately find three more that need fixing,' Marlene says. 'No, this'll have to wait.'

She raises her hands in front of her, as though the planters have pulled a gun on her, and backs over to the swing seat. It sways when she sits down. She replaces her old pinch of *snus* with a fresh one.

Cassi takes it as her cue to spread the playing cards out in front of her. It looks as though she's about to play solitaire. She's about to begin when Marlene asks why she's not using tarot cards. Marlene had expected illustrations. A more profound sense of magic. Cassi stares at her. A feeling of unease, which had only just subsided after her encounter with Hans, bubbles up again.

'Those are for beginners,' she says after a few seconds. 'Tourist traps and children. In London and Berlin, everyone, or well, anyone who knows what they're doing, uses this kind.'

Marlene looks at her, still not completely convinced. Cassi does her best to appear unperturbed. She picks up the jokers, turns them 180 degrees, puts them back in the pile.

'The power's in here,' she continues, tapping her temple. 'Not in some pretty pictures.'

'If you say so,' Marlene says, blinking. 'I've never had my fortune told in Berlin. Never been at all.'

Cassi gathers the cards back up, slamming them down against the table with a bang. She spreads them out again, like a fan, face down. She breathes on them, has her hands do a little dance in the air above them.

The first card she pulls out is the four of hearts. Cassi looks at Marlene, trying to come up with a compelling interpretation.

'I suppose my guess would be that this is my family,' Marlene does the job for her, looking to Cassi for confirmation.

'That's right,' Cassi says. 'You have two adult children and you're divorced.'

Marlene opens her eyes wide.

'Yes, spot on. What else can you see?'

'Hmm,' Cassi replies, delighted to have remembered

Marlene's personal situation correctly. 'You now live by yourself, after a long relationship. The person who wanted the divorce was . . . you? And you still live in the house your children grew up in.'

Marlene nods eagerly. Cassi guessed that last detail from the colourful marker lines she noticed on the frame of the front door when Marlene opened it. That turns out to be enough to make Marlene stop questioning Cassi's methods.

'I've lived here all my life. Ask me anything. I know everything, everyone. In one way or another, I'm related to half the people around here. And I've probably slept with the other half, at one time or another.' Marlene smiles, looking pleased with herself. It's a unique smile, in which one of her eyebrows shoots up while the other dips down.

Cassi puts more cards down on the table. The nine of clubs, two of spades, queen of diamonds. She casts about for more clues.

'Do any of these speak to you?'

Marlene scrutinises the cards.

'I imagine the two of spades has to do with last night.'

That smug smile again. Cassi can't be sure exactly what she means, but even though they haven't known each other long, she's already more than clear on what Marlene likes to hint at. Cassi herself hasn't had the slightest stirring of interest in the human body – hers or anyone else's – for over a year. All forms of touch, anything physical, have felt repulsive. She has more or less managed to shut down three of her senses, seeing no real use for anything but sight and sound. But for Marlene, the opposite seems to be true. The realm of the physical is what truly speaks to her.

Now, Marlene jabs the nine of clubs with her finger.

'I think this refers to my daughter's birthday. The ninth of March. She just landed a new job. The EU. She's moved to Strasbourg! And she's making enough money to join a country club!'

'That's exciting,' Cassi says, shuffling the cards again. 'Have you been to visit?'

Marlene shakes her head. Then, instead of expanding on why, she points to the queen of diamonds.

'That lady there,' she says. 'I don't know who that's supposed to be. A rigid old bat. Certainly not me.'

Cassi turns over new cards. Shows Marlene a future focused on kings and jacks, calling the ten of hearts 'a big party'. Wraps up proceedings with the ace of diamonds. A quick glance up at Marlene is enough to set her off.

'Well, well, if it isn't an orgy,' Marlene chuckles happily, before pointing out that she doesn't really believe in fortune telling. 'But that doesn't mean I don't enjoy seeing what's in store for me.'

Cassi gathers up the cards and kisses the deck with her eyes closed, before holding it out to Marlene, who follows suit.

Then Marlene stands up.

'Time for coffee! I'll go get it, you just relax.'

Cassi does as she's told. The sun has come out, like nature congratulating her on another successful session. The low rumbling of the combine lulls her.

Marlene returns with a clattering tray. She pops around the corner of the house again to reassess the shade, taking her cardigan off since it's getting warmer. Even after sitting down, Marlene seems to be in constant motion. She fills their cups with coffee from a red thermos, pushes the milk carton closer to Cassi. Runs a hand through her hair, scrunching up the sides, pointing to the road where a car is passing, commenting: 'Don't recognise that one.'

Then she puffs at the sun, asking if it isn't a bit too warm after all? Or maybe Cassi's cold? Cassi shakes her head, her mouth full of cake.

'Goodness, I just want to take all my clothes off,' Marlene says, peering down into her T-shirt. She hikes up her skirt. 'Said the actress to the bishop. No inhibitions when the sun's out. Or any other time, for that matter. Don't you want to take your blouse off, tan a little?'

Marlene adjusts her breasts in her bra. Digs the *snus* out from under her top lip with a practised finger movement and shoves up a new pinch from the tin on the table.

'That's better,' she says, leaning back. 'So, tell me about yourself.'

Cassi absolutely doesn't want to do that. On this particular day, she wouldn't even know where to start. What is she really, other than a shell, a surface, a piece of clay in the process of being moulded into something that makes sense.

'You seem like such an inspiring human being to me, Marlene,' Cassi deflects instead. 'You seem so good at living. Putting yourself out there.'

Marlene smiles and puts on the sunglasses she's just polished with a corner of the tablecloth.

'Life's short. A person has to live while they still can. Not limit themselves, put up boundaries. We have to look around, experience things, make the most of what we have.'

Marlene resolutely sips her coffee.

'But you said you've always lived here,' Cassi says. 'What was it about Bäcken that made you come back? You must have seen a thing or two before you decided this was the place for you?'

She's hoping for an answer centred on the tranquillity and sense of community in a small village, confirmation that she herself has made the right decision. But instead, she notices Marlene stiffen, only for a split second, before she answers.

'Mhmm. Personally, I've had far too many things going on in my life, always something new. So I haven't had time to travel much.'

Marlene strokes her eyebrow.

'At all,' she adds, almost swallowing the word. 'I got married, you see. I had children, a job. You know what it's like. You get stuck. But life is meant to be experienced! People should understand what they're missing when they don't challenge themselves.'

She fiddles with her earrings.

'Well, it's not too late,' Cassi says. 'You should go. See the world.'

Marlene fiddles with her earrings some more.

'Oh, sure. But you know, with my second child I had a caesarean, and they warned me that could cause intestinal obstructions down the line, when you least expect it. And I didn't want to go somewhere and end up with an intestinal obstruction in the middle of the street. Imagine, me sipping cocktails next to the Statue of Liberty and then boom, intestinal obstruction. And what if I'm in the jungle? How would I get home? No, I just wouldn't feel right about it. So I suppose you could say there are medical reasons why I have to stay here.'

Marlene half-heartedly shakes her fist at the sky. Cassi studies her. Marlene doesn't seem to want to be analysed.

'Go on, have another biscuit,' she says. 'You're so skinny your cheekbones stick out. Men don't want that. What made you lose so much weight? Death in the family? Or no, hold on, a relationship that went belly-up, of course. Tell Marlene. You were dumped. Betrayed. I have an eye for these things, let me tell you. Maybe I should have become a fortune teller too. I'm only thinking about Karl-Adam and Käthe because you're living in their house, but the stuff that was going on there, I was on to that from the start. But it's not the kind of thing you talk about.'

Marlene crosses her arms and nods. Looks away. Cassi's mind starts to run wild – what was going on with Karl-Adam? Could it have anything to do with—

'Speak of the devil,' Marlene interrupts her thoughts and stands up. 'Here's Pavel.'

'Pavel's here?' Cassi says, turning her head to see his orange Volvo pull up on Marlene's drive.

They silently watch Pavel's progress between two lush fields, up to the house. They both wave at him when he climbs out of the car. Marlene begins to yap about a series of seemingly random topics – Pavel's knack for languages, the colour of the flowers along the verge, a short tangent outlining when the deck they're sitting on was built. Cassi only has to listen and add an 'mm' of agreement from time to time.

'Good to see you, Pavel!' Marlene hollers when Pavel is

close enough to hear her. 'Go have a seat, I'll fetch another cup.'

Cassi smiles broadly at him.

'It's nice seeing you without having to put you to work,' she says.

Pavel smiles his tentative smile, raising a hand in greeting. He says nothing but heaves a soft sigh when he sits down in one of the chairs, pulling it over slightly so his face is in the sun. He takes off his baseball cap and hangs it on the armrest.

'Isn't this nice, now. And the weather today, just lovely,' Cassi says. She looks for something else to say, suddenly feeling awkward. She looks down at her hands, notes that there's almost always dirt under her fingernails these days.

'You wouldn't happen to have a nailfile on you? I have a broken nail that's driving me nuts.'

Pavel smiles again, shaking his head. Then he shoves a hand into the side pocket of his cargo trousers and holds out a tool to Cassi.

'But I have one for filing wood, if you'd like?'

It's not that funny, but Cassi laughs out loud, suddenly filled with relief and joy at sitting right here, in the warm sunshine, with people she likes and large amounts of refined sugar rushing through her bloodstream.

Marlene returns. The conversation picks back up. Marlene has no problem filling the silence, her personality takes up as much space as her hoarse laugh and the heavy, floral perfume she probably can't smell anymore and therefore over-applies. Marlene doesn't hold back, everything's out in the open with her, except the colour blindness she'd never admit to. Cassi and Pavel are filled in on the details of Marlene's latest conquest, which they most definitely didn't ask to be. Then Marlene leans back, studying her guests' reactions, looking pleased.

'I thought Berzan and Fia were together,' Cassi says, while Pavel has fixed his eyes on the horizon, looking pretty dissociated.

'My goodness, what kind of narrow-minded, heteronormative way of thinking is that?' Marlene says, shaking her head. 'I'd thought you'd be more open than that. Berzan isn't the type. He won't be exclusive with anyone. He's still in love with his ex. It is what it is.'

A van passes by on the road and Marlene can't stop herself from pointing at it.

'That's Alida. That's one way life can turn out, I guess,' she comments.

There's a moment's silence before Pavel asks the question, saving Cassi from having to.

'What do you mean?'

Marlene gives him a nonplussed look.

'You don't know about Alida, Pavel? She wasn't always a farmhand. She was a venture capitalist, one of those city-slicker types, and she made a fortune. Lollo told me. And then she blew it all on drugs. A proper junkie, that one.'

Marlene raises her hands.

'Not that I judge! Of course a person wants to try things. Anyone can get hooked. And she's clean now. It's just a pity she's such a bore. A real weirdo.'

Cassi says nothing. She feels professional for not gossiping about her patients – if patient is the right word? – but at the same time unprofessional for not managing to get this information directly from Alida. Or did Alida lay it all out while Cassi was busy thinking about herself and keeping the act going? It's not impossible. Cassi's no stranger to contemplating her own shortcomings. She's aware of her weaknesses. Most of them or at least some. That doesn't mean she necessarily thinks they're wrong, or that she even feels a need to work on them, but she is aware and that's what matters. And self-centred is a word that has popped up in rows she's had with people close to her.

Granted, she'd always thought that that was an unfair assessment. Surely it's OK for a person to know how they like things. Surely making a few demands is OK. Surely a person has to be able to do what's best for them, without being accused of only ever thinking about themselves, without being called selfish? Memories start flowing back and make her shudder. Marlene and Pavel turn to her. They've changed the subject.

Pavel's typing things into his phone.

'If you think of anything else, call me,' Pavel says to Marlene.

'Bathroom cleaner,' Marlene says. 'And kitchen roll. Pavel, I really appreciate you doing this.'

Pavel types some more.

'You don't like going to the shops either?' Cassi asks, wanting to get back into the conversation. 'Hans hates me. I don't know what I've done to offend him.'

Pavel and Marlene look at her, wide-eyed.

'Hans is a prick, and I don't have much good to say about Gretel either,' Marlene says. 'But that's a long story.'

Pavel leans back again, because a story being long has never been known to stop Marlene from telling it. Fifteen minutes later, Cassi has been filled in. In brief: Gretel and

Marlene became best friends in primary school, but fifteen years later, Gretel met Hans and things went sideways.

'That fusspot made sure everything went to hell in a handcart,' Marlene says. 'He felt I was a "bad influence" on Gretel. Me! All because I think life should be fun!'

Pavel has cocked his head to the side. Marlene purses her lips.

'So I avoid their shop as best I can, but I do need to eat.'

She shoves a biscuit into her mouth, signalling pleasure by closing her eyes for a moment and saying 'mmmm', before resuming her monologue, crumbs flying every which way.

'If Hans is being unpleasant to you, it's probably because he's against everything these days. Biggest killjoy that ever lived, that one.'

Pavel tilts his head in the other direction. Looks at Cassi.

'Now, to be fair . . . I know Hans's story. I think I know why he's hostile towards you. He'd likely object just as much if you were the Pope himself.'

Pavel would probably have preferred to leave it at that. Unlike Marlene, he's not one for long speeches. But Cassi's questioning eyes signal a need for more information. Marlene has crossed her arms again.

'Hans is against all forms of religion,' Pavel says. 'His mum was a Jehovah's Witness. She died when he was born. She wasn't allowed to receive a blood transfusion. So I reckon his behaviour's understandable, in a way.'

'But I have nothing to do with religion,' Cassi says, hoping Marlene won't bring up the fact that only a short while ago, when Cassi was deep in guru mode, she likened the forest to her church, her synagogue, her mosque. 'Your *moss*-que,' as Marlene had quipped.

'It doesn't even have to be religion anymore,' Pavel says. 'I think it's more about influence. Whenever a group of people think the same way. Anything that isn't science.'

Marlene looks at Pavel.

'I know you're the forgiving type, Pavel, but surely there are limits. The man's insane.'

'He may have taken things a bit far,' Pavel admits. 'Hans doesn't like big groups. People gathering. Anything kind of groupthink. Politics. Football games. Cities. Big corporations. You might have noticed The Market's not part of a chain.'

'Hans can talk all he likes about herd mentality,' Marlene counters. 'But is a bit of common sense too much to ask for? He won't even *enter* the church. When Käthe passed, he refused to go to her funeral. And that was Gretel's sister. And Karl-Adam's wife.'

'Hans is Karl-Adam's nephew,' Pavel explains, looking at Cassi, who apparently hasn't yet figured out all the familial ties in the area. 'And brother-in-law.'

Marlene shakes her head.

'And my second cousin,' she says. 'And a self-absorbed ass.'

'He stands on principle,' Pavel says, picking the deck of cards up from the table, shuffling it expertly.

'That's just another way of saying he's a knob,' Marlene says, making a fist on the armrest of her chair. 'So concerned with principles he cut off his only child simply because she chose to live abroad for a bit. My God. How does he live with himself?'

Pavel holds up the deck, pulls a card out, looks at it. Puts the card face down on the tablecloth.

'Think about the seven of diamonds,' he says to Marlene.
'Which card are you thinking about?'
'The seven of diamonds,' she replies.
Pavel flips the card over.
'The seven of diamonds!' he announces.

24

Cassi had always felt like she was an intrinsic part of her city's nightlife.

She'd landed a waitressing job after secondary school and never left. That hadn't been the plan. She'd just wanted to get away from her mother, away from her hometown, had planned on becoming something highly educated later on, but it turned out perfectionists like her were particularly appreciated in the hospitality world. So she stayed. Who could quit a job that provided that level of validation? Never before had she been commended for her attention to detail. Cassi learned everything about every aspect of the restaurant, worked in the kitchen, manned the bar, waited the tables. She took over as maître d' at the age of twenty-eight, when the previous maître d', a mild-mannered, sixty-three-year-old wrestling enthusiast with three Siamese cats, had died in his armchair one Sunday, just like that, while watching the ski jumping world cup.

Cassi was quick, fun, unabashed, foul-mouthed like one of those sailors everyone's heard of, but few have ever met. Her mood set the tone at the restaurant. She dominated any room she entered without even trying. That wasn't always a good thing. She wasn't universally liked; she expected the same high standards from others she did from herself and could have absolutely been cancelled for being rude to her employees if anyone had been bothered to organise a campaign against her, but luckily, she'd been able to avoid that.

Cassi was without a doubt outstanding at her job. She could sense who should be offered dessert on the house after having been forced to wait, who should have their water topped up more often, who was on a first date, and who deserved to be subtly put in their place. She was the first to arrive and the last to leave, not happy until every last napkin was folded neatly and in place for the next day.

And she loved her restaurant. Loved the jargon in the kitchen, the constant stream of people, having opinions about the dishes on the menu, the gratitude of the guests when she managed to find them a table even though they were full. The chats at the bar, the Friday atmosphere that often settled in as early as Wednesday lunchtime, the fear in the eyes of their new employees before they'd learned the ropes, even the desperation among the divorcees fifteen minutes before closing on the weekends.

It was at the restaurant, tending the bar, that she first got to know Jarmo. He was a duffel-wearing salesman for a wine importing company he'd started. He was quiet, tattooed, slightly bowlegged, spoke fluent Finnish and German, spent a lot of time at the gym but never did cardio, made a big show of 'not liking films', always had white deodorant lines on the outside of his washed-out black T-shirts, and shuddered at the thought of hot beverages. He was – and in hindsight, this was likely a red flag – always the right level of uninterested.

Cassi had never been very good at relationships, and it was only after a few years, after she'd been promoted to maître d', that she developed the confidence, or enough of a professional reason to seem unconcerned, to ask if he wanted to go for coffee. And it was only when he declined – which could also be seen as a red flag – that she became *really* interested. Five months later, she finally had her way when at a prosecco-sponsored industry party, decorated with lemons and plastic salami to live up to the Italian theme, she snogged him in the line to the bathroom to the dulcet tones of Gianna Nannini.

After that, their romance took off. If he had doubts, she had absolutely none. She was so used to getting her way that she didn't even notice. And he was almost always travelling around the country anyway. After a while, he was going to Norway, Denmark, Finland, and Germany too. His company grew and he could have opted to stay at headquarters, but claimed he enjoyed his jet-set lifestyle and the direct contact with his customers.

He moved in with her because she figured he might as well. They got engaged, because she'd found the perfect rings at an auction, and something about the way she felt she could never take him for granted made her want to tie him down. They, or maybe more accurately Cassi, adopted a dog. Jarmo had a son from a previous relationship, but the son and the ex lived in a different city and no situation ever arose where Cassi could have been organically introduced. But despite their lack of a normal, everyday life together, they had their favourite seats in the kitchen and their routines. They hardly ever fought.

They hardly ever had time off either. They only went abroad together once: to Thailand, where Jarmo was visiting a spirits manufacturer – a deal that never materialised. That's where they got engaged.

A third thing they didn't do was celebrate holidays together: Christmas, Easter, Midsummer, the lot. Jarmo's focus was always on his son, which Cassi was fine with, though she did think it would have been nice if she'd been included too. She would have liked being part of an open-minded, happy, blended family. And maybe not just part of it – sometimes she fantasised about being the hub of that kind of machinery, the kind of high-minded maternal figure who loves other people's children like her own, who has everyone over for dinners and holidays with beautiful, laden tables, and who spouts words of wisdom that will be quoted for generations. But Jarmo said his ex was prone to being irrational and jealous. That it would be better to hold off a bit longer. And Cassi didn't mind, she had her hands full anyway. She had her friends, she had her challenging and demanding job, busy and rewarding days. That her funny, stimulating, driven, loving husband-to-be was often elsewhere wasn't a cause for concern to her.

Why would it be?

25

The afternoon heat is stifling. Cassi has placed the beach chair in the shade of the barn doors. She feels an acute need for fresh air, but also an equally acute need for shade. Cassi has been drinking wine since the early morning, when a hormonally triggered rage coincided with not just the sudden resurfacing of an old memory, but also a sticky nightmare in which she was once again accused of being a fraud.

She has decided she's going to write a book about her life. An autobiography, a memoir, so the world will know and everyone involved will be sorry. When Pavel stops by on his bike, she's wearing denim shorts and a tank top, her current wine bottle's on the floor next to her chair, more than half empty, and her laptop's on her knees, screen fixed on a document that so far displays the words 'You can all go fuck yourselves'. He wobbles when he spots her in the gloom, then straightens back up, turns the bike towards the barn, and comes to a stop on the grass in front of her.

Cassi's wearing large sunglasses and is no longer in control of her facial muscles. She waves her right hand.

'I was going to ask if you need a bicycle,' Pavel says. 'I fixed this one up, but I have my own that I use. So I figured you could use this one for now.'

The bike is green, an old-fashioned ladies' model. He gets off and leans it against the barn wall. Pulls out a blade of grass that has woven its way between the spokes of the front wheel. Then he puts his hands on his hips and looks straight at her. The fact that his eyes don't glance past her means she's a sorry sight. He's never seen her drunk before. He probably doesn't even know she drinks. Drinks like this. This part of her life is unknown to him. Cassi feels scrutinised.

'Why are you shtaring at me today when you ushually refuse to make eye contact?' she thinks to herself.

Pavel immediately looks away. Oh, shit, maybe she said – slurred it, out loud.

'How are you feeling?' he asks. A new line has appeared between his eyebrows.

Her tongue feels too big for her mouth and the back of her head doesn't want to leave the back of the beach chair, so she lets it rest there. She points to the laptop as if to show she's very busy.

'Did something happen?' Pavel asks, this time bent over Maine, who has come over to say hi. He scratches the panting dog's neck.

'Would you like some water, Maine?' he says then.

He turns and walks off towards the house.

Cassi picks up her wine bottle, gulps down what's left in it. Wipes her mouth and chin with her bare arm. It's covered in dust and wine. Smells sour.

'Nothing happened,' she mutters.

'Pardon?' says Pavel, who's already back with a saucepan filled to the brim with water.

'I jusht shaid NUFFING HAPPENED,' Cassi says. 'What, I can't take shome time off? I can't have a glash of wine on a warm shummer day?'

The wine bottle topples over when she drops it onto the ground, but it's empty so she doesn't care. Pavel has set the pot down on the grass under a tree. Maine's drinking. Pavel takes a seat next to him, his arms on his knees.

Cassi can, her own state notwithstanding, see how she could be perceived. She can tell Pavel's uncomfortable, she can understand that, hard as she's trying, she isn't coming off as stone-cold sober. But she doesn't give a shit. She wants to be left alone. She slams the laptop shut. Her plan is to stand up and walk away, but her body won't cooperate. By placing one hand behind her neck, she manages to tug her head far enough forward that her back finally comes off the backrest. She leans forward to push up onto her feet, but immediately loses her balance and both the chair and Cassi topple sideways. Pavel jumps up, grabbing her arm and pulling her upright.

'Are you OK? I'll walk you back to bed. Maybe you have sunstroke.'

'Mhmm,' Cassi replies, clutching her sunglasses. 'Shunshtroke.'

She's unsteady, but Pavel holds onto her, making sure she doesn't take another tumble. He leads her, not very quickly, all the way to her bedroom. It feels cooler in there now and, once she's lying down, he opens the window a crack and pulls the dark-blue blind halfway down. The smell of wild strawberries wafts in from the forest.

'There's rain coming. It'll feel good,' he says. Then he goes out to the kitchen. She hears him digging through cabinets and drawers. When he returns, he's carrying water and a blister pack of painkillers. By then, Cassi's mood has changed.

'You're so good to me, Pavel,' she says. She picks a sweatshirt up from the floor and drapes it over her eyes. She wishes the room would stop spinning. 'What have I done to deserve you?'

She hears him take a seat on the chair in the corner; it creaks every time. It's a chair she bought at a flea market to use in the kitchen, but when she realised it struggled to hold the weight of anything heavier than clothes, it was relegated to the bedroom. Where her clothes are still on the floor.

'Careful with that chair, it . . .' she starts to say, because not even drunk can she bear to watch a rickety old man fall off a rickety old chair. When she peeks out from under the sweater, Pavel's already working on repairing it.

'I'll bring wood glue next time,' he says, sitting down on the edge of her bed instead.

He raises his hand as though he were about to put it on her arm but changes his mind and places it in his own lap instead. She puffs and pants under her sweater. Her head's throbbing.

'I'm going to be alone for the rest of my life, Pavel,' she says, suddenly weepy and pathetic. 'I'm never going to meet anyone. I'm never going to be someone's person. The centre of someone's galaxy. I'm no one's star. I never will be.'

She fumbles about for his hand or arm, ends up finding his knee.

'But I have you. I'm happy about that.'

It's the oldest, boniest knee she's ever touched. She lets her hand rest there. Pavel pats it gently.

'Remember the first time we met?' he says. 'Out on the

road, in our cars. I thought, just for a second, that you were a woman I knew a long time ago.'

But Cassi doesn't answer. She's fallen asleep.

Pavel carefully moves her hand from his knee. He goes back out to the kitchen and does the dishes, which have been sitting on the counter for at least a day. He puts several empty wine bottles in a bag, wipes down the surfaces, sticks a fresh twig of mock orange in the vase on the shelf, changes the water in it, throws away the old one. Spends a while unsuccessfully rubbing at an old dried-in stain on the hob.

'Wood glue and scouring pads,' he mumbles to himself, then he checks on Cassi one last time before stepping outside and closing the door behind him. He lingers for a second by the bell above the entrance, grazing it with his fingernail to make it emit a faint note. Then Pavel walks home through the woods, along the path only he and the hares can still make out.

26

The next morning, Cassi wakes up to a text from Pavel.

Good morning, my star.

27

Marlene has asked for 'whatever type of yoga's most popular in Berlin', and even though Cassi has spent the past few days trying to google what that might be and entail, the end result will, as usual, be something scrambled together from the recesses of her own brain.

'What does the twig signify?' is the first thing out of Marlene's mouth after she parks her car behind Cassi's and climbs out. Marlene points towards Cassi's head. Cassi doesn't understand what she means, but when she raises her hand to her ponytail, she realises a small pine twig's stuck in it.

'It's there to remind us of our connection with Mother Earth,' Cassi replies, instead of simply admitting that it must have ended up there by accident during her earlier walk in the woods with Maine. 'Nature is our origin. We're part of the cosmos. Sometimes, we need to return to it, take root, claim our rightful place in this sacred universe.'

Cassi puts her palms together in front of her chest and bows slightly. Dressed in her old gym leggings and a T-shirt she used to sleep in, she might not exactly look like the edgiest yoga teacher out there. But one thing she's good at is appearing as pretentious yet convincing as possible, regardless of her outfit.

Marlene has Berzan with her in the passenger seat. He climbs out when he's done with his phone, pausing between the door and the cab, placing a hand on the car roof, smiling broadly. Cassi is able to see now that Berzan's not quite as young as she took him for when they first met at the pizzeria. Probably closer to thirty than twenty. But he's as well-groomed today as the last time they met. Black hair slicked back, neatly trimmed black beard, black professional running outfit, with shorts layered over tights and a tight zip-down vest. He removes the latter, revealing an equally clingy top underneath.

'It's good to be here,' he says. 'Nice to see you again.'

Cassi replies with another small bow.

Marlene, dressed in pink leggings and a tight pink top that offers a glimpse of her midriff, takes in Cassi's property. The cottage, the barn, the broken beach chair, the stool, the dusty, relatively modern, mid-range sedan.

'It must be twenty years since I've been here,' she comments. 'If I didn't know better, I would have guessed it's been sitting empty since then. My goodness, the state of this place. It's shocking, actually. I thought Pavel helped you to get settled in? But maybe you're not interested in appearances?'

Cassi isn't offended. But she would argue there have been a lot of improvements since she moved in. She wants to point to the clothesline, which is no longer tilting, the geraniums in full bloom on the front steps, but is interrupted by Alida pulling into her driveway on her bike. She greets them without meeting anyone's eye. Alida's dressed in her regular clothes. She unstraps a yoga mat from the back of her bicycle. Then she puts a few deliberate metres between herself and the rest of them, while still facing them, making her both part of the group and an outsider.

From her jacket pocket, Alida pulls out a small juice box. In lieu of a straw, she pierces it with her bike key and squeezes the apple juice straight into her mouth, eyes fixed on Berzan the entire time . . .

'It's not polite to stare,' Marlene says.

'It's not polite to tell people off,' Alida counters once she's done drinking, her gaze still on the young man. She slips the empty juice box back into her pocket.

'And you're not special for having feelings,' she adds. 'That's just what it's like to be a normal human being. It doesn't make you better or worse than anyone else.'

It's Marlene's turn to stare.

'I would have thought you'd developed some manners,' she says, shaking her head. 'That you'd be a bit more polished. I mean, it's not like you were born in a barn.'

Alida mutters something.

'What was that? Speak up,' Marlene snaps.

Alida glares at her.

'I've lived more than most, but that hasn't made me any happier,' she yells.

Marlene looks sullen.

'Maybe you didn't have the right attitude,' she says.

Alida stomps off to roll out her yoga mat on the lawn near Cassi. Then she lies down, putting her arms over her face.

Cassi looks at Marlene, who shrugs. Berzan barely seems aware of the fact that he was just at the centre of a conflict. He's back on his phone, is waving it about, hunting for reception. Cassi walks over to him, grabbing his arm and pulling it down. Some days, the reception is shaky in her little clearing. All you can do then is wait until the glitch has been fixed, or the winds have shifted, or whatever it might be that's causing the problem.

She takes his phone from him and leaves it face down on her front steps.

'I want to encourage all of you to take a break from external impulses,' she says, turning to her guests. She chooses not to comment on the tension. 'Let's meet each other without shields. We're here to coax out the awareness that exists within us. Not to be distracted by the outside world.'

She also doesn't want anyone to record the class. No photos, videos or sound recordings to be passed around afterwards. To be used as evidence against her, should they ever realise she's a fraud.

Marlene and Berzan tear the rustling plastic off their newly purchased yoga mats and roll them out next to Cassi's. Alida's has the word 'Lollo' written in one corner, so it's safe to assume it's borrowed. Marlene and Berzan sit down. Cassi looks at each of them. She takes a theatrical breath, spreading her arms wide, mimicking an embrace.

'Before we start, I want to know more about your frame of mind going into this session. What's your intention today?'

Berzan and Marlene exchange a look. Marlene answers first.

'I want to try something new,' she says. 'That's just who I am. I don't sit still. I challenge myself. I need things to happen.'

Marlene motions with her head. Then she falls silent. Berzan smiles.

'My impression was that we were going to do some kind

of meditation, so I suppose I might say I'm the opposite of Marlene. I'm looking for serenity. There's a lot going on in here at the moment,' he points to his head and then his heart, smiling almost apologetically at Cassi.

Marlene rolls her eyes.

'Look, I didn't mean, like, a crazy experience. I'm not expecting anything life-changing to happen today. But this is something I haven't done before, so I'm in. OK?'

Berzan runs a hand through his shiny hair and mumbles: 'OK, OK.'

Everyone turns to Alida. She's still lying down, and her eyes look dazed, as though she's just woken up and doesn't know where she is. She sits up.

'I'm here because Cassi said it would be good for me. I don't know what I'm expecting. I don't know what we're going to be doing.'

She lies back down.

Their confusion about what's going to happen is, perhaps, understandable. In all honesty, Cassi's not too sure herself.

'What I want to tell you before we start,' she says, kneeling before them with her hands folded on her thighs, 'is that this is a type of soul yoga I've developed myself after many, many years of practice. There are, as I'm sure you're aware, many different types of yoga. This is mine.'

She looks at them, wants to make sure they understand. No room for doubt.

'Since none of you have done anything like this before' – she knows it's the first time for all four of them – 'I'll proceed with that in mind. Be mindful of your breathing and rest like a baby if you need. Chakra, my friends.'

That last part is a phrase she's come up with and begun to use because she thinks it sounds good. Like a cosmic starting gun.

They begin right away. Cassi comes up with a combination of breathing exercises, standing stretches, sitting stretches, beetle-on-its-back-type exercises. She tries hard to keep a very slow tempo, even though every part of her is itching with restlessness. Sometimes, she forces them to just sit cross-legged and yell 'gaaaaaaaaaah'.

After going at it for about forty-five minutes, she's out of ideas. Cassi's not displeased with the class, but she feels like something's missing. It doesn't feel like it had that extra oomph. It wasn't very interesting.

So she asks them to lie down on their mats and close their eyes. She spreads a weighted blanket, which is actually an old rug she found in the barn, over each of them. She walks in a circle, squeezing their body parts at random, trying to keep it PG – a foot, a calf, an arm. Then, she begins to chant. Sounds, random words, mutterings. At first, the others lie there silent, but a few minutes in, Alida joins in. It's some kind of singing, of the tone-deaf variety. Marlene can't let Alida be in the spotlight and Berzan doesn't want to be left out, so before long, all four of them are talking over each other. Disjointed sentences, long confessions, detailed fantasies, short words. Cassi starts to move in uneven circles with her arms in the air. The rag rugs slide off. Marlene starts undressing while Alida rolls back and forth on her mat. Is Berzan crying?!

This is absolutely inexplicable. Profoundly remarkable, and at the same time complete nonsense. Cassi's stunned.

It's as though the power she pretends to possess actually exudes from her.

After minutes or hours, no one can tell, a strange calm descends on the clearing. Cassi rests a finger on her lips to mark that they're done. She wants to make it look as though what happened here is normal, exactly what she expected, that this is how it always turns out. She winks, hoping that they'll see it as a sign of camaraderie. That they won't tell anyone about today's session.

They part ways in silence. Berzan picks up his phone but doesn't look at it. He walks over to Marlene's car and sits down in the passenger seat, eyes down, hands in his lap, ready to leave. Alida fetches her bicycle without a word and is already pedalling when she realises she forgot her yoga mat. She has to get off, run back to the lawn, pick up the mat, loosely roll it up, and emit a frustrated groan when it resists her attempts to strap it back onto her bike, fully unfolding again instead. It feels like the process is happening in slow motion.

Marlene makes eye contact with Cassi. She looks like she wants to say something, but Cassi puts her finger to her lips again. Marlene spreads her hands but Cassi shakes her head. Marlene cocks her head. Cassi waggles a finger back and forth. Marlene shrugs and sighs. Finally, she turns and walks towards her car, hips swaying wildly. They drive off quickly.

Cassi takes a seat on the front steps. She doesn't want to think about what just happened, and she doesn't have to, because at that moment the Village Shop delivery truck comes down the road with the crushed stone she ordered the other day. The man driving it wants to know where she wants it, and Cassi points to the clearing. He tips the flatbed and twenty bags of rock tumble down into a heavy, dusty pile.

Then, Cassi and Maine are finally alone. Cassi goes inside and downs a glass of wine standing up by the sink. After that, she pours herself another glass, which she decides to count as her first, since downed glasses have been filled for such a brief time it can barely be said to have been filled at all. The five-second rule, Cassi-style. If the wine wasn't in the glass for at least five seconds, it was never truly there.

She sits down on the steps, soaking in a ray of evening sunlight peeking through the trees, with her first proper glass of wine. Maine settles down next to her in quiet companionship. She pets him.

She's learned a few things by now. The thicker she spreads it on, the better. There are no limits to her performance, but she has to project enough confidence to pre-empt doubt. Showing weakness is like asking to be questioned. That was true in her former role as a manager and it's true now. What was it her group of friends always used to say? It's better to ask for forgiveness than to ask for permission.

Her group of friends. That feels so long ago. An eternity, a lifetime.

Shake that thought, she tells herself, shake the thought of them.

With a hand on Maine's back, she wonders if she'll be able to incorporate him in a session. Fur therapy? Puppy yoga? Dog-themed fortune telling. Aren't dogs able to sniff diseases in people's bodies before doctors can find them? That would be a cool service to offer.

No, not that, too grim. Cassi has to focus on a positive vibes-only approach. She won't be giving anyone bad or scary news. She will only bring inspiration. Joy. Community.

Three wonderful concepts, by the way. Should she write them down? Put them on a sign? Somewhere in the back of her mind, there's an echo of a memory, but Cassi's so wrapped up in herself she can't remember what it might be. She takes another sip.

She's going to spread strength and a zest for life across this entire village.

That thought, that decision, prompts her to commit to tackling her bumpy road straight away. Cassi toasts herself before knocking back the rest of her wine. Then she knuckles down. Sacks are dragged, stones tumble and skitter, holes are filled. She levels the newly filled patches as best she can with her foot. Counting on the flatness to sort itself out when cars drive over them. She fetches more stone and more wine. The evening sky is bright above her.

28

There are new buds growing from the half-dead plant. Granted, Cassi's starting to enjoy looking for signs and symbols, but this one seems a bit too on the nose. As though she and the plant exist in some kind of symbiosis and both of them are finally feeling better, happier. She's so focused on the plant she doesn't notice Pavel at the open front door until he knocks three times, impatiently.

'I brought the ladder,' he says. The ladder is tied to the roof rack of his car.

He sets it up against the wall by the kitchen window and climbs up. Should Cassi feel bad about a feeble old man helping her with this kind of rickety and potentially deadly stuff? The idea dutifully occurs to her but disappears just as quickly. After all, he did offer. In fact, he insisted. It's not like she's forcing him.

And he's humming his usual song up there, the one that sounds Russian, so she takes it he's happy. Then there are loud scraping sounds. Pavel climbs down, fetches something from the car, climbs back up. Still humming. There's hammering. Scraping. Cursing. Scraping. More scraping.

It goes on for a while.

Cassi gazes out the window. What else is there to do when someone you're fond of is up on your roof? She's not exactly holding her breath, but she can't focus on anything else either. And it would feel odd to go outside and stand there staring up at him, as though her gaze could keep him safe.

Eventually, Pavel comes back down. Cassi tries to open the window, but it's stuck, so she asks through the glass if he wants a cup of coffee. The sun is shining on the front steps. They sit on the stoop with their cups. Pavel is gazing into the distance, Cassi too. They know how this goes now between them. Maine comes back from a stroll from somewhere on the other side of the house and lies down on the gravel in front of them, rolling around.

'I haven't looked at the gutters yet,' Pavel says after a while. 'I can help you with that window too, if you want. And check the others. In case they don't open either. Since I'm here anyway.'

'Is there anything you can't do?' Cassi asks. 'You should teach me, so I know how to fix things as well . . . But then you might not come over here as much. And that would be sad.'

She looks at him and smiles, but Pavel's not so easily charmed this morning.

'I was thinking about the foundations as well,' he says. 'They're crumbling in places. The cracks will need repairing.'

We all have our cracks, Pavel, Cassi wants to say. He never asks about her past, and at times that makes her want to tell him everything. Make him see her, make him understand what she's been through. That she has scars too. The cracks in the house are nothing compared to the ones she carries inside her.

'What's the upstairs like? Any damp spots on the ceiling? I sealed everything up under those crooked roof tiles.'

'I haven't noticed anything, but I don't go up there a lot.'

'Want me to have a look?'

It's a rhetorical question. Pavel has never come across as the type to put things off, and he doesn't this time either. Maybe it's because of his advanced age? He sets his cup down immediately, goes inside, climbs the stairs to the first floor. Cassi can hear him walking around up there. There's creaking, there's shuffling. A thud. Then silence.

Cassi waits. She finishes her coffee and gives it another minute. Still not a sound from upstairs.

She stands up. 'Pavel?'

No answer.

She goes inside, following his dirty boot tracks to the stairs. Steels herself for what she might find up there. Slowly climbs the steps one at a time, hoping to hear signs of life.

When her head reaches floor level, she cautiously peers around.

'Pavel?'

She can hear him breathing now. Heavy, laboured old-man breathing, but that's normal for him, so it doesn't worry her. She can see him lying on the double bed that has no mattress. She rushes over, squatting down next to him. Suppressing the impulse to stroke his hair.

'Are you OK? Can I do anything? Should I call a doctor?'

Pavel keeps one hand over his eyes, the other is resting on his chest. He lets out a sigh.

'No, I'm fine,' he says, his voice rough. 'It's just overwhelming to be up here again. I had to lie down. The years go by so quickly. But the days go by so slowly.'

Cassi walks around the bed and lies down on the hard

slats. She knows how to read between the lines with Pavel. In a way, she doesn't feel like she needs an explanation. But she asks anyway.

'Would you like to tell me about the two of you?'

And so, she becomes the first person in the world to ever find out about the love of Pavel's life.

29

'When I arrived in Stockholm, I applied to the Royal Institute of Technology,' Pavel says, carefully stressing every syllable of the university's name.

'I was probably lucky, because term was about to begin and I was offered a place off the waitlist. The first day, I got lost on the way there and arrived late. At the entrance, I was given directions by a bloke with big hair and a big moustache. I felt so out of place. Barely spoke the language. Didn't know much about the city. But when I stepped into that auditorium, Karl-Adam was the first person I saw. And I knew right away. Even though I didn't have a clue. There was something about his eyes. The way he was leaning against the windowsill. I can still see it. I don't even have to close my eyes.'

He pauses.

'I've thought a lot about that, what made the penny drop. What made me understand.'

He falls silent again. Ponders it some more.

'But I don't know,' he says. 'I just saw him. And he saw me. And it was as though the lights suddenly shone brighter around us.'

Cassi lies still. Trying to breathe silently, as though the slightest sound from her might interrupt, ruin this moment between her and Pavel. She can picture it, the auditorium slowly filling up, young men, maybe a woman here and there, taking their seats in the rows. Late-summer heat outside tall windows, inside, a smell of cologne, cigarette smoke, sweat. Chairs scraping against a wooden floor. A young Pavel, shy eyes, neatly combed hair.

'It was different for him,' Pavel continues. 'His life was already in full swing. But mine began in that moment.'

Pavel scratches his cheek. Outside the window, swallows are swooping, the wall rustles as they fly in and out of their nest. He continues.

'It was complicated. He was struggling with himself back then. They were expecting, so they had to get married in a hurry. He used to go back to be with her during the breaks. Sometimes she came up to visit.'

He pauses again.

'But then it was the end of our first year of uni. A few of us were celebrating at a classmate's house, he lived near the school. There was schnaps. I know we talked about Midsummer, because ever since, Karl-Adam has teased me about forgetting to speak Swedish when I told them how we celebrate in Lithuania. I wasn't used to schnaps.'

Pavel smiles at the memory. He pinches the base of his nose with the fingers of his left hand.

'It was a late night. Going home, Karl-Adam and I were headed in the same direction, so we walked together. He was going back to her the next day. But that night, he took my hand.'

He strokes his own cheek.

'We walked off.'

Pavel takes a deep breath, sighing on the exhale. Then he's silent again. Cassi turns onto her side on the hard slats, studying him. She's unbelievably uncomfortable where she's lying down, but can't, won't get up. Pavel resumes his story.

'It was a difficult summer. He left, I stayed in Stockholm. I drank a lot. Found places to go. Secret clubs. I was . . . lonely. I didn't know what to do. It was a dark time. I don't like to think about it.'

He shakes his head. Cassi reaches out, puts a hand on his arm.

'But then, when he came back that autumn, it was as though everything had changed. We went out for coffee during the first week and then he came back to mine. After that, we were an item. He even moved in. From the outside, it looked like we were just flatmates, of course. What we had was kept between us. I didn't tell anyone that I loved him.'

Cassi feels like it might be time for her to say something. She clears her throat.

'But he didn't leave her?' she asks, instantly regretting it. It's so like her to focus on the negative, and to ask a question she already knows the answer to.

'It's such a romantic story,' she adds. 'So lovely to know you're meant for each other so soon.'

Cassi knows her answers are robotic. She, who has always been able to make small talk with anyone, has never been good at handling other people's grief or other strong emotions. It's as though the words she wants to say disappear, grow too big or too little, the questions become too intrusive or insensitive. One time, she was with a friend when the latter found out her sick father had passed away. All Cassi could come up with, after the tragic call had ended was: 'What a shame.' Nothing else.

Pavel's silent now. Cassi wonders if she's ruined everything, just like with her friend. Since then, she's tried to avoid that kind of situation. She doesn't trust herself, what might come out of her mouth.

But then Pavel pats her hand, the one resting on his arm, and relief washes over her.

'They stayed together, Karl-Adam and Käthe,' he says. 'They had a son, but he was poorly. Karl-Adam moved back home after graduating. I just wanted to be where he was. I even sent them a christening present. A bit brazen, perhaps, but I wanted it to remind him of me.'

He sighs again.

'I was lost. I didn't know what to do with myself. I had nothing to tie me to Stockholm. Nothing to tie me to anywhere.'

He wipes his eyes.

'Then, I received a letter.'

30

Cassi is recycling bottles behind The Market when she notices a couple approaching. They're holding hands, dressed in matching navy-blue gilets over knitted jumpers, smiling broadly at her.

The man wears tinted glasses and is carrying two paper carrier bags in his free hand. The woman's long, blond hair flutters in the breeze. Cassi's scalp remembers what it feels like to be so freshly washed, freshly blow-dried, freshly brushed. Her fingertips remember what it was like to wear a sweater that wasn't pilling.

They must be the Desgoffes, the alpaca farmers. Cassi's heard about them from Marlene and her description of their appearance was spot on. If they're also smug, posing wannabe swingers who can't hold their beer remains to be seen.

Cassi pushes a dirty strand of hair from her face, trying to secure it behind her ear. More and more often, she puts on what she calls her 'sacred face' when she interacts with people. She forces her facial muscles to relax, softens her gaze, and rolls her shoulders back and down. She reckons it gives her an aura of mystique, a Mona Lisa-style vibe, that of a person who has all the answers, but doesn't speak out of turn. Benevolent, self-sacrificing. Despotic.

She shoves the last bottle into the mixed glass recycling

bin with a graceful *plop*, hears its satisfying shatter when it hits the bottom.

'Cassi, right?'

She folds up her empty bag and puts it in her jacket pocket before turning to the couple. The blonde woman is looking at her with friendly, squinting eyes.

'Cassiopeia?' the woman adds, tilting her head, moving her outstretched fingers nervously.

'I'm Lollo,' she continues without waiting for a reply. 'We were just saying, it's so strange we haven't met yet. You know Alida already, she works for us. This is Simon. We're the people with the alpacas?'

'Of course, I've seen your magnificent animals,' Cassi reaches out with both hands, squeezing first Lollo's extended right hand, then Simon's. 'I've been meaning to stop by to introduce myself, but I've just been so busy. And a person has to take their time settling in. There's no room for stress here.'

With her arms raised and her palms open like that one famous statue in Rio, she looks around, smiling, seemingly beholding completely different surroundings than a cracked car park lined with recycling bins.

Simon smiles a straight-toothed smile.

'I understand completely,' Lollo says. 'Would you like to come by for coffee some day? It would be great to get to know each other.'

Cassi's hungry. She's put off shopping for days, and if visiting with the Desgoffes means another day without having to see Hans and Gretel, she's not about to decline. If there's one thing she can tell just from looking at this couple, it's that they keep a well-stocked fridge and a pantry to match.

'I could come right now,' she says. 'It's important to have days when you follow your natural rhythm, go with your impulses, see what life has to offer. And today is one of those days – maybe I was meant to meet you at this juncture.'

Simon looks at Lollo. Lollo's already nodding. She's clearly keen to appear every bit as life-affirming as Cassi.

'That's wonderful. Simon has to drive the children to their after-school activities in a bit, though. You know how it is, every day's packed. No rest for the wicked.'

Lollo smiles, apologetically and proudly at the same time.

'No, I don't have children,' Cassi replies. 'I wouldn't feel right making new humans, with the world the way it is. But that's me. I'm not saying it's wrong *for you.*'

She smiles at them.

Lollo nods slowly. Simon checks his smartwatch.

'So, do you want to go right now? We've already done our shopping, we were just going to recycle some cardboard. You can follow us with your car.'

Cassi drives behind them. Watches Lollo gesticulate as she talks while Simon drives. Sometimes, Lollo turns around and waves at Cassi through the rear windshield, as though to confirm she's still there. Cassi feels she can read the two of them even from afar. Lollo seems like a person who likes to curl up on the sofa in the autumn with a blanket and a cup of tea, not because she particularly wants to, but because she thinks it's what people like her should do. People who would have a colour-coded bookshelf behind said sofa. People who would watch *Love Actually* at Christmas.

Simon hasn't given Cassi much to go on yet, but she knows the type. Simon has no close male friends, but a loose gang he sometimes plays golf with. Or footgolf. Or frisbee golf. Sometimes, if they want to get a bit merry on the course, minigolf. Lollo likes to say Simon 'nerds out' about things, but in reality, Simon simply wants things to be uncomplicated. Sure, he might amuse himself pottering about the basement workshop Lollo has set up for him, he might enjoy flipping through a magazine about watches or phones if Lollo buys him one, sometimes he goes hunting because it's what's done, but mostly, he just wants to be left alone. To watch Second World War documentaries and eat crisps.

The alpacas are flocking around Alida, who's filling a metal cage with hay as they pass. Alida watches them and Cassi waves, but Alida doesn't acknowledge her. Cassi parks behind Lollo and Simon on the raked gravel drive in front of their white house. The drive encircles a lawn, in the middle of which is a tree, and hanging from a tall branch is a tyre swing swaying in the wind. Lollo and Simon have climbed out of their car and are lugging shopping bags and bulk packs of kitchen roll from the boot to the front door.

Cassi offers to help but is waved away.

'Come in, come in, and pardon the mess,' Lollo says, unlocking the front door with a code. 'So practical to not have to keep track of a key,' she comments, pointing and chuckling.

The mess is non-existent. The walls of the hallway are white and the grey floor is heated. Jackets are neatly organised on hangers and so are the clean shoes underneath them. Hanging from the wall next to the bathroom door is a family portrait taken in front of the big tree Cassi saw outside. Everyone's smiling.

The kitchen is modern yet rustic, the kind with a deep sink, white shaker cabinets, a sturdy, marble-topped island between the counter and the dining table. The surfaces are spotless. Pale-green apples sit in a bowl on the counter. Everything looks brand new. A bit like a display kitchen.

'You have a beautiful home,' Cassi says, since that's what people are expected to say when they enter a room like this one, a house like this one.

'Thank you, that's so sweet of you to say,' Lollo replies, cutting an inch or two off a bouquet of white roses. She puts them in a tall glass vase, which she then places at one end of the kitchen island. Then she shoves Simon aside so she can get to one of the drawers.

Cassi's not sure what else to say, because talking about interior design when you're the kind of person she is feels pedestrian. She walks a lap around the room, limping slightly after having tripped and fallen over a wine bottle a few nights ago.

Lollo watches her.

'What happened to your leg?' she asks.

Cassi sighs.

'I feel silly,' she says, shaking her head. 'It's an old injury from when I was shot . . .'

Lollo and Simon look horrified, freezing mid-unpacking.

'. . . in a previous life,' Cassi continues. 'Sometimes it comes back. I view it as a reminder that no one's immortal, but that we all live on. The air we breathe has been breathed by our ancestors. It doesn't matter how hard we work on our appearance, nothing can save us from the inevitable.'

Cassi touches her face and head, shooting Lollo a pointed look. Lollo runs a hand through her hair.

'Could I use your bathroom?' Cassi asks. Without waiting for a response, she walks out of the kitchen and into the bathroom, locking the door behind her.

She takes a little break in there, sitting on the closed lid, her bare feet on the heated floor and her cheeks in her hands. She stands up, flushes, washes her hands. Washes her hands again. Moisturises her hands with a lotion whose fragrance matches the soap, then does her arms and legs too. She peeks into the medicine cabinet, but the only thing behind the door is a box of painkillers.

It no longer washes over her as frequently, the feeling of 'Where am I?' and 'What am I doing?'. But it does happen on occasion, and on a day like this, after spouting rubbish like that, in a strange house with people she doesn't know, locked in the bathroom and smeared with someone else's heavily perfumed lotion, it's all kind of dizzying.

Life wasn't like this back when she was living in the basement and working in the hypermarket. That wasn't her normal life either, but it was familiar and never challenging. Here, everything's new, all the time. Every moment, when she's not alone or with Pavel, is an opportunity to get stuck in. She can never just be, always has to be on high alert. And granted, she likes it. After a year of isolation and silence, the change is unexpectedly welcome. She likes being this person, whom no one knows and no one knows anything about, always ready to help her fellow humans. She only wishes she could laugh at it sometimes, the absurdity of the situation she's put herself in. Roll her eyes, together with someone who understands. She wishes her old friends hadn't turned out to be false conniving rats, that she could share this with them.

On the other hand, if they hadn't turned out to be false conniving rats, she would never have ended up here.

It's quiet outside. Are they waiting for her? She should go back to the kitchen. Cassi pops two painkillers just because, swallowing them quickly with a cupped handful of water from the tap. A hand-lotion aftertaste. She smooths her hair down but then tousles it again before unlocking the door and stepping out.

In the kitchen, Simon's fiddling with the coffee machine and Lollo's putting her long hair up with a clip, checking with her hands to make sure precisely the right number of strands end up loose.

Cassi raises her arms above her head, moving her hands in sweeping circles.

'I'm reading the energies in this room . . .' she says. 'It's giving harmony and . . . playfulness . . . but sometimes things blow up too!'

Lollo looks delighted. She takes a glass jar of nuts from a shelf, sets it down on the kitchen table.

'That's hard to deny. But what would life be without passion?'

She winks and smiles at Cassi, puckering her lips.

'We have to make room for all of our emotions, that's one of the pillars of my philosophy,' Cassi says, running a finger along the windowsill. Taking note, Lollo quickly pulls a rag from a drawer and begins to wipe the counter in front of her. Cassi inspects the tip of her finger.

This couple irks her. They seem so successful, so beautiful, so in sync with life. And so very intent on making sure everybody knows it. As though they're shoving their well-organised lifestyle in her face just by existing.

'Oh, a lot of people find that challenging – a person might not want to be in touch with their rage, for instance,' she continues. 'Their envy. Their grief. We push down the complicated and the difficult, but in the end that only diminishes us as human beings.'

Pretty rich, coming from her.

'Life is both light and dark,' she goes on. 'We can't completely wipe our complicated feelings away.'

Lollo pauses her wiping.

'But surely keeping a nice home is a good thing?' she says. 'I'm happiest when things are neat and tidy.'

The look Cassi shoots Lollo is condescending. You can't tell from looking at Cassi that she used to feel the same way just a year ago. Lollo folds up the rag she's holding. Over by the coffee machine, Simon turns to Cassi, holding up two cups – one for espresso and one for cappuccino. Cassi points to the cappuccino one with a smile. Since she gave up on being a food snob, she's stopped following Southern European coffee rules. These days, she puts milk in her coffee regardless of what time of day it is. Simon places the cup under the spout and then holds up a carton of regular milk and another of oat milk. Cassi points to the regular milk. Simon nods and pushes a few buttons on the machine.

'We moved out here three years ago,' Lollo says, lighting a beige tealight lantern on the table with a gas lighter. 'Big cities are starting to feel scary, don't you think? So much crime and violence.'

She squints at Cassi, looking for agreement. Cassi says nothing.

'And Simon had just sold his company, which made it a lot more doable.'

Lollo smiles at her husband.

'What kind of company was it?' Cassi asks, turning to Simon, but Lollo beats him to it.

'Ha, not the interesting kind. No, they did commercial recycling. Simon's dad started the company in the seventies. But we were paid a lot for it.'

Lollo keeps talking while she stacks cinnamon buns symmetrically on a large plate.

'So we decided to change our lives around completely. I grew up with alpacas, my parents bred them, so it felt natural. If you live in the country, there should be animals. And Alida takes care of all of that. We're busy with other things.'

Lollo takes out her phone to show Cassi her Instagram account: @LooksByLollo. Pictures of interior design and gardening are interspersed with pictures of outfits, food, and happy, tousled-looking children.

'I worked in PR before, but I started this account when we bought the house and began renovating it, and people are starting to offer me interior design jobs off the back of it now. Have you been to Marlene's house? I helped her do her living room. And I work with various companies as well.'

Lollo looks pleased.

'I'm deeply passionate about inspiring my followers. And the environment's very important to me,' she says, putting a hand on her heart. 'Maybe more so because we live the way we do, close to nature? That makes it so easy to create content for that kind of collaboration.'

She quickly scrolls through her feed to demonstrate.

'Personally, I feel life should be lived here and now,' Cassi comments, looking stern.

Lollo swallows.

'Screens make us forget what truly matters,' Cassi continues.

Lollo opens her mouth to say something, but Cassi stops her.

'Let me finish,' she says.

She stands there, one hand raised. Lollo is silent.

'What was I saying?'

Cassi gazes out the window. Outside, the alpacas are chewing their hay, and the tyre swing is swaying back and forth. Alida's raking the gravel around a plastic flamingo chair.

'No, it's gone.'

Lollo looks down. Her lips look like they're forming a silent 'I'm sorry'.

Cassi puts her fingertips against her forehead. Looks as though she's contemplating something profound.

'Gut feeling,' she says at length. 'That's important. That's what should guide you.'

Cassi's own gut rumbles. She pulls out a chair to parry the sound and sits down. Grabs a fistful of assorted nuts from the jar on the table and chews them, one by one.

'We're all miracles,' she says. 'Just think of all the things our bodies have to do to keep us alive. It's dizzying.'

Cassi babbles on for several minutes, about her philosophy, her method. While talking, she devours half the jar. Lollo and Simon listen wide-eyed.

'Alida didn't tell us anything about the session, but I

could tell from looking at her she'd experienced something special over at yours,' Lollo says. 'Simon and I would love to come and, errr' – Lollo casts about for the right word – 'have an experience. We had this amazing couple's massage in Croatia once.'

Simon's leaning back in his chair, holding an espresso cup between his thumb and forefinger. One of his thighs is vibrating like one of those asphalt machines that turns pavement into rubble, the kind that was running outside Cassi's flat for what felt like six months straight. Without looking at him, Lollo puts a hand on his leg. It stops moving. Lollo places her hand palm-down on the table, fingers stretching towards Cassi.

'No one's more open than me when it comes to trying new things,' she declares. 'You're looking at a person who says "hello" to life. Like, "Hey, here I am!", you know.'

She smiles, raising her hand like at school. Then she suddenly claps her hands to her cheeks and opens her eyes wide.

'OK, hold on, I just had an amazing idea, Cassi! You and I should work together.'

She leans forward as though she wants to take Cassi's hands but stops herself before she reaches them.

'Let's live stream! Yoga! Wouldn't that be fun? You can spread your philosophy to more people, and wow, my followers would sooo appreciate it! I've noticed that wellness and health-related subjects really resonate with them. And it would be great for your business too – you'd get so many new clients! Amazing outreach!'

Lollo stops herself when she notices the look in Cassi's eyes, which has turned frosty.

'My *business?*' Cassi says.

It's been a long time since she had someone to boss around. Not since her days at the restaurant, when a frustratingly pliable sous-chef happened to coincide with one of Cassi's most stressful periods at work.

Lollo's cheeks flush. She doesn't know what she's done wrong. Cassi sighs.

'I don't think of my calling as a "business", Lollo.'

'No, but I mean, think of all the people you could help?' Lollo tries to course correct.

Cassi rests her gaze on the ceiling. Sucks on a piece of nut stuck in her teeth. Simon's eyes dart between the two of them.

'Fine,' Cassi says after a long pause. 'If it means I can help someone turn off their screen, even for ten minutes, I've accomplished something.'

Lollo seems to have detected ambiguity in what she just said, but the lines around her eyes quickly disappear and she energetically claps her hands together.

'Yay, that's great! Isn't it, Simon? It's going to be amazing!'

Simon nods, giving her two thumbs up. Then he reaches for a cinnamon bun, but Lollo moves the plate away so he can't reach it, holding it out to Cassi instead, who gladly takes one.

Simon stands up, almost knocking his chair over.

'May I offer you another cup?' he asks, or more accurately 'May I offew you anothew cup?', because as it turns out, his voice sounds like a child's, if that child had a speech impediment. If the situation had been different, Cassi would have assumed he was faking it, making a joke, but it doesn't feel like a funny moment.

Lollo swallows hard and stares out the window.

'Please. The coffee's delicious,' Cassi replies.

Simon turns his back to them, and the coffee machine begins to hiss.

'All organic, of course,' Lollo says, and Cassi thinks she could be talking about anything. Lollo's gaze has returned to the kitchen. She rotates the cinnamon bun plate, which scrapes angrily against the bare tabletop.

'Darling, get the boys' hockey things out. And don't forget Bianca's riding gear. You need to leave in ten minutes.'

Simon hands Cassi her refilled cup without a word and then walks out into the hallway.

'Simon's helping Max turn the campground into a holiday park,' Lollo says. 'He's a proper entrepreneur, always has been. We met on an online forum for young business owners, and I knew straight away he was the one. All he needed was the right kind of motivation, you know, like with his weight. You have no idea how big he was when we met.'

That last part is said in a theatrical whisper, from behind her hand. Then normal voice again, a weary look through the window.

'He was something else entirely back then. Not just appearance-wise.'

She doesn't clarify further. Cassi looks out too, watching the alpacas. There's no sign of Alida now.

'Yep, it took a lot of work.'

Lollo lets her hair down again, combing it out with her fingers. The smell of her shampoo – probably organic – wafts all the way to Cassi.

'It's been a struggle. It really has. Not always easy.'

Simon has reappeared in the doorway, drawing their attention by tapping the doorframe with the car key he's forced to hold with his teeth. His arms are full of hockey equipment, a small riding helmet balanced on his head. Lollo shoots her husband a brief glance, before turning back to Cassi. A new edge to her gaze.

'Next Sunday,' Lollo says. 'We'll live-stream. The whole world is about to meet Cassiopeia.'

31

'Did your life turn out the way you thought it would, Pavel?' Cassi asks. They're sitting on the front steps after Pavel has fixed the windows that were causing trouble, happily humming the entire time, and she's grateful for both his help and company.

He adjusts his grip on his cup, sighing slightly.

'I don't know what I thought. I didn't have a clear plan. But I grew up with a large extended family. I had a lot of friends. Got a degree in engineering. Things changed when I moved here, of course. But it doesn't matter now anyway.'

He trails off.

'And you? Is this your dream? You're still young.'

Cassi cocks her head. She doesn't bother telling him she'll be forty in a few years. Age is just a number, and this new life of hers has rejuvenated her. She might not be, but she does feel younger.

'I suppose I can honestly say I had never dreamed of this before, it just kind of . . . happened. The past twelve months have been rotten. Truly awful.'

She shakes her head.

'But now I'm here. This is how it is.'

To Cassi, every honest statement she makes about her life feels revolutionary when it escapes her lips. She has kept everything inside for so long. The memory of her failure, her humiliation. The reminder that everyone in the village has baggage to live with has made her own seem ever so slightly lighter.

'And seriously, things feel mostly OK. I like Bäcken. But my life used to be different, a few years ago. You wouldn't have recognised me. It's as though I was a different person. In a completely different world.'

The words stick in her throat a little. It's a bit taxing after all, this honesty thing. She clears her throat, as though it were phlegm and not feelings blocking it.

She smiles at him. 'Another cup?' she asks, standing up.

'Please,' he replies. He empties his nearly full cup over the side of the steps before handing it to her.

Cassi goes into the kitchen. Boils new water. Pinches her forearms. Through the window, she sees that Pavel has stood up and is throwing a stick in an attempt to engage Maine. Maine just looks at him. Wags his tail once, then turns onto his side to underscore his lack of interest. He then rolls over on his back to signal that he wouldn't mind a belly rub, in case Pavel's in need of something to do. Pavel obliges.

Cassi makes the coffee and goes back outside.

Pavel looks at her but says nothing. She knows he understands. Whatever it is he understands.

'Sometimes it's harder,' he says after she sits down. 'But that doesn't mean life will always be that way. That whatever it is now will continue forever.'

He continues to scratch Maine.

'But do you ever get used to it?'

It's a thought, but it slips out in word form.

'I don't know if life is something a person should have

to get used to,' Pavel says. He slowly stands up from where he's squatting next to Maine and sits down next to her on the steps again. He picks up his cup and blows on it.

After a minute, it becomes clear he doesn't intend to elaborate further.

'Have you never considered moving away from here, starting over somewhere else?' she asks.

'No. I chose this,' Pavel says. 'Maybe the thought occurred to me on occasion, early on. When I'd just got here. But not later. And I don't believe in running away from myself.'

'Oh, I don't know, I think it's a pretty neat solution,' she counters with a wry smile.

The corners of Pavel's mouth twitch. A shift in the mood.

'But you could have met someone else,' she says. 'Someone you didn't have to be so secretive with.'

'I never felt that way. We never lived together again, after those years in Stockholm, but we had a lot of good years. I didn't need anyone else.'

Pavel pauses.

'And we weren't all that secretive,' he continues. Looking down at his coffee. 'Not really. It wasn't something we told people. It was between the two of us. No one had to know. And Karl-Adam liked it best when it was just the two of us.'

Cassi gazes out at the woods. Wondering how a person hides from themselves. But the answer feels somehow too close, too familiar, so she drops it.

'But you seem so lonely. I'm sorry, that sounds harsh, but it's my impression. Maybe because you always have time for me. Even though I'm new here.'

'I don't have a big need for people. I like being here in his house. Or, well, your house. It feels safe. I have wonderful memories here. And as it turns out, I like you.'

Pavel almost smiles again.

'At first, I figured it was because you look like someone I used to know. But now I find I'm perfectly able to be around you just because you're you.'

Cassi rocks over towards him, nudging him with her shoulder. Rarely has she received a more amazing compliment.

'OK, I've made a decision,' she says. 'You and I are going on an outing. We're going to go visit him. Karl-Adam.'

32

Before she knows it, the day has come for Lollo to come set up an online yoga session in Cassi's barn. It's gloomy in there, but the evening sunlight manages to creep in through gaps in the walls. Cassi has tied string lights in between the rafters, particles of dust dancing in the bright spots. The atmosphere feels quite magical. At least Cassi thinks so. Lollo had tried to suggest that they host the session in her pristine study instead, with its white floorboards and walls, a beautiful birch tree outside the window. But Cassi had said no. Absolutely not. She'd been clear that if they were going to do this, she would not under any circumstances compromise on her method. Cassi's also becoming more strong-willed with each session she leads, and in Lollo's company she transforms into a full-fledged yoga dominatrix, if such a thing exists. Lollo's too afraid to object. The question is if she even wants to.

Has Lollo ever regretted not trying out Cassi's 'method' for herself before launching this idea? Wondered if maybe it was stupid not to take the time to sample that 'reiki treatment' or even visit Cassi's barn before nailing down their plans? Very possible. To Lollo, yoga's synonymous with cucumber water and pastel leggings, fit bodies and bright studios. That Cassi's not synonymous with any of those things had no bearing on her assessment. Perhaps Lollo counted on the bright studio setting to materialise and the cucumber water to be served the moment the mats were rolled out.

Not that it matters anymore. Because plans have been made. Tonight's the night and Cassi's ready for it.

Lollo has been granted permission to use her ring light on a stand, to which her phone is also stuck. Cassi's still capable of appreciating flattering lighting, she's not a barbarian.

Word of the event Lollo has invited people to has spread far and wide on social media. By now, five thousand people have marked themselves as interested in the free yoga session with 'the cosmic superstar of the deep woods of Värmland, Cassiopeia'.

Lollo's trying to sweep the worst of the debris off the dirty floor, but that only makes more dust swirl into the air. Cassi takes the broom from her and puts it to the side without saying a word. Lollo is dressed in floral tights and a matching tight crop top. Cassi hasn't changed yet, she's in her regular clothes, grimy denim shorts and a dirty tank top, but she is going to change, of course she is. Lollo hasn't dared to ask her about it, but she brought an extra set of clothes and held them up to her.

'I brought extras, just in case, figured yours might be in the wash or maybe it could be fun if you and I matched. Would it be fun if we matched?'

Cassi merely looks at Lollo, puts a hand on her shoulder, and demonstratively places her other index finger against her lips.

She informed Lollo yesterday they weren't going to talk to each other in the hours leading up to the class. Cassi needs to focus, needs time to shape the energies and forcefields they'll be working with. She's also asked Lollo to spend the hour before they go live in the woods 'cleansing her aura'. Cassi 'doesn't want anyone else's nerves or relationship problems hanging over her' while she finishes her preparations. Besides, Cassi needs time to burn her homemade incense in the barn, to further cleanse the space and perform a 'self-sacred' – a new term coined by Cassi – ceremony which requires complete solitude.

If Lollo flinched at the phrase 'relationship problems' or took offence, she hid it well.

'I was going to head over to The Market anyway, to buy some nuts and . . .' Lollo stops herself when she notices the look on Cassi's face.

'No, right, I'll go for a walk instead, that's much better.'

Lollo reapplies her lip gloss and grabs her phone before walking out the double doors of the barn. Cassi hears her voice fade away as she films a reel.

'In just an hour, my darlings, we'll get started on . . .'

Cassi checks that everything is in place, ready for the show. When she can no longer see Lollo through the trees, she exits the barn too and walks back to her house. She's given this a lot of thought. She was flattered to be asked, and the challenge is appealing, but she's acutely aware of the risks associated with taking her new role into the public sphere.

Cassi opens the fridge, takes out a cup of wine, ceremonially chilled, and carries it upstairs. That's where she's laid out her outfit for the evening.

Fifteen minutes later, she goes back downstairs. Refills her cup to the brim, sips it. She sprinkles dried tarragon from an ancient jar she discovered at the back of the pantry onto a plate. Then she grabs the matches. Back in the barn, she pushes the herb flakes into a pile and tries to light it. It crackles nicely and for a second, she's worried about setting fire to the barn, but as quickly as the flames ignited, they then die down, leaving nothing but a cloud of slightly suffocating smoke. Which is exactly how it's supposed to be, right?

She sits down on the yoga mat Lollo has rolled out and tries to collect her thoughts. Or let go of them, more like. She's noticed that's what she has to do. Let go of her need for control and any personal expectations, so she can simply let things happen. Let the words come. If she starts to think too much, she will stumble.

The cup is now empty and Cassi is ready. Lollo must have telepathically noticed because she knocks on the wall of the barn before entering again, rosy-cheeked and slightly sweaty. She picks pine needles out of her hair and sniffs, wrinkling her nose at the smoke lingering in the air.

'Are we ready to go?' she asks.

Cassi stands up. She's smudged black make-up around her eyes, not in a going-to-a-party-smoky-eyes way. No, she looks more like a burglar from a comic book. Her outfit consist of black tights and a black T-shirt, with spruce branches pinned to her shoulders. Cassi turns to Lollo, holding what looks like a mess of leaves and twigs in her hand. A closer inspection would reveal it to be a mesh bottle sleeve festooned with lingonberry leaves, but Lollo doesn't have time for that kind of scrutiny before Cassi gently starts to pull the thing down over her own head. She slides it down to cover her face like a balaclava, carefully straightening any greenery that has ended up askew.

'What—' Lollo starts to protest, but she stops herself.

Cassi knows she doesn't look anything like Lollo's idea of a yoga instructor. And that the barn looks nothing like Lollo's idea of a yoga studio. But Lollo agreed to this. It was her idea, in fact. And Lollo knows she's not allowed to question Cassi.

'Keep an open mind, Lollo,' Cassi says through the lingonberry leaves, breaking her own no-talking rule. Who wants to come off as closed-off and prudish? Not Lollo, that's for sure.

Lollo nods faintly. Both of them walk over to the ring light stand, where Lollo checks her phone one more time before pressing play on her livestream. As the number of viewers go up and the lower half of the screen fills with peppy messages – Marlene wires 'Let's go girlssss!'; Simon gives a thumbs up followed by a flexing arm and a lotus position – Lollo introduces herself and outlines what's going to happen.

'And I can promise you this isn't going to be just any old yoga class. I have the privilege to introduce to you our beloved guru, coach and yogi, the internationally renowned, cosmically famous: Queen Cassiopeia!'

Cassi steps into the frame. Lollo tries to hug her, but Cassi raises a hand to stop her. Lollo takes a few steps back and sits down on her yoga mat instead. The peppy comments in the box have slowed down quite a bit, replaced with '!!!!' and rolling-on-floor-laughing emojis, one or two Munch screams.

Cassi walks back and pays no heed. She sits down with her legs crossed, closes her eyes, asks her viewers to let her voice guide them.

'I want you to close your eyes and focus on your breathing. Let's sit in silence for a moment and take in each other's presence. Chakra, my friends.'

She can almost hear Lollo heaving a sigh of relief behind her, at there being at least an ounce of normalcy to this experience.

Then, the class begins.

JULY

33

Cassi laughs out loud at the memory the next day.
 The way she looked. What she did. How it turned out. When did she last laugh like this? Out loud, a proper belly laugh? She can't even remember. She's proud too, absolutely. Pleased she went through with it, happy so many people showed up. And she feels an unexpected love for them all.
 But there's shame there too. And concern. So many feelings, the entire spectrum, as far from her numb life in the basement as it's possible to get. And for that, another feeling: gratitude. She was so certain nothing would ever get better. It felt inconceivable she'd ever climb back out of that hole – she had no footholds and no motivation to find any. Disappointed in everyone, not least herself. Left with a single purpose in life: taking care of Maine.
 Everything is different now, especially after yesterday.
 Lollo comes by in the late morning bearing gifts: a potted rose and a new yoga mat. She says she's been approached by at least fifty people who want to hire Cassi. Lollo doesn't question Cassi's statements about her absence from social media or her aversion to modern technology, and has therefore printed out a bunch of DMs and emails that have come in.
 Cassi has obviously already been online. She's read comments and everything she can find about the class. It's even

been mentioned in a think piece about rural culture in one of the top-tier morning papers, written by a twenty-something columnist with bitingly sharp opinions.

'Get lost in the woods', the headline reads. The short sentences about 'the chanting lingonberry guru', who has not been identified, are difficult to gauge. Cassi reads the article several times. It could be positive, but just as easily negative. That's the good thing about having ended up in a field she never aspired to be in – that no one's more aware of her shortcomings than Cassi herself. It makes it easier to soak up the praise and let the criticism run off her back. She already knows it could have been done better. She can keep learning from her mistakes, grow, hone her craft. At the end of the day, all she cares about is that no one from her old life should recognise and unmask her. And she seems to have pulled that off. No one's seen the real person behind the lingonberry leaves.

During a trip to The Market, she's stopped by the chef from the pizzeria. He catches her just as she's on her way out, when she's eager to get away as quickly as possible from Hans, who's working the till again today, and who scrutinised her ID for so long she began to wonder if he was trying to memorise her personal identity number. But at least he didn't say anything. He stalked off and brought out her order without a word. Cassi has moved over to boxed wine so she won't have to deal with the racket of clinking glass, and when the chef stops her, her purchases are weighing her down like an anchor (or four).

She doesn't want to talk here, in front of Hans. She tries to lead the chef back out to the car park instead, but he's only just arrived and is enjoying the air conditioning.

He's looking to buy cigarettes before going back outside, but the queue's long, so he's in no hurry.

'I watched your performance with Lollo,' he says, hand on hip. 'Tell me about your philosophy. Who did you study under?'

The chef is smiling, he looks interested. Cassi shoots Hans a glance over at the till, meeting his gaze. Realises he's not going to look away. That he'd rather let his customers wait than stop listening. His contempt for her is frighteningly immutable. It's simmering away, like the lentil stew at the vegan restaurant Cassi used to live next door to. Day and night, whatever the season, at all times, the smell of cumin permeating in her flat, making it even easier to want to work late.

'I think it's interesting the way you mix influences,' the chef continues. 'You're bold. Modern. It's not like when I was growing up.'

Cassi smiles back. She doesn't mind Hans hearing this. The chef is liked by the locals. Cassi doesn't know him, but she's heard a lot about him from Marlene, who occasionally invites him over to hers because she's 'obsessed with Asian men'. Before Cassi could say anything, Marlene had raised a warning finger, adding that 'it's not racism if it's positive'.

'Cook's a poet too, Cassi,' Marlene has told her. 'I don't understand his poems, but they're incredibly beautiful.'

The chef has lived in Bäcken for over fifteen years but is still considered a newcomer. Everyone calls him Cook. Granted, they're right to, but it was 100 per cent the language barrier in his job application after arriving in town that made him change careers, at the age of forty, which turned out to be as welcome as it was unexpected. Cook, whose real name's pronounced but not spelled exactly like that, used to work as an accountancy consultant. He was part of the refugee wave that no one, except the ones who came, remembers now, and he has since amassed a larger Swedish vocabulary than most people around him.

Cassi cocks her head. She should have an answer to that question prepared, she knows that. But the truth is the answer is different depending on who's asking. And where she is when it's posed. She glances over at Hans. Chooses her words carefully.

'My philosophy,' she begins. 'I believe in the good in us all. I feel everyone deserves another chance. At heart, people want to do good.'

Cook's still smiling. Hans is scraping at the till with his fingernail, looking as though there's a stain on it that needs to come off before he can serve the next customer.

'I don't believe in rules,' Cassi adds, with another look at Hans. 'It's important to think for yourself. What I can provide is advice.'

She would have liked to see a nod from him. This would be a great opportunity to show him she's not some kind of cult leader. Not that she can see why that would be so wrong. If not for Hans's tedious attitude and the terror it instils in her, Cassi could have thought of worse things than being uncritically respected by a crowd of adoring people. Maybe even slightly feared.

'There's something to that,' Cook says, scratching his neck. 'You're a modern-day shaman. Those are simple words, but they do something to people. A spiritual experience that's both difficult and easy to take in.'

Difficult and easy? Cassi doesn't know which of those words to take as the worse insult. She has a sudden urge to scowl and do a reality-show storm-out, but she checks herself. Besides, the weight of the wine makes storming out difficult.

'Yes, it's a carefully developed blend of influences,' she says instead. 'I believe that in this day and age, people are ready for more. An updated spirituality, I guess you might say. We're open to impressions, fundamentally restless. We're chasing serenity.'

There it is. Complete with one-liners like 'chasing serenity' so everyone can hear how wise she is.

And Cook agrees.

'You're right,' he says. 'We need the familiar. The clichés. The security. Like a Margherita pizza. The good Margherita will never be taken off the menu. And then you mix it with things no one's ever heard before. Things that are kind of hard to comprehend. "Chakra, my friends", as you like to say.'

Clichés? And is he comparing her to a glorified toastie? Pressure is building inside Cassi. She tries not to but can't help glancing over at Hans. She can tell he's laughing. It sounds like sneering snorts. She has to control herself, even though rage is growing like a lather inside her, a toxic foam pushing to get out.

The best she can manage is a stiff smile.

'Is that the poet in you coming out,' she says, trying to sound light-hearted. 'That's an image I couldn't have come up with myself, but maybe it's one way of looking at it. Your pizzas satisfy one kind of hunger. The physical. My contribution speaks to something else. Something deeper.'

She's happy with that reply too.

'Queue's gone,' she says, pointing to the till. 'Nama-fucking-ste. As I like to say.'

34

It rained overnight. The bright blue of the morning sky clashes with the wet, neon green glass. The asphalt is sleek like freshly brushed cat fur.

She's finally managed to talk Pavel into it. Today, she'll be picking him up at his house and driving him all the way to that door. She's going to remain by his side until he's ready.

When she bends down to untangle Maine's lead, which is stuck on a lever underneath the passenger seat of her car, Cassi notices something sticking out of the mat. She slides her hand under and pulls out a small frame with a black-and-white picture in it. The memory crashes over her before she has a chance to stop it.

Jarmo is finally coming home after several weeks on the road and Cassi has taken the night off to celebrate. In all honesty, she finds having time off to be more taxing than being at work, because the buzzy restaurant is all she thinks about anyway, and when she's off, she can't control the way her colleagues behave in the kitchen, pre-empt issues in the service, ensure that every table has fresh flowers on it. Time off is like her own personalised circle of hell.

But she knows it's also important to nurture her relationship. Cassi and Jarmo haven't spent a lot of time together lately, their phone calls have been perfunctory and tense. So tonight has to go well. They're going to be like a perfectly normal couple: relaxed, in love, happy, committed. They're going out for dinner with two of his friends and three of hers. It was Cassi's idea. She's used all her restaurant pull to secure a good table for seven at the city's newest spot, one that's booked up for months if you're an ordinary mortal, but where Cassi knows both the head chef and the maître d'. She's calling it her belated birthday dinner.

Which is why it was unexpected when both Maggie and Andrea told her they couldn't make it anymore due to 'family logistics'. But Cassi wouldn't take no for an answer. They had to be there.

The restaurant's located inside a giant glass box, which in turn is located on the roof terrace of one of the city's tallest buildings, with a menu described as 'Modern Scandinavian Pure Fusion'. Since Cassi doesn't trust any of the others to do it, she has called the restaurant in advance, pretending to be another member of the group informing them that they'll be celebrating Cassi's birthday. Cassi has asked for a sparkler-adorned dessert to be brought out, but of course will protest when it happens. She hopes someone will take a picture of it too, that there will be a record of how happy and glamorous she looks.

On the day in question, Cassi hits the gym at dawn. She's done her hair and nails, cleaned the kitchen and bathroom again and bought new lingerie. It's important to feel good about oneself.

She starts her workday by arranging substitutes for waiters who have called in sick. Then, she moves six heavy kegs of beer some intern left in the wrong place, initiates the planning of a fiftieth birthday party for a successful music producer who wants to rent the entire restaurant, helps Jarmo's company with deliveries that are running late, chases down a vegetable supplier who has provided sub-par aubergines when one of the new dishes on their menu is a twist on *parmigiana di melanzane*, calls around to find a florist with peonies in stock even though peonies aren't in season, skips lunch, and changes her dinner reservation to a four-top since Jarmo has let her know his friends can't make it and her friend Liza has texted to say she unfortunately has a fever.

Cassi also has an emergency meeting at work about a chef with a gambling addiction and debts with the mafia, an upset phone conversation with the contractor who still has some skirting boards to install in her flat, and a check-in with the owner of the building the restaurant's in regarding upcoming renovations to address a damp problem in the basement.

To wrap it all up, she has to take a meeting with an artist who's been commissioned to 'interpret Stockholm from a bird's-eye perspective' for the back of the menus. The meeting ends up being a protracted discussion about which bird represents Cassi's restaurant the most.

'A sparrow has a completely different way of seeing the world than an owl, you know,' says the artist, who's in no hurry. He's a childhood friend of the owner and is not about to miss an opportunity to sample what he calls 'a selection of tasters' from the drinks menu: a beer, a glass of champagne and a shot of vodka. He immediately chugs the lemonade, wiping his mouth with the palm of his hand before running it over his head. Then he leans back and looks up at the ceiling, stretching his legs out in front of him. White, hairy ankles peek out between chinos and loafers, already sockless despite it only being early spring.

'Or is it a bird that doesn't belong in our climate originally? A flamingo? What would happen if I went with an extinct species – I'm picturing a dodo? That could be a many-facetted statement about animal rights, the environment, the wretchedness of humankind. Powerful. Potentially of interest to the media? Check out my arms, see the goosebumps?'

He points to his arm. The skin on it isn't particularly puckered, so maybe what he actually wants to show her is his expensive watch.

The pointlessness of the meeting is frustrating. The artist is so obviously drawing it out to continue getting free drinks. Cassi wishes they never went with birds in the first place.

Cassi needs to leave. Her and Jarmo never fight, but their respective work schedules are like opposing ocean currents competing to ebb or flood. She knows that every time she's late, the tide goes in his favour.

One way or another, she manages to be the first to arrive at the glass-box restaurant. The room smells of new wood, polished metal, maybe a hint of window cleaner. The carpet's plush, the noise level as opulently muffled as the view is sharp. A shimmering horizon, the city like glinting fairy lights below. Over by the bar, Cassi spots a blond waitress whose trial period she opted not to extend a month earlier. The waitress probably assumes Cassi can't tell she's talking about her with her colleagues as they sort cocktail ingredients into different tubs, but Cassi sees the pointed looks. She smiles, twirls her hair over her shoulder with her index finger, straightens up. If there's one thing she couldn't care less about, it's service staff badmouthing her behind her back.

Cassi picks up the wine list. Chooses carefully, noting that the selection's decent but unexciting. They really could have done a better job. She orders a bottle of white so it'll be ready in its ice bucket when the others show up. Pours herself some water. Cassi normally abstains from wine, beer and spirits unless it's a special occasion. Having grown up with Bea, that's always been an easy choice to make. Barely even a choice. She's never seen the appeal of intoxication, not even as a teenager. Sure, Cassi can understand why other people might feel differently, but for her, alcohol's in no way associated with pleasure. It's something else. A tool. A weakness.

She spots Maggie and Andrea at the door, waiting to be escorted to her. Andrea is short and petite with shiny hair and a sharp suit that hides her body. Maggie, who had a baby a few months ago, wears a formless grey dress that has an igloo-like quality to it. Is it really that hard to maintain some kind of sartorial standards when you have children? Cassi feels strangely annoyed, but quickly shakes the feeling and stands up instead, straightening her tight white top, as though it could possibly fit any more perfectly.

She's struck by the realisation that she can't remember what type of bird the artist settled on, but pushes away the thought. Focus, she tells herself. Tonight's about you.

Maggie and Andrea look stressed and flushed. Along with Liza, who sadly isn't there, they've been Cassi's best friends since elementary school. The four of them have done everything together, know each other's personalities and quirks inside and out. But they don't see each other as much now. In the past few years, the distance between them has grown. Cassi knows it's what happens when you grow older and jobs, partners and children come into play. But their group chat, which takes its name, The Smoke Signal, from the flat they all shared after secondary school, has been unusually quiet, almost too quiet, over the past few weeks. Cassi hasn't had time to give this any thought, but a spark of insecurity lights up in her gut as she watches Maggie and Andrea babble even faster than usual. Life updates follow each other in quick succession. Maggie's new baby life, Andrea's new shared-custody-life, Cassi's home renovation, Andrea's new role as a partner at her law firm, Maggie's dad's diagnosis, the fact that Andrea and Cassi, unbeknownst to each other, have invested in identical luxury handbags. Liza's health – something illness-related has come up every time Cassi's tried to call or meet up with her recently. How is she really doing? Maggie shows them pictures of the baby on her phone. Cassi says 'aaawwww!' with her head cocked and a hand on her heart. She's probably already seen several of the pictures, given the sheer amount that have been posted in their group chat, but she exudes enthusiasm anyway.

Maggie tells them she and her boyfriend have decided to move back to the town they all made very sure to flee the second they were done with school.

'We want to be able to buy a house when the baby gets a bit bigger,' Maggie says, scrolling through her pictures. 'A garden. And the schools are good there. It feels safe.'

'I couldn't bear living in a small town,' Andrea replies,

taking a big gulp of the wine Cassi has poured her. 'Stockholm's frankly on the small side for me, but there's no helping that.'

She smiles and raises her glass to Cassi, who clinks it with her water.

'I can't see myself ever moving back either,' Cassi says, shaking her head. 'I want to be where things are happening, don't you? I like people. And a house, nah, that's not a draw for me at all. When my flat, our flat, is done, I never want to move again.'

She smiles, pushing a strand of her blond hair behind her ear. Everything about the flat is hers, but she's envisioning a future where Jarmo's no longer travelling as much, where they're living there together and their shared life feels more concrete, not just like a promise. What's hers is his.

Maggie has practically inhaled her glass of wine and is now studying Cassi's face with a small smile, reaching out to take her hand. 'But it would be so great if our kids could grow up together, just like we did!'

Andrea glares at Maggie, but Maggie keeps on talking.

'And everything changes when you have a baby! I know you said it wasn't the right time before, but maybe soon?'

Cassi doesn't notice the moment Maggie realises her mistake and claps a hand to her mouth as if to stop the words coming out, because it is then that Jarmo arrives. He smiles at her but it doesn't reach his eyes. Cassi gets up and meets him halfway, it's been so long, she's missed him, but Jarmo gives her a mere fleeting peck on the cheek with his hands on her shoulders when she finally reaches him, followed by a quick hello to Maggie and Andrea. Maggie looks uncomfortable and barely gets up from her chair. Andrea waves from her seat on the other side of the table.

'I'm sorry I'm late,' he says, his hand back on Cassi's shoulder. 'I'm just nipping to the loo.'

Maggie and Andrea look at Cassi then look at each other. Cassi tops up their glasses, trying to ignore her thundering heartbeat. In a perfect world, her friends and her fiancé would have liked each other as much as she likes all of them. They've never spent much time together, so is it too much to ask of them to at least pretend to be friendly? The mood has already soured and the night has barely started.

'Blimey, the room's spinning,' Maggie says after another sip. 'I'm such a lightweight these days.'

Cassi smiles at her, remembering a different Maggie, a less tired Maggie . . . Andrea's typing on her phone.

'The sitter,' she says, wincing briefly. 'Apparently, we're out of ketchup. Cue utter mayhem.'

Jarmo returns, pulls out his chair and sits down. He picks up his wine glass, downing half of it in one go. Cassi can sense that something's wrong. Jarmo's barely making eye contact and isn't keeping up with the conversation. Maggie and Andrea talk almost exclusively to each other, busy with their own stuff. The wine bottle's already empty.

Cassi tries to shift their attention to the food.

'I have to figure out what I'm in the mood for,' Maggie says. She leans back and places her hands on her stomach, squints at the menu, a dimple forming in between her eyebrows. While Cassi has always found this endearing, the sight today makes her toes feel like they're about to turn inwards.

'I'll have the celeriac,' Andrea says, slapping her menu – thick, handmade paper attached to a thin pinewood board – down onto the tablecloth. 'Is there more wine? I have to get it while I can. I need to leave no later than half nine, that's as late as the sitter can stay.'

'I'll have the sole,' Cassi says. 'But I might swap the potatoes for the grilled Tuscan kale. What are you thinking of getting, Jarmo?'

He looks up, his eyes vacant as they meet hers.

'Huh?' he says.

'What would you like to eat, darling?' she asks again. There are many other questions she wants to ask him, but she can't make a scene. She would like him to volunteer some kind of explanation. Maybe something along the lines of: 'We're dealing with the crisis of the century at work and I really have to go, right now.' This wasn't how she'd imagined this evening going. Everything feels out of place.

Jarmo mumbles 'Food, right,' and looks down at his menu. Cassi smiles. The table is quiet until a waiter appears to take their orders. Andrea holds up the empty wine bottle and a single finger, Cassi asks for sparkling water.

They talk about a TV show. About a new workout method Andrea's tested – 'just twenty minutes of exercise, but with results as if you spent three hours at the gym!' Cassi starts to recount her meeting with the artist, but stops herself after a few sentences, because the words simply won't come out in the right order and it doesn't sound as funny as it did in her head. Andrea shows them a sketch of what her kitchen's going to look like when it's done. Jarmo tries to look engaged, but he doesn't say a word, his eyes more often than not glued to his phone.

At one point, Cassi notices Andrea staring at Jarmo. She's not sure what to make of it. Is Andrea, recently a divorcee, in love with Jarmo? Does she know something Cassi doesn't? *It can't be, just breathe*, she tells herself. Sometimes, it feels as though her head's about to fall off her body at any moment, as though it's somewhere else entirely. It's like vertigo on steroids.

But Cassi refuses to let anything ruin this night. She beams at her company and says: 'Cheers, everyone! To finally getting all together!'

Cassi heads to the bathroom after downing a glass of champagne, almost tripping in her high heels when the carpet turns into marble. The sleek ceiling lights are dimmed and the music that bumps from hidden speakers is melancholy, fragmented, experimental. Cassi runs freezing water over her wrists, stares into the mirror. The wall behind her is full of framed black-and-white photographs the size of postcards. Among all kinds of people she vaguely recognises – old royals, musicians, artists – a much more familiar face suddenly appears. The word 'mum' echoes in her brain, a word Cassi didn't even use as a child. Her mother was always Bea; Bea insisted on it.

Cassi snatches a rolled-up terrycloth towel from the shelf under the mirror, quickly drying her hands as she turns around for a closer look. It is her, she's not hallucinating. Bea climbing out of a taxi with a passport, cigarette and messy handbag in one hand, the other on the car door. Long, dishevelled hair, white tank top, short skirt. The necklace with the pink stone around her neck. Her eyes are pouty, unafraid, those of a barely twenty-year-old. Cassi breaks into a sweat. Unresolved mummy issues are the last thing she needs today.

She takes the picture off the wall and replaces it with that of a politician. Her first instinct is to drop Bea's into the bin, but she changes her mind and slips her, frame and all, into her new handbag.

When Cassi returns to the table, Maggie's covering her breasts with her hands.

'I'm leaking!' she says, sounding distraught.

Jarmo looks like he wishes he were somewhere else. Andrea's crying with laughter.

By the time the dessert with the sparklers is brought in, Maggie has already had to go home. Andrea snaps a few pictures after Cassi shoves her own phone into her hand, but Cassi doesn't even have to look at them to know she's going to delete them. Nothing about tonight is turning out the way it was supposed to.

Cassi had forgotten about Bea's picture until a few weeks later, when she was emptying her handbag and found it again. She'd decided to hide it again – maybe in an old Ikea bag? – and somehow, it had managed to follow her to Bäcken. Exactly when or how it ended up in the car remains a mystery to Cassi, but it doesn't actually matter, does it? She wipes the frame clean with her fingers, careful not to jostle the glass, which has cracked from side to side. She goes back into the cottage, puts the picture on a shelf in the kitchen. She talks out loud to herself all the way to Pavel's house.

35

Pavel's face is grey. He has shaved and put on an ironed, white – if visibly yellowed – button-down shirt. He tells her, again, that the outing probably isn't a good idea.

'Or maybe it's a great idea,' Cassi counters. 'You've missed him. I'm sure he's missed you. Besides, it's only a visit. You'll be back home before you know it.'

It takes Cassi twenty minutes to coax him into the car. The persuasion consists of a detailed account of Maine and Cassi's most recent walk in the woods, what Maine did, which directions Cassi thinks they walked in and why, what moss formations Cassi saw, things she thought about when she heard various sounds. It's as much a way of showing Pavel that she's not about to give up on their plan and go back home as it is a way to keep her brain away from thoughts she doesn't want to have.

Pavel's staring at his hands, his fingers wrapped around something small.

'What is it?' she asks.

Pavel's fingers stop moving. He shows her. It's a worn piece of round metal, yellow and green, a stag mid-leap. Cassi recognises the key ring he took off her house key the first time they met.

'It's just an old keepsake. It fell out of Karl-Adam's pocket one time, right after we first got to know each other. I picked it up to give it to him, but he said I could keep it. I thought of it as him trying to tell me something. A stag leaping towards freedom. Or the unknown.'

He smiles at himself.

'You see what you want to see.'

He studies the key ring.

'Only after moving here did I learn it's the logo of a tractor company.'

They sit in silence for a moment, until Pavel stands up, seemingly accepting his fate.

Cassi opens the passenger door for him, helping him climb in without hitting his head, like when a police officer shoves a criminal in their car on TV. The handcuffs are all that's missing.

'I brought coffee,' Cassi says, pointing to two plastic bottles in the cup holders. 'Yours is black.'

Cassi keeps babbling until Pavel reassures her that it's OK if she's quiet. Then they drive the rest of the way in silence. Cassi can see him physically shake next to her but doesn't say anything.

When they finally arrive, he suddenly doesn't want to get out of the car. They both stay seated for a while, until Cassi climbs out and opens his door, holding out a hand. He obeys and together they walk to the entrance of Green Grove Nursing Home. They step into a hallway with peach-coloured vinyl flooring and pale yellow walls. They run into a young nurse who tells them a room number. He pushes his dark bob behind his ears and adds:

'I think Kalle's asleep, though – I just checked on him.'

If they stop now, that'll be the end of it, that's how it feels. Their feet keep moving; Cassi almost has to drag

Pavel when they reach the right corridor. They stop in front of the door. He points at her: she has to do the knocking.

No answer from inside.

She opens the door a crack. She doesn't know what kind of behaviour's appropriate in this context, she's never been to a nursing home before. Is just walking in tantamount to breaking and entering? Either way, they're doing it. The blinds are down but angled to let in some light. A small blanket on the bed.

He's far from the tall, muscular man from Pavel's stories. Cassi stops right inside the door and leans against the wall while Pavel steps forward, legs visibly shaking. He takes a seat on a chair by the bed. He seems almost afraid to look at the head resting on the pillow.

'Do you want me to leave you alone?' Cassi asks in a hushed voice. 'I can wait outside.'

'No, stay,' Pavel says.

They wait. After a while, his eyelids flutter.

The air is still for a few seconds then a scream fills the room. It's like a shockwave of sound. Karl-Adam is now sitting up in the bed, thin arms flailing, trying to get his feet onto the floor as if to run away. Cassi rushes over to help Pavel, who's trying to stop Karl-Adam from getting out of bed, because it seems inevitable that that would end badly. The nurse comes running in too. He puts his arms around Karl-Adam and manages to calm him down. Karl-Adam stops screaming, but proceeds to let out a string of curses, obscene profanities that gradually turn into a recitation of the Christmas poem 'Tomten', all eleven stanzas. His visitors can only stand there and wait.

'. . . The *tomte* listens and, half in a dream, thinks he can hear time's endless stream, wonders where it is bound, wonders where its source is found?'

When Karl-Adam is done, he looks at the three of them in turn, lingering on Pavel. Pavel holds his hands out. Karl-Adam doesn't object when he takes his. With his hands still in Pavel's, Karl-Adam turns to Nathan, the nurse. Smiling.

'Does this place serve breakfast?'

Nathan nods and says he'll go get it. Karl-Adam lies back down.

'Thank you for stopping by,' he says to Pavel and Cassi. 'But I'm not interested in buying anything today. I baked just the other day, the freezer's full of biscuits. But good luck with your class trip!'

Pavel drops his hands and backs away, towards the door. Cassi tries to stop him, whispering: 'Aren't you going to say something?' but she can see that Pavel's eyes are full of tears and that all he wants is to get away. They step into the hallway and sit down on a bench. Pavel puts his head in his hands, Cassi drapes her arm over his shoulders. That's how Nathan finds them when he returns, pushing a cart with Karl-Adam's food on it.

'Don't take it personally, sometimes it takes a while before the drugs kick in,' Nathan tells them. 'The confusion goes away after he's been awake for a while.'

'So this isn't what he's usually like?' Cassi asks.

'No, the UTI is making it a lot worse. Are you family? Kalle doesn't get a lot of visitors, so it's a shame you came today, when he's in a bit of a bad way.'

Cassi looks at Pavel, then back at Nathan.

'Old friends. Or, well, I'm not, but Pavel is. But then I suppose we'll have to come back another day and try again. What do you say, Pavel?'

She puts a hand on his back but he stands up and starts walking towards the exit without looking back.

36

When Marlene's front door opens, Cassi and Maine are greeted by the sight of Berzan on his way out, squatting on the hallway floor and fastening the Velcro straps of his trainers. Is he always in workout clothes?!

He greets them before bidding farewell to Marlene with a – in Cassi's opinion – far too tongue-heavy kiss. Then he straps on his helmet, picks his bike up off the lawn and rides away.

'There's nothing he doesn't do well, that young man,' Marlene says, and Cassi braces for an onslaught of sordid details she has no desire to hear about today, or any day for that matter.

Marlene points to Berzan with one hand, holding her silky red kimono nearly closed with the other. The kimono is tied at the waist, but the fabric's so shiny the belt keeps slipping.

'Look how fast he's going!'

Berzan zooms down the gravel drive, turning off towards Bäcken.

'Did you know he does tattoos, too? Though at the moment, that's probably his weakest point – his so-called art.'

Marlene shakes her head, slamming the door shut behind her. As she turns to Cassi and puts her hands on her hips, the kimono pulls apart like a curtain at the start of a play. Cassi diverts her gaze.

'Same with the priest,' Marlene continues. 'I almost ran her over one time in the car park when she suddenly appeared in front of me, sketching the pizzeria. She seemed completely oblivious. And it wasn't a good sketch either. She doesn't even like painting. She only does it because she thinks buying art is too expensive.'

Then she bends down to greet Maine.

'Hello! I forgot to say hi to you, didn't I?'

She scratches Maine all over.

'Do you always bring him with you?' she asks Cassi.

Cassi ponders that.

'No, but I take him if he wants to go. I'd say he stays home most of the time, but when he follows me to the car, I let him come.'

'Aw, are you such a good helper, Maine, such a good boy,' Marlene gushes, bending down again, scratching him again.

'I'm going to get changed,' she says, heading to the bedroom.

Maine heads into the kitchen to sniff the floor. Cassi stays in the hallway. Along one wall are built-in cabinets, four in a row. Someone, presumably Josse, has written a name on each door: 'DAD', 'MUM', 'LULLE' and 'JOSSE RULES'.

'What does Berzan actually do for a living?' Cassi asks. 'I only ever see him when he's off work.'

'He operates the ferry across the river,' Marlene replies from the bedroom.

Cassi opens the 'Dad' cabinet door a crack. It's empty bar a single knitted hat on a shelf. Lulle's and Josse's cabinets have also been cleared out. 'Mum's is full of jackets and scarfs in every colour but black.

Marlene continues.

'He used to be the captain of a big ferry. But then there was some big scandal because he had an affair with one of the senior managers which got him fired. He almost collided with another ferry between Gothenburg and Denmark, so he really fucked it up. Quite literally!'

That's a lot of information to process at once, Cassi thinks.

A large cork noticeboard covered with photographs hangs from the wall on the opposite side of the wardrobes. Cassi leans in closer to look at the family pictures.

'Operates the ferry, eh,' she says. 'Yet another man coasting through life.'

A long, hoarse laugh from the bedroom.

'I like you, Cassi. You're funny. I'd never take you for a guru if I didn't know you are.'

Marlene comes back out, now dressed in a tight blue unitard. She stretches, tugging at her crotch to make the garment sit right.

'You guys look so nice,' Cassi says, still studying the pictures.

Marlene leans in for a closer look too. In the photos featuring her ex-husband, his head has been cut out.

'Don't we, though,' she says. 'My beautiful children.'

She reaches out to stroke the images of two happy teenagers with her finger.

'But my husband wasn't much to look at – even when he had a face.'

Her hoarse laugh leads the way into the living room, but Cassi lingers. She's stuck on a picture of a smiling Marlene in a red floor-length dress, a wine glass in one hand and high-heeled shoes in the other. A gold paper crown on her head.

'This is a great picture of you, Marlene! Who's this "Berit 50" you're celebrating?'

Marlene comes back.

'That's me,' she says. 'Berit. I changed my name to Marlene after the divorce.'

She meets Cassi's eyes.

'I became who I really am,' she declares. 'It wasn't popular with everyone. But the divorce is the best gift I've ever given myself. It came at a cost and it was hefty. But I could finally feel like myself again.'

She sighs quietly.

'Marlene has to be Marlene. Even though I did consider changing it again, to Debbie, just so everyone who was so shocked and said MARLENE, WHY? would say DEBBIE, WHY? And I could answer "Debbie or not to be". I always liked that joke.'

It's Cassi's turn to snort. Marlene smiles, looking pleased with herself.

'How long were you married?' Cassi asks.

'Twenty-five years. I got married because I gave up on myself, or that's how it feels, looking back. Everyone around me did it. I figured it's how it had to be. And I was a good wife, I don't think anyone would say otherwise. A good mother too! The old man, he turned dull before our wedding night was over, but I grinned and bore it.'

Marlene brushes invisible dust off her chest.

'Have you ever been married?' she asks. It's a perfectly normal question, but it makes Cassi clear her throat.

'No,' she replies. Then she adds: 'Never', as though there

were a number after the word 'No' that needed defining.

Marlene makes a sweeping gesture with her arm to get Cassi to follow.

'Come have a look, I redid this room!' she says. 'Only just finished. I needed a change. Lollo said she was happy to help.'

The living room is decorated in shades of beige, with a plush carpet, a low coffee table and a deep sofa. Two tan cushions on the sofa. Cassi had imagined Marlene's home as more of a firework display. Or at least a handful of sparklers. Animal patterns, risqué art, bear rugs, knick-knacks and naked men.

Marlene straightens a painting of a close-up of an orchid.

'I reckon she thought this room was too weird before,' she adds.

Cassi shoots her a questioning look. Marlene centres a tealight holder on the coffee table.

'When we got divorced, it was important to my husband that we split everything down the middle,' she says. 'It had to be fair. Half of everything. Down to the smallest thing.'

Marlene pulls on her bra strap, which is digging into her shoulder blade.

'He was counting cotton rounds, dividing them into two piles in the bathroom. After he went at the sofa, I had to hide the saw. I mean, you've seen the patio fence. I wonder if he's happy he has the other half, wherever he's living now!'

She sneers.

'I suppose the only reason the built-ins are still here is because he didn't own a crowbar.'

Marlene looks at Cassi.

'He wasn't the one who asked for a divorce, as I'm sure you've gathered. The way he saw it, our life was comfortable. I had to be the villain. I was the one they turned on.'

She shakes herself. Looks around.

'But I felt that now, after so many years, I was finally ready to revamp my space. Make it mine and *whole*. None of that fifty-fifty shit.'

Marlene blinks several times, her eyes sparkly.

'So when Lollo came over with her pictures and suggestions, I said yes. Give me something that feels like Marlene. Sexy. Fresh. Sophisticated.'

Marlene smiles. Cassi nods, says it came out great. Very Marlene. And very Lollo, too.

Marlene points to a door.

'I was thinking I could lie down on the table in there so I can hear the water feature,' she says.

They step into the conservatory. It's an overcast day, but the air is warm and the door to the garden is open. And through it, Cassi can in fact hear the splashing of the small plastic fountain in the flowerbed. The fountain's probably meant to be set into the ground, but instead it's been unceremoniously plunked down directly on the dirt.

Marlene climbs onto a chair to reach the tabletop. She's already rolled her yoga mat out on it. Maine's just about to settle down under the table, but Marlene shoos him away.

'Maine, I love you, but I would prefer if you could stay outside for now,' she says. 'I don't want to be bothered by your emissions. Said the actress to the bishop.'

Cassi walks him towards the patio door.

'I used to think it was because of the food I gave him,'

Cassi says. 'But he's back on the special diet stuff now. I guess it's something he eats in the woods.'

'We all have our flaws,' Marlene replies and lies down on her stomach.

Her feet dangle off the end of the table. Cassi hadn't heard about energy healing before Marlene requested it, but like with most things, all the information she could possibly need was only an online search away.

'All right, here I go,' Cassi says, cracking her knuckles. Then she starts kneading the air twenty centimetres above Marlene's body.

'I'm at the edge of your energy field,' she informs her. 'I'm going to have to use some force here around your lower back.'

Marlene puffs and writhes on the table. Cassi keeps massaging. She works in silence for a while.

'There's significant blockage in the shoulder area, Marlene.'

There's no response. Cassi keeps at it.

'It makes me wonder,' she eventually continues. 'When were you last truly happy?'

Marlene takes her time answering.

'Can I say this morning, with Berzan?' she replies. 'No, I'm joking. Let me think.'

She does.

'What even is true happiness?' Marlene asks eventually. 'I suppose I'm fairly happy. And that's all a person can expect most of the time.'

Cassi gently breathes on Marlene's shoulder blades.

'Sure, but as you like to say, one has to challenge themselves. Are you sure you do?'

'Oh, you should see the things Berzan and I . . .'

Cassi stops her by tapping on her arm.

'Not that way. This isn't just about your body. If you're completely comfortable with something, it's not really a challenge. I mean personally. Spiritually. In terms of growing. Sometimes, what a person needs is to step out of their comfort zone. To try things that seem scary.'

Marlene's about to interject, but Cassi pre-empts her again.

'Beyond sex, Marlene. In your case. For someone else it might be sex. But your boundaries in that area have been . . . well, they're non-existent. We've already established that.'

Silence again. Cassi kicks the air above Marlene as if she was in a boxing ring, about to deliver the final KO. If someone could see her now, she'd probably get sectioned.

'I'm going to pull a rope out of your spine now, Marlene,' Cassi says.

She tugs and yanks at something imaginary – is it weird that she can almost see it?

'This has been tying you down. But it's gone now.'

Marlene pants, arching her lower back.

'Gretel and I used to challenge each other,' Marlene says suddenly.

Cassi pricks her ears up. It's the first time she's ever heard Marlene talk about Gretel without sounding hostile.

'We competed at everything. Who could run the fastest. Whose hair was longer. Who could pick the most blueberries. Swim furthest in the lake. Eat the most sausages.'

Brief pause.

'And yes, I mean real sausages. Food.'

Cassi can tell Marlene is smiling.

'Do you miss that?' Cassi asks. 'That Gretel used to challenge you, I mean.'

There's another pause.

'I've never really given it any thought. But I think I used to enjoy it.'

Silence again. The only sound is the splashing of the fountain outside.

'We humans have different ways of holding ourselves back, both consciously and subconsciously. We need to take a good look at ourselves. Sometimes the empty spaces aren't immediately visible.'

Her words resurrect a memory of hyperstore manager Tiny Face stroking his chin. Cassi has to physically shake her head to make it go away.

'I've tried, but it's not easy,' Marlene continues. 'I honestly didn't think it would be this hard. I thought people would be more understanding.'

Cassi sweeps her hands above Marlene's body, again and again, big movements like she is moving through high waves in the sea. She huffs to communicate to Marlene the amount of effort required to cleanse her energy.

'I thought it was OK to change who you are, even as a mother. But it ended up doing the opposite. My children rejected me. They felt sorry for their dad and found me embarrassing.'

Cassi lets her speak.

'They don't visit, so I never see them,' Marlene continues. 'They don't call. And I'm too afraid to contact them. What if they say no?'

'Then that's how it is. Look at it as a challenge in itself.

If we didn't suffer even just a little bit, we'd never be able to experience real joy,' Cassi says.

She thinks that last part might be a quote from a film she's seen recently, but she can't recall which one. Marlene sighs again.

'Reality,' she says. 'It's hard.'

Cassi nods. Then she just waits. Her gaze wanders outside, taking in the nature. She spots a garden bench which seems to be dislodged from the ground, propped up against Marlene's shed. Are those marijuana leaves in the flowerbed?!

Marlene continues to lie there in silence.

37

Cassi and Pavel are standing in Pavel's garage. They usually meet up at hers, and even though she's been in his driveway and on his veranda several times, this is the first time she's actually crossed the physical thresholds into his home.

Cassi has never put much thought into what Pavel's house might look like – she no longer considers herself someone who cares about things like that. But when he slowly unhooks a large padlock and opens the garage doors, she feels like she's about to get a glimpse into his psyche, a side to him she hasn't been exposed to before.

There are boxes everywhere. And overflowing binbags, stacks of God knows what, overloaded shelves, wooden boards, tyres, furniture, paint cans, bicycle skeletons. The room looks like a recycling centre after an unexpected earthquake. Or a typhoon.

Discovering that someone you know is a hoarder feels especially violating. Cassi forces herself to smile, trying her best not to look alarmed or embarrassed.

'I can't believe you once had space for a car in here,' Cassi says, hoping the remark comes off as more diplomatic than judgemental.

Pavel grunts, tugging feebly at a metal rod sticking out of a cracked chest full of what look like tablecloths. They're here on his initiative. He was the one who suggested Cassi might be able to find something useful for her home in what he at that point called his 'storage space'.

Now, Pavel tenderly takes stock of his belongings. Then he pulls out three relatively intact wooden chairs and carries them outside.

'We can just put things here for now, and you can think about what feels OK to get rid of and what you'd like to keep,' Cassi says, because she can tell it's hard for Pavel to let her rummage through his things.

'And remember, I'm only borrowing them. Think of it as them being stored at my house instead. It'll give you more space. You can pick them up anytime.'

Pavel runs his hand along the splintery back of a chair.

'It's OK, don't worry,' he says. 'It's just that I hate getting rid of things that are still functional. You never know what you're going to need.'

He then takes an overfilled Ikea bag, pulling out what looks like a gold necklace, a doll's severed head, a jar full of white powder. Cassi didn't take Pavel for a drug lord but at this point, anything is possible.

Pavel is now focused on an unmarked cassette tape, which he flips over and over in his hands.

'I don't remember what's on this,' he says, looking around, as though the room could answer him. 'Probably something I recorded off the radio at some point. I used to own a cassette player, or, well, I still do, but it needs repairing.'

In an attempt to locate the promised kitchenware, Cassi carries box after box outside. Many are damp and at risk of falling apart, but Pavel helps her.

Finally, they find two boxes marked 'Britta kitchen 1' and 'Britta kitchen 2'.

'Britta lived over there,' Pavel says, pointing vaguely in the direction of the woods. 'There was an auction when she passed away. I took whatever wasn't sold. I wanted to help . . . I don't know. And because they were things I thought I might find a use for one day.'

They set the boxes down on the wooden chairs. At the top of one is some kind of grinder, a hand-cranked whisk, and a lemon squeezer made of chipped yellow porcelain. More and more kitchen utensils emerge from the box as if trying to escape. While rummaging around the very bottom of the boxes, Cassi finds a small stack of framed erotic photos. They're not overly pornographic – in fact, one might even consider them artistic. She holds them up to Pavel, amused.

'*Shunga*,' he says. 'Britta was some kind of expert in Japanese culture, I think.'

'We should give them to Marlene,' Cassi says, and a smile forms on Pavel's lips.

Cassi decides that she'll discreetly drive the rest of Britta's stuff to the landfill. But she still unties the piece of string around the cutlery to check what she's working with. The mix is as random as the rest of Britta's belongings: five dessert forks, eight teaspoons, a bent knife, two wooden butter knives, a cake cutter. There's curlicue writing on the handle of the cake cutter. Cassi holds it up and tries to decipher it. On one side, it says 'To many good years to come!', and on the other, 'Britta & Morten 1969'.

Pavel peeks over her shoulder and it's only when he gently touches it that she realises she's shaking.

'The engraving,' she says, pointing to the words. That's

not much of an explanation as to why she's suddenly tongue-tied and teary-eyed, because she has no relation to Britta or Morten, and more inspiring cake-cutter inscriptions have most certainly been composed. She's sick of her recent emotional flare-ups.

'Fine, should I tell you? It's a shit story from beginning to end and I really don't want to, but it's pretty ridiculous that you've told me so much about you and I haven't told you anything at all about me and my story. And now I'm suddenly standing here . . . crying.'

Pavel raises his hands.

'You don't have to say anything. As far as I'm concerned, there's no need for explanations.'

Cassi nods at him then pulls herself together.

'I'm so sick of being like this,' she says.

She stomps back into the garage. Looks around. She feels the need to tear down Pavel's stacks of boxes, his packed-up memories, and light the whole thing on fire. Instead, she carries out a cracked plastic tub full of flowerpots. Could she finally start growing her own food? Or should she maybe arrange a tasteful still-life at the bottom of the front steps?

She clears her throat.

'I wouldn't mind borrowing these too, if that's OK?'

Pavel bends over the tub, inspecting each pot. They're covered in soil that comes off like black dust to the touch.

'It's not that I don't want to lend them to you, it's just that I don't know when I might need them.'

Cassi points to the garage.

'There's a whole shelf of pots there.'

'Ah, well, then you take these. But I think I'll keep this

one.' Pavel holds up one of the dirty pots, brushing it off and putting it aside.

The words come out of Cassi's mouth before she can stop them.

'He never got his ring engraved.'

She sighs.

'It was that that made me realise something wasn't right. We'd been talking about what to write for so long. It had taken us months to decide, but finally we had settled on something and he was supposed to take them to the jeweller. I wanted his name, Jarmo, on mine, with a little heart. And mine on his of course. Gold bands. Oh, and the date. That's how I, we, wanted it . . . simple, clean, classy. I got mine, but he said something had gone wrong with his, so it was going to take a few more weeks. And then more time passed. But you don't exactly go around checking other people's rings, do you? Also, he never took his off. And I trusted him, why wouldn't I have? When I discovered his was blank, we'd been together for six years, engaged for three. Sure, it was some kind of long-distance relationship, but still. Still! His explanation was that he'd lost his ring and hadn't wanted to tell me; he figured he'd get a replacement. But I could tell something was off. I'd had a feeling for a while. Something had changed. Sometimes, you just know. Even if you don't want to face it.'

Pavel, who's been sorting Britta's cutlery into different piles, looks at her. Cassi turns around and fetches another box from the garage, filled to the brim with old magazines, newspapers and crossword puzzles.

'I might not keep all of them,' Pavel says shyly. 'We can go through them.'

Cassi puts the stack aside and picks up another.

'It turned out to be easily googleable once I got going,' she continues. 'The first thing I found out was that he was still officially registered to his ex-wife's address. The one he'd divorced long before we got together. They had a child, but he was only three when Jarmo and the mother got divorced – or didn't get divorced, as it turned out. The child was with his mother full-time, and since the two of them lived in a different city it made sense I'd never met him. In hindsight, it's clearer to me now what kind of father he was, seeing his kid so rarely, but back then . . . I knew nothing. I thought he was a good dad.

'Jarmo's a salesman. He imports wine. He's always travelling. Was always travelling. It was like that from the start, from when we first met. Sometimes we only saw each other once a week, but I was completely obsessed with him and I thought he was just as obsessed with me.'

Cassi feels unexpectedly composed. As though it's someone else's story she's telling, even though this is the stuff she hasn't even let herself think about for so long.

'I wonder if it was more about me having this perfect mental picture of what life should be, what our relationship should be, projecting it onto him. But that doesn't change how it felt at the time.'

She has sorted the magazines into two stacks, those with unreadable pages in one and those that a person could at least theoretically flip through in the other. Pavel has rolled a rusty wheelbarrow out of the garage and is taking the deflated wheel off it to see if it can be mended.

'I'm not even going to ask you if we should burn these,' Cassi says.

Pavel looks up but says nothing. Cassi dumps both stacks of magazines into the burn barrel and fetches a new box from the garage.

'I thought I was losing my mind. We'd been together for so long. We were engaged. It was him and me forever. I thought I knew him inside and out. When I found out what the real situation was, I couldn't bear to tell anyone at first. But when I talked to my friends, it turned out they already knew. That he had another family.'

She tosses another stack of magazines into the barrel.

'They'd known for weeks but hadn't said anything. And get this – it wasn't even his first family! There was another. A third. And that woman was pregnant! With another child!'

Cassi braces for tears, but none come.

'Do you have matches?' she asks Pavel. He goes into the house and returns with both matches and a lighter, holds them out to her. She notes that her hands are shaking. She lights three matches at once and drops them into the barrel. She'd hoped for instant roaring flames, but the damp pages only smoulder tentatively. The smoke makes her cough.

'Do you have lighter fluid?'

Pavel pops back into the house again. Cassi squirts fluid into the barrel.

'So the prick was running three families at once. Or, well, did the two of us even count as a family? When I got pregnant, he convinced me we weren't ready so I had an abortion. That child would have been three years old now. Same age as one of its siblings.'

She shakes her head, wiping her eyes. The smoke is increasingly acrid.

'Would you like some coffee? I was going to make myself a cup,' Pavel says, standing up from his squatting position by the wheelbarrow. His knees creak audibly, or maybe Cassi's imagining it. She feels all over the place.

'I'd love some,' Cassi says. 'Can I come in and see what your house is like?'

He waves for her to follow him.

She's curious to see if his hoarding extends to the house too. If it does, she'll have to seriously worry about his mental state, but as soon as she crosses the threshold it becomes clear there'll be no need for that. Pavel's cottage is immaculate. Suddenly she feels like the one with a derelict home. Given Pavel's otherwise well-worn style, it's surprising to find flowering geraniums on spotless windowsills, embroidered tablecloths and a fruit bowl on the dining table, a candle that burns a lovely floral scent into the room.

Pavel takes his shoes off in the hallway and goes into the kitchen. She follows his lead.

'Your house is so cosy,' she says, and truly means it. He takes coffee beans out of the freezer and fills up the coffee machine. The kitchen isn't new, but it is well-kept and clean.

'This thing here, it was a gift,' Pavel says, starting it up. 'I helped the Desgoffes lay some electrical cables last year and they gave me it. It makes really good coffee.'

She would never have taken Pavel for the kind of person who cares about the quality of his coffee. But who is she to say? She's the one who drinks it out of plastic bottles.

Pavel pushes the button for an espresso and places an Italian biscuit from a tin on each saucer, looking pleased.

'Sugar?' he holds out a bowl full of brown lumps.

Cassi declines, sipping her espresso and shoving the entire biscuit into her mouth. She walks back out into the hallway to peek into the bathroom, noting it's clean and tidy as well. The towels are hung neatly on a heated towel rack, the sink is sparklingly devoid of toothpaste remnants. In the living room, a TV guide sits on a wooden coffee table next to a box of gourmet chocolates.

'You're good at enjoying the little things, Pavel,' she says in the direction of the kitchen. She hears him chuckle.

Back in the kitchen, Pavel meets her gaze. That doesn't happen a lot. Every time it does, it feels special.

'What did Jarmo say?'

It's the first indication that he's been listening to her story, that she hasn't just been thinking it in her own head, and it makes Cassi physically react with a coughing fit. She tells herself it was brought on by biscuit crumbs before continuing her story.

'Right. He said "It just happened" and "I didn't want to hurt you". I guess that sums it up. I didn't get much of an explanation. Granted, I don't know what he could have said to make any of it better. So I upped and left.'

She doesn't mention that she also quit her job. That she sent a text the morning she found out, saying she was never coming back. She doesn't tell him she turned off her phone, isolated herself, cancelled the direct debit to the gym, the florist, the doggy daycare, the cryotherapy chamber. Turned her back on everyone and everything. That she got rid of her possessions. Sold her flat. She doesn't talk about how she fled back to her hometown, to a basement where no one could find her, which she barely left for months. She says nothing about her time at the hypermarket. It was like an involuntary parenthesis in her life, barely real. She doesn't tell him that buying the house in Bäcken was originally her running away again, away from everything.

Not that Cassi regrets her choices. But she now knows they were extreme.

She stands up, puts on her shoes and walks out. By the time Pavel joins her carrying a large watering can, she has managed to get a proper fire going in the barrel.

'Liza, one of my best friends, was the one who randomly ran into Jarmo at some fucking zoo opening or whatever. He'd been walking around with a toddler and some pregnant woman. And then Jarmo begged Liza to not tell me anything, told her that he was going to "take care of it".'

The magazines catch fire in the barrel.

'You might be wondering why my so-called friends didn't tell me anyway? I did too. How can anyone do that to a friend, to a person they've known all their life?'

Cassi throws a whole stack of newspapers in there.

'The answer is that they felt it would be better if Jarmo told me. That's what they said. Liza told Andrea and Maggie, then all three of them kept it quiet. They didn't want to have to get involved. It was too awkward, and anyway, he'd promised he'd do it.'

She wipes her eyes.

'The fire is making my eyes burn. Anyway,' she pauses for a brief moment without looking at Pavel. 'It did explain a lot of things. The way they'd been acting, why the last few weeks had been so weird. They didn't even tell me at my own birthday dinner! I'm not in touch with them anymore. They've tried to explain, apologise. But they crossed a line.'

Pavel tosses a few twigs into the barrel.

'People have their reasons,' he says. 'Everyone has their problems, even when they do us wrong. Things aren't always as black and white as they seem.'

Cassi looks up at him with questioning eyes.

'I'm not defending them,' he clarifies. 'I'm not saying what they did was right. I'm just saying that's how it is. Everyone has *stuff*, right?? Stuff they're going through.'

He bends down to pick up the watering can and douse the ground around the barrel. There's a short pause.

'But it's awful,' Pavel says, putting a hand on her shoulder. 'That you were let down by the people you trusted.'

Cassi presses her hands to her face.

'How are you feeling?' Pavel's hand is still on her shoulder.

Cassi looks into his eyes this time.

'He's still with that woman from the zoo, as far as I know. They have two kids now.'

Facts are easier to process than feelings. All she knows now is that there's barely any anger left in her, any self-pity. How strange that they seem to have shrunk. And how strange that she feels empty without them.

38

Pavel and Cassi are back at the nursing home. It took a lot of persuading on Cassi's part. And she had to call before they left Bäcken to make sure Karl-Adam was feeling better, that he would be capable of having visitors. Now, they're sitting on the bench in the hallway, just like they were the first time round. The mood is almost as tense as the weather outside, where a thunderstorm is looming. They're waiting for Karl-Adam to be done with whatever it is he's doing in another part of the building. He could appear at any moment. What state will he be in? The question is suspended between them. Cassi takes Pavel's hand. It's cold and she holds it tight between both of hers.

Pavel is leaning against the bench, his back straight. He's wearing his regular clothes today, the chequered shirt, the dirty cargo trousers. He's put his baseball cap in the cloth tote between his feet. Cassi can tell he washed his hair. He sits in silence, eyes fixed on his shoes.

Has Cassi ever felt this much anticipation and fear over anything? Felt so unsure about what was going to happen? Life with Jarmo was nothing but a long wait – for marriage, a family, company, even – but there were never any question marks. A lot of things can be said about Jarmo, but his knack for logistics and scheduling was unimpeachable. He was very rarely late, he always came on the day he'd said he would. As far as timekeeping went, he never failed to live up to expectations.

They've been waiting for twenty minutes now but the hallway is still empty and quiet. Pavel hasn't said a word either, except 'nah' when Cassi asked if he wanted anything to drink. She personally wouldn't have minded stepping outside to check out the supermarket next door. Now that she's rarely in a city, or any kind of urban area for that matter, shops have been imbued with a new sheen. She's beginning to imagine a life beyond porridge and pasta with tomato sauce. In fact, she's reached a point where memories of working at the restaurant cause a pang of longing. Even casting her mind back to the deli counter at the supermarket stirs up vague feelings of excitement within her. She's in a place now where she can see the draw of what used to be her primary interest, all the things that disappeared when her plastic-bottle-coffee life commenced. Olive oil pressings and artisan bakeries, *skrei* season, oyster harvests, paper-thin slices of Pata Negra, dusty wine cellars. Her mouth waters at the memory of the things that used to feel mundane, but now represent luxuries that Cassi can't afford anymore. Or rather, that don't represent her.

The automatic doors at the end of the hallway finally open, Cassi recognises Nathan. She doesn't recognise Karl-Adam – she'd barely had a chance to look at him properly last time – but assumes it must be him next to the nurse since Pavel stops breathing, lets go of her hand, and stands up.

Nathan spots them and smiles, but his focus remains on Karl-Adam, who seems to be telling him a story while laboriously walking in their direction. Karl-Adam is slightly shorter than Nathan, his hair is grey and neatly combed, he's clean shaven and, despite the summer heat, he's wearing a knitted jumper and dark-brown corduroy trousers.

Once he reaches his room, Karl-Adam finally looks at them. He studies Cassi with a puzzled expression, then turns to Pavel. Pavel takes a step forward. Karl-Adam stands there in silence, eyes filling with tears. Pavel steps even closer, holding his hands out. Then, realising Karl-Adam is unable to let go of his walker, he puts both hands on his arms.

'I . . .' Karl-Adam says. 'You . . . Where?'

A tear breaks free, trickling along the furrows of his face. Pavel wipes it away. He lets his hand linger on Karl-Adam's cheek for a moment, until Karl-Adam turns to Nathan, his nervous gaze bouncing back and forth between the two men.

'Would you like to ask your visitors to come in?' Nathan asks Karl-Adam. 'I can fetch a stool so everyone has somewhere to sit.'

Karl-Adam is staring at Pavel again now. When he nods, Cassi releases a deep breath she hadn't realised she was holding. Nathan puts the walker away and helps Karl-Adam settle into a velvet armchair by the window.

'You can sit here,' he then says to Pavel, patting a second armchair on the other side of a small table, 'and I'll go get another.' He smiles at Cassi.

She stays by the door, unable to take her eyes off the two men by the window. Pavel has leaned in towards Karl-Adam. They're holding each other's hands.

'I . . .' Karl-Adam says again, clearly confused. 'I don't remember. But this . . . feels somehow familiar.'

His eyes well up again. Pavel squeezes his hands, teary-eyed too.

'I should have come sooner. I was a coward. I thought maybe it would be wrong. That your son . . . It was stupid. I'm sorry.'

Nathan comes back with a chair for Cassi. He sets it down next to the men, but she pulls it away.

'I don't mind waiting in the hallway,' she says to Pavel.

'No, please stay,' he replies. Then he turns back to Karl-Adam, explaining: 'Cassi's your friend. She bought your house and lives there now. In Bäcken.'

'Bäcken?' Karl-Adam says. He looks at Cassi. 'What's that?'

'I moved in in spring,' Cassi says. 'And I love it. And I've been getting to know Pavel, and he's helped me with so many things. He's fixed the windows and the roof, there was something wrong with the pipes, and a lamp. The clothesline. And he told me about you, and we decided to come see you. See how you're doing.'

She makes a mental note to stop babbling.

Karl-Adam looks none the wiser. He nods, looking at her and then Pavel and then her again, but his memory doesn't seem to be jogged. Thankfully, Pavel came prepared this time. He picks up his tote bag and takes out a small stack of photographs. Holds one up for Karl-Adam to see. The house in the background, Karl-Adam and his son, early elementary school age, in the foreground. It's a summer day, they seem to be celebrating a birthday because the son is holding what looks like a wrapped present. Karl-Adam takes the picture and finally smiles.

'Is that me? Dashing, if I say so myself.'

Pavel smiles too. As does Cassi. They agree.

Pavel hands him another photo. An even younger Karl-Adam and an equally young Pavel are standing shirtless, arms around each other, in front of an enormous dead boar. Happy and dashing.

'Your wife took that picture. Käthe.'

There's a framed picture of a smiling Käthe on the bedside table. Pavel points to it. Karl-Adam doesn't take his eyes off the photo in his hand.

'We're good friends, I can see that,' Karl-Adam says. 'What's your name again?'

'Pavel,' Pavel says patiently. 'My name's Pavel. We were very good friends. We got to know each other in Stockholm. We were engineering students together.'

Karl-Adam studies the picture for a long moment. Goes back to the one of him and his son. Points to the house.

'That's a lovely house, but I don't remember it. But that's my sweet little Lars. I suppose he's at school now. And my darling Ludvig. I will never get over that grief. What time is it?'

All three of them are silent. Karl-Adam's still looking at the pictures. Should they tell him his son's not at school, that he's a grown man with a family of his own? Or would that upset him? Cassi looks around for Nathan, but he has left the room to give them privacy. Cassi hopes – more for Pavel's sake than hers – that Karl-Adam doesn't have another meltdown.

They look at more pictures, trying to jog a memory of anything, but Karl-Adam is losing focus again and doesn't say much. Eventually, he looks up at Pavel and announces that he's tired.

'It was nice of you to stop by,' Karl-Adam says. 'Thank you for visiting. But I think I need to rest for a bit now.'

Pavel stands up, putting the first two pictures and a few others down on the table. He takes Karl-Adam's hands and helps him stand up and move over to the bed. Karl-Adam pauses for a moment with Pavel's hands in his. Pavel leans in to give him a hug. They're almost exactly the same height. And just like that, Karl-Adam's head is resting on Pavel's shoulder. He nuzzles his face into Pavel's neck.

'I remember now,' Karl-Adam says softly after a few minutes. 'I remember you.'

His bony hands meet behind Pavel's back.

Pavel holds him in silence.

Cassi takes it as her cue to leave the room.

When Pavel eventually comes out, his eyes are misty and deep. Cassi stands up. They hug too, their first true hug, for a long moment, before walking out of the nursing home hand in hand. They cross paths with Nathan, but neither Pavel nor Cassi are in the mood for small talk. Cassi just waves at him and the two of them run to the car in the warm rain.

39

It's early in the afternoon and Cassi is sitting at a small table outside the pizzeria, feeling pleasantly full. She's forgiven Cook for having basically called her a cliché when they ran into each other at The Market. She can't afford to be petty. Risk making enemies. Besides, she really does like his Quattro Stagioni pizza, the way he separates the toppings into meticulous quarters. He's a perfectionist and she appreciates that.

She's pulling burrs and twigs out of Maine's fur. There will be more stuff to pull out once they get home, because Cassi and Maine walked into town through the woods and they'll be taking the same way back. Maine lets her do whatever she needs to do with his head in her lap. He seems to be enjoying himself.

Cassi spots a neon-pink windbreaker jogging towards her. It's Fia, who annoyingly keeps jogging in place after stopping to talk to her.

'How you doin'?' Fia says, checking her smartwatch before bending down to pet Maine. 'Have to. Finish. My steps. For this week.'

Cassi remembers that feeling. She wipes cheese grease from her lips with the back of her hand. She doesn't miss that lifestyle one bit.

'How have you been since we last spoke?' Cassi asks.

Fia keeps jogging, she's doing high knees now, but looks happy despite that.

'Yeah, you know, I think a lot of the stuff you said made sense,' she puffs. 'It got me thinking. Got my brain moving. It was fun.'

She puts her earbuds back in.

'Have to keep going, see you,' she says with a wave, setting off towards the trail that runs along the old railroad tracks.

Cassi stays put. Doesn't feel the word 'fun' is an accurate description of what she does. She would have appreciated 'life-altering' or 'rewarding'. 'Fun' feels trivial. She's going to show Fia. The next time she comes over for a session, there will be fireworks.

Cassi resumes cleaning Maine's thick coat, but loud hollering from the trail makes her look up. She sees Fia high-five someone running in the opposite direction, wearing a full wetsuit and a swim cap. It turns out to be Berzan, who sprints across the car park and stops in front of Cassi, bending over to catch his breath.

'What's going on?' It's the only question she can come up with that seems reasonable.

'Swimrun,' Berzan pants. 'Half swim, half run,' he adds when he notices Cassi's expression.

Berzan pulls off his cap. Underneath, his black hair is shiny and slicked back, as usual. The sun makes his wet beard glitter.

'And you?'

Cassi looks around.

'Maine and I have been on a . . .' She thinks about it for a brief moment. '. . . a *soul stroll* is what I like to call it. When you walk and let your soul roam freely. In the forest, of course.'

She inhales deeply, closing her eyes on the exhale.

'Mmm, I feel so fulfilled afterwards! Content!'

The role the Quattro Stagioni pizza played in her current state of well-being is something she chooses not to mention.

'Outstanding!' Berzan says. 'Amazing. You know, I was going to text you. That yoga class was . . . memorable. Do you happen to be free right now?'

'Absolutely,' she says.

Berzan nods towards the three-storey building across from the pizzeria and tugs on his wetsuit.

'I'd love to get out of this. Do you mind if we stop at mine?'

'Absolutely,' Cassi says again. She stands up, brushing away the pizza crumbs that have gathered in the folds of her top.

Maine trots after them across the street. The stairwell of Berzan's building smells of old rubbish and damp. Berzan takes the stairs three steps at a time to the second floor and Cassi hurries after him.

His flat is a one-bed with a small kitchenette. It looks like it belongs to a fugitive. The centrepiece of the room – if one could call it that – is a stool sitting underneath the window. The blinds dangle at strange angles. There are no wardrobes nor coat stands that Cassi can see – just jackets hanging off nails that emerge from random points in the wall. There are hooks in the hallway, but they seem to exclusively store Berzan's gym equipment, which is the only thing that looks somewhat presentable in this place.

There's no table in the kitchen, no chairs. Cassi spots three instant noodle packets on the counter next to a massive container of protein powder. On the fridge there is a card that reads 'Happy 25th Birthday!' Berzan notices Cassi looking at it.

'My mum sent it last week,' he says. 'I actually turned twenty-seven in February.'

He takes the card and holds it in his hand, his gaze darkening for a moment.

'Can I offer you anything to drink?' he then asks. 'Water? Energy drink? Protein shake?'

He smiles. Cassi shakes her head and politely refuses, so Berzan makes one for himself and glugs it down. He shoves the birthday card into the bin hanging off the back of a cabinet door. From where she's standing, Cassi can see lots of empty energy cans and banana peels. Tiny flies hover around the bag like it's their own pizzeria. Cassi smiles at the thought but forces herself to assume a more solemn expression.

'Could I use the bathroom and wash my hands?' she asks.

Berzan points to the hallway while filling an empty plastic container that once held some kind of takeaway with water for Maine.

The bathroom's small and damp. On two shelves above the toilet sit rows of hair and skin products. The soap on the edge of the sink is not the kind normal supermarkets carry. It smells expensive and Cassi's still sniffing her hands when she returns to the kitchen.

'Nice, huh?' says Berzan, who has wriggled out of the top half of his wetsuit. 'I order it online.'

'Smells expand our minds,' Cassi replies. 'They can send us hurtling back in time and space, to things we thought we'd forgotten.'

She can hear that she sounds stilted, but she can't stop herself. She wonders what she's really doing here.

'I'm going to have a quick shower, back in a minute,' Berzan says.

Cassi and Maine stand by the window. She sees Alida's van pull up outside the pizzeria, watches her as she goes inside to pick up an order. When she comes back out, her gaze shoots up, suddenly meeting Cassi's. Her face distorts for a moment, then Alida climbs back into the car and drives off in a hurry.

The van has barely left Cassi's eyeline when Berzan comes back with a towel wrapped around his waist. Cassi is about to compliment his cologne when her phone buzzes in her back pocket. It's Alida.

Cassi sighs. Somehow, she finds it more difficult to deal with her over the phone than in person. The first time Alida called Cassi, they ended up having an awkward stop-and-start conversation full of long silences, until Cassi had dared to ask the reason for the call. 'Why, are you in a hurry?' had been Alida's reply.

Since then, Cassi has taken to screening her calls, which have become particularly frequent over the past few days. She declines this one too, making a mental note to call back on the way home.

Berzan hangs up his swim cap on a loose hook.

'All right,' Cassi says. 'What did you want to talk about?'

Berzan looks at her, his eyebrows slightly raised.

'I guess we're done with the pleasantries! But that's good. Why waste time, right?'

He takes a pair of black jeans and slips his legs into them while Cassi takes a seat on the stool by the window.

There's a sketchpad on the windowsill full of drawings that look like warnings of an alien invasion. Next to it is a tattoo kit, and the combination makes Cassi's arms retreat deeper into her sleeves, as if to protect herself.

Maine lies down on the floor next to her. Somewhere in the building, a resident is playing the piano. Clearly, they're at the start of the learning process. The same tentative series of notes echo over and over again through the walls.

'The priest,' Berzan says, pointing at the floor. 'She practises at her friend's house, because she says she doesn't want to wear out "God's organ" unnecessarily. I reckon it has more to do with the church being too cold inside, though.'

Berzan walks around the room nervously, finding little tasks to fill the silence. He opens and closes the protein powder tub. Straightens his taekwondo kit, which is hanging from the wall. Then looks at Cassi.

'How's Pavel?' he asks. 'I ran into him at the shops the other day. He sounded positively chipper. He's usually so soft-spoken.'

'Pavel's the best,' she says with a smile. 'A true friend. You know when you meet someone you feel you've known forever? When everything's just effortless? That's how I feel when I'm with him.'

She pauses, pondering if she should add anything else, something Cassiopeia-esque, but decides she's said enough. The truth will suffice. Berzan looks touched.

'I know what you mean,' he says. 'That's actually what I wanted to talk to you about.'

Then he starts speaking. Cassi's had parts of his story from Marlene, but she pretends she hasn't. When Berzan tears up, which happens just a few sentences in, she asks him to lie down on a blanket on the floor. Cassi's getting used to strong emotions, but has realised she's more comfortable with them if they come at her from a horizontal position. She likes asking her clients to close their eyes so that she doesn't have to mould her expression to whatever they're feeling. Taking it all in is hard enough as it is.

Berzan stretches out on the blanket. Maine immediately joins him, snuggling in close and heaving a deep sigh. Cassi sits down with her legs crossed next to Berzan's head, moving her hands in sweeping gestures above his torso, not dissimilarly to her energy cleanse ritual with Marlene.

Apparently Berzan is in love with his former boss, a married woman fifteen years his senior who doesn't even live here. His story is one of a garden-variety broken heart. What happened to him has happened a gazillion times before and is going to happen a gazillion more.

'It was something that just . . . hit me,' Berzan says. 'The way she looked at me. I didn't plan for it to happen, but it was inescapable. Not that I wanted to escape it. But then it took over my life. She was like a magnet and I couldn't resist her pull. Until it was suddenly over.'

His voice breaks.

There are different versions of what happened in the lead-up to two ships almost colliding at sea. According to Marlene, it was because Berzan and his boss were having a 'steamy time' on the bridge of the boat which he was supposed to be driving. According to Berzan, the real culprit was a distracting, none-too-appropriate series of text messages. Anyway, all the papers in the country called it a 'double *Titanic*'. After botched attempts at crisis management, the company decided heads had to roll. More precisely, Berzan's and his lover's. She was given another role on another boat and Berzan was fired. Now, he operates Bäcken's small river ferry, and his love remains unrequited.

'She's asked me to stop contacting her,' he says. 'She says she's going to make things right with her husband.'

Cassi puts her hands on his shoulders. She's feeling inspired. She's good at things like this.

'Berzan, I see you. This is not your home. You want to be somewhere else but don't know how to get there.'

Berzan closes his eyes. Tears trickle down his temples. 'I don't know what to do. I feel like I'm falling apart.' Cassi speaks slowly.

'I see you, Berzan,' she says again. 'I see that you're lost. I see that you're fraying. I see your loose ends. You're looking for something to hold on to.'

She starts grabbing invisible threads above his chest, gesturing with force so that he feels the movement above his chest, senses that she is hard at work to help him.

'Now I'm pulling them up and tying them. Can you feel it?'

Berzan nods.

'Yes, I can feel it.'

'I've tied them into knots,' Cassi says, and ties bows in the air above him. 'You're in one piece now. You're not going to fall apart. You can grab onto them. I see you.'

She sighs heavily to signal that she's done.

'Take a step back, Berzan. Give her some space. If you hold on less tightly, you'll stand taller.'

Berzan wipes his eyes, a hand resting on Maine's fur.

Silence falls for a few minutes, until his phone dings in the kitchen. Berzan stiffens.

'Sorry,' he says.

Cassi puts her hands together.

'We're done for today,' she says, stretching. 'But do let me know if you want to talk some more. Go deeper. There's hurt inside you, Berzan. I can help you move on.'

They stand up. He goes into the kitchen and grabs some cash from his jacket pocket. Cassi seizes the opportunity to check her phone. There's a text from Lollo, inviting her to a summer party at the farm in August.

'Party at the Desgoffes!' exclaims Berzan, who's received the same text. 'Finally, something fun happening around here!'

40

Cassi never cleans the house and rarely showers, but today, she's making an effort.

She puts on the wrap skirt she found in one of Pavel's old boxes (and yes, she did air it out first). Only a faint smell of damp cardboard lingers when she ties it around her waist. The knee-length skirt is full and bright blue with an irregular tie-dye pattern. There's a large patch pocket too, with shakily hand-embroidered flowers on it. It was definitely sewn by someone creative. Pavel can't recall where he got it from. 'It must have been in some box or the other,' was his only guess when Cassi asked.

Cassi can't decide if she loves or hates it, but at least it's not a skirt that goes unnoticed. Its handmade, pre-loved, loud vibe matches her bohemian identity. It's a welcome change from her usual denim shorts or leggings, a deliberate one – she needs to look the part as much as she wants to play it.

The skirt is so wide it gets caught in the car door when she closes it and flaps like a pennant flag all the way to The Market. She's figured out that the earlier in the day she gets there, the lower the risk of finding Hans at the till. She now does all her shopping as soon as they open.

Inside, the air is cool, the chill seeping through the soles of Cassi's flip-flops. She moves stealthily through the aisles, hoping to go unnoticed. If this is meant to be her lucky day, there'll be an unknown temp at the till.

Crap. Gretel's at the dairy counter, mopping water off the floor. Cassi doesn't want to make herself known, but she really does need one of the cartons of milk sitting just behind the woman.

Gretel's eyes are fixed on the spill on the floor. When she looks up, Cassi notes that her eyes linger on the skirt before she forces them up to Cassi's face. Then they slide back down again. And back up.

'Am I in your way?' Gretel says. She sighs a little as she puts the mop down in the bucket, but not in a frustrated or tired way. She seems almost . . . pensive? She pushes the bucket aside, moving out of the way so Cassi can get by.

'I'm sorry to be a bother,' Cassi says.

'We have a leak,' is Gretel's only response. Her eyes wander back to Cassi's skirt.

Cassi turns and retreats towards the tinned tomatoes.

'Hey,' Gretel says behind her.

'Yes?'

Cassi whips around.

'I should warn you there's water over by the cheese too. I haven't had time to mop it up yet. Careful you don't slip.'

Cassi nods, overly animated. She even gives a thumbs up. She's so desperate for Gretel to like her. For it to rub off on her husband. It would be such a relief not to have to deal with the low-key dread his scepticism inflicts on her life.

'Thanks, I'll be careful!' she says.

She walks away with extreme caution.

'Where did you get that skirt?'

The words come out unusually quickly for Gretel and they sound brusque. Cassi turns around again, surprise painted on her face.

'Pavel gave it to me,' she says. 'We found it when we were cleaning out his garage. He's accumulated a lot of rubbish, that man.'

Gretel smiles. Has Cassi ever seen her do that before? Not that she can recall.

Cassi hurriedly adds: 'But a lot of nice things too! Isn't this incredible? The width! The colours!'

She twirls in the aisle.

'I bet you'd never guess it,' Gretel says, 'but Berit and I made that.'

Silence.

'Or rather, Marlene,' Gretel corrects herself.

Cassi stares at her.

'What?' slips out. 'I had no idea. I don't think Pavel knew either.'

Gretel has moved in closer and now reaches out to touch the fabric.

'We used to design clothes, a long time ago. We even had plans of starting our own brand. Thought we were going to take over the world. Young and naïve, you know.'

She smiles at Cassi again.

'That's amazing,' Cassi says. 'I love this skirt.'

'It makes me happy to see it worn and I'm glad you like it,' Gretel says. 'I thought everything we made was long gone. This really takes me back.'

'Incredible,' Cassi says. 'But why did you stop?'

She figures there's no need for her to let on that Marlene's already told her about the rift between the two childhood friends. Gretel looks around, straightening a few jam jars on a shelf.

'Oh, many reasons. We . . . fell out. But mostly it was

because Hans and I decided, together, to take over this shop. After that, I simply didn't have time for anything else. And, well, all kinds of things. Sometimes, friends grow apart.'

That last part said with a furtive glance towards the storeroom.

'That's a pity,' Cassi says. 'But you and Marlene are both still passionate about design, that much is obvious. You both have your own style, or whatever people call it. You've never thought about doing something together again?'

She knows the answer already, but she can feel she's getting somewhere. Gretel looks uncomfortable.

'Marlene stopped talking to me a long time ago,' she says at length. 'I don't know how well you know her, but there are a lot of feelings there. I've never met a person who can hold a grudge like her.'

Someone rings the bell that means a member of staff is needed at the till. Gretel pushes her glasses up.

'But it's great to see you in the skirt. We had a good time, working on that.'

Then she walks off, leaving Cassi behind. Cassi grabs a few boxes of pasta and kills time by the taco kit shelf. Then, spotting Hans's back through the warped plastic window in the door to the storeroom, she quickly retreats to a hidden aisle.

Gretel's now sitting at the till, staring vacantly out the main doors, which haven't closed behind the last customer yet.

'You know what,' Cassi says, as she puts her drily rustling shopping on the belt.

Gretel turns to her.

'I've been spending some time with Marlene lately and, without compromising my professional code of silence, I'd say she's very open to addressing what happened. Wouldn't it be beautiful if the two of you could reconnect? Life's too short to let old wrongs ruin a friendship.'

As usual, this idea doesn't come without its problems. For starters, not once has Cassi heard Marlene say anything about addressing things. And second, she shouldn't be mentioning a professional code of silence, she doesn't even have one. And who does she think she is, preaching forgiveness when she still carries so much resentment with her?

But Gretel doesn't know about any of that.

The door to the storeroom opens and Hans walks out, placing a pallet full of glass jars onto the shop floor. He has time to shoot Cassi a displeased glare before disappearing behind the shelves again.

Gretel scans Cassi's shopping in silence. Cassi pays, trying to make eye contact, but Gretel pointedly looks away. It feels surreal that they were having a normal, if not emotionally charged, conversation just minutes before.

'You have a lovely day, Gretel,' Cassi says. She's left her tote bag in the car so she has to carry her shopping inside her skirts like an apple-picker from another century. Gretel doesn't reply.

Only when she steps out of the shop and glances at the receipt does Cassi realise that Gretel has given her a staff discount. She looks back with a hopeful smile.

41

Now that she's consistently busy, Cassi doesn't even have to pretend to be content with her life, she genuinely is.

Almost every day, someone comes over to talk or get some kind of healing. She has now come up with a technique she's named *breathing therapy*, telling people they've had 'a breakthrough' when they pass out after holding their breath for an unnecessarily long amount of time. *Mossage* is when she crumbles and rubs dry moss from the edges of her garden on someone's back. Another time, she reads tea leaves, which is a real challenge considering the tea in question is from a powdery Earl Grey bag and often becomes a layer of goop at the bottom of the cup.

She drags a Norwegian man who's staying at Max's campground into the woods, but once out there, the *liberation dance* she prescribes him almost goes awry when the Norwegian, wearing a blindfold, trips over a root, falls over a tree stump, and almost breaks both his legs. In Cassi's version of the story, he took a tumble because he wasn't focused on being present in the moment enough. The dispute is settled amicably after she offers him a free tarot reading and introduces him to Marlene.

But she can't complain about occasional hiccups when everything has gone pretty much smoothly. Charging for her services – previously a point of internal contention – now feels normal. She deserves to be recompensed.

She's also been able to work out some days off during the week, which are spent either visiting Karl-Adam with Pavel or driving around the countryside visiting what Pavel considers local sights, which really aren't a sight to behold most of the time.

She's about to go pick him up for another aimless drive when Alida calls. With a sigh of frustration, she climbs back out of the car – she needs fresh air when talking to Alida. Cassi feels bad about not having called her back, realising it's been almost a week since she last heard from her. Maine, who had just settled into the back seat, lifts his head to see what the hold-up is, but thankfully decides to stay put.

'Hi, Alida. I'm sorry I wasn't able to talk when you called.'

Alida is breathing loudly on the other end.

'OK,' she says at length.

It sounds as though Alida can't be bothered to talk even though she's the one who called. You're a strange woman, you know that?! Cassi would love to tell her. But she just waits.

'I suppose you were busy with other things. As I could see for myself,' Alida adds. 'Busy with lover boy.'

'Yes, I've had my hands full with new clients,' Cassi says, ignoring the dig. 'And I'm heading out again now. Everything OK with you?'

Cassi hopes Alida will take the hint and get to why she's calling. But the only sound on the other end of the phone is Alida's breathing.

'Alida?' Cassi says after a few seconds. 'What's on your mind?'

Alida sounds as though she's about to speak, but if her mouth opens, it quickly closes again. The silence stretches, becoming almost painful.

'I have something I need to talk to you about. It's important,' she says at last.

'I'm literally on my way out, so I'm afraid it'll have to wait.' Cassi hopes this won't piss her off. 'But do you remember the exercises we talked about, the ones you can do when you're going through a tough time? Holding your hands above an anthill? Smelling the alpacas' ears? Or doing a few star breaths? Have you tried that?'

Alida's breathing sounds even more laboured. Cassi's chest feels tight.

'It's not like that,' Alida says. 'I've figured things out. I know now.'

'OK,' Cassi says, having no idea what the woman means. 'But I really do have to go now, Alida. It's technically my day off. You know how I feel about stress. Time is a gift to be handled gently. You take care, try and relax, and we'll talk later when you've cleared your mind. Look after yourself.'

She hangs up before Alida can say anything else. Does Alida have a problem with her now? Is she jealous? Cassi knows Alida has complicated feelings for Berzan. Alida makes life decisions guided by the principle of 'who cares?', which has fostered, among other things, an aggressive pickup style that's rarely acceptable or successful. According to Fia, she went over to Berzan's once and rang his doorbell, dressed in nothing but waders and a rain poncho, which she opened like a tent flap when he came to the door. Another time, she left a small plastic bag of alpaca fluff outside his door, with a handwritten note that said: *The alpacas don't bite, but I do.* It's unclear what she meant by that, because Berzan didn't call the number printed with boxy digits at the bottom of the note.

Now, Alida probably thinks Cassi and Berzan are seeing each other in a not-so-professional capacity. The idea makes Cassi uncomfortable. She doesn't want to be thought of as a member of the yearning village harem. But there's not much she can do about it. And at least it's not as though Alida has a big circle of friends she can spread her stories to.

Cassi gets back in her car and starts driving down her gravel. She's made it halfway to the main road when another car turns in from the left.

It's Gretel.

Cassi starts to reverse out of sheer surprise, back to the point she set off from. The two women park and climb out of their respective cars. They greet each other as though neither one of them knows what the other is doing here. As strange as it was for Cassi to see Gretel smiling at the shop, seeing her exist outside that building is even stranger. Gretel's dressed in flowy, dark-purple linen trousers, and an equally flowy, dark-purple linen tunic. She looks at Cassi through her glasses, lined with – of course – purple frames.

'I'm sorry to bother you,' Gretel says. 'I can see you're going somewhere.'

'No worries, Gretel,' Cassi says. 'I have all the time in the world.'

She doesn't, Pavel's waiting for her, but in Cassi's carefully contrived web of outright lies, faux facts and exaggerations, a fudged statement about time is neither here nor there.

'I've thought about what you said,' Gretel says. She looks up briefly, meeting Cassi's eyes before looking back down.

'I've thought about my relationship with Berit, or, well, Marlene. In a way, it would be good if we could meet up and talk it out.'

She rubs her thumbnail intently.

'But I don't think we can do it without some kind of help. Every time I've tried over the years, I've only made things worse. It always ends with us fighting even more. But since she trusts you, I was thinking it might work better with an external observer present. Whatever they call it, a mediator.'

Gretel looks up again.

'This warms my heart, Gretel.'

Cassi puts her right hand on her chest. She really means it. Having Gretel put her faith in her is validation she'd barely dared to dream of.

'How should we go about it, do you think?' Gretel asks. 'Because I personally don't see any need to tell Hans, at this point. I can't go to her house, it's far too close to the shop. And I don't want to do it here.'

She looks around again, eyebrows raised, as though there were something wrong with Cassi's messy garden.

'I was about to suggest we meet at the lake,' Cassi says, doing her best to ignore how annoying she finds it that everyone has to have an opinion about her property. 'The power of water is not only cleansing for the body, but also for the psyche. The soul. And the calming effect of waves lapping against the shore can work wonders.'

She lets her hands join in as she speaks.

'Waves would never allow a fight to get in their way. The wind doesn't stop for disagreements. Nature, life, everything is happening all the time, all around us. Within us. Time waits for no one. It can be good to be reminded of that when tempers are running high.'

Gretel looks as though she would have preferred to be anywhere but there, but she probably feels it's not the time to question the person she's just asked to help her repair a broken friendship.

'Yes, you might be right about that,' she says.

She takes off her glasses, cleaning them intently with the hem of her tunic.

'The reason I don't want to be here is that it was my older sister's house. Käthe was married to Karl-Adam and she was never very happy here. The place gives me a bad feeling.'

'I'm sorry to hear that,' Cassi says. 'For me personally, this house and its surroundings have been a port in a storm. But of course I understand the complicated feelings associated with memories and places. From what I know, your sister was ill?'

Gretel sneers.

'Sure, the cancer's what killed her, but it wasn't what made her life unhappy. One of their sons, Ludvig, died of leukaemia at the age of three. She was never the same after that.'

Cassi remembers Karl-Adam mentioning a Ludvig, but she didn't know about his passing. She looks at the house, trying to imagine the grief that must have seeped into every floorboard, every wall. Gretel continues.

'And her husband . . . their marriage wasn't a good one. He betrayed her. And it went on for a very long time.'

Cassi stares off into the forest. She's always had a hard time summoning any kind of feeling for Käthe. Her thoughts never linger on her, she's always been so clearly on Pavel's side. Now, she feels nauseous, a seed of discomfort lodges itself in her throat. She tries to shake it off.

'I really am sorry,' she says again. 'I could sense complicated feelings as soon as I moved into the house, but I've cleansed it thoroughly since. If you did want to come in, I think you'd feel that there are only good energies left.'

Gretel shakes her head.

'I'm sure you like it fine here, but for me, it's not about the house itself.'

Cassi considers offering her services as a medium if Gretel would like to contact her sister. After all, the step from mediator to medium is not that big. They're practically the same word. But it'll have to wait. She has to take things slow with Gretel.

'I'll talk to Marlene,' Cassi says. 'I'm sure we can come up with a plan you're both comfortable with.'

She puts her palms back together and bows slightly. Gretel goes back to her car and opens the door. Cassi follows.

'I hope this works out,' Gretel says.

She trails off, her eyes on the ground. When she speaks again, it's as though she's thinking out loud.

'Even if Berit and I can't get back the special bond we had when we were younger, it would be nice to not have drama anymore. My sister passed away with so many things unresolved.'

She looks up at Cassi's house.

'I don't want my life to end that way,' she says.

She sniffs. Wipes the tip of her nose. Cassi gently puts an arm around her, but Gretel turns out to be ready for a full hug, with both arms and her head on Cassi's shoulder. She smells like vanilla.

'I'm taking a chance with this,' she sobs. 'But it's a chance worth taking.'

The linen's rough against Cassi's fingers as she strokes Gretel's back.

'I hope you know how wonderful you are for doing this, Gretel,' she says. 'It's admirable. Life's too short to hold on to past wrongs.'

Gretel weeps openly into Cassi's shoulder. Her breath is hot and damp against Cassi's throat when she speaks.

'She was so busy with her own things,' Gretel says. 'Her grief. She didn't know. That he lived a double life. The way he cheated on her. How long it went on for. And I'm so sad for her. So very, very sad.'

Cassi feels the discomfort inside her grow louder. It's like a landslide, the entire side of a mountain collapsing, she doesn't know if she's standing up or sitting down, where her body ends, if her legs are going to buckle or her head explode. She has to let go of Gretel. Step out of the embrace. Squat down. Put her head between her legs.

'I'm sorry,' she says. 'I'm sorry.'

Cassi wraps her arms around her own head. This was unexpected. This wasn't how it was supposed to go. She wasn't supposed to be the one to break down. She has a flashback to the breakroom at the superstore, to that time when she just wanted to disassemble herself, fold up and disappear. Gretel stands there next to her, probably as surprised at the turn this has taken as she is. No one in the village has ever seen her show any signs of vulnerability, Cassi knows that. Using one sleeve of her tunic as a handkerchief, Gretel wipes her cheeks before sitting down on the ground next to her.

'What's going on?' she asks. 'Are you OK?'

Cassi's unable to answer at first. She doesn't know what to say.

'Yes,' she eventually replies. She forces her face into what she hopes is a smile and turns it to Gretel, who instinctively pulls away from the unnatural rictus.

'I just had an emotional collapse,' she continues. 'It happens sometimes when truly powerful forces are in motion.'

She's still hugging herself. Takes two deep breaths. Tries to compose herself.

'I'm so sensitive, it's as though I absorb everything that's radiating off you. All the energies that arise. Phew.'

Cassi lies down on the ground. She's not about to let her mind, her past, take the blame for what just happened. It's easier to keep living the lie and pretend Jarmo never existed.

'It happens sometimes,' she repeats. 'It means you've been relieved of a portion of those heavy feelings. It's as though you've poured a full bucket of feelings into an empty one, which I was holding out to you. And now you feel better. You've put it all on me so you can feel peace. And that's what matters, Gretel.'

Gretel looks around.

'Hmm. Your reaction freaked me out a bit. But I'm sure you're right. I haven't done anything like this before. Should I . . . apologise?'

Cassi stands up. Now Gretel's the one to extend a hand, to make sure she's steady on her feet. But her head is swaying. Cassi brushes some pine needles off her hands.

'No need,' she says. 'I'm used to it.'

'I have to go now,' Gretel says. 'But thank you for this, Cassi. I feel a bit shaken, maybe that's a symptom of my feelings being transferred to you. It feels unfamiliar. But not in a bad way.'

'Gretel. You're the one who deserves to be thanked,' Cassi replies. She almost feels like she's back to normal. 'And don't forget to hydrate.'

42

Cassi arrives at Pavel's house much later than they'd agreed. Pavel's tending to raspberry bushes and glances hesitantly at his watch when Cassi proposes going for a drive anyway, despite the delay.

'It's only half four. I promise to bring you back home in time for dinner!' she says, because she knows Pavel's a sucker for his routine, and she can guess what he's worried about.

'Just a short drive. There's time.'

She honks again. Pavel smiles. Few things fill her with joy like that sight. A cheerful old man in cargo trousers, always ready to drop whatever he's doing to be there for her, so long as it's within his strict timeframes.

'OK,' he says. 'I just need to wash my hands.'

He slips in through the front door, returning almost immediately.

When he's seated and buckled, he slaps his palms against his thighs and asks: 'So, what's the plan?'

He looks happy. She laughs.

'As usual, I don't have a plan,' she replies. 'But I was going to suggest riding the ferry. I still haven't seen it.'

'Sounds good,' he says, slapping his thighs again, staring straight ahead now, ready to go.

Surrounded by rural idyll, it's hard to take the yellow-and-red warning sign for the ferry dock seriously. But Pavel points and they turn left at a red barn. Further down a gravel road, a boom barrier blocks the way. The empty ferry's waiting on the other side of the river but casts off as they approach. Now that she can see it, Cassi can't understand why she hasn't come here sooner. The presence of a teeny, tiny ferry in the area gives low-key broken-down-theme-park vibes. The ferry can carry two or three cars at a time and its job is to connect two gravel roads. The 'river' barely looks like one, it's more like a very large stream. Cassi can make out two people up in the pilothouse, but they're little more than silhouettes. When she gets closer and rolls the window down, she sees Berzan waving down at her from behind the wheel of the ferryboat. She waves back.

The gate arms are lowered and they carefully drive aboard the small vessel before parking and exiting the car.

The late afternoon sun is blazing. Further down the river, children are playing on a jetty, their laughs echoing and melting with the mellow waves. Cassi and Pavel walk up to the prow.

Berzan sticks his head out again and shouts 'How's it going?' His black beard is neatly trimmed and his smile beaming and white. He looks much better than he did the other day in his minimalistic and bro-y home.

'We're on an outing,' Pavel replies. Cassi notes how his body language is open and joyful: arms extended in the wind, the sleeves of his shirt flapping as the ferry glides on the sparkly water.

'Perfect day for it,' Berzan says.

Then he turns back to the other person on the bridge, whose long black hair dances in the wind. Cassi can't make out what they're saying, but she can hear Berzan laughing.

This would be a perfect place for a party, Cassi thinks. Going back and forth across the river, swimming, drinking cocktails. She mentions it to Pavel. He laughs as though it were the craziest idea he's ever heard, but then he says he agrees. They decide they're going to do it, soon. Maybe invite Karl-Adam to come with them, just for the day. They're visiting the home at least twice a week now.

'Not knowing how he was doing was excruciating,' Pavel says. 'Seeing he's well taken care of makes me feel calm.'

Pavel has even been granted special permission to spend the night, thanks to Nathan. Though that did make Cassi wonder about how Karl-Adam's really doing. Is this a sign he doesn't have much time left? Maybe Nathan wants to make sure his last days are memorable and happy.

The trip to the other bank only takes a few minutes. They disembark and wave goodbye to Berzan. Maine has crawled into the front seat of the car and is now perched on Pavel's lap. They drive on. Pavel points out the start of a narrow path that leads to what he claims is the best mushroom-picking spot in the county. He shows her a place where a dramatic lorry crash happened thirty years earlier, covering the entire road with flour. Oh, and in a meadow beyond that, there was a big brawl once, but it didn't involve anyone he knew. Before that house over there was built, there used to be a different house in that spot. At one point, he saw a bear right here. Or, well, not here, but a mile or two into the woods from here. And it was at dusk, so he didn't see it that clearly. But it could have been a bear.

AUGUST

43

It was Fia's idea. Lollo heard about the plan when she was shopping for a new sprinkler at the Village Shop. Together, they've talked Cassi into doing a séance. Or, what they're calling a séance. As usual, Cassi's not sure what they're expecting, but as usual, they're going to get whatever Cassi sees fit.

They're going to be seven people in total. Fia, Lollo and Simon, and Simon has invited Max the estate agent, who in turn is bringing a woman called Nadia, who Cassi doesn't know. And Marlene's on board too, of course.

By now, Cassi has achieved a sense of security in her persona. A confidence that isn't shaken even when new people come into the picture. It's been weeks since she last had a nightmare about being exposed as a fraud. In the most recent one, which she can in fact still vividly recall and shudder at, her subconscious served up an investigative reporter who was out to catch her with a hidden camera. The video, in which she was talking about the sacred power of pine needles, internal light diodes, and the human body's magnetic nerve endings, went viral online, identifying her by name and showing her face. Then the dream cut ruthlessly to clips of former colleagues and friends laughing at her, of hurt Bäcken neighbours. Hans, pointing his finger. Cassi had woken up in a cold sweat.

Thankfully, this hasn't deterred her. She feels good

about the séance. She's come up with a plan and she's going to stick to it, while remaining open to any inspiration that might materialise along the way. Cassi went out into the woods in the early morning to set out the torches Pavel's made for her, and as evening falls, she changes into the clothes she'd laid out that morning.

The main purpose of the outfit she wore for the live-streamed yoga was to keep her anonymous. This time, it's about showmanship. You have to push yourself, be avant-garde, give your participants something they didn't know they wanted. Black leggings and a black top to start. Instead of the hideous boa she wore to the yoga session, she'll be wearing a skirt made of sticks. She has also improved on the mask concept, because last time, the lingonberry twigs kept scratching her face and the scratches were visible for days afterwards. Today, Cassi will be using a mask made of black plastic, onto which she has glued the little twigs. She won't even have to put make-up on, how convenient.

Late-summer darkness is enveloping the clearing when she carries a box full of small lanterns outside, setting it down on the front steps of her home as the first of the evening's participants, Marlene, pedals up towards the house with a sweeping headlight.

Lollo pulls up behind her in her Land Rover, and with her in the car are Simon, Max, and a woman with long black hair who must be Nadia. Nadia looks vaguely familiar and is quite obviously drunk. Maybe it's rude to assume but if there's one person who knows what being drunk feels like, it's Cassi. But she can't help but feel that this is disrespectful to her as a shaman. Should a person be intoxicated when doing something like this? Cassi hasn't had a drink all day, and barely any yesterday either. She's doing better of late, every piece of the puzzle falling into place. If anyone were to doubt her, she'd point to the plant in her living room, which used to be on the verge of death and is now growing big healthy leaves.

Nadia flounces over to Cassi and holds her hands out to her.

'Oh, this is so beautiful,' she says. 'I love nature. It's just incredible, the way it grows and grows. Are we all wearing masks?'

After touching Cassi's mask, Nadia's hands wander lower. They trace circles on her skirt – 'Forsythia!' – and down all the way to her toes.

It's a motley gathering. Cassi on the steps in her twig skirt and leggings. Maine next to her, his collar also adorned with twigs. Simon's dressed like he's going hunting, Fia is in a full white outfit, while Marlene is wearing a red floor-length dress cinched at the waist by a green belt, and she explains with a wink that she was aiming for 'sultry and culty'. Lollo's dressed in floral leggings and a large knitted jumper. Max has on blue jeans and a white T-shirt, both tight around his limbs. Nadia's wearing blue jeans and a T-shirt, too, both baggy. Cassi glares at Nadia and closes her eyes, breathing deeply. The mood becomes suddenly solemn, the small talk hushed. Even Marlene is keeping her voice down – her sickly sweet perfume now the loudest thing about her.

'Do you remember meeting me before?' Nadia asks Cassi. Nadia's curly hair falls like a cape down her back. 'At the pizzeria, just after you moved here,' she continues before Cassi has time to say anything back. 'I've been wanting to see you again ever since.'

'Yes, Cassi, we're so happy you've agreed to do this,' Max adds. 'Nadia's going through a rough patch in her relationship right now, but we think a proper séance can point her in the right direction.'

Nadia nods.

'I was with this man, accidentally,' she says, as though it were a muddy puddle she happened to step in. 'It's made me question what I want with my life.'

'The Berzan effect,' Marlene says, winking again. 'We must all walk that path, sooner or later.'

Lollo lets out a chuckle.

'Here's hoping,' she says, shaking her head at Simon when he shoots her a questioning look.

It's time to start. Cassi has lit the lanterns and now hands them out to each participant. Then she raises her arms above her head and leads the group into the barn, which is dimly lit by the fairy lights hidden among the rafters. She strides into the middle of the room and instructs the others to form a semicircle facing her.

'We live in a time when we forget our innermost desires. We forget ourselves.'

Cassi beats her chest with a closed fist.

'The theme of this evening will be a celebration of our self-love. *Selfebration*!'

Marlene lets out a chuckle, but Cassi shoots her a stern look.

'We're going to dig deep into ourselves, find our core, raise it up, and put it on the throne it deserves. By finding ourselves, we find the world.'

Cassi looks each one of them in the eye. She lays out her rules. All phones have to be put into a bin and left in the barn. Everyone has to find the ceremonial place alone. And no physical contact.

'If you don't find your way, it wasn't meant to be,' she tells them. 'And if you stumble on your path, it means you need a stronger sense of direction. Anyone who doesn't make it, we'll come and find afterwards. Just sit down and wait.'

When Cassi sees that Nadia's about to open her mouth, she adds: 'And absolutely no talking. Think about the questions you need to ask. The answers are already inside you. Life is an experiment that is meant to be experienced.'

Nadia looks up at the ceiling.

'I want you to be part of this night, not analyse it. Be here. Be now.'

She tells them to spread out more inside the barn and then she and Maine step out through the door, into the woods.

Maine leads the way and Cassi's bare feet, hardened by a long summer of country living, follow the path they've walked many times. Once she's safely hidden by the trees, she pushes her mask up and turns on the flashlight on her phone, which she has most definitely not left in the barn – who says that shamans have to agree to their own rules?! – so she can see better and walk faster. A few minutes later, she has reached the place she has designated for the séance.

The torches are easy to light and once that's done, she pulls her mask back down, slips her phone into her waistband, and sits down on a tree stump in the middle of the lit circle. Maine lies down next to her.

Marlene is the first to arrive. Simon appears soon after, followed by Fia, Lollo and Max. Only Nadia has not yet found her way. The darkness around them deepens as the minutes tick by. Then they hear sobbing and see a faint point of light approaching.

Nadia looks like she's just made it out of an active warzone. She sits down at the edge of the circle, pulling her knees up to her chin and hugging them in tightly. Cassi sits in silence with her legs crossed and her arms hanging by her sides, palms up. She focuses on the sensations around her to get into character: the rustling of the leaves, the fragrant smell of moss, the splinters from the tree stump that pierce her through the leggings. She lets time pass until Nadia's sobs subside.

Cassi stands up. Moving softly, she walks a lap around the clearing, circling each torch, moving her hips, her hands straight and strong above her head. The real reason she's doing all this is that she desperately needs to shake out the splinters and loosen the leggings that the day's sweat has stuck to her skin without having to resort to something as pedestrian as tugging on the fabric covering her bum. It doesn't feel like behaviour worthy of a shaman, especially during a séance.

Cassi eventually stops in the middle of the circle, planting her feet wide. She can see distant glimpses of stars and treetops through the eyeholes of her mask. She speaks in staccato bursts, taking her inspiration from Pavel.

'Sometimes, empty spaces are invisible until we really look for them. Find them. Fill them.'

Cassi stomps her foot firmly.

'No one. Is built. Like you. You design yourself.'

One thing she forgot to do was set her phone to airplane mode. It's now vibrating against her ribs. Thank God it's on silent. She wraps her arms around her middle, muffling any noise. The others emulate her and are all holding their middle section now.

'If you want something you've never had, you have to do something you've never done.'

She chants. She marches. She places small stones on everyone's head. She waves a large branch about. She strikes the tree stump so hard with it that pieces of wood go flying in every direction. She stands perfectly still and silent for two full minutes. She burns a piece of paper. She asks everyone to stand on one leg with the other leg and both arms out, like the stars they are.

But then her phone starts up again. The buzzing against her stomach is drawn out and persistent. It's someone calling. Cassi wraps her arms around herself again, worrying about the light from the screen shining out through her jumper. She starts to chant again, this time loudly and incoherently. Incomprehensible noises, disjointed words, wild grunting, howling. She can't focus enough to form intelligible sentences. She takes large strides, waving first one, then the other arm wildly. Anything to draw attention away from her stomach.

But the person calling isn't deterred.

As soon as the phone stops buzzing, before she can even get a full sentence out, it starts up again.

'Lie face down on the ground,' Cassi orders brusquely. 'Feel the moss. See your core! Shout at the top of your lungs!'

As soon as everyone's down, she peeks down into her

top to see who's being so disruptive. At the same time, she walks around with heavy steps, chanting atonally. Having to keep so many things in mind at once almost makes her lose her balance.

It's Alida calling. Always bloody Alida. Always so unrelenting.

Cassi screams, a primal scream at the stars, and this time she really feels it. It's cathartic. Maine joins in with what might be his first ever howl. Taken aback, Cassi looks down at him for a second, then shoves her phone back in her waistband. It's the third time Alida's called, and Cassi's legs and voice are getting tired.

'Follow your feeling,' she says. 'Let the spirits in, let your ancestors live through you. Find yourself as you get lost among their souls. Tarot! Tarot! Tarot!'

What she's saying is incomprehensible even to her, but the participants take it as permission to stand up. Cassi waves her arms in the air, upwards, like a conductor, like a child throwing an armful of leaves. The others take that as a signal to start moving and making noise. Cassi notes that Marlene is tugging on her clothes again today.

Cassi takes a seat on her tree stump, rocking back and forth, hissing and humming by turns. And that's when she sees the light. A blinding, swaying light in the distance, hovering above the ground. Moving closer. Cassi holds her breath. Has she summoned a spirit? She calls Maine to her with a finger snap, hoping that even the laziest dog in the world can become a hound when their owner is in danger.

One by one, the others notice that she's gone quiet. They follow her gaze. One of them, probably Nadia, lets out a long, trembling 'oooooh'. Marlene stiffens with her dress halfway over her head.

'ARE YOU OUT OF YOUR DAMN MINDS?' a voice booms through the trees.

'The woods are dry as a bone, and you're dancing around with torches!'

Hans has now reached the clearing, flashlight in hand, and is so agitated and close to her that Cassi can see spittle flying from his lips.

'Pigeons have bigger brains than you! Mice! Peas!'

He points to the flames.

'One little spark from one of those and everything could burn! And that would be the end of this forest.'

He points at Cassi. He's not shouting anymore, but his voice is thunderous.

'Ever since you came to Bäcken, everyone's completely lost their minds. They come into my store, asking for incense. They want "healing herbs". They ask me directions to "the guru". It's a-b-s-o-l-u-t-e rubbish from beginning to end. Are you praying to your God or what? Is this satanism? Are you burning down the forest as a murder-suicide attempt? If I could, I would call the police on you!'

Silence falls. Cassi feels a sudden, intense gratitude for Hans's aversion to practically all forms of modern technology, the till at The Market being the only exception. According to Marlene, he doesn't own a mobile phone, only uses car keys you stick into the lock and turn, and has personally made sure the area is still on the 3G network.

Cassi has a feeling that this is it, that this is the point after which it'll all be over. The moment Hans gets home to his landline, the jig will be up. On her right, Fia sighs loudly.

'Seriously, I can't even. Just go away, Dad.'

Hans, who was about to launch into another rant, stops dead in his tracks. Peers into the darkness where Fia is covering her face, her white clothes almost fluorescent in the sharp beam of his flashlight. Cassi is taken aback – Fia is Hans's daughter?!

'Leave,' Fia says. 'Go home.'

Hans stares at her with mellowed eyes. He looks like he's shrinking in size right in front of them, his power taken away by shock.

'Fia,' he says. 'I didn't know you were here.'

He looks around at his neighbours. Simon gives him a tentative nod. Lollo looks down at the spruce twig she's holding. Marlene's putting her belt back on, looking the other way. When Hans's eyes meet Maine's, Maine gives him an encouraging tail wag. He turns back to Fia.

'Eh,' he says. 'I . . .'

But that's all he manages.

Fia doesn't even look at Hans. She steps forward. From her back pocket, she pulls out her phone, which she apparently kept in breach of Cassi's prohibition, and Cassi, who is now standing behind her, watches her open Google Maps. Once Fia has located their position, she turns on her phone's flashlight and walks away without saying a word. The beam from Hans's torch follows her until she disappears in the forest.

Then he turns to the group.

'Making fire in the woods. At this time of year . . .' he says, but the gravitas his voice possessed when he first appeared is fully gone.

And then, the torches go out. One after the other, just

like Pavel had said they would. 'About an hour's burn time,' he'd told her. Cassi had envisioned a grand finale, she was going to pose as the ruler of fire, able to blow them out with her mind. Why did Hans have to ruin everything?

When he turns his beam of light on her again, Cassi squints into it.

'Welcome, Hans,' she says. One of her hands is clutching a fistful of pine needles she's picked up without realising it, the other is resting on Maine's head. 'It might have been easier to book a family therapy session during office hours.'

Cassi knows she shouldn't antagonise him. She has nothing to gain from it, but right now it doesn't feel like she has much to lose either. She lets go of the pine needles, brushing her hands together. Behind her, Marlene giggles. The situation is what it is. It's perfectly conceivable that Hans might make good on his threat to call the police as soon as he gets home.

But Cassi's mind is still processing the fact that Fia is Hans's daughter. That Hans and Gretel are Fia's parents. How did she not make that connection herself? What else has she missed? She feels stupid. What kind of guru doesn't instinctively sense familial ties? She'll have to do something to impress Fia very soon.

In the meantime, Hans is looking down at his feet. He evidently doesn't even have the energy to argue with Cassi at this point.

'I thought there was a fire,' is all he says. 'I was in the kitchen and I saw the flames. I thought there was a fire.'

Only now does Cassi realise Hans is holding a fire extinguisher in one hand.

'Maybe you could lead us out of the woods?' Nadia says, taking a step forward. 'It's very dark now.'

She turns to Cassi.

'Because the séance is over, right?'

'Yes,' Cassi replies. 'It most certainly is. A bit of an abrupt ending, not the one I had planned. But energies move as energies will. As they should. It's not their job to tell us things. It's our job to interpret them.'

Hans starts walking. The others follow, taking each other's hands. At least Cassi's phone has stopped buzzing. She wonders what it is Alida wants, what could be so important. She feels a vague sense of unease and tells herself she'll call her first thing in the morning, make sure everything's good before they inevitably see each other at the Desgoffes' party.

But by the time Cassi arrives back at her house, she has already forgotten about her.

44

The lake is still and has a dull shine to it, like a mirror someone's tried to polish unsuccessfully. The water near the beach is lukewarm after a long day of good weather (and children peeing in it). Cassi spreads out a large quilted blanket – which, like so many of her possessions, is infused with the stale smell of Pavel's garage – on the grass a few metres from the water's edge. She has brought sparkling water and a punnet of strawberries, which she places in the middle of the blanket.

A group of teenage boys are hanging out on the diving platform, but other than that, everyone has left the beach for the day. Families have gone home to put lotion on their burnt shoulders and their dinner on the barbecue.

Marlene comes sauntering along with a mesh bag over her shoulder. She's dressed in a sheer pink tunic with a bikini underneath, and her knees dance as she walks.

'Any visits from the cops?' she asks in mock concern.

Cassi, who's trying to look as though she hasn't been nearly as worried as she has since the séance, shakes her head and smiles, the image of serenity and carefreeness. Marlene seems to buy it.

'That man's not right in the head,' she says. 'And even knowing that, you insist on making his wife and me reconcile.'

She has agreed to today's set-up, but is still sceptically eyeing Cassi, who in turn tries to make her smile as big as possible.

'It's going to be fine, Marlene,' Cassi says. She actually feels confident about this. Self-assured. 'Gretel's really eager for the two of you to be friends again. And wouldn't it be wonderful if you could be? Dwelling on old quarrels is not what life's about.'

Marlene doesn't reply. She drops her mesh bag onto the bedspread and takes off her tunic.

'You're a lover, Marlene, not a fighter,' Cassi says.

'You're right about that, Cassi. But Marlene has her limits,' Marlene replies. 'I'll hear her out, but I'm not making any promises.'

Marlene walks down to the water and throws herself in once it reaches her thighs. Then she swims out to the platform, gracefully heaving herself up onto it, making the teenagers crowding it part like the Red Sea. The platform bobs up and down. Marlene dives back into the lake as the teenagers whistle and clap. Ignoring them, she swims back to the beach, where she sits down and shoves a large strawberry into her mouth.

She probably isn't even aware that Cassi's studying her. Cassi tries to imagine what it would be like to be Marlene. To feel so confident in your own body and personality. To have no doubts about who you are and what you think, to just react instinctively, like an animal, to whatever's happening around you. To not care what people think about anything or anyone, about you. Isn't it the same feeling she tries to exude as a guru? How wild is it that she's managed to do it successfully?

Her thoughts are interrupted by Marlene letting out a snort.

Cassi spots Gretel walking towards them along the

water's edge, her sandals in one hand and her feet in the water. She's moving slowly, as though walking hurts or as though she's not sure she wants to get to where she's going.

Marlene turns in the opposite direction.

Cassi stands up, spreading her arms.

'Hi, Gretel, welcome!'

Gretel waves with her sandal-free hand.

'I'm not sure I can get back up if I sit down, so maybe I'd better stand,' she says. 'My hips, you know.'

Marlene immediately crosses her legs. Her knees are almost flat to the ground. She reaches her arms up, stretching first to one side, then the other.

'To each their own, sit, stand, whatever's comfortable for you,' Cassi says. She holds the strawberries out to Gretel, who takes one, but doesn't eat it, just holds it between her fingers. Cassi positions herself between the two women, so she can turn back and forth between them. She reckons she might as well dive in, so as not to give Marlene a chance to get cold feet.

'We're here today to see if the two of you can find your way back to the beautiful friendship you once shared.'

Cassi speaks solemnly, the waves in the background a great soundtrack to her inspiring speech.

'I understand that there have been feelings of betrayal in the past, but what we need to do now is look forward. To forgive, put the past behind us and move on.'

She looks at Marlene. She looks at Gretel. This is a mission she takes seriously.

'Refusing to forgive is a type of vengeance. To some, it's a defence mechanism. Sometimes, we can be under the impression that holding on to something guarantees it won't happen again.'

Marlene purses her lips, but Cassi raises an authoritative hand to pre-empt her from speaking. Cassi closes her eyes for a second. Then gets up and she resumes with newfound ardour.

'I figured that, since this is a sensitive situation, we might start by acquainting each other with our everyday lives. It will help if we understand one another, where we are in life and how we're doing. I can go first, to give you an idea of what I have in mind.'

She takes a step back, then a step forward, as though starting fresh.

'I'm Cassi,' she says, putting a hand on her heart. So far, so true. 'I woke up early this morning and went out into the forest to meditate, like I do most days. The forest makes me feel good, but today I've been thinking a lot about a friendship I want to help give new life to. It was a fairly hectic afternoon. First, I coached a client who feels stuck in a rut, then I led a tantric dance, which can be very challenging. But I'm grateful to be me. I love having the power of guiding people. Helping those who need me.'

'It was Fia, wasn't it?' Marlene asks.

Gretel's eyes dart to Marlene at the mention of her daughter.

'I obviously can't share information about my clients, Marlene,' Cassi says. 'Who would like to go next?'

Gretel stares at her. Doesn't look as though she has any desire to be part of this, but probably realises there's no way around it.

'All right, I'll go,' she says. 'I'm Gretel.' Gretel briefly moves her hand to her general chest area, before letting it dangle limply by her side again. 'I've been at work all day. There are a lot of tourists this year, which means a lot of traffic at the shop. Someone broke a glass bottle of squash in the middle of the pre-dinner rush. And I slept poorly last night, so I'm feeling pretty tired. And a bit nervous about this meeting, to be honest.'

Cassi nods to her.

'Thank you, Gretel, well done. It's so good of you to share. Marlene?'

Marlene looks up at her.

'Honestly, this is ridiculous. But, OK, fine.' Her tone is hostile but she obeys.

'I'm Marlene. I woke up when Berzan left my bed to go to work. So I haven't *slept* much either, *Gretel*!'

Gretel sighs.

'It's so hard to be you, isn't it? Always has been,' she says. Cassi is taken aback by Gretel's sudden fierceness, but tries not to let it show on her face.

Marlene continues.

'I feel grateful *every* day that I'm not stuck with some tedious old geezer like Hans. And knowing I don't have to stack jars day in and day out fills me with so much *energy*.'

Cassi intervenes.

'Marlene, I feel like you're bringing a lot of aggression into what is meant to be an open exchange.'

Gretel has turned her back to them and is now gazing out across the lake. The teenagers are still larking about on the platform, taking turns pushing each other in.

Marlene shrugs. She pulls her tunic back on over her bikini.

'I told you this was a stupid idea.'

'But what is it that makes you feel so angry?' Cassi asks.

'Why is it so hard to understand?! I'm angry because Gretel was my best friend and because she didn't hesitate for a *second* before choosing that dead-boring man over me! She just slammed every door between us shut. She stopped talking to me, for God's sake!'

Gretel turns back to them.

'It wasn't like that, and you know it. You had these insane ideas about us moving to London and making it big as artists, moving to Paris and becoming fashion designers. You wanted to go to Moscow and dance in the Red Square, then to Machu Picchu to build new temples! How does that make sense?! You were manic, Marlene. And I was married. I wanted children. I needed to sort out my life. All you did was try to make Hans leave me.'

'I don't know about manic,' Marlene mutters, also taken aback by the resentment behind Gretel's words. But she quickly bounces back, as she always does.

'We were young, Gretel! Young people are meant to *do things*! Party! Explore!'

The teenagers on the platform are watching them now. Cassi would also find this pretty entertaining if she wasn't so worried about this discussion escalating into a physical fight. She steps closer to the two women.

'In Machu Picchu?' Gretel scoffs. 'But you've never even left the county!'

'There was nothing objectionable about how I chose to live my life. It's your idea of how to live that's so mind-numbingly fucking dull.'

'It's called reality,' Gretel counters, but no one hears her, because Cassi steps in again, raising her voice.

'Marlene!' she says. 'We have to be able to stay clear of that kind of language. Let's keep the conversation dignified.'

She feels that the mediator role suits her. She just needs to lead with authority, make them talk. Her only role is to help to de-escalate the conflict without invalidating their feelings.

Gretel sighs. She lets her sandals fall to the ground and spreads her arms wide, the wind making her sleeves flap.

'Marlene, I feel like we're not going to get anywhere if we only discuss the past. What I want you to know is that I'm so sorry about how things turned out. That this has been going on for decades. You were my very best friend. I've never met anyone like you. And I miss you. I apologise from the bottom of my heart for letting you down. I'm prepared to grovel.'

Marlene picks up another strawberry and pops it in her mouth, leaves and all. Red juice trickles down her chin. She angrily wipes it with the back of her hand.

'Well, if you're going to grovel, I might as well stop yelling,' she says. 'But I'm still angry. I appreciate the apology, but it's just words. If you really care about me, you'll tell Hans we're going to be spending time together. And alone. I obviously realise the reason we're meeting here is so he won't find out,' Marlene looks up at Gretel defiantly as she delivers her final line.

Cassi can see their dynamic, who they used to be around each other before the rift, that neither one of them has changed very much. Which ought to mean reconciliation is possible. Marlene wants the stability, Gretel the impulsiveness. Neither one of them has moved on, they still miss each other.

'Forgiveness is something that happens within,' Cassi says. 'It's about achieving inner peace. It can also mean forgiving yourself.'

Marlene and Gretel stare at her blankly. They're beyond this kind of talk.

'Come by my house on Friday, we'll get shitfaced,' Marlene says. 'Like we used to. Cassi can come too, if you need a "mediator" to feel comfortable.'

She draws air quotes with her fingers. Gretel lets out a chuckle.

'OK. You're on. But I don't drink moonshine anymore.'

She smiles. Cassi smiles. Marlene doesn't.

'Moonshine? And you think I do?'

Marlene pulls out her *snus* tin and shoves a fresh pinch up under her lip.

'Though I don't turn it down when offered. I don't think it's a biggie.'

The mood's beginning to bristle again, but Cassi sees a chance to salvage the situation.

'Said the actress to the bishop?'

Marlene can't help but laugh. Gretel rolls her eyes, but Cassi can see there's new light in them. Cassi feels warm too, as if joy had sparked in her belly and spilled into her bloodstream. Maybe she's actually good at what she does. Maybe this is a sign everything has worked out. That her life is actually really, really good, and nothing will ever come close to ruining it again.

45

Cassi wakes up on her yoga mat in the living room with a giant crick in her neck. Her lips feel like sandpaper, her eyelids have been glued shut, and when she touches her head, her hair is sticky and matted together in stiff strands, thick as drinking straws.

There was a party at the Desgoffes' farm last night. That much she remembers. But she has no idea when she got home. Or how she got home. The button-down shirt with the pale blue stripes she's wearing is covered in yellow and red stains, the cuffs grimy with dirt. Her body is hurting all over – her knees and the palms of her hands look scraped and swollen.

Her phone's lying on the floor next to her, the screen cracked.

She still manages to respond with a ♥ to Pavel's *Good morning, my star*.

Cassi tries to stand up, and both her head and her body protest. She takes a sip from the glass sitting next to her without knowing what the clear liquid is, hoping for water. It turns out to be wine. She must have continued drinking when she got home.

She pathetically crawls over to the bed and lies down. Stretched out on her back, with her head on the pillow, she closes her eyes, her gut screaming at her that something has gone very, very wrong.

*

The next time she wakes up is several hours later. Her heart is thrumming with anxiety. There's dirt and mud on the sheets now. Her muscles are still sore.

She manages to rinse off in the shower, change into clean clothes and put her hair up. She also manages to drink a glass of water, take a double dose of painkillers and feed the dog. She then sits in the beach chair with Maine on her lap, trying to focus on a podcast she's been listening to about a charismatic cult leader. She tries not to think about anything other than the pine trees and the clouds dancing above them.

But then a rusty red pickup turns into her driveway, Fia waving at her from the driver's seat.

Cassi has no memory of scheduling a session. She can feel that her new life was somehow altered last night, but can't put too much thought into it now. She remains seated as Maine goes over to say hi. Cassi pulls her cardigan tighter around herself instead and gets up, too.

Fia has climbed out of her car and squatted down, going so far as to let the dog lick her face.

'Hiya,' Fia says after standing back up, as Maine trots back to Cassi. 'You all right?'

'I'm grand, thank you,' Cassi lies, wishing she could believe it. 'Quite a night last night.'

'Yes, I imagine it was a late one for most people. I left early, though. I don't like it when everyone gets super drunk. People always seem to go insane. Did you stay long?'

Cassi's not in the mood. Maine takes up position right next to her, as though he can sense he's needed for emotional, moral, physical support. She shakes her head slightly. Cassi wishes she'd left early too. It was the plan, but it seems she abandoned it. If you've decided to live a lie, you have to keep at it meticulously and never let your guard down. She fears she might have yesterday. All she knows for sure is that her head is scrambled, her body feels shaky, and nausea is churning in the back of her chest.

'Give me a minute, I'll get set up,' she says, heading back into the kitchen. Maybe a teeny, tiny helping of hair of the dog?

Fia replies: 'No rush on my account.' She takes out a stick and throws it towards the forest. Maine looks at the stick, then at Fia. Then he lies down.

'But I'm annoyed I left my phone at the party,' she says to Cassi through the open door. 'I feel completely cut off from the world! I have to stop by the Desgoffes' later – I couldn't exactly go before work.'

Cassi finds the yoga mat and spreads it out on the grass. Being outside in the open air feels easier.

Fia lies down on it. The grass smells freshly cut and the sun's warm, but not clingy. Fia closes her eyes, places her folded hands on her stomach, smiles a big smile. Her shirt comes up a little, revealing a fresh tattoo, a crooked smiley face grinning cross-eyed on her abdomen. The skin around it is red and angry.

'Let's begin with silence,' Cassi says.

She needs to get in the right mindset, and to try to recall what they talked about the last time Fia came by. Something about her moving to Oslo and the people she lived with there. Cassi has thought more than once that she should start taking notes after her sessions to aid her memory, as her clientele keeps growing. But it's still little more than an idea.

And besides, she feels she ought to be able to keep it all in her head. Just over year ago, she was known for her excellent memory, she never missed a thing. It was her job not to. And maybe it's still her job, but things are the way they are.

Cassi walks a few laps around Fia. Counterclockwise, then clockwise when she starts to feel dizzy. She opens and closes her hands. When she notices that Fia has opened her eyes and is watching her, she finishes her pacing off with some large circular arm movements before taking a seat by Fia's head. She covers Fia's eyes with her hand.

Cassi counts down from twenty in a mumbling voice.

Then she starts humming an improvised melody. How long can she drag this out before it becomes too obvious she's stalling?

'All right,' she says at last, putting her hands on Fia's shoulders as a sign for her to go ahead.

'I've been talking to my magic rock,' Fia says, patting her jeans pocket.

Right, the stone. Cassi can see the bulge by Fia's hip, just below the wonky tattoo.

Cassi makes a vague sound of encouragement.

'Do you feel the stone's helped you?' she asks. 'Has it fulfilled its purpose in guiding you?'

Fia wrinkles her nose but keeps her eyes closed.

'Honestly, yeah, maybe,' she says. 'I think it's helped me be more confident when talking to people.'

Cassi makes vague noises. She can barely bring herself to listen, that sunken feeling in her stomach, like freefalling in a dream, is refusing to subside. It can't just be because she's hungover. Did she do something stupid last night? Did she do something inappropriate? Was Hans there?

Fia keeps talking. Cassi tries to focus. It's another Oslo story. About work and relationships. Fia filmed a documentary about her friends, she was dating a guy who wanted to put it on TV.

Cassi can feel herself zoning out. Flashes from the night before start to resurface.

46

No one has ever felt better than she does in this very moment.

'The Real Slim Shady' plays in Cassi's earbuds as she pulls her bike from its resting place by the wall and pedals off to the party. She's not usually the type to listen to music while cycling. Not since high school, when a classmate was hit by a dustcart while – according to his still-functional MP3-player – listening to the previous year's Eurovision winner on repeat. But Cassi is making an exception tonight. She feels practically invincible after the past few days. It's been success after success. Business is booming. Since telling Pavel her story, she's also realised it no longer controls her. This means she's able to move on. Like, truly move on. She's free.

She's even resurrected herself in the Smoke Signal group chat. Andrea had written something about an awful date she'd been on, and Cassi suddenly broke her long silence with an idyllic picture of her cottage in the sun, Maine on the front steps. That triggered a cascade of messages from the other three. She's read them all but has yet to reply. All in good time.

The village gleams golden in the late-summer sun. The sweet scent of the forest, the balmy temperature and the absence of traffic give Cassi a boost of confidence.

When she finally arrives at the farm, she feels like she's

beaming too. Everyone else is dressed up, while Cassi's wearing her usual denim shorts and sandals. Her cotton button-down shirt is, like so many other things, a relic from Pavel's garage. She has a wreath on her head, made from leftover flowers she'd picked for Lollo, which she hopes people will appreciate with the right level of intoxication.

She locks her bike against the fence of the alpaca enclosure. She grabs her handmade bouquet and turns around with a smile, ready to be received with the enthusiasm she deserves. The mood's already lively, she can tell. Summer hits are blasting out of a speaker in the kitchen window. Simon's swaying by the grill, dressed in a Hawaiian shirt and pale linen trousers, surrounded by men Cassi's not sure she's met. They turn to look at her. She winks at them. Over by the house, there's a huge canopy tent that hosts a buffet table laden with drinks and crisps and several long tables covered by white tablecloths. Cassi salivates at the sight of canapés and giant bowls of tangy, golden potato salad, but resists the temptation to fix herself a plate. Serving herself first in front of everyone wouldn't work for her brand.

Marlene spots her first and greets her with a kiss on both cheeks and a sloshing plastic cup in either hand. She spins around so that her short red dress twirls around her, exposing her toned legs. She then hands Cassi one of the drinks, pushing her sunglasses up.

'Have you heard what's happened?' she says. 'After our session by the lake, I gave myself a pep talk and called my daughter to congratulate her on her new job. It turns out that made her happy. I thought she'd be furious. But she invited me to come visit!'

Cassi's eyes go wide.

'That's incredible, Marlene! I'm so happy for you!'

And she genuinely is. But it's nothing compared to Marlene. Marlene does a little dance, puckering her lips at two men passing by on their way to the grill.

Lollo comes over, throwing her arms around Cassi. She's dressed in a pink floral maxi dress and has daisies in her long hair, which is styled in a half-up-half-down ponytail, meticulously casual as always.

'You're here, finally!' she says, grabbing Cassi's shoulders. Her eyes look glazed and sparkly.

Cassi hands over her bouquet – if a few anaemic flowers and wooden sticks can be called that.

'A ceremonial summer bouquet,' she says. 'It will bring success, fertility and joy, and once it dries, you should throw it in the firepit and dance as it burns.'

Cassi bows.

Lollo turns the bouquet this way and that, looking thrilled. She touches the leaves, picking a few and sticking them in her mouth, smiling mischievously. Then she takes Cassi by the hand and drags her over to the buffet.

'What would you like? You need a drink. It's tradition.'

Without giving Cassi the time to ask what tradition that may be, Lollo picks up a glass and fills it halfway with thick liquid from a large plastic jug, which she tops off with some kind of fizzy drink before handing the glass to Cassi.

'Cheers! To success and friendship!'

'Or maybe the other way around,' Cassi says, since correcting Lollo is what she does. Lollo nods, but doesn't look browbeaten, the way she would have if she'd been sober.

Cassi sips her drink. The alcohol content is high enough to make her cough. It occurs to her that without having given it any real thought, she's been sober for several days. It kind of feels regressive to start drinking now, but she can sense she's going to need it at this party. Anyway, she's planning to leave early. She's not comfortable drinking in public. That's something she does alone.

'There are a lot of people here I want to introduce you to. I've told everyone so much about you!'

Alida watches them from the corner of the house. Cassi meets her eyes and feels bad for not returning her phone calls. She meant to, but something always came up. Cassi wants to hide behind Lollo, but she can tell from Alida's stare that this isn't the time for jokes.

Alida walks over. She's holding a bowl of peanuts and is clearly chewing a handful. Her jaw moves furiously as her eyes dart between the two women.

'I have a bone to phhwick with you,' she slurs in Cassi's direction, which feels a bit awkward, not only because of Cassi's plans for a carefree night of mingling, but also given Alida's history of drug abuse and her recent sobriety. Has she fallen off the wagon? Alida makes a fist, a single finger jutting out, in case it was unclear who she had a bone to *phhwick* with.

'But first, I need to hit the head.'

Alida storms towards the front door.

'Should she really be . . . ?' Cassi starts to say, but then realises Lollo has not been paying attention. She puts her arm around Cassi's shoulders, pointing at someone standing in a group of people, someone Cassi can't see. Cassi waves at no one in particular and knocks back her drink, promising herself to take it slow from now on. Maybe she can even slip out before Alida finds her again.

Marlene is back, empty-handed this time, and kisses Cassi on the shoulder, leaving lipstick marks on her shirt. She laughs.

'Isn't it weird that Strasbourg's in France when it sounds so German? SHTRASSBURRG!'

Then she's gone again, making a runner for the grill, yelling: 'Siiiimon, is that a tiny lighter you have in your pocket or are you just happy to see me?'

Further away, Cassi sees Fia waving at her, raising her glass in a toast.

'I was sober this morning, but it's being taken care of,' Fia hollers.

Cassi toasts her back with her empty glass. Her head's crackling. It's been a long time since she was last at a party. The buzz of it fills her with energy. It's as though reality's morphing into a rapidly changing kaleidoscope, the colours warped, sparkling. The booze might have something to do with it, too.

Lollo pulls her into the tent and over to a group of people at the far end of one of the long tables. It's Lollo's 'old work gang' from the city, a besuited, slightly more under-control troupe keeping to themselves, standing slightly apart. Lollo introduces Cassi as 'my completely incredible yoga instructor and life coach. You should have seen the magical bouquet she brought! She's the local shaman!'

Cassi smiles a smile she feels would look both intriguing and friendly.

'I watched your live-stream yoga session,' says a woman

in a crisp button-down shirt and a party hat. 'It was fun! Really . . . different.'

She smiles at Cassi. Cassi feels irritated by the snarky tone in which she said 'different', but she bows nonetheless, the need to stay in character more important than her pride.

'It's an honour to meet any friends of Lollo,' she says mildly. 'It's beautiful to see that you would travel so far for an old friend.'

They smile, looking flattered, but don't quite seem to know what to say to her. That's life when you're a shaman. Some people shy away when confronted with that kind of power. Part of the challenge of the profession, Cassi muses, is exactly that, knowing how to handle the expectations and prejudices of this world.

'Wine?' someone asks, having noticed her glass is empty, holding up a bottle they've brought.

'Please, but only a little,' she hears herself answer. 'I'm not usually a big drinker.'

It seems her plan to take it slow lasted for about a minute. But at this point, she tells herself, it's a matter of survival. This time, getting drunk isn't just what she has to do to endure. It's a way to blend in. But she *is* going to leave early, she is.

A drinking game is in full swing at the other long table, and over by the tyre swing Simon seems to be trying to head off a fight. Marlene is dancing with a man Cassi's never seen before, her face turned away, and by the house, Alida's slowly walking down the front steps, carrying two cases of beer. She manages to balance them all the way over to the buffet table, setting them down without having dropped a single can.

Cassi tries to keep her attention on Lollo's friends. The wine's beginning to loosen them up, and they ask if she can read palms.

'Of course,' she says, since it's preferable to making small talk. She downs the rest of her wine and hops to it.

Cassi's three palms in, and a small group of onlookers have gathered to watch her, when Simon enters the tent with a large platter of grilled sausages. He sets it down next to the potato salad and puts his arm around Lollo, who has danced up to him with a microphone in her hand, happy to be the centre of attention. She pulls her hair out from under his arm, then claps her hands and whistles.

She clears her throat theatrically and launches into a welcome speech.

'Dear friends and neighbours, welcome to our summer party. It's become quite a tradition by now! We're so happy you're here! New for this year is, as you can see, a karaoke mic! Do-re-mi-fa-so-la-ti-dooooooo!'

Lollo may be pretending to be drunker than she is, but she's truly giving it her all.

'Fia, promise you'll give us a chance to hear your lovely voice! And I promise I'll try to keep Simon from rapping.'

Lollo winks and raises her glass to Simon, who makes a clumsy peace sign in return.

'I also want to remind everybody that the toilet's to the RIGHT when you enter the house, not the left. Last year, someone took a wrong turn and I'd love for that not to be repeated. To the RIGHT! But now, it's time to say dig in, everyone! Eat, drink, dance, snog – let's do this! Woo-hoo!'

Lollo raises her glass in a victory salute and everyone cheers. Wine, beer and mixers are raised and lowered, people flock to the tent and sit down, the smell of grilled meat and spices dense in the air. Marlene walks over to Lollo and asks to borrow the microphone.

'A doctor?' she says into it, her lips so close they rasp against the metal. 'Is there a doctor?'

Then Alida turns the music back up and the intro to 'Money for Nothing' thumps out across the fields so loud that the alpacas bolt, disappearing off to the far end of their enclosure.

Marlene knocks back her wine.

'No one?! All right,' she says, sitting the microphone down and walking over to Cassi. 'I've never slept with a doctor! Might be nice with a man who knows his way around the female anatomy!'

Cassi laughs and shakes her head before turning her attention to Berzan and Max, who are talking about weight training.

'We need top-ups,' Max notes.

Cassi turns to the drink table and her eyes fall on a bottle of vodka with just enough shots left in it.

'We're out of shot glasses,' she says. 'Sorry in advance!'

She grabs the vodka bottle in one hand, a bottle of soda in the other and takes a swig from each in quick succession. Berzan watches her with delight, then holds his hands out to take the bottles and does the same thing. Max laughs. Berzan gives him the bottles, and he then hands them back to Cassi. Dizziness pumps in her bloodstream. She's not been this drunk in ages. She feels feral.

'Check this out!' Cassi says.

She takes a mouthful of vodka and a mouthful of fizzy drink, then grabs the back of Berzan's head and presses her lips against his, pushing the foaming mixture from her own mouth into his. He takes it, but then leans forward and laughs, some of the drink dribbling from his lips.

Cassi feels embarrassed. This is *so* far outside of her comfort zone. She's not used to spirits.

Max is getting ready to follow suit and has her in his crosshairs, but Cassi dodges his attempt, and he swallows instead. She points to the food.

'Wanna go get something to eat?'

The three of them manage to get separated during the short walk over to the table. Cassi goes straight for Marlene, who's dancing with herself while enjoying generous spoonfuls of potato salad straight from a serving bowl.

'Marlene! Why are you all alone?' Cassi says, her volume higher than expected, picking an abandoned hotdog up from the table. She smothers it with ketchup and fried onions before eating half of it in one bite.

Marlene licks the serving spoon she's holding, gesturing towards the seated group.

'Pretty disappointing selection, honestly. Been there, done that,' she says, pointing vaguely at various people. 'Unless one of Lollo's old mates turns out to be more fun than they look.'

Cassi finishes her hotdog. The floor sways before her eyes. Marlene serves herself another helping of potato salad from the bowl, says yes to wine when Cassi holds up a bottle and two empty glasses she's just found. They drink them in one gulp before topping themselves up.

Marlene throws an arm around Cassi, her breath hot in her ear.

'Tell me something, Cassi.'

Cassi looks at Marlene. Her eyes are suddenly filled with tears.

'How am I supposed to find the courage to go to France? How?'

'You can do it. You're going to be fine,' Cassi replies. 'People go abroad all the time. I'll help you.'

Marlene takes Cassi's hand, raises it to her cheek.

'I like you so much, Cassi. You're such a wonderful friend.'

She cocks her head.

'But why is Alida staring at you like that?'

Cassi shrugs, refusing to turn around and face Alida. She has a bad feeling about this. She really should go home, but somehow her glass seems to have refilled itself. 'Pata Pata' starts blasting out of the speakers. Marlene lets out a whoop, ready to go again after her quick display of emotion. She sees someone she knows on the dancefloor and says: 'So long, sister' to Cassi before sashaying away.

Lollo calls her from her chair further down the table, where she's sitting with more people Cassi doesn't know.

'Cassi! Come here! We have big plans for you!'

Cassi downs the rest of her wine. Tops herself up – yes, again – and goes over. The alcohol-fuelled kaleidoscope in front of her is changing at an ever-faster pace, the colours increasingly garish. Cassi's insides are cheering, it feels like the entire party's about her. Everyone wants to be near the guru. And why wouldn't they? They are lucky to be in her radiant presence.

Hours that feel like minutes pass. Cassi saves someone's relationship. She performs what she calls an 'energy transfer'. She predicts the future by reading leftover food. She initiates a dance circle, in which each member takes a turn in the middle, and is ecstatic when seemingly everyone at the party joins in cheering her when it's her turn. She slow dances with Marlene. She agrees to something waltz-like with Max, but when his hands begin to wander, she says she needs the loo.

Cassi thinks to herself that she should go get her bike and go home, and yet her legs take her into the house. Loo – she needs the loo. Through the door and to the right.

But before she reaches it, she's stopped by a loud 'oy!'.

Alida is sitting on the hallway floor with her back against the wall. She's holding a half-eaten sausage, a mustard stain in the corner of her mouth.

'You fucking cow,' Alida hisses. 'You've been avoiding me, Cassi. I've called. I've texted. Why don't you answer? You bitch. If that's even your real name.'

Cassi wants to tell her she's never claimed her name to be 'bitch', but the aggression has taken her by surprise and it's most definitely not time for jokes. She's upset with Alida for wanting to kill the joy bubbling inside her. That's what Alida is: a killjoy! Cassi's mind replays every interaction they've ever had, moments flash before her eyes, bright and distorted. Her take on the situation is that this is all about jealousy. That Alida has managed to build up some ridiculous fantasy involving Cassi and Berzan, and that falling off the wagon has exacerbated her aggression. Cassi would do anything to go back to her night of partying.

She squats down next to Alida with unsteady legs. She

takes a deep breath. She needs to be understanding and stern.

'Alida. This may sound harsh. But you have to pull yourself together.'

At least she doesn't have to put on a front to say those words. Every part of her means them. Cassi holds out a hand to help Alida back onto her feet.

'Stand up, wipe your face, finish your sausage.'

A *Sliding Doors* scenario pops into her head. If she'd gone through with her pregnancy three years ago, it might have led her to utter that same exact sentence, in this exact moment, to someone else. The person in front of her now is very different from a defiant two-year-old, but is unexpectedly obedient. Alida obeys and gets up, wiping her mouth with her T-shirt.

'I've told you so many times I need to talk to you,' she says. 'And every time, you've ignored me.'

She pulls out her phone, chopping the air in front of her with it.

'This really isn't the time, Alida,' Cassi breaks in. 'But how about tomorrow morning? You could come by?'

'You're always putting everything off,' Alida snaps. 'You're not listening to me! But if you refuse to listen, I'm going to tell the others instead. They deserve to know.'

She drops the last piece of her sausage on Lollo's pristine floor and heads for the door.

'But there's nothing between me and Berzan!' Cassi calls after her. 'We're just friends. There's nothing to tell!'

Alida is already outside, marching towards the crowd, and Cassi has no desire to run after her. It feels too undignified. She'll have to sort it out tomorrow.

Cassi picks the sausage off the floor and throws it in the bin. On the kitchen counter, she finds both wine bottles and glasses and before she knows it, she's poured herself one and raised a solitary toast. Large pies and bowls of whipped cream are waiting to be carried outside. Giggling, Cassi finds a spoon, digs into the middle of one of the pies, and scoops out a large piece. Welcoming the tangy, sweet taste that explodes in her mouth, as well as the seemingly first moment of silence she's had all day, she walks over to the big window to observe the party. The long tables look like a drunken version of that one Jesus-dinner painting by Leonardo da Vinci, only with Lollo holding court in the middle, singing a drinking song while standing on her chair, her hair wild across her face. Microphone in one hand, phone in the other, filming herself and her audience. It's a beautiful scene.

Cassi almost feels sentimental when she's struck by how much her life has changed. How good she has it. The kind of turn things have taken, how everything's fallen into place. To think that all these people are her friends. Someone like Lollo would have never befriended her a few months ago, but now Cassi is the main attraction. This is her life now. Not always easy, but inspiring and varied.

Lollo accepts her guests' applause. Cassi laughs to herself, raising her glass as if she was out there with them. She digs through her back pocket for her phone to commemorate this triumphant moment for Lollo. What a good friend she is!

When Cassi looks at the screen, she notices a text from Alida, received over an hour ago. It's a picture and it opens at the exact moment the music is cut as the result of a quarrel over the loudspeaker.

'Give it here,' she hears Alida say into the microphone that Lollo would prefer to keep. There's a tug of war, which Alida wins.

Cassi's internal bliss is quickly replaced by mounting panic.

When she steps out onto the front porch, Alida has just regained her balance after climbing onto the main table. She stands up there, feet planted wide, eyes wild, her hair a halo of radioactive candyfloss around her head. She points to Cassi, making everyone at the party turn to look at her. Cassi can't breathe. She knows what's about to happen but she can't stop it, it's as if she were watching it happen to someone else.

Her life is about to be smashed to pieces again, only this time, in front of a live audience. A very drunk one.

47

No one has ever felt worse than she does in this very moment.

The memories from the previous night come flooding in, turning Cassi's insides into ice. She gulps loudly, pushing down the bile that's risen in her throat. She wants to explode or maybe implode (less messy), right here and now.

Fia doesn't notice and continues talking.

'But my guy friend, who I did have some kind of feelings for, took me out for a walk. He made me feel better again, helped me see what really matters. "This is all we need", he said. "A couple of cigarettes, a cup of coffee, and a bit of conversation. You and me and fifty *kroner*."'

Nope, that doesn't add up either. Cassi's neurons feel paralysed, but apparently her brain has the ability to function on several levels at once, at least in certain areas, and now it's telling her something's wrong. There's not a chance you could buy coffee *and* cigarettes for fifty *kroner* in Oslo.

Besides, Cassi has heard this story before. Has she become clairvoyant? She helplessly casts about for an explanation. Fia keeps talking about something her friend did.

'And then his dad died?' Cassi asks. 'And you went on to be with him?'

Fia breaks off. Looks up at Cassi with her eyebrows raised and a tentative smile.

It's not the first time something's felt off about Fia. Not wrong exactly, not weird, just a few degrees off. Cassi hasn't been able to put her finger on what it is. She's wondered if it's the age difference, or just their different backgrounds. Or if it could be something as simple as Cassi's complete lack of counselling experience.

Fia sits up. The vibe in the clearing is deflated.

'Fine,' she admits. 'That wasn't entirely true.'

Cassi should be enraged but feels nothing.

'*Reality Bites*, right? Possibly not the best film to go with when talking to a woman my age,' she says. She doesn't have the energy to feel disrespected. Soon enough, Fia will find out about last night, so why even bother.

'Has everything you've told me been from films?'

Fia looks away.

'No,' she says, looking up to meet Cassi's eyes.

She pulls her shoulders up towards her cheeks.

'There were TV shows too.'

Cassi nods. Of course Fia's lying. The whole world's a lie. Nothing's real. And she's the biggest liar of them all.

Fia continues.

'I just feel like talking to someone is the right thing to do. Everyone does it. But my life's so dull, I have nothing to talk about. Nothing ever happens at the Village Shop, not much happens at all, really. Before I started coming here, I went over things I could present as my issue, you know, what kind of "internal wounds" I might have. Call me crazy, but I have nothing I need to process. No scars. No anxiety. So I've talked about other things.'

There's a brief pause.

'It's nice to lie here and talk. It's uncomplicated, I don't have to perform, I can relax. It's peaceful. And I like it when you talk. You say wise things. Things I have thought about but didn't have the courage to admit to myself.'

Cassi wants to cry. If her new life hadn't crashed and burned last night, this would have been one of her favourite sessions ever.

'For a while, I thought about pretending that I wanted to discuss my relationship with Berzan, or my dad, but those things are so uninteresting to me,' Fia continues. 'I get that they might sound like something to talk about, like me dating a guy who's sleeping with every woman in the county, but honestly, if anyone has issues, it's him. Why are you only allowed space to vent if you're depressed or anxious? Why does everything have to be so serious all the time?'

To Cassi, this all sounds perfectly reasonable. But Fia's not done yet. Maybe she sensed her fiction wouldn't be able to fly under the radar forever. Maybe the words have been dormant in her, longing for this moment. The sentences pour out of her.

'What I like best is staying in, watching a film. The kind where things look hairy for a bit, but you know everything's going to work out in the end. Lawyers. Tom Cruise. Not action, exactly, but a bit of action. I want to do whatever I want. I don't want to have to change for anyone else, unless I choose to.'

She pauses briefly.

'When I was younger, so much of life was about fitting in. Having the right hairdo at school. Staying on people's good side. Making sure not to provoke Dad at home. No, don't make that face, I don't mean in a horrible way, it was never like that, he's just grumpy, you know? I don't like it. I like when things are easy. Comfortable.'

'He seems a bit . . . complicated, your dad,' Cassi says. 'I'm not surprised there's been tension between the two of you.' She tries to go easy on Hans, but there's so much more she could say.

Fia looks sceptical, turning her head to the side.

'Fine. But to me, it's not that interesting. It probably looks more intense from the outside. Oooh, a father shunning his daughter. It's the kind of thing people like to gossip about, I get that. But that's not what my reality looks like. He's just a surly person. He wants everything to be his way. He named me Sofia because it means "wisdom". He'd always tell me that when I was little, but it's not for him to dictate what I should be, if I should be smart or dumb. So, when I was thirteen, I decided to change my name to Fia. Why let that old grouch rule my life? I don't think arguing with him is worth the effort. But I'm not going to roll over either. I've got nothing to apologise for. I don't give a shit.'

She stands up. Cassi tries to do the same, but wobbles and has to sit back down.

'How are you feeling anyway?' Fia asks. 'You look a bit peaky.'

She holds out a hand, pulls Cassi to her feet.

'Did my bluff break you?' she continues with a smile. 'Look, don't take it personally. I'm here because I like you. I like talking to you. Sorry I made stuff up. It's really not that deep.'

Cassi tries to return the smile, shaking her head.

'No, no, don't worry about it,' she says. 'But I actually don't feel great. Maybe I'm coming down with something. I think we'll have to leave it there for today.'

They walk over to Fia's car. There are no more words to say, so Fia climbs in and drives off.

Swallows warble high above the treetops. Maine sleeps on the front steps. Cassi finds her cracked phone next to him. Notifications of missed calls and texts blur in front of her eyes, her lungs feel like they might catch on fire. She decides to not bother reading them – what's the use? Everyone knows she's a fraud. Her new, wonderful and fulfilling life is over before she's had a chance to enjoy it.

She sits back down in the beach chair, waiting for what's to come.

48

The party has gone silent. Alida's standing on the table, empty glasses and dirty plates at her feet.

'Turn down the music,' she says into the mic. She waits a few seconds, but nothing happens. Then she shouts the same thing, so loudly that her voice breaks and the loudspeaker growls.

Simon rushes over to pause 'Dancing Queen', which was just getting going.

Everyone has turned away from Cassi again, now they're staring at Alida. She looks hesitant up there. Not used to being in the spotlight, uncomfortable with it, but she pulls herself together. Taps the microphone lightly to make sure it still works. Then she raises her eyes, looking straight at Cassi.

'That one,' Alida says, pointing. 'Cassi. She's not who she says she is. She's a *complete fucking fraud.*'

Lollo tries to take the mic from Alida but can't reach it. She grabs Alida's ankle and says: 'Come back down, we can talk in there instead,' but Alida kicks her hand away with her foot, hitting a plastic cup full of red wine in the process, every last drop of its contents ending up on Lollo's dress. And if that wasn't enough, Alida hisses at Lollo like some prehistoric lizard.

Then she says: 'Stop. Everyone needs to hear this.'

It's so quiet now you could hear a pin drop.

'Hey,' Cassi says, in a voice she doesn't recognise, a voice that sounds both shrill and feeble, a voice she doesn't want to be associated with. 'I think Alida's fallen off the wagon tonight.'

It's a desperate attempt to draw focus away from what the woman is about to reveal. But it's the truth too. Surely everyone at this party's hammered, surely no one's going to take her seriously?

Alida's eyes darken in response, black holes of fury.

'You really suck, Cassi, you know that?! What are you talking about? I've been sober for nine months. It's the reason I'm able to stand here today!'

They lock eyes. Cassi realises Alida's telling the truth. That the drunkenness she noticed in Alida's behaviour was all in her mind, that she's chosen to interpret reality in a way that suited her. Cassi's about to say something but is pre-empted by Marlene who, in her Marlene way, is starting to get restless.

'Fine, Alida, so what has she done? Don't just stand there. Tell us. Some of us are trying to party.'

Cassi can tell Marlene doesn't take Alida seriously. Smiling, she turns back to the man she was talking to, one of Lollo's former coworkers, and raises her glass with a wink.

Alida holds her phone close to her face.

'Everyone deserves to know who she really is.'

Cassi starts walking towards her. Who she really is. Who is she, really? By now, not even Cassi knows. Has she ever known? Does anyone?

Alida looks at Cassi but Cassi can't – won't – react.

'Our *genius* Cassi over there, she's not a guru,' Alida spits out the last word. 'She's not a therapist. She knows *nothing* about any of the stuff she talks about. She's played all of us for fools. She works at a restaurant. She's nothing but a waitress.'

Is that a murmur rippling through the crowd? No, probably not, it's probably just the ringing in Cassi's ears growing louder, making her feel like her head is about to fall off her body.

She starts running. Crossing the gravel, sprinting up the road. It's not a pretty sight nor a dignified experience. Cassi falls and pushes herself back up, keeps running. She can still feel everyone's eyes on her, and it's only when she's almost home that she remembers she left her bike at Lollo's. But there's no chance of her going back now.

There's one thing she wishes she could correct Alida on. She wasn't a waitress. She was a restaurant manager.

49

Once Fia leaves, it feels like reality as Cassi knows it ceases to exist.

She quickly finds herself back in front of the kitchen cabinet where she's kept her wine ever since she moved into the house. The alcohol has been there for her before, and it will be again.

She locks herself inside with Maine, and if anyone does come by during the days that follow, which is not necessarily the case because it's become unclear what's real and what's a product of her imagination, she pretends she's not home. The front door only opens when Maine scratches, needing to go outside. The only texts Cassi opens and replies to are Pavel's *Good morning, my star.*

Her mind races like when you have a fever or have accidentally binge-watched several seasons of a reality TV show too quickly. Characters and events blend together, confrontations and conflicts melt into one another in a never-ending loop. How she feels ought rightfully to upend the laws of physics. How she feels ties itself in knots. How she feels makes Einstein's theory of relativity seem uncomplicated. It is, plainly put, impossible to describe in the words of human language.

Not that she's even trying.

Most of the time, Cassi's convinced she needs to do another runner. Leave everything behind again and get out of Bäcken. It's a familiar impulse. It's what she usually does. It would be easy. Get away, and quickly, before everyone she's met here is standing outside her door, yelling, crying, possibly demanding their money back. Could they report her to the police? Should she flee across the border to Norway and, if so, how do extradition treaties work? How far can she go before the police catch her? She can already picture it, her and Maine in the car, racing through the forest, a line of police vans trailing behind them like a slithering, flashing blue tapeworm.

But the fact is it's not hypothetical emergency vehicles that worry her the most. Her most abject feelings are associated with what Pavel's going to think when he hears about this. Does he already know? Should she call him? Shouldn't he have come to see her? But what if no one's told him? Would he be disappointed or furious? Should she smash her phone so no one else can reach her? She doesn't have an answer to these questions. Everything is a mess of gigantic proportions and she's caught in the middle of it, right in the eye of the tornado.

She thinks about everyone she's met since coming to Bäcken, everyone who's trusted her, confided in her. This is just like the nightmares she's been having, only much, much worse. There's no waking up from this. The only thing she can do is put the pedal to the metal and leave all of it in the rearview mirror. She can't bear even the thought of looking them in the eye.

Days pass and her blind remains closed. Sometimes, she hears tyres on the gravel outside, but that only makes her lie even more still in her bed. She confines herself to the bedroom, only leaving it when she needs to fetch more wine and use the loo. Since she'd been cutting back on her drinking, her reserves weren't sufficient to begin with, and it's getting to a point where she'll be out of it very soon. But she can't think about that yet. It'll have to work until it doesn't.

So many things to think about, so many things to sort out. Could she talk Pavel into running away with her? No, he wouldn't go. Not while Karl-Adam's still alive.

But then, maybe, after that? Karl-Adam's very old. Of questionable health. If Cassi can hold on just a while longer, keep to the house, keep calm, things might be all right. She's used to being alone, she can handle living like a hermit while waiting for Pavel to be ready. Eventually he might agree to start a new life with her somewhere else. If she broaches the subject the right way. Somewhere by the sea, maybe? They could move south. To a different country? Someplace warmer?

The shame hits her as she imagines cracking open a cold beer with Pavel in the Costa del Sol. Here she is, fantasising, by extension, about Karl-Adam's death. She truly is a horrible person.

Cassi squeezes the last few drops out of the boxed wine straight into her mouth, cursing herself for not being more diligent about her supplies. She thought she'd built a new life for herself, working her way up from rock-bottom, transforming into something new, something better. But now she's alone again. Exposed as a fraud. And this time, she has no one else to blame, there's no grand betrayal. It's all her own doing.

She's forced to fetch the last of her reserves, her mother's old silver flask, from its hiding place in the planter. It's like she's on the edge of a familiar abyss, about to throw herself in fully. The flask is covered in potting soil. The cork has ended up crooked and won't come out. She works on it until the bottle feels warm to the touch. She throws it against the wall with a loud grunt, leaving a dent in the wallpaper, and the cork finally pops out. Lukewarm vodka pours out onto the floor.

50

She's woken up at what feels like the crack of dawn by the sharp ringing of her phone.

The man on the other end introduces himself as 'Nathan from Green Grove'. It takes her a few seconds, and for him to mention the name 'Karl-Adam', to make the connection. In her hungover daze, she has to ask him to repeat himself several times.

'Oh, sure, so, I'm calling you because I realised we don't have Pavel's number,' Nathan says. 'Kalle's deteriorated overnight, it's been a bit touch and go, so I think it might be good if the two of you, or just Pavel, could come by. It might be time to say goodbye.'

Cassi sits up. Panic sinks its claws into her. It's a different kind of panic compared to the one she's lived with the past few days – how many has it even been? – since the Desgoffes' party. This kind is pure, overwhelming, alive.

'I'll go get Pavel, we'll be there soon,' is all she says before hanging up and running to the bathroom to throw up last night's wine.

She tries to call Pavel, but he doesn't answer, so she sends him a text saying she's on her way, that he should get ready to go see Karl-Adam. She somehow finds the energy to pull on her shorts, find a clean sweater in the piles that lie all over the bedroom floor, grab Maine's collar and lead and shove the dog into the back seat. She throws up one more time, leaning against the car door, but quickly pulls herself together.

It's a beautiful morning, the forest lush and bright green, the air clean and warm. Cassi's headache is excruciating. She can barely breathe as she drives to Pavel's. She rolls down all the windows, letting the wind whip around her. For her, it's a matter of survival, but to Maine, who takes the opportunity to stick his head out the window, this is pure enjoyment.

She has no idea whether Pavel knows that she's a fraud yet. Maybe not? He might have been holed up at home taking care of his vegetable patch all this time.

She tries to drown her thoughts. She'll find out in due course. Within minutes, most likely. But she won't be the one to bring it up. He can talk about it if he wants to, and in a way, it might be good if he did, it would probably be healthier for him to be angry at her than sad about what's happening to Karl-Adam, if you can even call death something that happens rather than something that simply is.

Her mind is spinning. It's a swirl of messy thoughts chasing each other's tails so there's no room to think about anything real, anything important, and she's about to turn into Pavel's driveway, but he's already waiting by the side of the road, and oops, she almost runs him over. He jumps out of the way, she slams on the brakes, coming to an abrupt stop. Without a word, he climbs in and shuts the door. She doesn't say anything either, just sets off again.

Many minutes pass. They make it all the way to the motorway before Pavel asks if it's OK if they close the windows. She nods, pushing the buttons on her side of the door. Now she can tell him about the phone call. Pavel asks what happened, but Cassi realises she didn't ask Nathan any follow-up questions. They just have to get there.

They're minutes away when Nathan calls again. Cassi's too scared to answer, but Pavel isn't, he swipes a finger across Cassi's cracked screen and holds the phone to his ear. Cassi's afraid to breathe, but it's not long before Pavel looks at her with a teary smile and she knows it's not the end. He hangs up.

'Things are looking better,' he says. 'I think Nathan overreacted a little. He apologised. Karl-Adam's having breakfast now.'

A sob escapes Cassi, bursts out of the hand that was already covering her mouth. She turns into the nursing home car park, stops the car and kills the engine, tears begging to be let loose.

'You go ahead, I'll be right behind you,' she says to Pavel in between sobs. He looks at her, puts his hand on her shoulder and squeezes before climbing out. She watches his unsteady steps disappear in through the nursing home doors before fully breaking down behind the wheel.

She bawls loudly for a while, feeling profoundly sorry for herself. It's too much at once: the shame, the guilt of having fantasised about a world in which Karl-Adam is dead, the hangover, the lies. Why is she even alive? She's hunched over with her throbbing head on her forearms when there's a knock on the window. Nathan's outside with his dark hair tucked behind his ears. She rolls down the window, looking up at him with red, swollen eyes. He hands her a glass of water.

'Pavel told me you were out here,' he says. 'He said you might be thirsty.'

She takes the glass and downs it. Maybe it's placebo or maybe she's dangerously dehydrated, because the headache pounding across her forehead seems to subside a little.

'I'm sorry I called and got you all worried about nothing,' he continues. 'But things were looking bad when I went in to see Kalle this morning. He couldn't speak and his pulse was weak.'

Cassi wipes her nose on her sleeve.

'I'm glad you called,' she said. 'And I'm so relieved he's doing better.'

A shudder, the aftershocks of crying, runs through her. She leans back and closes her eyes.

'I honestly don't think I have it in me to go in there,' she says. 'And I don't think anyone in there needs me. Would you mind telling Pavel that I'll be here when he's done? No rush. And thanks for the water.'

Nathan clinks the glass against the half-rolled-down window.

'No worries,' he says. 'You stay here. I'll see you soon.'

It's very possible she dozes off. When she checks the time, half an hour's gone by. Exhaustion has crept in, replacing the panic. She tries to breathe through it. She takes Maine for a walk in the park across the street and buys coffee for herself and Pavel in the kiosk there. When she gets back to the car, Pavel's waiting for her. Cassi puts the cups on the roof and wraps her arms around him. Their bodies intertwine in silence for a few minutes.

'How was it?' she asks when they're back inside the car. Cassi reverses out of the car park and heads towards the highway.

Pavel takes a minute to respond.

'Karl-Adam was his usual self,' he says eventually. 'Maybe a bit tired. But he talked and laughed. And he knew who I was. So that felt good. I'm glad we went. Thank you for taking me.'

Cassi shakes her head.

'You really don't have to thank me. It's a given. I'd go anywhere with you, at any time.'

She smiles weakly at him, and he smiles back. Then Pavel turns to look at Maine in the back seat, waving his hand under his nose, saying: 'Oh, Maine, that might be your worst one yet!' Things almost feel normal. But not quite. She can tell he knows.

'Marlene called,' he says at last. 'She told me about the party. What Alida said.'

Cassi's eyes well up. At least she doesn't have to tell him herself, endure the shame of revealing her own lies. There's silence.

'I'm so horribly ashamed,' she whispers. 'I never meant for things to happen this way. One thing led to another and suddenly it was as though I'd become a different person. A person I liked.'

She forces herself to look at him. A quick glance, then back at the road.

'But not with you, Pavel. I haven't pretended with you. You probably don't believe me, but it's true.'

Pavel says nothing. Cassi breathes in and out slowly.

'I've really put my foot in it, huh?'

She wants him to say no, that it's not so bad.

'Yes, I believe you have,' he replies.

Silence again. They're usually good at being quiet together, but today, the silence is sticky and uncomfortable.

A rest stop appears and Cassi quickly pulls over, turning to look him in the eyes.

'I can't bear knowing I've disappointed you, Pavel. There's nothing I won't do to make things right, if I can.'

He looks at her with questioning eyes.

'My goodness, you don't have to apologise to me. I can't say I understand why you did what you did. But between you and me, I don't know if it matters. To me, you're Cassi. The person I do things like this with.'

He gestures towards the road ahead, the one that leads to their respective homes.

'I know that you're my friend. There's no doubt about that.'

He reaches out and strokes her cheek gently.

'Regardless of the lies.'

He says it with a smile, to show her everything's all right. She doesn't believe him but still leans towards him, crumbling with her head against his chest.

'I'm sorry,' she says, sobbing again.

He puts an arm around her.

'You don't have to worry about me,' he says. 'We're good. But I don't know how the others feel. Marlene was . . . upset. You should talk to her.'

No, she thinks to herself. No, no, no. But she knows he's right.

'Yes, I'm going to have to deal with that,' she says. 'You have to believe me when I say I feel horrible. It wasn't planned, it just happened. I thought I was buying a house. I thought I was going to be all alone, just me and Maine. But then people started assuming things about me. And then things snowballed, and lately, they've been going so well, I figured maybe it wasn't so bad after all.'

She's babbling now. Trying to justify what she did, realising that might be difficult. Pavel's mouth twists but he says nothing. Cassi sighs and starts the engine up, turning out onto the motorway. She feels shaky. For the first time since she moved to Bäcken, she's dreading going home. They drive in silence for a while.

'I'm shocked it was Alida,' she says, 'who was the one to dig up that old rubbish.'

She can sense Pavel giving her a disapproving look.

'Fine, fine, not rubbish,' she says. 'The truth.'

51

Cassi drops Pavel off at his house. She watches him in the rearview mirror, sees him pause on his front steps and look back at her, and at that point she revs the engine and shoots off, gravel spraying. Then she waves out the window and he unlocks his door. This is their usual routine. This is what they always do.

If Pavel's on her side, then she's not completely alone.

She's tired, so tired, as if she's been awake for months and not a mere few hours.

When she pulls up to her house and turns the engine off, the world goes quiet. The murmur of the forest is the only sound. Everything looks the way it always does.

She opens the car door. Maine sniffs the air. They climb out. Cassi closes the door gently. It feels like any loud noise might just kill her right now. The sweet, motionless smell of pine needles and moss, of the heather over by the treeline, envelops her like a blanket.

She manages to make it to her bed and falls into one of the deepest sleeps of her life.

52

Pavel climbs the three steps to his front door. At the top, he turns around, with a hand on the key, looking back at Cassi who's about to drive off. She usually makes the gravel fly everywhere, it's their little game, and this time is no exception. She sticks her hand out through the window, waving back at him. He goes inside with a soft smile on his face.

He feels shaken and tired, but also relieved. The sofa looks unusually inviting, he thinks that maybe he should lie down for a minute before dinner. Pavel likes his routines, but if he were to push dinner from six to half six this one time, it would hardly be the end of the world. And everything's prepared. He already peeled three potatoes and put them in salted water earlier today. A piece of salmon is defrosting on the counter.

Pavel slips his feet into his worn slippers and walks into the living room. Pinches two dead leaves off a geranium, putting them down on the coffee table. He'll throw them out in a moment, he just needs to rest first.

He's had his sofa for over twenty years and it wasn't new when he got it. But the brown corduroy still retains a certain glow and since he's been careful to use all three seats equally, neither side sags more than the other. He puts his head on one armrest, which is just the right height, and his feet fall on the opposite side. He's never slept a full night here, but there have been many naps. Pavel takes in all the familiar noises of his home: the ticking of the clock in the kitchen, the rumbling of a passing lorry outside, a bumblebee in the window, thudding dully against the glass. He closes his eyes.

He's sitting on his mother's lap, eating a biscuit on a bus somewhere in the countryside, watching bright yellow fields outside the window.

He and his little brother cuddle a litter of kittens they found in the basement of their house.

He's on a fieldtrip with his graduating class, standing on a sand dune between a lake and the sea, wind whipping around him.

He's camping in the woods with his best friend.

He's taking the ferry over to Sweden with the girl he's engaged to, the one who looks so much like Cassi.

He tells her he needs the loo after they get off, but instead he jumps on a bus to Stockholm. He's never felt freer, never happier than in that moment.

Until his eyes meet Karl-Adam's on his first day at the Royal Institute of Technology.

Until his hand grazes Karl-Adam's in the darkness of the Draken cinema in February.

Karl-Adam kissing him under a budding willow on Gärdet.

Days, nights, hours, minutes, all the moments they shared – he sees them all pass by and he smiles.

He'd always felt like half a person. But suddenly he was whole, he *is* whole, and his life turned out the way it was supposed to. Not perfect, but he never expected that anyway. He has known love, he's had solid friendships, he's had good days and sure, he's had bad ones, but what is there to regret? He could have done things differently, but it's impossible to know if that would have made his life better.

When Pavel falls asleep forever, he feels content. Joy was always relative and fleeting, but it was there. His existence has come full circle – a clean, precise one – and he's happy for it to be closed.

53

For the first time since the tradition began, there's no *Good morning, my star* text from Pavel.

Lunchtime rolls around — still nothing. Cassi texts him. Pavel doesn't reply. He's probably angry after sleeping on it. She tries calling. No answer.

Halfway through the afternoon, she decides to go over there and do whatever she has to do to regain his trust. Apologise again, grovel, find a way to keep his friendship. She calls Maine and together they take the path they've walked so many times by now.

Everything is as it always is until they step out of the woods. Then, Maine growls.

The door was unlocked. She knocked, then let herself in when there was no answer. Everything looked normal in the hallway. Shoes and jacket in their places. A piece of raw fish on the kitchen counter, which explained the nauseating smell. Pavel's house usually smelled of coffee and warmth.

He was lying on the sofa. Peacefully sleeping from a distance. Unmoving and cold from up close. The shock made her fall to her knees. Somehow, though she can't remember how, she managed to call a doctor. Somehow, an ambulance appeared and took the body – Pavel – away.

'Do you have someone you can call, to keep you company?' the doctor asked before he left, and Cassi said 'yes', even though Pavel was the first person who came to mind.

Then the house was empty and familiar again. As though Cassi and Maine had stopped by for a completely normal visit. Everything was the same as when they stepped out of the woods a few hours earlier.

Maybe she dreamed it. Life didn't make sense anymore. Maybe Pavel was just making himself a coffee. Maybe he was rummaging through his wardrobe for the right shirt to wear on his next visit to Karl-Adam. Maybe he was in the garage, staring at fifteen-year-old biscuit tins, trying to decide which one he was least likely to need in the near future and could therefore lend her.

She tidied up. Put everything the paramedics moved back, binned the salmon. There was a pot on the hob. She boiled the potatoes and ate them, crying because they once rested in Pavel's hands, because they were carefully peeled by his fingers, even though it turned out he'd salted them a bit too much.

She turned off the heated towel rack in the bathroom, unplugged the TV, watered the flowers in the windows, put the contents of the fridge in a tote bag to take home. Thinking that as long as Pavel's belongings still existed in some way, he was still alive.

When dusk began to creep in, she put his grimy shirt, the one he used as a jacket, over her shoulders, picked up the bag of food and slipped the small stack of framed erotic pictures waiting in the hallway into another one. She closed the door behind her and locked it. Whispered to herself: *Good night, my star.*

Then she must have gone home.

54

Days pass in a daze. The least painful thing she can do is sleep, so she sleeps, and when she's not sleeping, she and Maine wander aimlessly through the forest. She has not taken Pavel's shirt off since her last – ever – visit. She found his key ring in the breast pocket. The metal deer leaping towards freedom. Cassi clutches it so tightly that red indents form in the palm of her hand. At some point, her phone buzzes with an incoming text so she turns it off and throws it under her bed. Pavel's name will never pop up on the screen again. Nothing else matters.

Another night, as Cassi and Maine return from yet another long, meandering walk, her gaze falls on the tote bag she brought home from Pavel's house, which has been sitting by the front door for days. The bag isn't empty like she thought. At the bottom, she finds several printed photographs and a plastic folder, the ones Pavel had brought to Karl-Adam a few weeks ago. Cassi sits down at the kitchen table. She's never seen the folder before. She picks it up and an envelope with Pavel's name and a faded Stockholm address falls out of it.

Dear Pavel,
I thought I saw you the other day when I went swimming, but it was just someone who looked like you from afar. But it made me want to write to you. I want you to know you're in my thoughts. I

hope you're doing well. I think a lot about my time in Stockholm.

Here, life goes on. Ludvig's back from the hospital, and we're hoping for the best. I've built cabinets upstairs and put new flooring down in the kitchen. My late sister's husband has given me a job, you might recall he runs the hardware shop, so I help him out with all sorts of things. (I repaired a tractor engine the other day. Imagine what they'd think of that at the Royal Institute of Technology!) Käthe's teaching my nephew Hans at school. She says he's doing well, but that he keeps to himself a lot.

It's almost moose hunting season. Have you done any hunting? Because I was going to ask if you'd consider coming down here and joining my hunting party. It's usually a great couple of days. I was going to pack a tent and a camping stove. That way you get to see this part of the country, see where I'm from. It's a beautiful place, take my word for it.

I thought about what you said, that you'd love to have a house of your own. I've looked around and there are some nice ones for sale around here, where you could settle down, and the prices are much lower than in Stockholm.

I'm sitting on the front steps of my cottage. I hung up the bell you sent for the christening above the door. Käthe calls it 'Ludvig's bell', but every time it rings, I think of you. Do you still have the key ring?
Yours sincerely,
Karl-Adam

55

It's been a week since the party, three days since the unimaginable happened.

Cassi walks into her clearing from a long walk in the woods to find Alida sitting in her beach chair.

'You're late,' Alida says, looking at her wrist as though there were a watch there. 'I've been waiting fifteen minutes. And this chair's broken.'

Cassi stares at her. Thinks she must be hallucinating. When was the last time she had a proper meal? Maybe the hunger is driving her mad.

Maine has gone over to Alida and is enjoying an ear scratch.

'What's the matter with you?' Alida asks. She checks her imaginary watch again. 'Can we start? I have to feed the animals in an hour.'

Cassi's legs are threatening to buckle under her. She sits down on the front steps of the cottage. Her legs feel like jelly.

'What are *you* doing here?' she finds the strength to ask. Her voice comes out raspy, she hasn't spoken for days. Since the unimaginable happened, that is.

Alida frowns.

'Why wouldn't I be here? I paid in advance. I have two more sessions.'

'But I thought . . .' Cassi says. What she really wants to say is: *You betrayed me. You think I'm a fraud. Well, you found* out I'm a fraud and you told everyone I know. I'm a horrible, worthless person and there's no one in the entire world who cares about me because my only friend just died. Nothing comes out.

'What?' Alida says. 'What's the hold-up? You thought I was going to stop coming because of that thing at the party? Nah!'

Alida stands up.

'I was mad at you!' she says. 'And I thought people deserved to know. When I found those pictures, I wanted to talk to you about it. But you avoided me! Suddenly, it was more important to hang out at Berzan's than listen to what I had to say.'

Alida does a thrusting motion with her hips that would have been unseemly in any context, but in this moment is outright revolting. Cassi looks away. Puts her elbows on her knees, her face in her hands.

'And always whispering away with Marlene. And Gretel. Even Fia, that vapid little thing. But Alida, oh no, no time for her!'

Alida kicks a pinecone.

'I told you we'd met before! And you were all, like: "No, Alida, you're wrong again." But I wasn't! We had! I used to be a regular at your bloody restaurant. I could have painted every inch of Bäcken Church white with the amount of cocaine I did in the bathroom at that place. I reckon it's my bills, my tips, that paid for this shack!'

Cassi lifts her head back up. She sees Alida's red, angry face. Alida puts her hands on her frizzy hair, pulling it back.

'Remember me now? With my hair slicked back? They used to call me Alan.'

Cassi does remember now. She remembers a former

regular. An oftentimes problematic woman who always tipped well, with a ton of make-up and slicked-back hair. She was always in the company of at least three male colleagues with identical haircuts, identical clothes. They used to take turns carrying each other out at closing.

'Once I started going through my phone, I found lots of pictures with you in the background,' Alida says.

She seems to have calmed down again. She takes a seat on the stool.

'We were always at the same table, the round one on the left. Remember? But then you disappeared. No one seemed to know why. Where'd you go?'

Cassi doesn't reply. She runs her hands through her hair and shakes her head.

'I'm sorry,' she says. 'But I can't do this now . . .'

That's as far as she gets. She starts sobbing violently. It's been mostly slow, quiet tears over the past few days, like an extra lens over her eyes or a slow drizzle, but now that she has company she can no longer hold back. The crying is loud, it's wet, she's overcome by it, so violent that it feels like her features are erased and rearranged with each racking sob.

Alida's on her feet again, confused by her reaction. She shifts from one foot to the other in silence before walking over to her car and returning with a packet of tissues.

'Pavel?' she asks. 'I heard about that at the Village Shop.'

Alida sits down on the steps next to Cassi and places an awkward hand on her shoulder. They sit like that for a while.

'I'm really sorry,' she says. 'I know you were friends. He was a decent man.'

Cassi is sobbing so hard she can barely breathe. Maine has come to lay by her feet, his eyes alert and alarmed.

'He helped me when the water pipes burst in the stable last winter,' Alida continues. 'And with the fences last summer. He wasn't a big talker, was he? Didn't say much unless he had to. I appreciated that.'

She pauses, giving Cassi an encouraging smile.

'But I could tell you made him happier,' she says. 'He'd tell me about things you'd done together. You should know that.'

Alida removes her stiff hand. She's silent again, before eventually standing up. She sets the packet of tissues down next to Cassi.

'All right, I'll come back another day,' she says. 'We'll set up a new session when you're feeling better.'

Cassi looks up at her.

'Thank you, Alida,' she says. 'And I'm sorry I didn't listen to you before. I should have. I . . . I have no excuse. It just happened.'

If Alida heard the apology, she doesn't show it, but she's studying Cassi with a look of concern on her face.

'Still, it's strange,' she says after a moment. 'Because I remember you as really good-looking. Always perfectly groomed.'

She draws a circle around her face with her index finger.

'You're pretty puffy now, you know. A cold compress wouldn't hurt.'

Alida kisses Maine on the head and walks back towards her car.

'Hey, by the way, your bike,' she yells over her shoulder. 'It's still at the farm. Make sure you pick it up soon!'

56

She wakes up the next morning knowing she has to pull herself together. Her eyes disagree, they still haven't recovered from the torrent of tears of the past few days. She makes herself a weak cup of coffee and sits down on the front steps. Maine goes for a wee over by the treeline before trotting a lap around the garden with his nose to the ground.

In a way, it's like her first morning here. Solitude, an empty fridge, people to avoid. But minus the sense of adventure. No fresh start, nothing to look forward to.

Cassi downs her coffee. She may have several – many – flaws, but she's not lazy. Before she can leave this place where everyone hates her, she has things to sort out. She needs to talk to the priest and arrange a funeral. She needs to do whatever needs doing with Pavel's house. Even if that means sorting through and clearing out his garage, she's going to do it.

On her way to the church, Cassi drives slowly past Marlene's house, peering up at the window to see if Marlene is in. But there's no sign of her, neither half-naked in a sun lounger or completely naked by the living room window as usual.

The priest's wiping down the church vestibule with a chlorine-smelling cleaner when Cassi enters. For reasons unknown, or maybe no reason at all, the priest is wearing a bowler hat on her head which, coupled with her stern facial expression, helps Cassi get through explaining why she's there without bursting into tears. In her office, the priest rummages through one of her overflowing cabinets, after first pointing firmly at a brown bottle of hand sanitiser on the desk.

'It's somewhere around here,' she says. 'Oddly enough, Pavel came to see me just a month or two ago to give me an envelope. Maybe he could sense it coming.'

Cassi drowns her hand in sanitiser. She sits down on the edge of one of the visitor's chairs.

'This isn't how it's normally done, but we're a small congregation,' the priest says when she finds the envelope in a drawer by her desk.

'I see,' she says after reading its contents. 'What do you know.'

Cassi waits. She doesn't want to jeopardise this rare moment of calmness and dry eyes by speaking. Instead, she focuses on the priest's idiosyncrasies. A coat rack by the door is home to an impressive collection of hats. The top shelf of the bookcase displays what appears to be household cleaners from around the world. The desk is covered in liquorice sweets wrapped in colourful plastic.

'That man knew how he wanted things,' the priest says at last. 'What I have here is both a will and instructions for his funeral.'

The priest puts the papers down on the table. Cassi has never seen Pavel's handwriting before – it's elegant yet simple, just like him.

As far as the funeral goes, Pavel had modest requests. The priest reads aloud from his list. The ceremony is to be held in Bäcken Church. It's to be kept brief. He doesn't want any eulogies, but he does want a minute of silence. He wants the decorations to be green, no flowers. He wants Karl-Adam to attend, if he's able and it won't cause too much hassle for the nursing home. He wants a piece of music called 'Palangos jūroj' by Danielius Dolskis to be played, and he wants people to wear black. After the ceremony, he wants everyone to enjoy a Fanta and a Black Forest cake, because that's what he had during one of the happiest moments of his life.

The will is just as uncomplicated. A date at the top – which Cassi will later recognise as the day after the second time they went to see Karl-Adam – and a few short lines.

I leave my house and anything of value in it (subject to exclusions listed below) to Giedrė Žvirblytė. She may go by a different surname now. She was born on 29 April 1950 in Pajūris, Lithuania. Tell her I'm sorry.

I leave my coffee machine and everything that goes with it (beans, cups, etc.) to my friend Cassi. Thank you for everything. You're wonderful and you've made this old man's life so much better, in so many ways. The bottled coffee you make is the only thing about you I'm not crazy about.

This will be my way of saying 'Good morning, my star' forever.

57

On the way home, Cassi musters up the courage to make (a few) things right and parks in Marlene's driveway. She fully expects to be asked to leave before she can even knock, but the front door remains closed. Is it weird to prefer confrontation over silence?

Cassi climbs out of her car, letting Maine tag along. Not a sound from inside. She walks around to the patio in the back. There's no one there either. Maine investigates the deconstructed trellis piled up by the gate. The grass is getting tall around it.

Back at the front door, Cassi places the small stack of erotic paintings from Pavel's garage on the doormat, leaning them against the wall. She told Marlene about the paintings just a day or two before the party. She'd envisioned a repeat of the coffee klatsch on the patio from earlier in the summer as the setting for the handover. Her, Marlene, Pavel, giggling together on the plush garden swing.

Marlene's home feels eerie without her there. On her way back to the car, Cassi tries, unsuccessfully, to push down thoughts of Marlene lying dead on her sofa. Only when she notices the open garage door and the missing car inside can she breathe a sigh of relief. Though that's an unusual situation as well. It's rare for Marlene to drive anywhere, she prefers her electric bike, so long as it's not raining horizontally or freezing.

'The body needs to breathe, Cassi,' she's told her more than once. 'The feeling of the wind between my legs is just delightful.'

Cassi drives home. She eats the last of Pavel's food. She thinks to herself that she has to fetch her bike. His bike. The day he gave it to her, she didn't realise what that meant to him. What a gift he was giving her, not the bike itself, but the very gift of trust.

She sets off as the August night begins to fall. Following the same paths as the day of the party. It's so much slower on foot. She remembers the unadulterated joy she felt then but can no longer find her way back to it. How could she let herself believe life could be that easy? She must have come back the same way that night. It's a miracle she didn't get lost. Her body aches with love for this place, with grief for Pavel, with shame at the mess she's made.

When she reaches the Desgoffes' driveway, she tiptoes up the grassy verge, avoiding the gravel. She can see that all the lights are on in the house. Someone's even bothered to straighten up and plug in the plastic flamingo. Its pink glow is a poor fit with the surrounding rural idyll.

Having reached her bike, Cassi fumbles with the key. She doesn't want to turn on the flashlight on her phone and risk someone noticing her.

'I see you, you know,' a voice says behind her, as though Cassi's thoughts were visible too. She has no choice but to turn around. She can just about make out Lollo's shape in the darkness under the tree. Lollo is on the swing. Her long, white skirt is dragging on the ground behind her like a ghost.

'Hi,' Cassi says. 'I didn't want to bother you, so . . .'

'Yeah, I suppose you don't want to be seen,' Lollo interrupts. 'I suppose your plan's to just keep hiding, hoping we'll all forget, right?'

The sound of a can being opened hisses in the air.

'It's not even that I feel duped,' Lollo continues. 'It's because nothing makes sense anymore.'

Gulping sounds.

'Because I don't even get why you did it,' she continues. 'Was it, like, an experiment? Have some fun with the country bumpkins?'

Cassi shakes her head, searching for words.

'Marlene talked to Pavel the day after,' Lollo says. 'He said you'd had a tough year.' She chuckles dryly. 'What's that supposed to mean, a tough year? Like that's an excuse? I don't even know who you are. I've had tough years too. But did I lie? No, I didn't. I might not have told you about it, I might not have let on at all, but I don't owe you any of my secrets now, do I? No, I don't!'

Cassi realises Lollo's drunk. Properly drunk. Not all-in-her-mind-Alida-at-the-party drunk. Cassi carries her unlocked bike over to the gravel. Lollo throws a beer can at her. It lands by Cassi's feet, warm liquid spilling on her shoes.

'Don't go out there, the lights will turn on,' Lollo says, pointing to the large gravel driveway. 'Far too bright. And then they don't turn off for ten minutes. They're automatic. Like most things in this house.'

Cassi takes a step back. Lollo bends down, picks something off the ground, opens another can.

'And the party,' she says, pausing for a long swig. 'That went completely off the rails after Alida's reveal. And not in the good way. It died. And you just fucked off. Ran away like the coward you are. It was all people could talk about. I had stuff planned, you know. But we didn't even get to the dessert. We had to eat cobbler for days afterwards.'

Lollo sighs.

'I'm sick of it, just so you know. Sick of everything. Sick of my bloody children, sick of my dweeb of a husband, sick of my fucking followers who comment on every fucking part of my life, sick of the damn algorithms that keep changing, sick of fucking collaborators who are never happy. Sick of it taking three fucking hours to have extensions put in, and so fucking sick of having to look so goddamn happy all the goddamn time.'

Lollo tilts her head back and drinks.

'So stop then,' Cassi says. 'Just stop.'

The sound of a can being crumpled up. Then a string of curses.

'Now I've gone and cut my damn hand open too.'

Lollo stands up. Still swaying, even without the swing. She turns and starts walking towards the door. The lights turn on. Blood is dripping from the hand Lollo's holding high above her head, trickling down her arm, dripping onto her white skirt, which is sheer in the backlight. She almost looks triumphant.

Only when Lollo calls out 'It means something different in Sanskrit', does Cassi notice that the middle finger of her raised hand is extended.

Since the lights are on now anyway, Cassi wheels her bike down the gravel drive. She checks to make sure there's air in the tyres and fiddles with the headlight. It's an old-fashioned dynamo, the kind that's powered by the spinning of the back wheel. The kind you can't trust to function correctly. But when she takes off, it does. The headlight shines brighter as she speeds up, lighting her way. Pavel, she thinks. It's his way of telling her that she will be OK.

58

The priest informs her that Hans will be seeing to the funeral reception.

'He says Pavel discussed it with him,' she says. 'And since Hans won't be attending the ceremony, I suppose we should think of it as his way of saying goodbye.'

Cassi doesn't have the strength to object. Fine, let Hans do it. She's going to keep her distance.

On the day of the funeral, Cassi arrives early to help with the preparations at the church.

'At least the weather's beautiful,' the priest comments, as though the mood on this late-summer day could somehow be mitigated by sunshine and balmy temperatures.

Right before people are due to arrive, Cassi takes off with Maine. Her plan is for them to sneak back in just as the ceremony's about to start. They're going to sit in the last row and then slip out before people can see her and be upset by her presence. She doesn't want to cause a scene. Pavel's funeral has to be a dignified affair.

The church is almost completely full when Cassi returns, which takes her by surprise. She had no idea that Pavel knew so many people, but she assumes that in this kind of sparsely populated backwater, it might also have something to do with showing one's appreciation for long and faithful service.

When she slides into her seat, her chest tightens. It

feels wrong. As though she's not participating properly. If there's one thing Cassi's proud of, it's her friendship with Pavel. And that means she can't sit back here and hide. He wouldn't approve.

She stands back up and brings Maine with her to the front, where the entire first row is unoccupied. When she gets there, she notes that Marlene's seated two pews back. She's wearing a small hat with a black veil and a dramatically low-cut black dress. If they were still friends, they would have been able to joke about her being dressed like a widow who's just murdered and buried her husband in a soap opera.

Cassi almost hopes to be told off, that Marlene cares enough to spit a small, chewed-up lump of paper at her. Even a poison dart would be preferable to the indifference.

The priest sticks to her instructions. Cassi doesn't hear a word of her sermon, because in a misdirected effort to fight her tears, she focuses on recalling that W. H. Auden poem from *Four Weddings and a Funeral*. When she tries to wipe her face with her jacket sleeve, she notices her whole body's shaking.

Only when she feels the warmth of another body next to her does she realise that someone's joined her in the pew. A cloud of powerful perfume envelops her, a hand with crimson nails takes hers. The priest keeps talking, standing next to the coffin.

'Receive him into your peace and give him, in the name of Jesus Christ, a joyous resurrection.'

Marlene's hand squeezes Cassi's.

'Said the actress to the bishop,' she whispers.

Cassi laughs through her tears, gratefully laying her head on Marlene's shoulder.

Then it's time for silence.

The church is still. Heads are bowed. Only occasionally is there a scraping against the floor or a rustling of clothing, and then, right at the end, a frail old voice asks: 'Is this my funeral?' Cassi hears Nathan answer Karl-Adam: 'No, you're good.' Even without seeing it, she can almost feel him putting his reassuring hand on Kalle's.

Then the music Pavel requested is played. Cassi didn't recognise the name of the piece when the priest read it to her, but when she hears the melody, she knows it instantly. It's the one Pavel was always humming when he worked on her house, when he was riding in her car, when he was fiddling with his coffee machine, when he threw sticks for an uninterested Maine, when he cheerfully planned what his next DIY project was going to be. Now she hums along too, possibly too loudly, through a stream of warm tears.

59

The parish hall is decorated with paintings by the priest herself, depicting various locations around Bäcken. In all honesty, the subjects would have been hard to figure out if it weren't for the printed descriptions pinned at the bottom of each frame.

The mourners, if that's the right word, have gathered into small groups and are chatting away. Cassi is relieved, from her position in the corner. Mingling is out of the question.

Marlene comes over and puts an arm around her. Cassi knows better than to assume that means she's forgiven, that what happened is behind them now. Everything has to wait until Pavel has been put to rest, she knows that.

Gretel joins them, hugs Marlene. She gives Cassi a puzzled look, but doesn't mention what happened at the party either.

'Pavel talked to Hans about how he wanted things only a few weeks ago,' Gretel says quietly. 'He wasn't a man of many words, but Hans said his description of the cake was the longest speech he'd ever heard him give.'

All three of them look over at the long table where Hans has prepared everything and is now serving people. The Black Forest gateau is fluffy and white, decorated with chocolate thins.

'Pavel must've really loved cream,' Gretel says, wiping

the corner of her eye. She goes over to pick up the plates of cake that Hans has cut, passing them out to the guests. Cassi knows. It was important to Pavel that the cake be exactly like the one he and Karl-Adam shared the first time they went for coffee together, somewhere near the Royal Institute of Technology in Stockholm, in the autumn of 1968.

She's not hungry – hell, she can barely remember when she last was – but she eats anyway. The sweetness of the cake transports her to another time and place. She can almost feel their elation, their apprehension. The glint in Karl-Adam's eyes. Pavel's tentative smile. Karl-Adam's hand, brushing against Pavel's knee under the table.

Cassi excuses herself and steps outside with Maine. In the sunny car park, she finds Max the Estate Agent leaning against his car, smoking a cigarette. He flips her off when he spots her on the church steps.

'It means something different in Sanskrit,' he comments.

Cassi realises they've been talking about her. That the village gossip mill's been running at full tilt all week. It's perfectly natural and she knows there's nothing she can do about it. She just nods and walks off in the opposite direction. She thinks of leaving the reception. It's not like anyone would miss her. But no, she has to stick with it. For her friend.

She touches his key ring, which she now always carries in her pocket. She goes back inside the hall and sits down on one of the chairs lining the walls. She feels people's eyes on her and she lets them stare. On the other side of the room, Lollo, Simon and their three children are seated at a table. They have cake and Fanta, and Simon's unsuccessfully trying to keep the children's clothes cream-free. Lollo looks annoyed. Fia comes over and takes a seat next to Cassi, tucking her blond hair behind her ears. She's dressed in a black tank top and a long, black skirt. She looks beautiful, mature and solemn.

'How are you doing?' she asks.

Cassi raises her arms, forcing Fia into a hug. Fia hugs her back.

'I'm sorry, Fia,' Cassi says. She doesn't know what else to say.

'Seriously, you think I care?' Fia says with a chuckle. She keeps talking in that leisurely way of hers. 'I knew something was up right away. But like I told you during our last session – I enjoy talking to you. And that's what counts, isn't it?'

She leans back in her chair, surveying the room.

'I was obviously surprised to hear what Alida told us at the party, but at the same time, not *that* surprised.'

It's hard for Cassi to accommodate any feeling but grief on this particular day, but a hint of relief and surprise sparks in her chest regardless. Cassi tries to look up and meet Fia's gaze but fails.

'Remember that time we talked about meditation, and I brought up TM?' Fia continues. She chuckles again. 'And you thought I was talking about trademarks? That seemed odd to me. Someone like you should know what transcendental meditation is. And there were a lot of other things too. That middle-finger thing was too hilarious. Mum might have told some people, now that it's become, you know, topical.'

Fia puts a hand on Cassi's shoulder.

'But honestly, what difference does it make? Even the séance was top notch, until that old muppet crashed it!'

Fia's being slightly too loud for a funeral reception. Cassi looks over at Hans. He's still standing over by the cakes, talking to Karl-Adam. Hans meets her eyes.

'He misses you,' Cassi says. 'I hope you realise that. How sorry he is about the way things are between you.'

Fia picks at her eyelashes. One comes off and she rolls it between her fingertips, studying it briefly before blowing it into the room.

'Fine, then he can go ahead and tell me that,' she says.

Cassi notes that Nathan and Karl-Adam are getting ready to leave. She puts a hand on Fia's knee.

'I'm just going to say goodbye to Karl-Adam,' she says, standing up.

He doesn't seem to recognise her when she walks over to the wheelchair, extending her hand. But he looks happy.

'Have you had a piece of cake, Karl-Adam?' she asks, holding his hand between hers.

He nods and smiles.

'Black Forest,' he replies. 'It was always my favourite.'

Cassi smiles at him and at Nathan, who's standing behind the wheelchair.

'I wanted to thank both of you for taking the time to be here,' she says. 'It was really appreciated.'

'It was our pleasure,' Karl-Adam says, sounding jolly. 'It's not every day I get to go on an outing and have cake, you know. Where are we, again?'

Nathan beats her to it.

'We're in Bäcken, Kalle,' he says. 'We came for a funeral.'

Karl-Adam looks at them questioningly before smiling again.

'Wonderful cake,' he says.

Then he turns to Cassi.

'Are you coming back with us?' he asks.

She shakes her head and puts a hand on his shoulder.

'No, I'm staying here. But I can come visit you again soon.'

She means it. He looks at her.

'Why?' he asks. 'Do we know each other? And where are we again?'

Nathan gives Cassi a look.

'It was lovely to see you, Karl-Adam,' Cassi says. On a whim, she puts her hand in her pocket and pulls out Pavel's key ring. She holds it out to Karl-Adam.

He takes it and studies it in the palm of his hand. When he looks up again, his eyes are solemn.

'Pavel?'

Cassi takes a deep breath.

'Pavel,' she says.

Karl-Adam closes his fingers around the key ring. Puts his hand in his lap, the other one on top. He looks down. Nathan looks at Cassi.

'It was a lovely ceremony,' he says, patting her on the shoulder. 'Take care.'

Cassi nods in reply, can only hope he knows she wants to say the same thing back, but that the lump in her throat and the tears in her eyes are in the way.

Nathan wheels Karl-Adam out through the door, down the ramp, over to the nursing home car waiting for them. He and the driver manoeuvre the old man into his seat.

Then the wheelchair is folded and put in the boot. Karl-Adam doesn't look up again. Cassi watches the car drive away and exhales a deep sigh. Surely this must be over soon.

Hans is hovering around the cake table, reorganising the glasses now. Cassi walks over to him. Whatever tension exists between them, she feels she has to thank him for pitching in. Pavel would have appreciated it. Hans is visibly misty-eyed and before Cassi can say anything, he asks if she'd like a Fanta.

'Pavel wanted it to be cold, preferably served with two ice cubes per glass,' Hans says, his voice trembling. 'But no straws, that was important. He absolutely didn't want straws.'

Hans wipes his eyes. He's placed the bottles of fizzy drink in an ice bath, and there's a large bowl full of ice cubes and tongs sitting next to it. On a small, water-stained note, a message: *Best enjoyed with two ice cubes. – Pavel.*

Apparently, Hans has agreed to a truce between them. He pours a glass and holds it out to her. Making small talk with him feels less strange than Cassi had thought it would. It's hard to accept that this is the same Hans she's been fearing all summer. That this man has scolded her. That she has fled at the sight of him in the supermarket.

To be fair, there is very little for Cassi to be fearful of at this point. What she thought would be the worst thing that could ever happen to her has already happened. And it turned out to be nothing compared to the very thing there were all gathered here to mourn.

'He was a good man,' Hans says. 'He should have had more time. Life . . . it's too short.'

Cassi almost wants to hug him but holds herself back.

'He had a long life. And I think he was happy when he died, at least. He looked so peaceful when I found him,' she says, successfully keeping her own feelings at arm's length. 'It was as though he were sleeping.'

'But all the things he still had to do,' Hans says, running a finger under his eyes. 'All the people he loved. He worked so hard.'

Cassi has the feeling Hans isn't really talking about Pavel.

'Pavel had no regrets,' she says, and now she has to pause to swallow. 'He was at peace. He'd taken charge of his life.'

Fia walks by them, eyes on someone else, and Cassi reaches for her arm, stopping her in her tracks.

Hans looks at Fia. Fia looks at her father. He reaches out for her and takes her hands. He whispers: 'I'm sorry!' and pulls her close. He cries into her hair. 'I'm sorry! Forgive me! I've been so stupid.'

Gretel comes over too, joining the hug. Cassi stands next to them. She can, even through the grief, see herself from the outside, now cast in a new role, that of a doula in the process of bringing a family into the world. The hug lasts for several minutes. The impact of it on the room is noticeable. If people were holding back before, they now speak no louder than a whisper. After the embrace dissolves, Hans puts one arm around his wife and the other around his daughter, not ready to let go of them just yet. He clears his throat.

'I'd like to say a few words,' he announces, his voice echoing across the hall.

His face is red and puffy, but his voice is steady again. The whispered conversations stop. Hans takes a deep breath.

'We're here today to honour our dear friend Pavel. He was well known in Bäcken. He was what I'd like to call a pillar of society.'

As much as Cassi heartily despises this side of Hans – that he assumes he has a right to speak for everyone, that he's convinced he knows better and therefore should and will tell the rest of the world what's what – she appreciates this initiative. She would have liked to eulogise Pavel herself. But with her situation being what it is, she would never have dared to.

'Pavel has been there for as long as I can remember,' Hans continues. 'Pavel was a handy man. A decent man. He lived the way a person ought to – he looked after his house and minded his own business. He was appreciated by everyone. He may have been frugal with his words, but always generous with his help.'

There's nodding all around the room. Pavel helped virtually everyone in the village at some point.

'My uncle Karl-Adam got to know Pavel while studying in Stockholm and must have spoken well of the area, because Pavel eventually moved here. I doubt many remember now what things were like here without Pavel. I remember him from my childhood. To me, he always felt like a part of my family. Karl-Adam and Pavel had a special friendship. You'd often see them together, talking, laughing. And of course, the moose hunt! The most special day of the year. I remember how excited they were about it,' he pauses, his eyebrows furrowing. 'And some might remember how much Pavel helped, how he was always there for Karl-Adam after Käthe passed away.'

Cassi looks around furtively. Could it be that not

everyone knew the truth about Pavel and Karl-Adam's relationship? It's hard to read people's faces. Gretel studies the floor while Fia winks furtively at Cassi. Hans continues with his speech.

'Pavel lived alone all his life. But this summer, he seemed happier than he'd been for years, I'm sure you'll all agree. And the reason for that is Cassi.'

Cassi's lungs seem to deflate inside her. It hasn't been nearly long enough since she was last the subject of a spontaneous public speech. She would have loved not to have to repeat the experience. She considers walking out but forces herself to stay put. She shuts her eyes, trying to regulate her breathing.

'I've always been sceptical of her,' Hans continues. 'From the very beginning. I remember the day Max came into The Market, telling me that what he called a "self-help guru" was moving into Karl-Adam's house. I knew right then she was going to drag a bunch of hogwash and flim-flam into our wonderful village. Tantra festivals, we've all heard about these things from neighbouring counties. We don't want that here. And then she almost started a forest fire with one of her rituals.'

He shakes his head, as though he's still recovering from witnessing such stupidity.

'And as it turns out, she is exactly what I said she was all along. A fraud.'

He holds a finger up. Now he looks like the Hans Cassi knows.

'I'm not excusing her lies! The whole thing's appalling.'

He drags out the second a, pronouncing the word more like 'apaaaaalling'.

'And her methods are obviously . . . unorthodox and utter garbage from start to finish. I heard something about rope therapy?'

He turns to Gretel.

'And what were you talking about the other day, Gretel? Moss?'

'Mossage,' Gretel whispers.

'Mossage, right. And psycho-aura synthesis?'

Gretel nods, but then shakes her head. She doesn't want to be dragged into this. Fia's elbow meets her father's abdomen.

'But anyway, that's not the point here,' Hans continues after rolling his eyes. 'The whole thing's despicable. But you know what, I will admit that she has accomplished a number of things.'

Now, this is a plot twist Cassi hadn't seen coming. Surprise makes her look up.

'It wasn't just Pavel. My wife has, how shall I put it, cheered up as well. And she's told me about several other people here who have been helped by Cassi. And so I'm asking: is a person really a fraud if they succeed at what they say they're going to do?'

Cassi recognises her own line of reasoning. She'd begun to doubt it, but now, hearing Hans, for whom her feelings keep shifting so dramatically, say the same thing, it sounds plausible again. He's about to carry on when he's interrupted.

'All right. That's enough. Wasn't this speech supposed to be about our beloved Pavel?'

Marlene has stepped out onto the floor.

'It's just like you to put on the big speaker's hat and tell the rest of us what to think. But we – or I, because I'm not going to be like you and make out I'm speaking for anyone but myself – don't need your help.'

Hans looks at Gretel, as if for support, but Gretel merely shrugs.

'Everyone can go back to eating their cake,' Marlene continues. 'It was nice of you to set this up, Hans. Thank you. Pavel would have liked it.'

She waves a hand in the air and the chatter resumes. Fia playfully slaps Hans's shoulder, smiling at him. He briefly stares at Marlene, shaking his head, but then he turns back to his daughter.

Marlene holds a hand out to Cassi. Cassi doesn't move, unsure of how she's expected to react. Marlene is unpredictable. This could just as easily be an invitation to a fistfight as to dance. Then Marlene steps in closer and she doesn't seem to have violent intent.

'Dear lord, that man can be tedious. Always telling people what to think and how to react. Thanks, but no thanks, Hans. You mind your business, I'll mind mine.'

The veil on Marlene's hat has whipped-cream remnants at mouth level, as though in her eagerness to scarf down cake, she forgot it was there as her spoon approached her mouth. She lifts it.

'You know what, Cassi, I've been so furious with you. And devastated! I was never going to speak to you again.'

Marlene has put her hands on her hips, as though to underscore that she's serious. Cassi nods.

'I understand, Marlene. I'm so sorry about how things turned out.'

Marlene raises a hand, palm dangerously close to Cassi's nose.

'No, no, no, don't give me any of that "turned out" nonsense, you're only going to get me worked up again. Nothing "turned out", you made choices. Again and again and again.'

Marlene looks as though she's ready to slap her. Cassi breathes a weak sigh of relief when she lowers her hand.

'But regardless of how it happened, you've done a lot for me. I have Gretel back. I found the courage to call my daughter. And we've had fun together, you and me. I've laughed a lot with you.'

Cassi nods. Gretel has come over to them. For a person who moves so slowly, she certainly seems to be everywhere at once at this reception. Marlene smiles at her friend.

'And I wanted to tell you about our trip,' Marlene continues. 'Next week, Gretel and I are off to Strasbourg. Can you imagine! Marlene's going abroad!'

Marlene takes Gretel's hand, holding it up above their heads, like a silent celebration.

'And I'm in charge of booking the tickets, so it's not impossible we'll stop by Berlin on the train. I have a passport now!'

Marlene winks at Gretel. Gretel laughs. Cassi beams at them through silent tears.

'Amazing,' she eventually manages to squeeze out. 'Amazing.'

She wipes her forehead with the sleeve of Pavel's old polyester suit, which she couldn't help but wear for her final goodbye. Cassi reaches out to Marlene and Gretel, wanting them to understand what this moment means to her, what they mean to her, but all she can do is grab their arms and squeeze them. She can't quite find the words, but they seem to understand. Cassi presses her palms together as she backs away towards the exit. Maine, who's been napping by the door this whole time, follows. In the doorway, Cassi runs into Cook, who's coming back in after stepping out for a smoke. He flips her off.

'It means something different in . . .'

She nods.

60

Cassi and Maine continue to live an isolated life. It's perfectly possible Maine doesn't notice much of a difference from what his days were like before, but for Cassi, it feels like they're in a bubble. They sleep late, they take long walks in the woods, they go over to Pavel's house to harvest what's left in his vegetable patch. They water his plants, pick his raspberries, make sure everything looks the same as it always did.

On this particular day, they're at the lake. Cassi sits quietly on a bench, gazing out across the water. It's late afternoon and a chill wind is blowing.

All of a sudden, Lollo is standing right in front of them, feet wide. She's there with her children, keeping an eye on them as they play by the water's edge. Lollo's wearing a shapeless dress and her hair is in a ponytail. Not her usual pristine ponytail, but a messy one that matches Cassi's. The pink polish on her nails is chipped.

'I wanted to ask you something,' Lollo says.

Her face is neutral. Cassi doesn't have time to reply before Lollo continues.

'Or, well, I suppose it's less of a question than it is a job.'

No one seems angry with Cassi anymore, not exactly, but no one seems eager to hear what she has to say either. Cassi's role, she's noticed, has become to listen to what people say to her. She no longer gets paid for it, and they're barely interested in a reaction or an option. But they still want to tell her things.

When Cassi last picked up a pizza, Cook told her his first collection of poems is going to be published, that after the debate about rural culture that followed in the wake of her live yoga, he turned out to be the right poet at the right moment. Jogging by her one day in the woods, Fia gave her a hug and said she's going to take over The Market, that Hans and Gretel were beginning to plan for their retirement. A text comes in from an unknown number. It turns out to be Nadia from the séance, wanting to tell her she's not going to leave her wife after all. 'The séance helped me see how much of what we do is pointless nonsense and I'm grateful for that. We have to cherish the things that aren't.' And Alida came by the other day to tell her she's now dating Max. 'Estate agent and stockbroker, it's a match made in heaven,' she said. 'So hands off!'

Cassi had promised.

'I've noticed my followers respond well to me showing them the crappier parts of my life,' Lollo tells her now, one hand on her hip and her eyes still on her children. They're filling buckets with sand and water, periodically emptying them into the lake and starting over.

'So I'm working on a new style I'm calling "pure crap". It requires me to work differently. But my new reach is record-breaking.'

She puts one foot up on the bench, scratching under her heel with a brazenness Cassi has never seen. When Lollo commits to something, she goes all in, Cassi will give her that.

'So that's one good thing you contributed to, at least.'

Lollo doesn't smile when she says that either. A small part of Cassi wants to challenge Lollo's attitude, the aggressiveness in her voice which doesn't feel necessary anymore. But Cassi's not confrontational, she never was.

'I was thinking you could write down those things you used to say, your so-called mantras, so I can use them instead? They'd go well with this so-called natural way of living. And you won't be needing them, I assume. You can bill me for it.'

Cassi looks down at her hands. Lollo's proposal sounds all right. Cassi's costs are currently low, but eventually she will have to make a living somehow. Writing for other people sounds like a good gig. Perfectly doable. Could she call herself a scriptwriter then? Or published author, plain and simple? Maybe this is the start of a new gig.

Cassi's about to accept the offer, but Lollo pre-empts her.

'Anyway, think about it. It's all the same to me. I remember some of it, so I'll be doing it whether you're on board or not.'

61

It's a few days later. Cassi's gone down to the main road. She's getting rid of her junk mail, stomping down the piles of dirt marking where her sign once stood. Maine's out in the field, sniffing around as usual.

Cassi looks up and down the road, towards the village, then the other direction. She spots a green figure cycling down Hans and Gretel's drive. Tears begin to stream down her face yet again, it happens without warning these days. She wipes her cheeks and eyes with the bottom of her T-shirt.

'Crying again, I see,' Marlene comments after coming to a full stop in front of her. 'You're going to have to give that a rest soon, you know.'

Marlene's dressed in low-cut skinny jeans and a green, tie-dye crop top. Cassi smiles with watery eyes.

'I don't mind the tears,' she replies. 'Do you know what it feels like? Like it's all the love I had for him finally pouring out. I never had the chance to really express it.'

Marlene rolls her eyes.

'Seriously, this is the cringiest thing I've ever heard. You have to stop wallowing in your grief. Pavel's gone, but life's still happening. I think you need something to do. And to spend less time alone.'

Marlene looks firm as she takes her *snus* out, flicking it into the ditch.

'Let someone else in. Talk to people. It's time,' she says. 'I was just over at Gretel's, we're planning what to pack. We're leaving the day after tomorrow.'

'When will you be back?' Cassi asks. She's starting to view her existence as divided into alternating periods of sociability and solitude. Perhaps she's coming out of the latter now.

'The plan is to be gone for two weeks,' Marlene replies. 'But part of me thinks we're going to fall out over her calling me Berit before we even get on the train. Oh well. We'll see how that turns out! You can't plan for every single thing in life, can you.'

Cassi nods, impressed.

'Insightful,' she says. 'Very zen of you.'

Marlene laughs. She spreads her hands and closes her eyes like an unholy Buddha statue.

'Life needs a pinch of crazy,' she chants. 'Sometimes you just have to let things happen.' She opens her eyes and looks at Cassi. 'A wise woman once told me: if every day's the same, there would be nothing to remember.'

Marlene's eyes narrow and she stares at Cassi until she looks away.

'Did you hear about Berzan, by the way?' Marlene asks then, rubbing the bike's handlebar with her thumb. 'He went to Norway. His ex called and offered him a job on a Hurtigruten cruise ship.'

Maine comes over and Cassi bends down to brush the grass out of his fur with her fingers.

'How does that make you feel?' Cassi asks before she can stop herself. Granted, it's a perfectly normal question to ask someone, but as a retired fraudulent therapist, maybe not from her.

Marlene sneers, confirming Cassi's anxieties.

'Ha, how is it supposed to make me feel? I suppose I'm happy for him. If nothing else, Hurtigruten is supposed to be amazing. It'll suit him.'

She thoughtfully gazes out at the forest, then she cocks one eyebrow.

'Said the actress to the bishop?'

Cassi giggles. At first, it's just a small snigger. But then it bubbles up from deep inside her and it grows, turning into a full belly laugh. Marlene watches her with amusement. Then she squats down to scratch Maine's head.

'How do you do it, Maine,' she says, 'living with this nutcase?'

Maine rolls over. Cassi wipes her eyes, smiling at the black thong that sticks up from the waistband of Marlene's jeans. Some things truly never change.

'Your lower back tattoo,' Cassi says. 'I've been wondering for a while now. What does it say?'

Marlene turns her head as though to refresh her memory.

'It's the Chinese character for happiness,' she replies.

It's Cassi's turn to raise an eyebrow. Marlene hears her unspoken question.

'I mean, literally, that's what it says,' she clarifies. 'I told Berzan I wanted the Chinese character for happiness, but he didn't realise I meant the symbol. So he wrote the full sentence. What an idiot.'

Marlene shrugs.

'I obviously couldn't see what he was doing, but sure, I did think it was taking longer than I'd thought. But I'd never gotten a tattoo before. I had no idea how long it was supposed to take and since he's a beginner, I assumed he was taking his time. But hey, mistakes can be beautiful too.'

Marlene buries her face in Maine's neck, pretending to bite him.

'And full disclosure, I'm told he misspelled it too,' she says.

She stands up and brushes the dirt off her knees.

'All right, time to go home and pack. But stop by for coffee tomorrow, if you want. Because after that, I won't be here. And who knows if you'll ever see me again.'

Marlene tries to look nonchalant. But her smile is an anxious one.

'It's going to be amazing, Marlene,' Cassi says. 'You're going to love it. The world was pretty much made for you.'

Marlene nods. Then she gets back on her bike, raises one hand, and rolls off without a sound. Cassi and Maine make their way home.

When they get to the cottage, she has another go at figuring out Pavel's coffee machine, hoping the result will be an espresso. The black-and-white picture of Bea now sits above the machine, and Cassi studies it while coffee bubbles and hisses. She will forever associate the smell of coffee with Pavel. She's been having dreams about him. Dreams of walking into his house, seeing him in the kitchen, with that content look he always had on his face when he measured out the beans. She hears him explain some indescribably dull detail about the roast and where he ordered the beans from this time.

Going back out, she strokes the bell above the door. Cassi is about to set the cups down on the front steps when she spots a spider scurrying across the concrete. The scene feels familiar. The spider appears to lift its head to peer up at her, giving her a microscopic nod before hurrying on. Cassi sits down. Maybe she's fully lost her mind, but who cares? The stakes of her life are at their lowest.

She thinks about Pavel arriving in Sweden by ferry. About how he thought his future was set in stone. He was going to go back home after his trip, to live his life with the woman whose relatives they were visiting. They were going to have children and he was going to take over his father's workshop. It was all settled. His life had been planned out. But it didn't turn out the way he'd thought it would. And even though he sometimes regretted the way he acted, Pavel never regretted the decisions that led him there.

The sunshine gives the clearing a golden glow. Cassi sips her coffee and stares at the trees. She flips through the junk mail, which she should have thrown in the bin on her way back, but instead discarded on the front steps when she got home. There's a postcard nestled among the flyers, which she hadn't noticed before. It has her name and address on it, but the message consists only of three small, puffy, hand-drawn clouds, one above the other.

☁
☁
☁

But Cassi understands. She knows who sent these smoke signals and what they mean. She misses her friends as much as they miss her, if not more. And finally, she feels ready to forgive them. Marlene is right. It's time to talk to people.

Cassi goes into her bedroom, rummaging under the bed for her phone. She plugs it in to charge.

Back on the steps, Maine sits down next to her. His fur warming the sliver of bare skin between her T-shirt and shorts. The murmur of the forest the only sound, their breathing the only movement.

Cassi wasn't always like this. She's been someone else, she's been something else. She will keep changing. And for the first time, it's a reassuring thought. Regardless of what her future looks like, regardless of where life takes her, she will always be grateful for this place and what it's given her.

Cassi downs her coffee, turning her face to soak in the last rays of the setting sun. She catches herself smiling. Maine heaves a happy sigh. She thinks to herself that it's a good thing they're outside.